PYRENEAN BANDITTI

Gothic Classics

PYRENEAN BANDITTI.

A ROMANCE.

THREE VOLUMES IN ONE.

BY

ELEANOR SLEATH,

AUTHOR OF

ORPHAN OF THE RHINE, WHO'S THE MURDERER?, &c., &c.

Know'st thou not,
That when the searching eye of Heav'n is hid
Behind the globe, and lights the lower world,
Then thieves and robbers range abroad unseen,
In murders and in outrage bloody here?
But when from under this terrestrial ball
He fires the proud tops of the eastern pines,
And darts his light through ev'ry guilty hole;
Then murders, treasons, and detested sins,
The cloak of night being pluck'd from off their backs,
Stand bare and naked, trembling at themselves!

SHAKESPEARE.

WITH AN INTRODUCTION BY
REBECCA CZLAPINSKI AND ERIC C. WHEELER

Kansas City:
VALANCOURT BOOKS
2011

Pyrenean Banditti by Eleanor Sleath
First published by A. K. Newman in 1811
First Valancourt Books edition 2011

ISBN 978-1-934555-92-7

Published by Valancourt Books
Kansas City, Missouri

Composition by James D. Jenkins
Set in Dante MT

10 9 8 7 6 5 4 3 2 1

CONTENTS

INTRODUCTION

The Real Eleanor Sleath

THE novel you are about to read, *Pyrenean Banditti*, has been out of print for over two hundred years. One need only to pass through a local bookstore to see that there are already plenty of romance novels in print, so why resurrect a musty old tome? Why Eleanor Sleath? Who was Eleanor Sleath? Our research has revealed that Sleath's life was as tempestuous as those of her heroines. Before examining the new biographical information about Eleanor Sleath, one first must deal with the conjecture of past scholars. One of the misconceptions about Sleath's life, that she was Catholic, was begun in 1927 in a paper presented to the English Association by Michael Sadleir, who discusses the Northanger Canon, novels mentioned in Jane Austen's parodic Gothic novel *Northanger Abbey*. These novels are *The Orphan of the Rhine* (Sleath), *The Mysteries of Udolpho* (Ann Radcliffe), *The Necromancer* (Karl Friedrich Kahlert), *The Midnight Bell* (Francis Lathom), *Horrid Mysteries* (Carl Grosse), *Clermont* (Regina Maria Roche), *Castle of Wolfenbach* (Eliza Parsons) and *The Mysterious Warning* (Parsons). Sadleir regretted he was unable to find even a single copy of *The Orphan of the Rhine* to read as part of his research. However, by the time his paper went to press, a copy of *The Orphan of the Rhine* had been found. Sadleir categorizes the novel with Roche's *Clermont* because of its "affinity to the Radcliffian school of sensational landscape-fiction staged abroad".[1] Sadleir surmises that Sleath must be a Catholic because "the monks and nuns of *The Orphan of the Rhine* are all wise and of a spiritual disposition".[2] The idea that one must be a Catholic to treat nuns and monks kindly seems a little silly today, but Eleanor Sleath was writing in a period of animosity between Protestants and Catholics. She wrote in a genre which often used the perceived secrecy and medievalism of Catholic traditions to depict dark secrets and clandestine activity.

Devendra Varma perpetuates the idea of Sleath's Catholicism

in his introduction to the 1972 Folio Press edition of *The Nocturnal Minstrel* (1810). Varma asserts, "Mrs. Sleath's ecclesiastical figures are all of noble and virtuous pattern, sane and wise and spiritually inclined. This indicates that Mrs. Sleath had strong leanings toward Roman Catholicism".[3] However, our research reveals that her generosity and kindness toward monks and nuns stemmed from a kind spirit rather than a religious affiliation. Eleanor Sleath was the daughter of a gentleman,[4] raised as an Anglican, and married an Anglican minister, Reverend John Dudley of Sileby, England, thirty years after the death of her first husband.[5]

Varma is also the source of other mistaken information about Sleath. In his introduction to the 1968 Folio Press release of *The Orphan of the Rhine,* Professor Varma recounts his investigation through interviews with people who supposedly knew someone who knew the author and archival work that, rather than simply a *nom-de-plume* for an anonymous writer, Eleanor Sleath was a real person. He did discover that Sleath was a Leicestershire name; in fact, Leicestershire was the county in which Eleanor Sleath spent much of her life. Professor Varma erroneously concluded that Eleanor Sleath was Eleanor Martin who married Joseph Sleath of Leicestershire in 1784. However, recent archival evidence proves that this cannot be the correct woman or marriage because Eleanor Sleath, the novelist, was born in 1770 and died in 1847 at the age of 77.[6] If Sleath was born in 1770, she could not be the woman mentioned by Professor Varma who stated, "Eleanor Sleath, at the time of her marriage in 1784, stood before the altar of the Church in Gilmorton, Leicestershire; she was a tall slender woman in her twenties."[7] In 1784, Eleanor Sleath, the author, was only fourteen.

Fifty years after Professor Varma wrote his introduction to *The Orphan of the Rhine*, our research reveals details concerning the life of this interesting author. Eleanor Sleath was born Eleanor Carter and baptized at Loughborough Parish Church on 15 October 1770. The youngest child of Thomas and Elizabeth Carter, Eleanor had four older siblings: John Edward (1753), Mary (1755), Judith (1757), and Ann (1766).[8] As an upper-middle class family of the minor gentry, the Carter family moved from Herefordshire to Leicester during the seventeenth century.[9]

Eleanor's father Thomas was one of five surviving brothers;

his siblings were John, Laurence, Isaac, and Henry. If one were not the eldest son who inherited and managed the estate, choice of professions of landed gentry at the time included only a few options such as the clergy, law, and the military. John Carter became a cleric, while Thomas and Isaac entered the legal profession. Little is known of Thomas's early life until his marriage to Elizabeth Cousins at Wimeswold, Leicestershire on 6 October 1752.[10] The demands of a country attorney forced Thomas and his new family to move multiple times before they settled in the market town of Loughborough where Eleanor was born in 1770.[11] Thomas Carter died while away from home, more than likely unexpectedly because he died without a will. He was buried at Sileby on 29 October 1773.[12] Elizabeth, his widow, and his brother Isaac administered the estate until John Edward reached his majority. The family had land wealth to provide a living and allow for the education of the children.

Although the details of Eleanor's upbringing are unknown, we can assume she was educated in social and practical skills involving managing a household to the standards of a young woman of her status. In the late eighteenth century, women were either tutored at home or sent to small local schools in someone's home. An accomplished woman of Sleath's time would be taught "drawing, dancing, penmanship, piano playing, grammar, spelling, elementary arithmetic" and often French.[13] It is evident that Eleanor Sleath was an educated woman. By tracing the epigraphs of her first novel, *The Orphan of the Rhine* (1798), one can imagine some of the authors she had on her shelf: John Milton, Oliver Goldsmith, Robert Burns, William Mason, Alexander Pope, and, of course, William Shakespeare. She may have owned the popular collection of essays and poems called *Extracts, Elegant, Instructive and Entertaining* (1791). Or she could have owned *The Lady's Poetical Magazine* (1781) or *The Tea Table Miscellany* (1755), since both also contained several of the works she references. In addition to having the resources to select an apt epigraph, Sleath demonstrates a familiarity with conventional plotting and stock characters of the gothic romance novels so popular at the time.

On 14 September 1792, Eleanor Carter married Joseph Barnabas Sleath of Calverton, Buckinghamshire.[14] Details about Joseph are limited. He was summoned as an officer cadet "for the artillery of the Bengal Establishment" in 1783 but had found a substitute to go in his place by 1784.[15] Whether or not he went to India is uncertain; however, he was connected to the military and was named a surgeon of the Leicestershire militia in 1794. It is possible that Eleanor met her husband through the Leicestershire militia with which her brother John Edward was also associated.

By the time of her marriage, Eleanor was twenty-one; Joseph was five years her senior and a bachelor. It is interesting to note that Eleanor's marriage, unlike those of all her siblings, took place outside of Leicestershire; she was married instead at Calverton, the home of Joseph Sleath. No member of the Carter family signed the Calverton parish register as witness to the marriage.[16] These seemingly minor details raise questions: Did her family frown on the marriage? Could she have been pregnant? Could she have been acting against the wishes of her family? The newlyweds settled in the large market town of Nuneaton, a distance from both of their families. Joseph established himself as a surgeon and apothecary with an early account referring to him as "Mr. Sleith Doctor."[17] Eleanor went about setting up her home, as is evidenced by the minute details provided in her surviving bills of expenditure: from buying curtains, carpets, tables, and the painting of the parlour, to the repair of her watch for two shillings.[18] Eleanor soon gave birth to a son: Joseph Barnabas Sleath. Surviving records paint a picture of domestic bliss, hopes for the future, and new beginnings; however, that happiness was not to last.

The Leicestershire militia began to recruit more troops because of the threat of a French invasion. Joseph resigned from the military in 1794; the first in a chain of events that would shatter Eleanor's newfound happiness. In September Eleanor and Joseph lost their child, who was buried in Nuneaton parish churchyard on 4 September 1794.[19] Four weeks later, Eleanor's husband died at the age of twenty-eight.[20] Eleanor was left with mountains of debt, mostly household expenses and unpaid business accounts.[21] No record exists of any money or property left to Eleanor by her husband, although she probably had income from previous Carter family legacies. Records do show that John Edward, Eleanor's brother, her mother Elizabeth, and her brother-in-law J. S. Cardale administered the debts of Joseph's estate. One by one the debts were discharged over the winter and spring of 1794 and 1795. In November, after returning to Leicester, Eleanor fell ill, no doubt from stress and grief.[22]

From this period until the publication of *The Orphan of the Rhine* in 1798, little is known about Sleath's life. It is unclear whether her writing was a serious hobby, a career path, or a means of providing income to discharge her debts. Eleanor met frequently with a small group of intellectual and literary minded neighbors who often shared their work and received critiques and support. One member of the group was Susanna Watts, a well-known poet and resident of Leicester. A descendant from Sleath's great-grandfather's first marriage, Susanna Watts's family suffered economic difficulties. She was self-educated and of a genteel nature. To help get by, Watts published poetry and her own translations of French and Italian literary works,[23] as well as the first guide for the town of Leicester: *A Walk through Leicester* (1804). Susanna Watts's determination, her love of nature, and her persistent advocacy against social injustice, particularly slavery, has earned her a place in history as a strong female leader in a time when women's roles were restricted. In addition to Susanna Watts, the group consisted of Eleanor Sleath and Reverend John Dudley, vicar of Humberstone, as well as a few others. Sleath completed and published at least one novel after *Orphan of the Rhine* while meeting with this group. *Who's the Murderer?* was published in 1802 while Eleanor was living in the small village of Scraptoft, four miles east of Leicester.

In 1801, John Edward Carter moved his family, including Eleanor and their mother, from Leicester to an estate he leased called Scraptoft Hall. Located a short distance from the busy town of Leicester, Scraptoft Hall, with its gardens, grottos, and lush grounds, provided a retreat for Carter.[24] The Carters mixed with the local gentry of the area including the Watts, the Coltmans, the Simons, the Heyricks, the Frewens of Cold Overton, and the Dudleys of nearby Humberstone. The Carters, Frewens, and Dudleys often called on each other for tea in order to catch up on local business and gossip. They also stayed at each other's homes. For example, in 1803 John Dudley notes that he stayed at Cold Overton Hall for seventeen days;[25] and Mary Frewen and

Susanna Watts stayed with the Dudleys the same year.[26] The group of friends often traveled together. The letters between John Dudley and John Frewen indicated that they frequented the fashionable resort, Bath, where they attended balls, the theater, social functions, and other activities.[27] In February 1804, a party including John Dudley, his wife Ann, and Mary Frewen set off for Bath. They were joined by John Frewen, and Ann Dudley's father and sister.[28] Later that year, John Dudley notes in his diary that "Mrs. Sleath set off with Mrs. Dudley and myself on a journey into North Wales," and they were joined later by the Carters, the Miss Bagnalls and their maid, and a Miss Lutwidge.[29] Eleanor Sleath moved in a close knit circle of families affording her social and intellectual stimulation. Thrown into each other's company as a result of friendships and literary interests, Eleanor Sleath and John Dudley developed a platonic friendship. John Dudley tells John Frewen in a letter, "various literary occupations led me to frequent intercourse with Mrs. S and Miss Watts."[30] Mrs. John Dudley developed a resentment of their relationship, when in 1807, at a gathering of friends and family, Eleanor's sister-in-law, Mrs. John Carter (Elizabeth) commented sarcastically about the nature of the friendship between Eleanor and Rev. Dudley. The sarcastic remark sparked gossip inflaming a simmering jealousy in the heart of Mrs. Dudley, resulting in a slanderous scandal, a strained marriage, and shattered friendships. In a letter to John Frewen, Dudley complains that the "sarcasms of Mrs. Carter, which were very unfriendly, fostered by the Watts laid . . . the foundation of jealousy in the mind" of his wife.[31] According to John Dudley, his wife hid her jealousy until she eventually "became hostile to Mrs. S. and injured her indiscreetly and secretly in various ways," all while maintaining a civil and friendly facade. Dudley naively chose to believe that his wife's "discontent" would diminish when she realized that his "acquaintance with Mrs. S produced no change in [his] behaviour or affection toward her."[32]

Despite his continued insistence that his relationship with Mrs. Sleath was purely platonic, Ann Dudley's jealousy grew. Dudley believed that he had done nothing wrong and felt that he had to protect Eleanor's honor, which had been tarnished by gossip and rumors, and increased his wife's anger. Dudley enlisted the help of

John Edward Carter and his brother Isaac, but to no avail. Finally, Mr. Pochin, a mutual friend, suggested that Mrs. Dudley make peace with Eleanor. She agreed to do so "but her very first step rendered the thing improbable. Her violence now was no longer controlled and the worst of language was too often used."[33] John Dudley finally gave up seeing Eleanor when his wife insisted that her health was failing; however, her ailment proved to be a ruse when she made a miraculous recovery.

The circle of friends became polarized with Susanna Watts and Elizabeth Simons siding with Mrs. Dudley and fueling her resentment. Eventually Mrs. Dudley's machinations led to her undoing when she spread a rumor that Mrs. Sleath went to London with the Isaac Dudleys in order to have a child—the love child of her husband, John Dudley.[34] Rumors began circulating around Leicester that Dudley fathered a bastard by Eleanor, and an anonymous letter was sent to Eleanor instructing her to forgo the acquaintance of the Dudley family for the sake of Mrs. Dudley's "peace."[35]

Frustrated and angry at the attacks upon both his and Eleanor's character and reputation, Dudley charged Mrs. Simons with giving a "slanderous report," and later he also filed a citation against her in ecclesiastic court for defamation. He also visited Susanna Watts, accusing her of authoring the anonymous letter and threatening her with a lawsuit. However, loss of friendship and a crumbling reputation were not his only troubles. In the letter to John Frewen in which he explains the sad course of events, Dudley asserts that Mrs. Dudley "is now desperate and her only object is revenge which is chiefly directed against me. She rides about to defame me." He goes on to explain that she knew he was about to sell everything and "run away with Mrs. S." Mrs. Dudley also told "Mrs. Isaac Dudley that she was hired to murder her." Dudley also accused his wife of feigning injuries so that she could accuse him of assault.[36] Dudley decided to remove his wife from Humberstone, the center of the gossip, and moved to his other vicarage in the village of Sileby, seven miles north of Leicester. The move also allowed the Dudleys to live in separate houses with Ann and the servants in the larger house and John in the smaller.

As a result of the scandal, acrimony, and separation, the

Dudleys' social circle was diminished and as a result the flow of letters stopped, reducing the source of details about the lives of the Dudleys and Eleanor Sleath. We do know, however, that these years of upheaval were a very creative period with three books published between 1809 and 1811: *The Bristol Heiress* (1809); *The Nocturnal Minstrel* (1810), and *Pyrenean Banditti* (1811). John Dudley too published a poem, *The Metamorphosis of Sona: A Hindu Tale*, in 1810. The preface to his work hints at Eleanor's encouragement and again mentions her Indian novel which he alluded to in a his diaries six years earlier: "The author of this work was induced to relate in verse, the following legendary tale from the Vayera Parana, at the suggestion of an ingenuous and esteemed friend; who, intending to write upon a subject connected with Hindusthan, imagined such a poem might be properly introduced in it."[37] Sleath's novel of India hinted at by Dudley has yet to be discovered, nor has it been determined if it was written. *Glenowen; or, The Fairy Palace* (1815) does contain Indian material; however, it is hardly "connected with Hindusthan." This preface also implies that Dudley and Sleath were still working together.

Eleanor faced another upheaval in 1813 when her brother John Edward Carter died without issue, and his large estate was divided among his wife and his four sisters. Eleanor was bequeathed a house on High Street Leicester, and a quarter share in a small estate called Brickman Hill in Kirby Muxloe which she would inherit after the death of Elizabeth Carter. She received a lump sum of £2000 to be paid out of the Barons Park Estate inherited by her sister Ann Carr, and £1000 from John Edward's personal estate. She earned interest on these bequests for two years after John Edward's death. Eleanor, along with her brothers-in-law George Carr and Joseph Spencer Cardale, were the executors of John Edward's estate which granted them a financial reward through a division of the residue of John's personal wealth and real estate after all bequests, debts, and funeral expenses were settled.[38] Six months after her brother's death, Eleanor lost her mother.

Little is known about Eleanor whereabouts between 1814 and 1816. Records place Eleanor in Loughborough, a market town, where she remained for six years in a house on the Leicester Road that she purchased for £500 on 19 December 1816.[39] It is interesting to note that Loughborough was the location of the petty sessions court where local magistrates, including John Dudley, came to try cases. Also Loughborough is only 5 miles from Sileby, where Dudley continued to live alone after Ann moved to Leicester in 1811 after a getting a deed of separation.[40] Although the details of Eleanor Sleath's life for the next six years are unknown, one can assume she lived a comfortable life as an independent widow with means of her own. Since John Dudley was separated from his wife, he was free to see Eleanor. When they received news of Ann Dudley's death in February of 1823, they became betrothed and married on 1 April 1823 at the Loughborough parish church.[41]

Eleanor and John Dudley settled in Sileby. Eleanor would have been kept busy as a vicar's wife for two congregations, and his partner as he remained active in various clerical and civic duties. In 1847 Eleanor's health began to decline, and she died of liver disease[43] at home at the Sileby vicarage on 5 May 1847 at the age of 77.

Like the lives of her heroines, Eleanor Sleath's life included drama, scandal, loss; like her heroines, Eleanor Sleath faced adversity headlong with a strong faith in God and the power of a loving family; like her heroines, Eleanor Sleath achieved happiness and married the man she loved after many trials.

Pyrenean Banditi

Eleanor Sleath wrote romances during the rise of the popularity of novels through circulating libraries in the late eighteenth and early nineteenth centuries. Her early works are deeply entrenched in the Gothic tradition as established by Horace Walpole's *The Castle of Otranto* (1764) and Ann Radcliffe's novels, including *The Mysteries of Udolpho* (1794), *The Italian* (1797) and *Romance of the Forest* (1791). Sleath's 1798 novel *Orphan of the Rhine* remains in print because it is mentioned in Jane Austen's parodic Gothic novel, *Northanger Abbey,* as a "horrid novel," evoking a spine-chilling fear and horror. *Pyrenean Banditti* can be classified as a "horrid novel" in the sense that it evokes fear and horror; however, the horror and fear are evoked mainly by the immoral behavior of people, rather than the appearance of supernatural apparitions—although Sleath does include one specter.

Sleath follows the Gothic conventions popular during the early part of her lifetime, particularly those used by Ann Radcliffe. Sleath's Gothic romances fall under the category of Female Gothic. First, supernatural events are explained as created by humans to frighten or distract. Second, her works are didactic, demanding that the reader reflect on the lessons of the novel, grow morally and accept the conservative views held forth. Third, the heroine in Sleath's novel is strong and morally sound, while many of the peripheral characters are immoral. Finally, the heroine has a strong bond with another woman in the novel.

Pyrenean Banditti depicts a fallen world in which the protagonist must face tests and trials in order to achieve a greater understanding of herself, her relationship with others, and, in the case of this novel, to the divine. Like other Gothic novels, *Pyrenean Banditti* examines power relationships and the arbitrary nature of gender-based power imbalances.

The greatest symbol of medieval secular power is the castle. Functioning as a positive image, the castle standing on a hill guarding all within its sphere represents safety, home, and vision. Functioning as a fallen image, the castle teetering on the edge of a chasm surrounded by mist, fog and darkness represents danger and prison resulting in terror, despair, and evil for all within. The first castle in *Pyrenean Banditti*, that of Count Saint Angouléme, is furnished comfortably and open for visitors; however, the female occupants are isolated by this sinister and menacing Count. The two main female characters, the Countess and Adelaide, are emotionally manipulated and abused, as well as socially immured, in effect jailed by Count St. Angouléme. Later in the novel, in a rare outing from the castle, Adelaide is waylaid by banditti and incarcerated in a second, more remote and decrepit castle where she is a physical prisoner. Adelaide moves from one place of incarceration to another through a series of misadventures involving two castles, two chateaus, and two prisons. Adelaide's final prison is one of silence and secrecy resulting from a bond of filial loyalty in which she faces certain torture and perhaps death rather than betray her newfound father, a man she can neither love nor respect. Despite having gained a father, Adelaide remains alone.

The lonely Adelaide, a recent orphan, as are many Gothic protagonists, falls from a state of happy innocence, secure in the love of her father, the Chevalier St. Angouléme, to a state of confusion, which shakes her very self-image, while she attempts to navigate a confusing world of truths, half-truths, and falsehoods, all while retaining her personal integrity and faith in God. While Adelaide's body is in the power of her uncle, or a variety of other villains, and seems to be a prisoner, she remains a bastion of selfhood and faith, constantly seeking strength in herself and in her relationship to the divine, while learning from even the most frightening experiences. She resists becoming cynical and world-wearied by her trials; she emerges as a confident, powerful woman who survives the fallen world of the novel because of her own inner strength.

Adelaide must draw on her reservoir of fortitude in facing a deception created to manipulate her and undermine her social status. Adelaide is told that her loving, aristocratic father was not her blood relation; she discovers instead that her alleged birth father is a man of reprehensible character and low birth. By reducing Adelaide from an aristocratic heiress to a female of the servant class, Sleath undermines her power and limits her ability to navigate in the landscape of the novel. Facing powerlessness forces Adelaide to further strengthen her faith and fortitude. This plot twist also allows Sleath to explore some class anxieties. The evil Count responsible for Adelaide's tribulations and exile is counter-balanced by a kind male servant who rescues her and provides her with refuge, expressing faith in the seemingly ignorant, yet moral working class while expressing disillusionment with the old ideals of the aristocracy. This reversal of roles by class reveals the upward mobility hopes of the early nineteenth century working class and the anxiety of the aristocracy at their weakening hegemony.

Another source of tension in the book is the image of beautiful, moral, and honorable Adelaide and her potential to be either angel or whore. Adelaide through her beauty becomes the supernatural force in this novel as the fear and horror is evoked by extraordinary human malice. Adelaide, as "more than woman," has all of the physical and psychological attributes of the ideal woman: she is beautiful, pious, submissive, and naïve; yet, she has a firmness, an unyielding, self-righteous, stubborn impulse to remain loyal to an undeserving father-figure. Through her silence about the mystery surrounding her circumstances and her new father De Launé, Adelaide's past is misconstrued. She spends some time in the care of a woman of low status and ill-repute, thus inadvertently tarring herself with the same brush, despite her vulnerability and ignorance of the woman's past. Adelaide's confused love interest Montroi seeks the help of an old friend, Father Athanasa, who perceives Adelaide's beauty and accomplishments as "lures held out for [Montroi's] destruction." Before Father Athanasa meets Adelaide, she is cast as the seductress, the temptress, the Eve who will lure her male victim to sin. In contrast, Adelaide's beauty, demeanor, and gentility cause admiring gentlemen who meet her to perceive her as angelic: her "rosy health, associating with innocence, or what appeared to be such, gave her more than human splendour to her beauty, and exhibited her to his enraptured fancy as something truly angelic." Sleath, herself the subject of gossip, also strove to maintain her own reputation as an honorable and moral person. Her concerns about gossip and deportment are apparent in the didactic passages of the book when the narrative voice comments on moral behavior.

Only time will tell where Sleath's out-of print works will fit in the growing corpus of newly rediscovered women writers. *Pyrenean Banditti* is an interesting book with the potential to add to the discourse surrounding women writers of the eighteenth and nineteenth centuries.

Rebecca Czlapinski and Eric C. Wheeler

December 6, 2010

NOTES

1 Michael Sadleir, *The Northanger Novels*. 1927. p. 22
2 Ibid.
3 Devendra Varma, "Introduction." *The Nocturnal Minstrel*. New York: Arno Press, 1972.
4 3D42/13/49. Undated. Record office for Leicester, Leicestershire and Rutland (ROLLR).
5 Loughborough All Saints: Marriages 1815-1826. "John Dudley of the Parish of Sileby & Eleanor Sleath of this Parish were married in this church by License 1 April 1823."
6 3D42/13/49. Undated. ROLLR. Sleath's birth records. Death Registered 8 May 1847: Eleanor Dudley 1847 – Quarter 2, Barrow upon Soar District Vol. 15 p. 24.
7 Devendra Varma, "Introduction." *The Orphan of the Rhine*. London: Folio Press, 1968.
8 Joseph Spencer Cardale. "Copies of Parish Reg[iste]rs respecting the Carter Family", nd. 3D42/13/49. ROLLR.
9 Ibid.
10 3D42/13/49. Undated. ROLLR.
11 Ibid.
12 Eric C. Wheeler. The Parish Registers of St. Mary Sileby Leicestershire Vol. IV: Baptisms and Burials 1765-1812. Burials 1843-1846. Sileby: 2003. p. 83.
13 Barbara Swords. "Woman's Place in Jane Austen's England." *Persuasions* 10 (1988).
14 3D42/13/49. Undated. ROLLR.
15 IOR/L/MIL/9/255/70v, 74 British Library 1782-84. Also: Major Hodson, V.C.P. *The Officers of the Bengal Army 1758-1834* Vol. 4 Part 1 S-V. London; 1947. p. 112.
16 Calverton, Buckinghamshire. Parish Registers—Marriages 1559-1836. Centre for Buckinghamshire Studies. p. 22.
17 3D42/13/66 ROLLR.
18 Various accounts: 3D42/13/69, 3D42/13/74, 3D42/13/81 ROLLR.
19 A birth or baptism date is not known. His existence is known from his burial record: St. Nicholas, Nuneaton. Parish Register Burials 1577-1812. 4 September 1794. DR 61/5 Warwickshire County Record Office.
20 St. Nicholas, Nuneaton. Parish Register Burials 1577-1812. September & October 1794. op. cit.
21 Various accounts: 3D42/13/65-71, 75-78, 84 ROLLR.
22 Account of Thomas Teasdale, 13 November 1794. 3D42/13/69 ROLLR.
23 Shirley Aucott. *Susanna Watts 1768-1842*. Leicester, 2004. p. 10.
24 Lease dated 31 May 1801 between Edward Hartopp Wigley of Little Dalby,

Esq and John Edward Carter of Scraptoft, Gentleman. 3D42/13/507 ROLLR.

25 Misc 338. op. cit. p. 55 ROLLR.

26 FRE 2314 East Sussex Record Office (ESRO).

27 Letter from John Dudley to Mary Frewen with his impressions of Bath, 12 April 1801. FRE 2786 ESRO. Also FRE 1231 ESRO. John Frewen at Bath in 1784.

28 Misc. 338. op cit p. 57 ROLLR.

29 Misc. 338. op cit p. 67 ROLLR.

30 Letter from John Dudley to John Frewen dated 20 September 1808 FRE 1832 ESRO p. 1.

31 Letter from John Dudley to John Frewen dated 20 September 1808 FRE 1832 ESRO p. 1.

32 FRE 1832 ESRO. ibid. p. 1-2.

33 FRE 1832 ESRO. p. 2.

34 FRE 1832 ESRO. p. 2-3.

35 Letter from Susanna Watts to Mary Frewen dated 8 August 1808. p 3 FRE2817 ESRO.

36 FRE 1832 ESRO. p. 3.

37 John Dudley, *The Metamorphosis of Sona*. London: Black, Parry, and Kingsbury, 1810. ROLLR.

38 Will of John Edward Carter of Scraptoft, Gentleman. Dated 21 October 1811. Codicil dated 7 June 1804. Proved at London 26 July 1813. PROB 11/1546 National Archives.

39 Conveyance: John Heathcote of Tiverton to Eleanor Sleath of Loughborough, widow. Dated 19 December 1816. DE 2018/15 ROLLR.

40 Deed of Separation mentioned in the will of Ann Dudley, dated 2 October 1821, proved 3 May 1823 PROB 11/1670 National Archives.

41 Loughborough All Saints: Marriages 1815-1826. "John Dudley of the Parish of Sileby & Eleanor Sleath of this Parish were married in this church by License 1 April 1823."

42 Death Registered 8 May 1847: Eleanor Dudley 1847 — Quarter 2, Barrow upon Soar District Vol. 15 p. 24.

CHRONOLOGY

1770 Eleanor Carter born in Loughborough, Leicestershire.

1792 Eleanor Carter marries Joseph Barnabas Sleath in Calverton, Buckinghamshire, moves to Nuneaton, Leicestershire.

1794 Joseph Barnabas Sleath, son and husband, both dead, Eleanor lives with brother John Edward Carter, Leicester.

1798 *The Orphan of the Rhine* published by William Lane's Minerva Press.

1801 Eleanor moves with brother's family to Scraptoft Hall, Leicestershire, part of a literary group in the area, including Susanna Watts and John Dudley.

1802 *Who's the Murderer?* published by Lane's Minerva Press.

1804 Travels to Wales with Ann and John Dudley, joined by brother and his family.

1808 Scandal erupts of illicit affair between Sleath and John Dudley; John and Ann Dudley separate.

1809 *The Bristol Heiress: or Errors in Education* published.

1810 *The Nocturnal Minstrel* published.

1811 *Pyrenean Banditti* published. John and Ann Dudley legally separated.

1813 John Edward Carter dies, Eleanor inherits property and cash; mother Elizabeth dies at 83.

1815 *Glenowen; or, The Fairy Palace* published.

1816 19 December: Eleanor Sleath purchases a house in Loughborough.

1823 Death of Ann Dudley; John Dudley and Eleanor Sleath marry in Loughborough, live in Sileby.

1833-4 High Street Bridge over Sileby Brook dedicated to John and Eleanor Dudley.

1847 5 May: Eleanor Dudley's death.

1856 John Dudley's death.

NOTE ON THE TEXT

The Valancourt Books edition of *Pyrenean Banditti* follows the original three volume edition published by Anthony King (A.K.) Newman of London in 1811, under the Minerva Press imprint, to which he succeeded after his business partner William Lane's retirement. One or two obvious printer's errors have been silently corrected; otherwise, the text reproduced here is unabridged and unaltered. No effort has been made to modernize or standardize spelling or punctuation.

This 200th anniversary edition of the novel is the first reprint since the original edition, copies of which are known to survive only in the collections of Yale University, Harvard University, and the Corvey Library.

PYRENEAN BANDITTI.

A ROMANCE

IN THREE VOLUMES.

BY

ELEANOR SLEATH,

AUTHOR OF

THE NOCTURNAL MINSTREL, BRISTOL HEIRESS, WHO'S THE MURDERER, &c., &c.

Know'st thou not,
That when the searching eye of Heav'n is hid
Behind the globe, and lights the lower world,
Then thieves and robbers range abroad unseen,
In murders and in outrage bloody here?
But when from under this terrestrial ball
He fires the proud tops of the eastern pines,
And darts his light through ev'ry guilty hole;
Then murders, treasons, and detested sins,
The cloak of night being pluck'd from off their backs,
Stand bare and naked, trembling at themselves!

SHAKESPEARE.

VOL. I.

LONDON:
PRINTED AT THE
Minerva-Press,
FOR A. K. NEWMAN AND CO.
(Successors to Lane, Newman, and Co.)
LEADENHALL-STREET.
1811.

CHAP. I.

IN that wild tract of country which separates Barrége from St. Girono, in the little district of Gascony called the Conserance, stood, in the year 1653, the Castle of St. Angouléme, a venerable and lofty pile, for many centuries inhabited by the family of that name. It had been fortified with the care necessary to defend it from the incursions of the enemy, when the burning zeal of religious fury broke out, and raged with unabated violence under the factious government of Charles the Ninth and Catherine De Medicis; when the Huguenots,* driven by persecution to acts of desperate violence, took arms against their fellow-subjects, and involved the whole country in civil tumult and desolation.

The family of St. Angouléme had attached itself to the royalist or Catholic party, and till the period when Henry, Prince of Navarre, mounted the throne of France, had retained considerable interest and authority at Court, amid all the political revolutions and intrigues which disgrace the annals of that celebrated æra.

The disgust which naturally attends the triumph of the opposite party, the coalition of new interests, and a fresh system of state politics, drove the family of St. Angouléme from a Court, where its influence had ceased to be felt, and where its interests were no longer courted: the high posts of honour it had hitherto occupied, were transferred to other families, and the descendants of a once-noble house, reduced by poverty to a situation which scarce enabled them to maintain an appearance suitable to the rank of the chevaliers, or private gentlemen of the country.

The Castle seemed now to be the only vestige of the former opulence and extravagance of the family, guarded on one side by the Pyrenees, on the other by ramparts and battlements, which appeared, but for some breaches which the fury of civil war had made, to have been almost impregnable, stood this venerable remain of antique grandeur. It was surrounded by a moat, now partly filled up, but broad, and once deep; in which several kinds of water-fowl lived secure and unmolested, amid the reedy grass and weeds which fringed its sides, and whose cries were often heard with those of the vulture, which was seen cowering round the neighbouring cliff, or the eagle, as she sought her eyrie among the rocks, which either jutted out into immense crags, or rose in giant masses above the walls of the Castle.

A bridge, now seldom drawn up, was the only means of access. The entrance was through a stone arch, to a hall, lofty and extensive, and adorned, like the rest of the apartments, with the heavy magnificence of former times. No alteration had, for several years, taken place in the furniture and decorations of this once-splendid mansion; nor was it in the power of its present inhabitant to repair the breaches which time and war had made in it.

The Count, as he retained not the opulence, neither did he possess the virtues of his ancestors; these Nature seemed to have bestowed exclusively to enrich the mind of his brother, the Chevalier St. Angouléme, who having, through an advantageous alliance by marriage, and an elegant, not niggardly economy, realized the means of enabling himself to maintain an appearance of splendour and affluence far above that of the Count, had become the object of his direst hatred and detestation.

Count St. Angouléme never forgave an injury, or what he conceived to be such. He had loved Madame St. Angouléme, previous to her marriage with his brother, had offered himself, and was rejected. The loss of the lady he could have borne, but that of her fortune, which was immense, and which was the principal object of his wishes, was a stroke as fatal to his interests as it was mortifying to his pride; and when, in a brother, whom he had never loved, he beheld the rival of his hopes, his interests, and his ambition, his rage and disappointment knew no bounds.

Till the death of Madame St. Angouléme, which happened to the inexpressible grief of the Chevalier, about ten years after their marriage, the Count had never seen or written to his brother.

He had been informed by the Chevalier, in a letter dictated in the most affectionate terms imaginable, of the birth of a daughter, with which Madame had unexpectedly presented him, about five years after their marriage: but the letter, after having been coldly received, was thrown aside, though it contained, with the most earnest solicitations, an invitation for the Count to visit Avignon, to perform the office of sponsor to his infant niece, who had already been baptized by the name of Adelaide.

From that period till the death of Madame St. Angouléme, nothing passed between the two brothers; but as the Chevalier thought it right, notwithstanding his brother's neglect of him, to inform him of this sad event, he again ventured to address him: and received in return a letter, containing a few common-place condolences, conceived in formal and concise terms, and so little expressive of a friendship towards himself, that it seemed to have been drawn from him rather by necessity than inclination.

The Count, during several years, had spent much of his time at Paris, and had mixed occasionally in the dissipations of that voluptuous city: he had made several unsuccessful attempts to ally himself to the heiress of some illustrious house, whose ample fortune might remedy the deficiencies of his own, and enable him to support an appearance equal to his rank and situation. He had reached his fortieth year, without having obtained the object of his wishes: he saw with mortification and regret, that he was destitute of those arts of insinuation which are necessary to secure an interest in the heart of a young and beautiful woman, as richly endowed by fortune as by nature; and, after a number of unsuccessful efforts, resolved to make fortune, as it was his first, his only object of pursuit.

Whilst partaking of the amusements of the metropolis, he found means to introduce himself to the widow of a rich Portuguese merchant, the daughter of a private gentleman in the neighbourhood of Rouen, a lady who, though past the bloom of life, possessed a sufficient portion of beauty to attract admiration, even at Paris: her manners were amiable, her disposition was sweet, her fortune large. The Count made overtures, and was accepted: the marriage was celebrated without delay, though not without some secret dissatisfaction on the part of the Count; the lady having insisted that the half of her property should remain at her own disposal, in consideration of a nephew, who had been left an orphan to her care, and for whom she had promised to provide. The youth was pursuing his studies at one of the seminaries at Paris, at the time of his aunt's marriage, and was sent for, to join in the festivities usual on such occasions.

Theodore St. Leon, for that was his name, was then only seventeen years old: his countenance was prepossessing: his figure, for his age, tall, and finely proportioned; his address graceful; his disposition frank, ardent, generous, and sincere. The new Countess having had no children by her former marriage, had attached herself to her nephew with the tenderness of a parent; it was perhaps rather in compliance with the ambitious wishes of her family, than her own inclinations, that she had consented to make his happiness in some degree dependent upon the will and power of another.

It was not, however, till several months after her marriage, that she began to feel anxiety for the fate of her nephew. The Count had assumed an appearance of kindness and affection for his new relative, which being only assumed, it became difficult for any length of time to support: he grew indifferent, and at length severe. His lady was accused of an undue partiality to one who, from some traits of character he pretended to observe, would soon prove unworthy of her care: every trifling defect was magnified into a fault, every excellence concealed, or repressed; what would have been a virtue in others, was a vice in Theodore; what in others would have been termed an error, was in him a crime.

The prejudice which his uncle had conceived to the unfortunate youth, causeless as it appeared, became at length a source of sorrow and regret to the unhappy Countess; it was unjust, and therefore could not be removed: and it was easy to perceive, that any mark of affection discovered to him by herself, occasioned an increased disgust in the heart of her husband; and that this disgust (although, in their now frequent conversations on the subject of her concern and solicitude, she still continued to practice the utmost gentleness and forbearance in her behaviour to her Lord) was extending rapidly to herself, and threatened to become the cause of much domestic uneasiness.

The school-vacations were no longer welcomed by Theodore as they had been formerly; two had already been spent at the castle, and one at Paris, when the Countess, with eyes swimming with tears, and a countenance on which the anguish of her heart was faithfully delineated, informed him, that he must spend the next with a distant relative of hers, in Provence; and that, as he had discovered an early predilection for a military life, she had determined to purchase him a commission—"Go, my child," added she, "and may Heaven protect and bless you! Alas! I can no longer offer you an asylum in the castle: your uncle, whom, I now too late perceive, had no motive in marrying me, but to make a considerable addition to his own fortune, upon my refusal to relinquish that part of my property which I had reserved for you, insists that you shall never more enter those doors."

Theodore mingled his tears with those of his affectionate relative while she uttered these words, which were frequently interrupted by deep and heavy sighs; he earnestly conjured her to submit to his uncle's will, lest, by a steady adherence to her first resolution, she should involve herself in difficulties and distresses, which, he added, would be infinitely more painful to him than any loss he could himself sustain—"Allow me not," said he, "to interfere with the interests of one so dear to me, one to whom I owe a debt of gratitude too vast ever to be repaid; suffer me not, I conjure you, Madam, to be the cause of domestic broil: sacrifice what you would for my sake retain; allow me, after what you have so generously promised, to depend solely on mine own exertions—let me seek my fortune in the field of honour; and may no care or sorrow intervene to disturb, on my account, the peace and happiness of one so dear to me."

"Generous and noble youth," exclaimed the Countess, again weeping bitterly—"But you are not yet acquainted with half my causes of distress; alas! never again can happiness or peace visit this unhappy bosom!—Your uncle is not only avaricious, but necessitous—he is in debt, deeply in debt; and when last at Paris, lost, I have been since told, considerable sums at play: the reserve I would make is not, therefore, more necessary on your account than my own. Oh, why was I ever persuaded, for the acquisition of an empty title, to sacrifice my fortune and my peace!"

Theodore now perceived that his aunt had a double motive for persisting in her determination of resisting the persuasions and threats of her Lord: he trembled at the review of a situation so replete with difficulties and even dangers: he knew not what to advise: for, of the haughty and tyrannical disposition of the Count, he had already had repeated proofs.

"You, Theodore," resumed the Countess, after a pause of some moments, "may yet taste the blessings of prosperity. The estates of your family are considerable, though, as the descendant of a younger branch, your title to them is not immediate. It is not however improbable," added she, "but you may succeed, in a few years, to that of your late uncle: the present heir, now about sixteen years of age, is said to be consumptive; and has been ordered, as a letter from my friend Madame Boileau has this day informed me, to try the effects of a foreign climate. His health may be restored; but on his death, should this happen, your claim to an estate of upwards of twelve thousand a-year is indisputable. I shall then behold my Theodore elevated to a situation which he is every way calculated to fill with honour and dignity."

"Could I see you happy, Madam," said Theodore, tenderly taking his aunt's hand, "I should have no thought or care for myself. Oh that I could indeed instruct you in what way to act! but, alas! in a matter of such moment, I feel myself utterly incompetent to advise. Think only of yourself, and let not your child, your Theodore, occasion you one moment of anxiety."

The Countess tenderly embraced her nephew. While she

pressed him to her throbbing heart, the agonizing idea presented itself that she might never see him more: she wept anew; her audible sobs penetrated the heart of Theodore—it was with difficulty that he could restrain the expression of his grief; a thousand melancholy forebodings communicated to his heart—"Alas!" said he, "how much uneasiness have I cost you! how much may I yet cost you!—Adieu, my more than mother; may Heaven reward and bless you!"

"Adieu, my beloved child," feebly ejaculated the Countess; "write to me frequently, my Theodore; and may the holy virgin protect and guard you!"

CHAP. II.

The Countess retired to her chamber, to give free vent to a sorrow she was afraid openly to express, and which she was utterly unable to restrain. It was near the dinner hour: the Count, who had been absent, returned with a party of guests; the Countess, unable to compose her mind, or remove traces of her grief, pleaded indisposition, and dined alone in her anti-chamber. When she again met the Count, she affected to appear cheerful; but the effort was ineffectual. He observed the uneasiness she would have concealed; and knowing she had lately parted with Theodore, was not insensible to its cause—"I did not know, Madam," he said haughtily, "that when I received your hand at the altar, I was to hold but the second place in your heart. It is well, however," added he, "that I am at last effectually rid of that rival in your affections, whose artful insinuations have been but too successful in their purpose. But recollect, Madam, though the inconvenience may be mine, the punishment may be yours: except on the conditions I have mentioned, you see Theodore no more."

"No more!" reiterated the Countess—"Oh, my Lord, you will not, you cannot be so cruel!"

"Sign those papers," cried the Count authoritatively, "and I will instantly issue an order for his return."

"*Never*," said the Countess emphatically.

"Decide not too hastily," cried the Count—"you may repent. You love the boy?"

"As my life," said the Countess.

The Count reddened, and looked contemptuously—"Shall I then send for him back?"

"Never, dear as he is to me, on the conditions you impose."

"You have resolved then to see him no more?"

"I have resolved not to see him again at this castle, if, by so doing, I shall greatly offend you," answered the Countess mildly, but in a voice extremely agitated; "I may, however, see him elsewhere."

"*Hear* me," cried the Count, in a tone of voice elevated by passion to such a pitch, that, to the ears of the unhappy lady, it sounded almost tremendous, "while I swear *you shall not*; within these walls he shall never come, beyond them you shall never go."

"How, my Lord," rejoined the Countess tremulously, "am I then to be your prisoner?"

"Till you have consented to obtain your enlargement, by a relinquishment of your daring and obstinate purpose of disobedience to a husband's will," returned the Count, "you must be contented to remain a prisoner in this castle: this is my determination, Madam, nor is it in your power to alter it."

As he said this he withdrew, leaving the Countess in a state of mind too agonizing to be described. The mournful presentiments she had experienced when she last parted with Theodore, although since conceived to have been the mere effects of momentary anguish, now seemed to be realized: the rest of the day was devoted by the unhappy Countess to the most melancholy ruminations on her own fate, and that of her beloved nephew.

Shortly after this event, the Count received a letter from his brother, the Chevalier St. Angouléme, in which he informed him that he was then languishing under a nervous disorder, which had been for some time undermining his constitution, and which had hitherto resisted the effects of medicine. He was advised, he said, to travel; and had some intention, should it be agreeable to the Count, to spend a few weeks at the Castle, on his way to Barrége. He was anxious, he added, to introduce to him his daughter, then about seventeen years old, who, in the case of his demise, would, at so early an age, be in want of a protector. He then spoke of his affairs; adding that he had made his will, leaving the Count and Countess, the latter of whom he yet knew only by report, joint executors and guardians of his daughter's person and property, till she should be honourably disposed of in marriage, or till she should have attained the age of one-and-twenty: in case of her death, if she died unmarried, or without issue, during the period of her minority, all her property and estates were to devolve to the Count. At the conclusion of his letter, he expressed great pleasure in the hopes of seeing his brother, who he hoped, he said, would receive him with as much affection as he himself felt; and should he be restored to his former health, that the most friendly interest and brotherly regard would be revived and established between them.

The Count could not but feel this new instance of fraternal regard and affection from a brother whom he had cruelly slighted, if not injured; and conceiving his disorder might possibly prove fatal, although the danger might not be immediate, he resolved to answer the letter as it deserved, and invite his brother and niece to the Castle.

He communicated the contents of this letter to the Countess, to whom his manners became, on a sudden, more mild and obliging than they had been of late: Theodore was never mentioned; and the Countess, engaged in the necessary arrangements for the reception of the expected guests, seemed to have lost the immediate recollection of her recent sorrows and vexations.

The Chevalier no sooner received his brother's letter, than he made preparations for his journey; and attended by Mademoiselle Adelaide, his daughter, and a few of his domestics, set off from Avignon, and performing his route by short and easy stages, arrived at the Castle.

CHAP. III.

The Count received the Chevalier and his lovely daughter with every outward expression of affection and regard: he observed the altered appearance of the former, an alteration which seemed to be the effect of long illness and confinement; and was much struck with the personal graces of the latter, who seemed to him even more lovely than her mother, when in the full bloom of youth and beauty.

The Countess felt an immediate prepossession in favour of her lovely visitant, whose regard she endeavoured to conciliate with the most winning courtesy and politeness. The admiration which her extreme loveliness, her sweet and engaging manners, first excited, soon ripened into an attachment the most tender in the heart of the Countess; yet, though animated by the society of her amiable friends, though beguiled by their conversation, from a review of her own melancholy and forlorn state, the idea of her loved Theodore would sometimes intrude, and with it all her former uneasiness and apprehensions concerning him—"How charming would be the society of this Castle," she would sometimes say, "were he here! How would the Chevalier admire a youth possessed of so many virtues and graces as adorn my Theodore!—What a charming companion would he be for Mademoiselle Adelaide! how would they walk, read, and sing together! what an endless source of delight might they find in each other's society!" Then reverting to the Count's late cruel prohibition, she would burst into tears.

The Count's behaviour to the Countess, since the arrival of his brother and niece, had been uniformly polite and attentive. Her amiable and obliging manners soon endeared her to the Chevalier, who often spoke of her to his brother in the highest terms of commendation—"Should my illness prove fatal," said he, in one of his conversations with the Count, "I can desire nothing so much as to put my daughter under the patronage of your excellent Lady, who, I am sure, is every way calculated to take the charge of a young creature situated like Adelaide."

"You do the Countess great honour," cried the Count, affecting to be pleased with this new instance of attachment to his wife, though in reality vexed at it.

"I am convinced," resumed the Chevalier, "she is as amiable as she appears to be."

"Or as women usually are," said the Count, smiling, but in a tone that seemed to imply a sarcasm.

"I am inclined to consider her as superior to most of her sex," returned the Chevalier; "nor do I believe I overrate her merit."

The Count bowed, but was silent.

CHAP. IV.

Nothing was wanting on the part of the Count, that could contribute to the amusement and satisfaction of his guests: the mornings were usually devoted to rides, or strolls among the mountains, the evenings to the reception of various parties of the Count's friends, in which the Chevalier was allowed either to continue or retire.

Change of air, of scene, the altered behaviour of his brother, who, he now believed, had buried for ever the remembrance of his former vexation and disappointment, conspired to produce the most favourable effects imaginable upon the Chevalier's health, which was now visibly improving.

Adelaide, who had hitherto seemed to droop under the melancholy presages of her father's fate, suffered hope again to visit her heart: her features, which had hitherto been overcast with a shade of interesting melancholy, were now animated with an expression of the most lively joy; and Adelaide, to all with whom she conversed, appeared more lovely, more enchanting than ever. It is scarcely possible to conceive a face and form more touchingly beautiful than were those of Adelaide St. Angouléme: her complexion was of a transparent whiteness, her cheeks glowed with the blushes of health, her features were regular, and finely turned; when she spoke or smiled, a thousand dimples played about her rosy lips: her teeth were like rows of pearls, and the expression of her dark hazel eyes varied every moment to the emotions of a heart full of energy and softness: light-brown locks, inclining to yellow, shaded her brow, and descended in natural ringlets down her waist; these were suffered sometimes to hang loose, sometimes confined with a golden comb in the Grecian *costume*, displayed the fine symmetry of her neck: her form was of the most exquisite proportion—every turn was grace; the painter might have studied it, and from it the statuary have taken his purest model of perfection. Such was our heroine: but it was not beauty only that made Adelaide St. Angouléme so charming; it was the look that went to the heart, the ease and dignity of her manners, and an entire unconsciousness of the power of her charms and superiority in attainment over others, that rendered her so lovely and alluring.

Every day discovered some new trait of character to endear her to the Countess; but never did she appear so attractive, as when attending, with a filial tenderness almost unequalled, her revered and beloved parent. That attendance became at length more and more necessary: the Chevalier had taken cold in one of his evening rides about the Castle, and his disorder had returned with more violence than ever; it was attended by hectic symptoms. The best advice was procured; the disorder became, nevertheless, more and more obstinate; and the Chevalier, after languishing some weeks, expired in the arms of his beloved daughter; having previously committed her, in the most solemn and impressive manner, to the care of the Count and Countess St. Angouléme.

CHAP. V.

LANGUAGE can but feebly describe the sensations of the unhappy Adelaide, on the death of a parent to whom she was so fondly attached: though prepared, by a long series of indispositions, for this awful event, her heart seemed bursting with the excess of its emotions. In vain did the Countess endeavour to inculcate the necessity of fortitude and self-exertion, and the imprudence of yielding to unavailing regret; Adelaide, in the fullness of her grief, could not reason, she could only feel.

"Think of him, my love," said the Countess, when the throb of agony had begun to yield to the softer feelings of distress, "think of him as being translated to a happier region—a blessed eternity of joy. Would you, when the bitterness of death is past, recall him, to suffer again the agonies of his parting moments? Would he have reason to bless his Adelaide, had she the will and power to reanimate his breathless clay with that now beatified soul which has so lately quitted its earthly tenement?"

"He is—yes, I cannot doubt, he is a blessed, accepted spirit," exclaimed Adelaide, "receiving, at this instant, the reward of his faith and patience."

"He is the companion of the blessed Virgin and the saints," cried the Countess; "and would you draw him, if you could, from such a heavenly society?"

"Oh no, I would not; I think I would not," said Adelaide: "I would go to my father, but I hope I do not now wish he should come to me."

"This is the language of a Christian, my dear," said the Countess; "and, as such, becomes you. Look up, my sweet Adelaide; many years of happiness are yet in store for you."

"I should be in the highest degree ungrateful, Madam," said Adelaide, her eyes meanwhile beaming tenderness and sensibility, "if I could entertain any fears for myself while I am under such a protection as yours."

"That protection, while Heaven spares me, you will never lose," rejoined the Countess; "at least—at least I hope not. Oh, how much delight and satisfaction do I promise myself in the society of my amiable and beloved Adelaide!"

The Count, who was a complete adept at dissimulation, appeared sensibly affected by the death of his brother, and spared no pains or efforts to rouse the sometimes yet deeply depressed spirits of his orphan daughter, to assure her of his entire affection, and of the deep interest he meant to take in every thing that concerned her: he instantly perceived the advantage that would accrue to him, as guardian of his niece's property, during a minority of some years, and he resolved to deport himself in such a manner as to win her entire esteem and confidence. To succeed in this scheme, it was necessary to appear to be upon good terms with the Countess who, he found, had greatly insinuated herself into the affections of his ward: he dropped therefore all mention of the requisition he had formerly made, and even sometimes condescended to ask concerning Theodore, from whom the Countess frequently heard, and who, he was at length informed, having entered into a regiment of horse, was shortly to leave France.

The Countess, surprised and reassured by these inquiries into the situation of her nephew, assumed courage to solicit permission to see him before he joined his regiment. This, however, the Count opposed, though with less vehemence in his manner than formerly—"You must not," said he, "see him at present: we will talk these matters over some other time—I have not now leisure to think of them."

"Alas! who knows," said she, in a mournful tone, "but he may be called to a post of danger?"

"He will have the same chance as others, I suppose," interrupted the Count.

The Countess sighed, but made no comment.

"It may be unnecessary, perhaps ineffectual," continued the

Count, "to remind you, that, in your situation, it will be highly improper for you to acquaint Adelaide with the little altercations we have had on a subject which I do not intend at present to resume; certainly not at present, unless provoked to it."

"It would be highly improper, my Lord," rejoined the Countess, "to inform Mademoiselle St. Angouléme of events and circumstances which are, or ought to be, confined to ourselves."

"You judge very prudently," returned the Count:—"these are affairs in which she can have no concern, and of which she certainly ought to have no knowledge. I am glad to find you seem to have, in one instance, a just idea of what is due to me as your husband."

"It is the duty of a wife, my Lord," resumed the Countess, "to endeavour to conceal every thing in the character of a husband, which can have the least tendency to injure him in the opinion of his friends, or of those with whom he associates."

She uttered these words with more spirit and energy than she usually assumed in her manners towards her Lord. The Count looked angrily, but made no answer. The Countess withdrew.

CHAP. VI.

No visitants had appeared at the Castle, for several weeks after the death of the Chevalier. The room in which he breathed his last, as also the chapel where his remains were deposited, had been hung with black, and adorned with the hatchment of the family; the domestics were habited in the same colour, and a general gloom seemed to have been diffused throughout the mansion.

These emblems of woe were at length removed, parties were again admitted, and the Count, in honour of his niece's birthday, gave a sumptuous entertainment at the Castle. Adelaide's grief was yet too recent to allow her to mingle with satisfaction in the festivities of this scene: she thought of her father, of his joy, had he been there, to witness her attainment of her eighteenth year; and notwithstanding the frequent resolutions she had formed to think of him only as a glorious beatified spirit, removed from a state of trial and infirmity, to one infinite in happiness as in duration, she could not sometimes forbear secretly wishing he was present, or always repress the gushing tear, which the memorial of him often brought to her eyes.

The guests were numerous, the assembly gay and brilliant; for several of the most distinguished families in the neighbourhood were invited to attend.

The Count introduced his niece, for whom he affected an extravagant fondness, as an heiress of great wealth; spoke, even in her presence, of the high hopes he had conceived of a future alliance for his ward; and lamented, again and again, the loss of a brother, for whom he had the confidence to declare he had always entertained an extraordinary regard and affection.

Music, feasting, and dancing, by turns succeeded. Adelaide's attractions were generally acknowledged: her beauty, her reported fortune, her fine and various accomplishments, became the theme of every tongue; all were eager to recommend themselves to one possessed of so many charms and endowments, but few could hope to succeed, when the prize was so great.

No sooner had she appeared in public, than the Count received various proposals of marriage, all of which he rejected almost as soon as heard—"I will not," said he, "bestow such a gem unworthily; she shall never marry beneath her rank, nor even to an equal in birth, if inferior to her in fortune. Adelaide has charms enough to command an empire—she shall not dispose of herself but to her own honour and emolument."

Careless and unconcerned as to what might be her future destiny in this particular (for, though susceptible of the finest emotions of the human heart, love was yet a stranger to her bosom), Adelaide placed her whole satisfaction and delight in conciliating the affections of her uncle and his lady. The latter, she perceived, was unhappy. She thought, too, she discovered an indifference, though untinctured with harshness when she was present, in the behaviour of her guardian towards his amiable, and, as she could not doubt, unoffending wife: she had sometimes caught her in tears; but, on her observation of them, she would endeavour to suppress her grief, and smile away the sadness she could not otherwise conceal. She observed that she never left the Castle for a ride, or even a walk about the ramparts, without the invitation, or implied permission, of her husband; yet no complaint escaped her.

The Countess's woman, who attended also upon Adelaide, sometimes gave hints she was afraid to hear explained. She felt the impropriety of interrogating her on a subject of this nature, or even of listening to her—"If my aunt withholds her confidence," said she, "she has doubtless good reason for such concealment. My uncle may fail in expressions of attachment to her, yet I think he must love her; for how, kind and obliging as she is to him, can he forbear to love her? at least, however, he must esteem her, for her numerous excellencies and virtues."

"It is now near twelve months," said Bertha, which was the name of the Countess's woman, as she was one night assisting Adelaide to undress, "since the young Chevalier Theodore last left the Castle."

"Theodore!" repeated Adelaide; "is not that the name of the Countess's nephew, of whom I have, I think, more than once heard her speak?"

"Yes, Ma'moiselle, it is the same, sure enough; if my poor lady did not take it so to heart, she would talk of him oftener: he was a sweet young gentleman indeed; no wonder she cries and frets about him. Holy saints! when he went, there was not a dry eye in the Castle, except my Lord's, and he was a hunting in the forest: and as to my poor Lady——"

"If your Lady is so much attached to him," said Adelaide, "why does he not revisit the Castle?"

"Alack, Ma'moiselle! he is never to come again!"

"How! never?" repeated Adelaide.

"No; for all he used to be so free and so kind, that every body loved him; and would sing and play upon the music, and might have been such a fine companion for my Lord, making the Castle, which is but a poor lonely place, you know, Ma'moiselle, quite alive; he might never rest, poor dear soul—every thing he did was wrong. Holy Saint Peter! how often have I cried to see how he was used!—But my Lady knew little about the matter; for he never told her, lest it should make a difference, I warrant, between her and my Lord. Ah, Ma'moiselle! there must have been some black doings somewhere; for how could he hurt my Lord?"

"Had the Count taken up some strange prejudice, which you conceive to have been unreasonable?" demanded Adelaide.

"Yes, a strange prejudice, Ma'moiselle, nobody knows how, nor why; for, la! as to Monsieur Theodore, he would not harm a fly; and then he is so handsome and so genteel, and speaks so sweetly, as if he thought himself above nobody: but all this is nothing now, for they say he is turned soldier, and gone to the wars to seek his fortune, though, as we all say here, more likely his death; and if he should die, I think verily my poor lady will die too; for truly I think she likes him better than herself, or even my Lord."

Adelaide, who had long perceived the traces of a concealed grief in the countenance and manners of her aunt, for which she had been unable to account, now discovered its cause: often, in the midst of an assumed cheerfulness, would she sink into fits of melancholy and abstraction; and then, as if fearful of observation, suddenly recall her spirits. Yet had she discovered nothing austere in the behaviour of the Count; it was civil, it was sometimes obliging; it was nevertheless unmarked by that endearing tenderness and solicitude which affection dictates, and which, from the nature of their connexion, to her young and amiable mind seemed so indispensable, that their absence could hardly be atoned for, even by the most scrupulous and rigid attention to the other duties of his situation.

The Count, unsuspicious of observation, however prepared for it, affected a degree of fondness for Adelaide which he was far from feeling, and which he was indeed incapable of experiencing for any object, however amiable and endearing. The memory of a brother whom he had never cordially esteemed, was soon erazed from his mind—he had never really lamented his loss; and his thoughts were now wholly employed in considering what way he should act, so as to make the greatest possible advantage of the power with which he had been invested by the will of his late relative, as guardian of his niece's property and person. She could not marry during her minority, without his consent: if suffered to go abroad, her youth, her beauty, her accomplishments, and, most of all, her fortune, would render her an object of almost universal pursuit. The choice of a husband for his fair ward, it is true, remained solely with himself, till she should have accomplished her twenty-first year; but might she not form an attachment to some person he could not himself approve, and whom it might be his interest to reject? and was she not, at a prescribed period, to become her own mistress, when his former authority over her would avail nothing, and serve only to add to his own chagrin and vexation?

It may be supposed, from the Count's eager anxiety to elect a husband for his niece, that he was desirous to fix her in a situation equal to her pretensions and deserts; and that he was only following example of many affectionate, but ill-judging parents, who think they are promoting the happiness of their children, by elevating them to stations of wealth and consequence. But the Count, although he was not destitute of ambition, nay, though he had more than an ordinary share of it, was not highly solicitous that Adelaide should advance herself by marriage; his intention was to dispose of her in a way better calculated to promote his own interest, and the design he had formed of being freed from his present difficulties and necessities; and it was this hope, and the sanguine promises of success which his somewhat enterprising mind hourly gave him, that determined him to desist, for the present, from that scheme of persecution which he had meditated against the Countess, on her refusal to resign, at his most earnest solicitations, that portion of her property which she had reserved for Theodore. This scheme was not abandoned, it was only superseded by another, which demanded for a time all his energy and ability.

The Countess knew enough of the unrelenting temper of her Lord, to be convinced that he had by no means abandoned the hope of acquiring what he had demanded; nor was she much reassured, by the circumstance of his having lately ceased to trouble her upon a subject which had been the cause of so much uneasiness and perplexity to herself: the calm, she feared, would not be of long duration—again the tempest would burst over her; and though the native fortitude of her mind, aided by religion and the feelings of conscious rectitude, would have supported her under any difficulties she might have to encounter while they affected her herself only, she could not bear to reduce to indigence and obscurity a youth she so tenderly loved, and whom she had brought up with expectations of inheriting at least part of her fortune, and who, except in a reversion depending upon the life of another even younger than himself, had not the most distant claim upon any one, even for a bare subsistence. It is true, she had purchased him a cornetcy;* but how, unassisted by her, could he live upon this slender supply?—He might indeed be promoted; but could she bear to blast his former hopes, and cloud with care a brow hitherto animated with the genial smile of peace? No; it was impossible—she could not endure it; and so agonizing was the thought, that she resolved to brave the utmost efforts of the Count's vengeance, rather than sacrifice to his base and selfish views, the future prospects of her beloved nephew. She had heard from Theodore since his regiment had reached its destination; he had written in high spirits, and expressed himself highly pleased with a military life.

CHAP. VII.

In her letters to Chevalier Theodore, the Countess blended advice and instruction with the most affectionate expressions of regret and tenderness: she warned him against the dissipations of which young men in his situation too often largely partake, and to which the warmth of his heart, and the vivacity of his disposition, might too generally incline him; she endeavoured, by her representations, to tear off the seductive covering which gives such a bewitching appearance even to vice itself, and to display it to his eyes in all its native deformity. Many faults, from the peculiar construction of his mind, he was not likely to fall into; a mean and unworthy action he never could commit, for Theodore possessed a loftiness of soul which few could emulate: frank, open, and undesigning, he ensured a general affection, and obtained an almost immediate ascendancy over all who knew him. Yet vice alone is not exposed to the temptations that await us here; virtue too has her trials, and often the most affecting trials. She feared the power of artful beauty over the mind of Theodore, who had a susceptibility of it, when united with the bewitching accompaniments of taste and sentiment, which, while it rendered him extremely interesting and fascinating, exposed him to no small degree of danger, particularly in the station he now held. It was possible, led on by the example of his associates, he might form an attachment dishonourable to himself, and which might serve to embitter all his future days; she counselled him, therefore, not only against those vices which are included in, and glossed over, with the general name of gallantry, but against yielding his affections too hastily, and without a thorough knowledge of the person to whom he attached himself— "Reserve your heart," said she, "my Theodore, till you have found one worthy of your entire esteem and confidence. Beauty may charm, taste and elegance may delight; but these, unless united to something more solid, are of little value; they will neither comfort you in sorrow, nor delight you on the bed of sickness. Remember always, that those qualities which to the eye of youth and inexperience, are the least shining and attractive, are those to which we must look for real comfort and satisfaction, amidst the trying and often melancholy vicissitudes of human affairs."

Theodore's reply to the anxious endeavours of the Countess to guard him against all the dangers and temptations to which the sanguine and ingenuous mind of youth is too often exposed, was dictated by every sentiment of respect and tenderness to herself, and expressed the most earnest resolution of profiting by the excellent precepts she had given him—"I can never," said he, "be enough grateful to one who, beholding my situation in every point of view, seems determined if possible to guard me against every evil that can assail me. Oh, may I always profit by counsels so sweetly, so affectionately delivered! May the Countess St. Angouléme never blush for her nephew!"

At the latter part of his letter, he adds—"We are to-morrow called into the field. Our regiment occupies a post of danger, but it is a post of honour. Pray for me, my dear aunt, pray for your Theodore! Think not I am alarmed at the prospect of death; yet I do not feel that contempt of it which I observe in some of my companions; it is the contempt of insensibility; sometimes the effect of intoxication; sometimes of a desperate violence; both equally removed from true courage: yet some of them are brave, and promise to signalize themselves, as they have already done, in the field of battle."

The Countess perused Theodore's letter with sensations which partook equally of joy and sorrow, mingled with the most affecting apprehensions as to what might be his fate, thus exposed to all the hazards of his situation. It was the last she received from him; it had been given to her in the presence of the Count, and she had communicated to him a part of the contents—"Oh, why, why," said she, in agony, "was I not permitted to see him before he left France?"

"Are you surprised," said the Count, "to find your nephew exposed to the dangers inseparable from a military capacity? Did you imagine he was to bear only the ensigns of his profession, without partaking of its hardships? You thought, I suppose, the military dress becoming—it would set off his handsome figure; his commission, too, would render him independent of my authority: you did not imagine, nor does it seem ever to have entered into your politics, that he would be called into actual service."

"I did, my Lord, believe he would; but I did not suppose he would so soon be ordered to the field of combat, to prove that courage which is inherent in him, and which, if he survives, will do him so much honour."

"He has had great opportunities of proving his courage," retorted the Count sarcastically, "yes, great opportunities," after a pause, "great opportunities, in his insolent behaviour to me."

"To *you*, my lord?"

"To *me*, Madam."

"When, and on what account?"

"I am not to be interrogated by you, Madam; it is sufficient that I say he was insolent, highly insolent!"

"Oh, never, never!"

"This is arrogant indeed!" resumed the Count—"Do you dispute my words? Do you dare——" He arose in anger, and paced the room in sullen thoughtfulness.

The entrance of Adelaide recalled him from his abstraction: he addressed her with the same appearance of good humour which he usually preserved in her presence. The Countess was in tears: she arose, and left the room. Adelaide could not forbear casting a look of gentle reproach at her uncle. He did not notice it. The morning was fine, and he proposed their walking together along the ramparts.

Adelaide had always expressed great delight, when viewing the magnificent scenes of nature; and nothing could be more magnificent, or more striking, than those which the Castle commanded; wherever she turned, some new object, either of beauty or sublimity, courted her attention. The eminence on which the Castle was situated, commanded, on one side, a deep and extensive valley, rich with dark woods, beyond which appeared forests of pine, mountain tops, and narrow glens opening among the Pyrenees, and retiring from the sight, into regions almost inaccessible; on the other, a wild and desert tract of alternate wood and heath, bounded by rocks of a majestic height, and surrounded, at the edge of the horizon, by mountains of almost Alpine grandeur.

The Count amused her, as was his custom, by pointing out the various features of the landscape. He was desirous she should be pleased with a residence which, except its situation, had little to recommend it: he feared that Adelaide would be weary of her retirement, which almost entirely secluded her from the society of young women of her own age and station; yet, for reasons we have before unfolded, could not prevail upon himself to relax from the resolution he had formed, of keeping her as much as possible unseen.

The Countess herself had but few acquaintance, and with these she was seldom allowed to mix: pride prevented the Count from suffering her to associate with her inferiors, and the dislike which prevailed against him amongst people of his own rank, a dislike which, for some reason, had of late greatly increased, occasioned many, who would otherwise have paid their respects to the Countess, to delay, and afterwards forbear their visits.

The Count frequently had parties at the Castle; but, though they were often composed of people nearly of his own class, they were not of the highest respectability; and at these parties, neither the Countess nor Adelaide were present. When, in honour of her birthday, he had introduced the latter to a notice more public than he had since done, the homage which had been paid to her had convinced him that she had only to be seen, to be surrounded by admirers, and receive the most brilliant and advantageous offers. He was in perpetual fear lest, weary of her present situation, which afforded so little novelty and amusement, she would solicit a removal to Paris; for although steadily resolved not to yield to any entreaties or remonstrances which might be employed to this end, he nevertheless dreaded them, partly because he scarcely knew on what plea to refuse, and partly because he was apprehensive she might penetrate his reasons for wishing her to remain in the retirement of her present residence.

CHAP. VIII.

The Count, in his conversations with Adelaide, seldom spoke of the Countess; nor did Adelaide dare to inquire the cause of the distress she had witnessed, or revert, however slightly, to the subject: she saw he was anxious to conceal from her his own ill humour and vexation, and prevent the observation of his wife's uneasiness. She felt, however, that restraint which his presence, under such circumstances, could not but impose; and when alone with him, hastened to disengage herself, that she might fly to indulge the compassionate interest she felt for this amiable and neglected woman: to sooth, to comfort her, without appearing to perceive that attention and consolation were necessary, or that her situation in any way required them, became the chief aim of her endeavours.

The Countess felt the full value of these attentions; they were delightful—they became at length necessary. She was fond of reading and music; and the frequent absences of the Count left them often at leisure to pursue their favourite studies and amusements. The Countess, having received no new command to the contrary, sometimes ventured from the Castle; and sometimes, attended by Adelaide, extended her walk to visit the cottages on the heath, whose inhabitants received frequent relief from the donations of their benevolent visitors.

Several weeks had passed since the Countess had last heard from Theodore: her anxiety now partook of distress: he had promised, in case of his survival, to write to her after the engagement, which was then immediately to take place. Every day augmented her distress, and encreased the power of her apprehensions.

One night, when Adelaide had retired to her chamber, Bertha suddenly entered the room: her face was pale, and she seemed in great agitation—"La, Ma'moiselle," said she, seating herself, "what do you think?—The saddest news!—Oh, my poor Lady, it will surely break her heart!"

"What is the matter?" asked Adelaide fearfully—"Surely nothing—" concerning Theodore, she was about to add.

"Oh, it is all over!" interrupted Bertha—"he is dead! the Chevalier Theodore is dead!—He is killed! he is killed!" added she—"Oh, my Lady, who will tell my Lady? I am sure I cannot—I would not be guilty of such an action for the world; though my Lord says, either you, Lady, or I, must; for he will not tell her himself."

"Are you sure it is true?" said Adelaide—"Who has said so? what authority have you? May you not have been listening to a mere idle report?"

"Oh lack, Ma'moiselle, no! it is as true, holy Virgin protect us! as the gospel; for my Lord told me, and Benoit says he heard one of my Lord's company talking about it last night, as they were playing at cards, and said there was not a doubt, not a shadow of a doubt; and so the sooner my Lady knew, the better; and so in truth I think; for, poor soul, she sits expecting to hear from him, day after day, and no letter comes; and she will never have one from him again: and when she knows the worst, if it does not quite break her heart at once, she may look up again, and be as cheerful as she used to be."

"Alas!" said Adelaide, "how much will she feel! how difficult, how melancholy will be the task of unfolding to her this new cause of distress, perhaps the severest she has ever known!"

"Had you not better go to my Lady's room, Ma'moiselle, to-night, and try to prepare her for it?" said Bertha.

"By no means to-night," answered Adelaide—"besides, I would first have the melancholy information confirmed by undoubted testimony: let us not unnecessarily inflict a wound—it is possible he may be yet alive: reports of this kind are often circulated, and afterwards proved to have had no foundation in truth."

"Ah, Ma'moiselle, you have a good knack at hoping; but, for my own part, alas! I always thought it would be so. I always said, when he first came to the Castle, quite a youth, he was too clever and too handsome to live; and when they talked of his going to battle, I could not get him out of my head, for I thought of my own words; and so, in truth, it has fallen out. Oh, you don't know, Ma'moiselle, how he was beloved here! it would do your heart good to hear how they are all lamenting him in the servants' hall: poor old Ursuline is crying, as if he was her own son; and all the servants are bemoaning him, and blaming my Lord the Count for not keeping him in the Castle, instead of sending him to the wars."

"Alas, poor young man!" said Adelaide sighing—"But my aunt, who must tell my aunt?"

"You, Ma'moiselle, because you will tell her so kindly; for if it should be left to my Lord——"

"I will think about it," said Adelaide; "but I would first see my uncle."

She then dismissed her attendant, and retired to her bed.

She arose at an early hour in the morning, for she had slept but indifferently, her mind being entirely engrossed by the melancholy subject of the night's conversation: she met the Count in the breakfast-room, of whom she instantly made inquiries relative to the report of Theodore's death. His answer left her no doubt of its authenticity. "I fear," said she, "it will be a heavy stroke to the Countess."

"I have no doubt it will sensibly affect her," answered the Count; "but she ought to have considered such an event as probable, and to have prepared for it accordingly. A military profession was, I suppose, his choice; he embraced it with the acquiescence, if not the approbation of the Countess; I was not consulted, I have therefore nothing to reproach myself with. I am sorry the young man is dead; and concerned, if the event of his death is likely to be attended with any unhappy consequences to my wife, that she did not dispose of him more prudently." He then desired she would, as soon as possible, inform the Countess of her loss; adding, "I hope she may bear it better than we expect."

CHAP. IX.

It was long before the sympathizing girl could assume the courage to enter the apartment of the Countess; when she did, her countenance, the faithful index of her heart, displayed, in characters the most legible, she had a tale of sorrow to relate.

"You are pale, my dear," said the Countess—"are you unwell? or has anything happened to discompose you?"

"My dear madam," said Adelaide, taking both the Countess's hands, "I am indeed discomposed; but it is on your account only. I have something—something that I would unfold to you."

"What is it?" said the Countess, in a faint and agitated tone of voice.

"Exert all your fortitude, my beloved friend," resumed Adelaide; "recollect what you once said to me; apply to your own wound that sweet, that healing balm, you once infused into mine. The Chevalier Theodore——"

The Countess shrieked—"Oh Heavens!" exclaimed she, with a look of agonizing wildness, "he is dead then! he is killed!—Oh, my Theodore, my Theodore!"

"Moderate these transports, I conjure you, Madam," cried Adelaide, weeping bitterly—"He is gone indeed; but remember, he is gone to his Father and your Father, to his God and your God. Think of him, as you said to me, when grief for a parent's loss lay heaviest at my heart, think of him as a glorious beatified spirit; and let no selfish pang prompt you to wish him back again, from among that heavenly society into which he is now joyfully admitted."

"I know all you would say, all you can say," cried the Countess, whom a violent gush of tears had now somewhat relieved from the faintness which had almost overwhelmed her; "but oh, first," clasping her hands in agony, "first I must think of him as a mangled corpse, left amongst heaps of slain, without a friend to close his eyes, or perform for him the last mournful offices of humanity; denied perhaps a grave, or thrown into the rude unhallowed earth, the rites of burial unperformed!—Oh, Theodore! was it for this I consented to thy too pressing importunities to fight in thy country's cause? So soon, so very soon, to end that career of glory thou hadst but begun!"

Tears now stopped her utterance: she leaned upon the arm of Adelaide, and continued weeping—"Just and righteous Heaven," added she at length, "support me, I beseech thee, under this, the heaviest of all your afflictions with which thou hast thought fit to try me: and let me not, in the bitterness of my present sorrow, in the midst of an anguish the most exquisite, forget thy manifold, thy abundant mercies—Theodore revered thy laws, and he is blessed."

A sweet composure, the effect of religious hope, and an entire confidence in the beneficent dispensations of that Being whose very chastisements are mercies, stole by degrees over the before-agitated features of the Countess. Adelaide, with the look and accents of an angel, bent over her: she took her hand, she pressed it tenderly to her lips—"Suffer me," said she, "to supply the place of him whom you have lost. Oh that I were indeed worthy to supply it!"

"Excellent young creature!" exclaimed the Countess—"yes, in those pitying eyes," added she, "I have long perceived a compassionate interest, above what I was then able to account for—they spoke a language beyond what tongue can utter; and obeying the overflowing feelings of my now breaking heart, I could almost call you daughter."

"Oh, say not almost," cried Adelaide—"Such a mother I once had; but, alas! I lost her when I was too young to estimate that loss, and now I am an orphan."

"Forget, forget that you are so," said the Countess—"He who was to me indeed a child, is gone, and you only can supply that chasm in my heart which his loss has left in it."

"Promise me then," said Adelaide, "to bear with patience, nay, with fortitude, the present sorrowful event; rouse yourself from the indulgence of an unavailing grief; it is your Adelaide asks it of you—your daughter, your newly-adopted daughter."

The Countess pressed her hand in silence, while a deep involuntary sigh heaved her breast.

Adelaide continued with her, in her room, throughout the day. The Count sent a message by the Countess's woman, to inquire after her health, but did not himself appear. "How unkind!" thought Adelaide—"but he is unwilling, perhaps, to witness her distress. He ought, however, to make a sacrifice of his own feelings, to impart comfort to her—I fear, indeed, he does not love her."

For several days after the account of Theodore's death had reached the ears of the Countess, she confined herself in her own apartment. The Count had visited her only twice in that interval: he addressed her in accents of affected kindness, but his countenance yet bore traces of that unrelenting sternness it usually exhibited when he condescended to accost her. He spoke little, made some general inquiries about herself and Adelaide, but never once mentioned Theodore. Adelaide thought this too unkind; "but perhaps," said she mentally, "he is afraid of reviving her grief." So much candour was there in the disposition of Adelaide, that she frequently conceived an action, in itself culpable, might have originated in some amiable or worthy motive.

Weeks, and even months, rolled on without any new event, except that the Count, having allowed, as he imagined, a sufficient interval for the Countess's grief to have evaporated, urged anew his former remonstrances, and even threats, to induce her to make the resignation he required. She paused: ruin, perhaps inevitable, awaited her; but it would affect herself only: she deliberated, and at last consented—"Alas! what I have relinquished," she said mournfully, "may retard, but cannot prevent the approach of an evil I have long foreseen—the Count's affairs are, even now, desperate."

Whatever prejudice he might be inclined to indulge against his wife, the Count still preserved the same uniform appearance of kindness in his deportment to Adelaide, who hoped, by the power she possessed over him, to attach him to her aunt, who was now, more than ever, the object of her compassion and tenderness.

CHAP. X.

THE Count having thus arbitrarily obtained possession of the residue of his wife's fortune, now found it necessary to visit Avignon, in order to inspect the estates, and manage the affairs of his deceased brother. In his absence, he addressed a letter to the Countess, in which he informed her, that he had met with an unexpected delay in the business which had called him thither, owing to an extraordinary report which was circulated in that country, deserving, as he believed, of little credit, but which had nevertheless occasioned him some concern, and much embarrassment: he had, however, he added, little doubt but that the affair would terminate fortunately in respect to his ward; though it was possible some further difficulties might occur, before her affairs in Provence could be finally arranged. These, however, he observed, might be more vexatious than important, as he could not suffer himself to doubt Adelaide's right of inheritance, or allow himself to listen, without the fullest evidence and conviction, to a relation of events and circumstances, which appeared highly improbable, and even romantic.

On the subject of the nature and import of the rumour which, according to his account, prevailed in the neighbourhood of Adelaide's former residence, the Count was silent; nor did the letter contain any explanation, or even hint of what might be its purport or tendency, except what was conveyed in the few succeeding lines; from which it seemed that Adelaide's claim to the property of the late Chevalier St. Angouléme appeared to be, in some way or other, questioned. Yet how, since she was his daughter, and only child, could this be possible?

The Countess perused the letter again and again, which appeared so extremely mysterious and perplexing, that it mocked all her efforts to comprehend it. Her curiosity being thus excited, a curiosity which sometimes partook of apprehension, she awaited with some anxiety the return of her Lord; from whose lips, since he had graciously condescended to write to her (a circumstance which had somewhat surprised her), she hoped for a thorough elucidation and explanation of that part of his letter which, at present, appeared wholly obscure and inexplicable.

Her anxiety was not dissipated, when, on the Count's arrival at the Castle, she learned, in answer to her inquiries, that it had been rumoured in various parts of Provence, that Adelaide was not, as had been supposed, the daughter of the Chevalier and Madame St. Angouléme, but the child of a woman of the name of De Launé, lately deceased; to whose care, immediately on its birth (Madame St. Angouléme being then apparently in a dying state), the infant daughter of the Chevalier had been committed, to be fostered with her own child; and by whom the confession had, as was said, recently been made.

The child, which was also a female, and of the same age as that to which the poor woman had given birth, died, according to this confession, when only a few days old; and the woman, at the instigation of her husband, and with a view probably to her future interests (for thus ran the report), had been persuaded to conceal its death; and, by a daring imposition upon the parents of the deceased, placed her own as the future heir, in the family of St. Angouléme.

The Countess, on this intelligence, eagerly demanded if the Count had seen the husband of the woman, by whom, according to this report, the deception had been practised? The Count answered he had not, the man being found, upon inquiry, to be in a distant part of France; but as he was inclined to treat the whole of the story as a ridiculous fabrication, he had not given himself much trouble about the matter.

The Countess, who felt an almost maternal interest in her

niece's fortunes, was reassured by the manner in which the Count seemed to treat the subject of her concern; though she could not forbear wondering if, disposed to consider it as wholly unworthy of notice, he should have mentioned it at all, particularly to her, to whom his communications, in respect both to himself and Adelaide, had been always made with so much reserve, that she could hardly be said to have any share in his confidence.

CHAP. XI.

Several weeks passed on, during which no future reference was made, either by the Count or his Lady, to the subject of their former interesting conversation; when one day, the Count having just returned from one of his accustomed rides into the forest, was informed that two people, a man and a woman, meanly dressed, and apparently in a very low situation of life, had gained admission into the Castle, and on the plea of some business highly important, had demanded to speak with him. They were shewn into a private apartment in the Castle, and remained for some time in close conference with the Count.

The Countess, who had gained from her woman some description of the strangers, and had marked an extreme perturbation in the manners of the Count, on the news of their arrival, instantly concluded that their visit had some relation to Adelaide, and the estates in Provence; and she waited, with an anxiety almost painful, the conclusion of an interview, which would probably throw some light upon a subject which, notwithstanding the apparent indifference and unconcern with which the Count had treated it, appeared to involve circumstances not wholly unimportant.

She had remained for some time in anxious expectation of the departure of the new guests, when she received an order from the Count, to attend him in an anti-room. She started, on her entrance, on finding the strangers were not, as she imagined, departed; and her surprise was converted into apprehension, when the Count, arising from his seat, and putting into her hands a paper signed with the name of De Launé, said—"I sent for you, Madam, as joint executor with myself (for so runs the will of my late brother) in the affairs of the person calling herself, and hitherto supposed to be, the daughter of Julien and Elinor St. Angouléme."

"Good Heavens, my Lord!" ejaculated the Countess, interrupting him, "you do not—you cannot doubt!"

"That paper, Madam," resumed the Count, "contains, as you will find, the deposition and confession of Agnes de Launé; and will, on examination, be found completely satisfactory, on the subject of the birth and claims of the young woman, hitherto considered as the natural and legitimate heir of our deceased and much-regretted brother, Julien St. Angouléme."

The Countess, trembling with agitation, prepared to examine the paper. It contained, as the Count had observed, the confession of a woman called Agnes de Launé, was written in bad French, in many places misspelled, and ran thus:—

"I, Agnes de Launé, do hereby declare, that on the seventeenth of May, in the year one thousand six hundred and thirty-five, I received from the hands of a woman, called Blanche Munée, the infant daughter of Monsieur and Madame St. Angouléme, of the city of Avignon, in Provence, to be fostered with my own child, a female of the same age, the children being both born on the same day, and nearly at the same hour. The child, which had been sickly from its birth, died in the middle of the night, on the same day that I had undertaken the care of it—my own was alive, and healthy. I was poor, and friendless: my husband proposed that we should impose our own child upon the parents of the deceased, by which we should obtain a provision for it in future, and the promised pay for its support, which I could ill afford to lose. I was somewhat frightened at the proposal, for I dreaded the discovery, and the punishment which might follow, should the deception be detected; but my husband persisted that, if we kept but our own counsel, a discovery was impossible: and held out so many promises and advantages, that I length consented. It passed off without suspicion or inquiry: the child, on the recovery of its supposed mother, was received into the family of Monsieur St. Angouléme, and nothing further transpired.

"In the year one thousand six hundred and fifty, I, Agnes de Launé, was attacked with a severe disease, which seemed to threaten my life. In the course of my illness, I often thought of the injustice I had been guilty of towards the Chevalier and his family: as my disorder encreased, I grew more and more unhappy. My husband endeavoured to quiet my mind, but to no purpose: I told him I could not die easy, unless I confessed the truth; for I had been tormented with dreams and visions, which had greatly disturbed me. He desired I would be quiet, and say nothing about the matter; but I was still restless and unhappy. I could not forbear wishing to do an act of justice before I died; so one day, feeling myself a little better, I resolved to put the account down in writing; and in a few days growing worse, I made my husband promise to declare the truth on the death of the Chevalier, who was then said to be dying; having been grievously disturbed and afflicted by my own conscience, which never suffered me to rest, and which had raised to me many fearful apparitions. This is the whole account, and the last confession of me,

"AGNES DE LAUNE.

"So help me, holy Virgin and the blessed saints, as I have here spoke the truth.

"*Avignon*, June 28, 1652."

The Countess having examined the paper, the man, who now introduced himself to her notice as the husband of the deceased and the father of Adelaide, confirmed, by oath, the intelligence contained in it, an oath, he said, he was willing to repeat, when called upon, in any court of judicature in the kingdom.

The woman who attended him, now his wife, also entered her deposition, which was committed to writing by the Count, and signed by her hand. She could swear, she said, to the hand-writing of the deceased Agnes de Launé, having many times seen it; and she had more than once, having attended her in her last illness, heard her express much uneasiness and remorse respecting some deception which, she said, had been practised upon the family of St. Angouléme; and once, her fever running so high as scarcely to allow her to know what she said, she had given some insight into the business: that, owing to this, some of the rest of the neighbours being present, the report, then prevalent in the neighbourhood, had been circulated; and that her husband and herself had at length resolved to confess the truth, having been much disturbed and perplexed by its concealment, and to take back the girl, whom they were now willing to receive and acknowledge as their daughter, and who, as she was now grown up, would be able to get her own living, and, providing she was strong and hearty, assist her parents.

"Never!" exclaimed the Countess—"Oh, my Lord, you will not, you cannot part with Adelaide!"

"This affair," rejoined the Count, "must undergo a complete investigation; the deposition of these people must be given in form, and undergo an examination.—You are ready, you say," addressing himself to the man, called Gaspard de Launé, "to confirm, by oath, what you have asserted relative to this business, wherever it may be required?"

"Anywhere, my Lord," returned De Launé.

"That, I believe, is quite sufficient," said the Count—"You may now, Madam, if you please," to the Countess, "retire, and summon Adelaide to attend; her presence will, of course, be necessary."

"Adelaide, my Lord?—Oh, not so suddenly!"

"I would see her immediately," resumed the Count.

"Let me at least prepare her for an interview that will surprise, and for intelligence that must greatly shock her."

"The less preparation, Madam," said the Count, "the better. Tell her I would see her immediately."

The Countess withdrew, and trembling with an agitation she was utterly unable to suppress, repaired to the room in which Adelaide was sitting. The traces of astonishment were yet visible upon her features, mingled with a concern so tender, as to leave little room to doubt but that something of an equally extraordinary and affecting nature had occurred. To her eager inquiries the Countess could make no reply; but, taking Adelaide's arm, she requested (for, while she spoke, the Count's bell rung violently) that she would immediately accompany her to the apartment where, by his orders, she had been summoned—"Prepare yourself, my dear," said the Countess, "to hear something that will greatly surprise and affect you; but remember, you may always rely on my protection, my care: think of me always as a mother, and be assured, nothing shall prevent me from performing the duties of that sacred relationship; no, though even death should be the penalty, never, never will I forsake you!"

Adelaide had not time to reply, before the Countess, urged by the seeming impatience of the Count, had thrown open the door of the apartment in which the Count and his guests were sitting—"By a paper which has been just submitted to our inspection," proceeded the Countess, forcefully recalling her spirits, for she feared the effects of such a communication from any other quarter, "it appears, though it may not yet be fully proved, that you are not, as was supposed, the daughter of the Chevalier and Madame St. Angouléme, but of the persons now present: nevertheless, under our protection, you will suffer nothing by the change, but the mere loss of fortune, a loss of which you will soon cease to be sensible, for, into a mind like yours, no mercenary or selfish wish can, even for an instant, gain admission."

"Adelaide, I hope, can have no doubt of our protection," said the Count, in a low voice, and in no very energetic tone.

Adelaide was thunderstruck—"Oh, Heavens, Madam!" she at length exclaimed, "what do I hear?—I not the daughter of St. Angouléme! How can this be?—It is not, it cannot be possible!"

"You are my own daughter, I believe, Ma'moiselle," returned the man, "my own flesh and blood; and she that stands there is your mother—your step-mother, I should have said; for poor Agnes——"

"My father, my mother!" interrupted Adelaide, almost fainting with her emotions—"Oh tell me, Madam," leaning upon the arm of the Countess, "can this be real? are you not amusing yourself with me?—Yet you are not wont to do such things. Great and righteous Heaven! what can this mean?"

"It means, Ma'moiselle," replied the man, who appeared thoroughly insensible of the poor girl's distress, "that you are not, as was supposed, a rich heiress, but the daughter of mean but honest parents, who are willing, if so be it shall please his Honour, to take you home again, and provide for you to the best of their power. You can sew, and work in the vintage; and if you should like a service better than staying with your parents, who, God knows! have hard work enough to live, I have one in my eye that will suit you to a tittle, and you may be as happy as a little princess."

"A service!" repeated the Countess, in a tone between surprise and contempt, and fixing her eyes upon the man, as she spoke, with an expression which seemed to say, "Can this be the father of my Adelaide?" for never had she witnessed so much apparent insensibility, ignorance, and indifference, united to a face and figure so thoroughly disgusting, as in the object now before her. He was a middle-sized man, thin, and swarthy: his small, sunk, grey eyes, had an expression of cunning approaching to roguery, which was indeed the only character of his countenance: his figure was not only lean, but bent; his shoulders were high, his limbs ill-formed, and extremely disproportioned.

The woman, who, from her appearance, seemed to be some years younger than her husband, was scarcely less ugly and disagreeable. She was of a low stature, thick-set, and corpulent; her features were harsh and forbidding; and her large black eyes, the whites of which were horribly contrasted with the extreme yellowness of her skin, denoted the vixen, if not the fury.

They wore the garb of one of the lowest orders of peasants: the man was somewhat better dressed than his companion; but their appearance seemed, upon the whole, to correspond with the account they had given of their own indigence and obscurity.

Adelaide shrunk involuntarily from the observation of her newly-discovered parents; surprise had so completely overwhelmed her, that she was scarce able to comprehend the distressing change in her situation, or believe that change could be real. The air of solemnity that marked the manners of the Count, while, engaged in the examination of their claims, he continued to converse alternately with the man and the woman; the ill-concealed distress of the Countess, whose eyes, now humid with tears, now lighted up with an expression which seemed to partake of disgust, and almost of horror, as she contemplated the objects of her astonishment; the confidence perceptible in the manners of the people by whom the claim had been made; the confession of Agnes de Launé, a confession wrung from her, as it seemed, by remorse, at the season of approaching death—all these collected, seemed to compose a host of proofs, to confirm the veracity of the assertion she had been listening to; and Adelaide could no longer doubt. But her parents—could Adelaide love her parents, her parents whom she had never before seen, and who were probably incapable, by their nature, as well as from the effects of time and absence, of experiencing the least particle of affection and tenderness for her whom they now called their daughter?

To the conviction that all she had heard was real, not imaginary, the most agonizing reflections succeeded; and Adelaide sat drowned in tears of the deepest sorrow. Of these, of her griefs, all, except the Countess, appeared perfectly regardless.

Anxious to pour into her bosom all the consolation it was in her power to administer in this truly affecting situation, the Countess at length arose, and whispering something to the Count, led Adelaide from the room.

As the latter was retiring, she was struck with the impropriety of withdrawing without first addressing her father—"If he is my father," said she mentally, "ought I not to ask his blessing? Let me not forget the duty due to those to whom I owe my being. Oh, St. Angouléme! were you not, as you seemed, my father?—To you—to you I was indeed a daughter!"

She paused—she would have uttered something; but the agitated, the embarrassed Adelaide, knew not what to say; and she stood confounded and perplexed.

"You may go, Ma'moiselle, if you will," said he, with the same air of indifference with which he had at first accosted her; "you will hear from us again anon."

Adelaide bowed, and retiring with the Countess, vented upon her maternal breast that grief she could no longer stifle, a grief which, while it seemed to encrease with reflection, seemed boundless and irremediable.

These feelings of affliction were, however, converted into those of the most lively gratitude, when the Countess, pouring forth fresh assurances of protection, declared she would never part from her, and that she now considered her as more than ever her daughter.

The power of the Countess, while under the arbitrary controul of her husband, was so limited, as to allow of but little hope that she could perform the engagement she had made, without injury to herself; and Adelaide, however grateful, could not have been fully assured of the continuance of this protection, had not she, on the departure of her father, after having been again admitted into the presence of the Count, heard from him a repetition of the same promises and assurances which she had before received from the Countess—"I cannot," said he, "think of consigning you to the low connexions of the people who now claim you as their daughter, and who, it seems, unassisted by your own exertions, are unable to afford you even a scanty provision in their family: nor can the claim they have made be fully ascertained and established, till it shall have undergone the necessary examination before the Parliament of Paris, to the judgment of which Court it will be now speedily referred. That it will stand the investigation of the Parliament, I cannot myself doubt; for would it not be unreasonable to suppose that two people, utter strangers to both of us, in a matter too in which their interests cannot be any way concerned, should wilfully assert a falsehood, or that they could indeed have fabricated a story of this kind, a story so circumstantial, both as to time and place, as to bear all the features of truth, and narrated with a simplicity which falsehood cannot assume? Though unconnected with me by the ties of blood, this castle may still be your home; you may still, in every thing but the name, be the niece of Count St. Angouléme."

Adelaide gratefully expressed her thanks; and secure of the protection of her late guardian and his highly revered Lady, began at length to taste again the sweets of that repose which the late extraordinary events at the Castle had, for some time, banished from her mind.

It was the severest of Adelaide's griefs, and indeed the only one which could gain a permanent place in her heart, that she could not love, as she had thought she ought to do, her newly-discovered father. All the filial tenderness of which she was capable, had been lavished upon St. Angouléme—with his memory it was still cherished; and if she thought of De Launé, however anxiously she strove to avoid it, as an act of undutifulness she could hardly herself pardon, she could not help comparing him with *him* she once imagined to be her father; and that these moments, as they arose in affecting contrast to her mind, her saddened heart and tearful eyes told how greatly she venerated the one, and how little, notwithstanding her utmost efforts, she did, or ever could, regard the other.

CHAP. XII.

The Count, who, in consequence of the discovery of the failure of Adelaide's right of inheritance (a matter which, nevertheless, remain to be proved before the Parliament of Paris, ere he could formally put in his claim), was the undoubted and acknowledged heir to the estates, and other property of the deceased Chevalier. Fully satisfied as to the decision of the Parliament, he entered at length into all those gaieties and extravagancies to which he was so much addicted: his parties at the Castle were more frequent than ever, and became less and less select; for they were composed chiefly of people whom he had accidentally met in Paris, in the houses of persons not always respectable, or on occasional visits at Barrége, whither they had fled for the recovery of that health which they had voluntarily and culpably sacrificed at the shrine of luxury and pleasure.

The Countess, from inclination, and an almost unconquerable disgust to many of the invited guests, had by degrees so entirely absented herself from these parties, that her presence was now always dispensed with; she was therefore somewhat surprised, on receiving an invitation from her Lord, for herself and Adelaide to attend a sumptuous entertainment he had ordered to be prepared, which was to be honoured with the attendance of two Parisian ladies of high fashion, whom he seemed anxious to introduce to them, and whom he spoke of in terms of the highest respect and commendation.

One of these was the wife of a Monsieur le Mousin, citizen of Paris, a lady more remarkable for the gaiety of her disposition and the levity of her conversation, than the rectitude of her conduct, or the purity of her manners: the other, who was introduced to the Countess and other guests, to all of whom she was a stranger, by the name of Signora Violanta Sforza, was Italian, as her name imports, who had only lately appeared in France. She was the daughter of a famous Roman courtezan, with whom she had resided almost from her birth, and who had bequeathed to her, on her decease, a fortune large enough to maintain her in affluence, if not in splendour.

To the figure of a nymph, and the attractions of a Grecian Laïs,* Violanta, under the tuition of her mother, united all the blandishments and allurements which are possible to become concentrated in one object; and to render that object completely dangerous and elusive, one charm only was wanting, a charm, without which every other must be defective—the charm of modesty; and this her instructress had not found necessary to impart to her; indeed she had it not to impart.

The accomplishments of the Signora were various and enchanting: she sung, she played, she conversed, with an ease and grace which are scarcely to be acquired, and seldom equalled. The Count admired—he was at length fascinated; for though inferior in beauty to Adelaide, as to real perfection in loveliness, so much was there of attraction in all she said or did, that he seemed unconsciously to have resigned himself to the effects of her charms, and to have been drawn by her enchantments from all consideration of what was due from him to the rest of the assembled guests.

A variety of occupations divided the time devoted to the evening's festivities, when a splendid collation was spread; after which, when the exhilarating wine, which rose high in the sparkling goblet, had been liberally diffused around, the boisterous spirit of inebriation broke forth; and the Countess, who had hitherto been amused by the variety and novelty of a scene in which the accomplished Italian was the principal actor, now experienced only sensations of disgust and uneasiness. Violanta and her companion, elated beyond all rules of decorum, betrayed, in their manners, that utter disregard of it, which can only be found in societies the most depraved and immoral.

The night, or rather morning, was far advanced before the company began to separate. The Countess was surprised, and somewhat hurt, in finding the ladies were to continue there the night. The next morning, she was told they were to remain some days at the Castle; that the Signora, charmed with the romantic scenery of the country, had hired an elegant chateau, at the distance of about half a league from the Castle, and was shortly to become resident in the neighbourhood.

The necessary preparations for the reception of the Signora, and her establishment at her intended future habitation, were already begun; the Count and the ladies took frequent excursions about the country; the Countess, on a plea of illness, excused herself from attending; and Adelaide was not invited to accompany them. The day appointed for the departure at length arrived;

the Count attended his fair guests on their way to Paris, as far as Thoulouse, and then returned to the Castle.

Shortly after the removal of Signora Violanta and her companion from the Castle, Adelaide was informed by the Countess's woman, that a man, whom, from the description she had given of him, Adelaide instantly concluded to be her father, had again visited the Castle, and had been for several hours closetted with the Count. This intelligence surprised her, as the Count, whom she had since seen, had mentioned nothing of the circumstance, though the business upon which they had met must doubtless concern herself; nor was the Countess, as she afterwards found, informed of it.

The next day, she was told he had been again, and was a second time admitted to a private conference with the Count. Adelaide's astonishment was now greatly encreased—the affair they were engaged in must concern herself principally, if not entirely: how strange then that the Count should not have informed her of his arrival, and the motive and occasion of his visit! how strange too, if indeed her father, he should not desire to see her!—"How insensible," cried she, weeping, "must he be to the feelings of parental tenderness!—Yet why do I complain, when I feel, notwithstanding my full sense of the duty I owe to such a relationship, I cannot love him as a father?"

Urged by curiosity to know something relative to the business which called him thither, and the nature of these now frequent conferences, she was more than once tempted to make an inquiry of the Count; but his manners, the alteration in which she could not but remark, though the cause was unknown to her, for he was suddenly become thoughtful and reserved, repelled every effort to this end; nor could she, for she had sometimes attended it, draw him into a conversation, which might lead, however remotely, to the subject of her present concern and embarrassment.

These somewhat mysterious visits, after having been regularly repeated for several successive days, were at length entirely discontinued; and Adelaide heard no more of her father, who, she now concluded, had left Gascony, and was on his way to Provence.

CHAP. XIII.

Several weeks passed on in the usual routine, when one evening, as Adelaide was passing from the Countess's chamber to her own, she was surprised by an unusual bustle below, and the sound of several voices. Curiosity detained her for some minutes in the corridor: as she listened, she heard the Count give orders for someone to be conveyed to the north tower, a part of the Castle that was not inhabited, and the interior of which she had never seen. "Confine him," said he, "in the chamber of the turret, and take care he has no means of escape—I will see him in the morning."

As she paused, she heard the clinking of a chain, and a low murmuring sound, too indistinct to be articulate, but which seemed to be the utterings and moanings of distress. Several footsteps then passed along the hall, the great door was opened and closed, and all was again silent.

She had just entered her apartment, when she was startled by the sudden appearance of Bertha, whose countenance expressed terror and amazement. Adelaide eagerly inquired what had happened?

"Dear Ma'moiselle," cried Bertha, "have you not heard what a fluster we have all been in below? My Lord the Count has been stopped and robbed, or as good as robbed—he has been frightened out of his wits; and if he had not been overtaken by two of the servants, who had followed him from Barrége, and happened not to be far behind, would have been murdered too. Never did I see such an ill-looking dog! Here he is, Ma'moiselle, at the Castle; for they seized and brought him hither. Holy Saint Peter! I wonder how they durst touch him!—I declare, if it was not for being sure he could not come near us (for my Lord has ordered him into the north tower, and has had him chained from head to foot), I should not have a wink of sleep to-night."

"The Count, I hope," said Adelaide, "has received no injury from the attacks of this outlaw?"

"Oh no, Ma'moiselle—no injury at all, except being frightened, as I was saying, out of his wits; and so, in faith, well he might."

"What is to be done with the poor wretch?" said Adelaide—"He is confined, you say, in the chamber in the north turret?"

"Yes, Ma'moiselle, and a poor comfortless lodging he will have of it; for my Lord has let that side of the Castle go to ruins, for want, they say, of money to put it in repair; and so the stones are all tumbling in; and if the night should prove stormy, they will be all rattling about his ears, and it will be well if he escapes without a broken pate; though, if he should be killed, it won't much signify, as he is sure to be either broke on the wheel or sent to the gallies, for stopping my Lord the Count, as may as well die one death as another."

"Alas, poor soul!" said Adelaide, "how melancholy must be his reflections!"

"Melancholy indeed, Ma'moiselle," replied Bertha; "and I am sure if they were not, the place he is in would make them so. Holy Saints! I had as lief sleep in the haunted Castle as in that turret!"

"The haunted Castle!" repeated Adelaide.

"Goodness, Ma'moiselle! have you never heard of the haunted Castle? Why, it is only about three leagues from this place. La! I thought every body in Gascony had heard of the haunted Castle!"

"Is it so celebrated?" cried Adelaide—"Pray where is it? and how has it acquired the reputation of being haunted?"

"It was shut up, Ma'moiselle," continued Bertha, "for several years; and, though a very fine old place, was suffered to go to ruin; for the person who owned it lived almost constantly abroad, and never came near it. It fell at last to a new heir, who determined to have it modernized and repaired: well, and so it would have been; a number of men were set to work, but what was done in the day was always undone at night; and so it never could be finished."

"And was the cause of this extraordinary circumstance never known?" asked Adelaide.

"Oh yes, Ma'moiselle, it was soon known; several people were set to watch, and it was at length found out that the Castle was haunted."

"And how was this discovery made?" demanded Adelaide—"Were the spirits detected in the act of removing the stones?"

"Why no, Ma'moiselle; for they never could tell when and how they were removed: but, at the hour of midnight, just when the great clock at the Castle tolled twelve, lights used to appear at the windows, and a ghost in a bloody sheet was seen stalking about the apartments. Blessed Virgin defend us! I would not go near that dreadful Castle, no, hardly for my Lord's estate!"

"And are the same extraordinary appearances observed now?" rejoined Adelaide, with an incredulous smile.

"Oh yes, for people used formerly to go out of curiosity to see the lights; and many that have been to see them, have never returned, and could never afterwards be heard of. A cousin of mine, who was travelling amongst the mountains, says he saw the western side of the building illuminated, as if it was all on fire; and if he had ventured nearer, might have seen the ghost, who always takes his nightly rounds about the Castle at the hour of twelve."

"This must be all delusion," rejoined Adelaide.

"No, Ma'moiselle, it is all true. Ask my Lord or my Lady, and they will tell you the same."

"Where do you say the Castle is situated?" asked Adelaide.

"Somewhere amongst the mountains, Ma'moiselle, and not many leagues off. La! I almost tremble to think we are so near it; though they say the ghosts are never seen out of the Castle; indeed they have a fine range there, and cannot be hampered for want of room."

"Well, I shall make some inquiries about it to-morrow," said Adelaide; "for your relation partakes so much of the marvellous, that it will require at least to be authenticated by further testimonies, before I can venture to give credit to it."

Although disposed to treat the circumstance of the haunted Castle as ridiculous, Adelaide did not forget to mention what she had heard from Bertha, the next morning to the Countess, who, to her surprise, being somewhat addicted to superstition, did not treat it as the mere effects of ignorance and credulity. She had heard, she said, some extraordinary things relative to the Castle of Ponteville, usually called the Haunted Castle, which never were, and to all appearance never could be, accounted for: lights certainly did appear at the windows, though it was known to be uninhabited; and it had been authenticated, by the corresponding evidences of various respectable persons, who, from motives of curiosity, had approached it at the hour of illumination, that a figure, covered over with a bloody sheet, passed and repassed the apartments where the lights were seen.

"And has nobody had the courage to venture into the interior of the Castle?" asked Adelaide.

"Two men," resumed the Countess, "in consideration of a large premium were mad enough to make the attempt; but they were punished for their temerity, for they never afterwards appeared, and consequently perished in their rash and fruitless enterprise."

"And the ghost has really been seen?" cried Adelaide.

"A figure," rejoined the Countess, "has certainly, and I suppose does at this time regularly appear, at the windows on one side of the edifice, which is called the western building."

"But may not this appearance," observed Adelaide, "be the effect of an artifice which has hitherto remained undetected?—Such a circumstance is at least possible."

"It is only barely possible," resumed the Countess; "as, had such an artifice been practised, it must have been detected long ago. The only entrance to the Castle is by a bridge, which, since the unaccountable disappearance of the two men who had engaged to enter it, has been constantly drawn up; for so strongly has the idea of supernatural appearances and supernatural horrors fastened upon the public mind, that no person will venture within a certain distance from the Castle, where the lights, at the hour of midnight, are always discernible, and the shadowy movement of the spectre that haunts its dreary and deserted labyrinths. Screams and dismal yells are also said to proceed from the Castle; and on the wild heath that supports its walls, now crumbling into ruins, dismal forms flit before the eyes of the traveller, as he takes his adventurous course through the neighbourhood of this scene of horrors, that wraps him, as he goes along, in superstitious dread, and wonderstruck astonishment."

"That the sight of a spectre should conjure up a host of terrible apparitions, and excite in the mind a strange variety of horrible imaginations," said Adelaide, "is by no means wonderful, or even extraordinary: the awful appearance of an inhabitant from another world, bursting suddenly, unexpectedly upon the view, must instantly rob the mind of all rational perception: I cannot conceive that any thing can excite ideas more horrible, and at the same time more sublime; for it is a horror that must partake more largely of sublimity than the view of such a being as you have described; and while my very blood chills in my veins at the mention of them, I can almost wish myself to be a spectator of the scenes you have been delineating."

"How!" exclaimed the Countess—"Have you courage to visit the haunted Castle?"

"I would view it," said Adelaide, "from the place where it is usually seen, at the hour when the lights appear at the windows of the western building."

"You must see it then," resumed the Countess, "at midnight."

"But it is some leagues from this place," said Adelaide.

"Yes: and the path intricate, lying, for the most part, amongst mountains, and through forests; but, over the lesser range of the Pyrenees, a nearer track may be found. I would not, however, advise you to brave the dangers such a journey would expose you to, however well escorted and defended.—But you are not in earnest, Adelaide?"

"Seriously, I am in earnest—I should like to see this Castle."

"Not surely at the hour you mention?" said the Countess.

"If I could be conveyed thither in safety, I would be there precisely as the great clock of the Castle tolls twelve," answered Adelaide.

"You're laughing, I see, at my story," cried the Countess, "and have as much faith, I find, in the now-almost-exploded doctrines of witchcraft, as in the appearance of spirits."

"I should, I think, sooner incline to the latter than the former," said Adelaide: "yet, allowing that I admit the possibility of one, I see no reason why I should absolutely reject the other."

The Countess was about to reply, when the Count entered the room; and the conversation turned upon the adventure of the preceding night.

The gentle Adelaide, who could not contemplate distress, however merited by guilt or vice, without experiencing the tenderest feelings of compassion, inquired if the Count had examined the prisoner in the north tower? The Count hesitated, and at length answered he had. "Alarmed as I was," added she, "to hear you had fallen into the power of this outlaw, now I see you safe and unhurt, I cannot forbear wishing the poor creature might escape: perhaps it is the first offence; perhaps the horrors of his situation, the terrors of apprehended punishment, may have worked in him a resolution never to repeat it: who knows," said she, laying her hand upon the Count's arm, her sweet entreating eyes fixed earnestly on his face, "who knows but, were an act of mercy extended, were it allowed, in this instance, to supersede the higher claims of justice, he might live to be a blessing, instead of a scourge, to his fellow creatures?—Might you not at least make the attempt?"

"I am willing to make it," said the Count, in a low voice.

"Are you—are you indeed willing?" reiterated Adelaide, in a tone as animated and expressive of delight as if she had herself obtained a reprieve from condemnation—"My dear, dear Lord, you know not how happy you have made me!"

"If I do it," rejoined the Count, his countenance changing, as he spoke, to an almost ashy paleness, "the last night's adventure in the forest must not be mentioned: I shall be blamed—perhaps called to a strict account: it will be said, I ought to have entered a prosecution; that, in screening him, I am myself committing an offence against the laws of my country. The poor fellow's story has, I confess, interested me in his behalf: he has been criminal, but his misfortunes have been greater than his crimes. He has promised to abandon the lawless course he pursues, and become an honest, peaceful member of society; and on these promises I have ordered him to be set at liberty."

"How kind!" exclaimed Adelaide—"oh, my Lord, you know not how happy, how very happy you have made me! The poor man himself can hardly feel more grateful for your lenity than I do."

"Remember, however, Adelaide," cried the Count, rising from his seat, with an agitation he seemed struggling to conceal, "that this affair must be kept strictly secret: I have already given you my reasons." As he spoke, he withdrew.

The Countess expressed great satisfaction on finding the prisoner was released; it was, nevertheless, not unmingled with surprise: that the stern unrelenting disposition of the Count should have been melted into tenderness and pity by the story of a robber, one too who had even attempted his own life, seemed extraordinary—it was even wonderful; for she well knew him to be fierce, and even terrible, in his resentments; and though so great a master of dissimilation that he could assume almost every virtue at discretion, sad experience had convinced her, that his mind was the receptacle of every vice that can deprave and disgrace the human heart.

CHAP. XIV.

Soothed and reassured by the endearing manners of her young friend, who became every day more and more dear to her, the Countess's spirits, which, since the melancholy intelligence of her beloved Theodore, had been greatly depressed, were now somewhat revived; her health had, however, suffered too much from the pressure of grief and anxiety, to be speedily restored; and Adelaide still spent most of her time in her apartment.

The Count was not so often absent as formerly; he was observed to be much alone, and he frequently wandered about the Castle, with his arms folded across his breast, in an attitude of deep thoughtfulness; his brow sometimes overcast with the gloom of melancholy, sometimes distorted with an expression which partook of horror.

Whatever might be the cause of this alteration in his appearance and habits, and whatever circumstances or feelings had given rise to it, he seemed anxious, when not entirely occupied by his own ruminations and reflections, to elude all observation of it in others. When addressed, he would often start, as from a dream, and endeavour to assume an easy and disengaged deportment, from which he would again almost instantly relapse into his former state of silence and abstraction. His attentions to Adelaide had, of late, greatly decreased; he seemed no longer either to court or desire her regard. She feared he was displeased with her; yet, when and how could she have offended him?

"You stay too much at the Castle," said he one evening—"you are become paler and thinner than formerly—you will lose your health, if not your beauty—you must walk abroad."

"Will you accompany me, my Lord?"

"No; I have other occupations. You may take your ramble unattended, within a certain distance from the Castle—You know the path along the mountains. I would not, however, have you venture too far—your own discretion will direct you; but I must not suffer you to be thus constantly confined. I will attend the Countess in your absence."

Adelaide loved to wander alone, and, to enjoy the beauties of the adjacent scenery, had been wont to ascend some of the eminences a little beyond the limits of the Castle—a gratification she had of late resigned, for the no less pleasing one of soothing and supporting her beloved friend and protectress. But, still delighting in the lonely ramble, and anxious to oblige the Count, by an attention to what he had recommended, she gladly availed herself of his promise of remaining with his Lady in her absence, and took a stroll along one of the dingles* near the Castle; and, cheered by the freshness of the air, and eager for an extended view, she even crossed one of the mountains.

The track was lonely; but as she gradually wound among the heights, they opened to scenes of such enchanting beauty, that she was led insensibly on, till the sun had sunk low in the west, and a dim purple haze began to spread over the surrounding objects. She now came to one of those streamlets which tumble, in a series of interesting cascades, from the heights, when, seating herself upon a rock overhung with dark beech, she sat admiring its playful waters, till her attention to these passed to other thoughts, and soon became wrapped in pensive reverie.

These scenes, only a few months ago, she had visited with St. Angouléme, that friend now separated from her by death, but on whom her thoughts, though soothed with the sweetest hopes, had never ceased to dwell, with soft but melancholy tenderness; fancy recalled his image to her mind, while memory, from her treasured store, brought back his words, with every look and gesture that had accompanied them, and tears of tender regret, and affection truly filial, stole to her eyes. From the recollection of St. Angouléme, her supposed father, her thoughts reverted to him whom she was now taught to consider as her real father—But what a father!—How distressing, how affecting was the comparison!

She was engaged in these reflections, when she was startled by a rustling among the trees which overshadowed the ledge of rock on which she sat, and hastily quitting her seat, ere she had time for apprehension or conjecture, two men, of a ruffian-like appearance, issued from the side of the wood. One of them seized her by the arm; she shrieked, and called loudly for help. "You may as well be quiet, Lady," said the other—"you must go with us."

Adelaide, whose presence of mind had at first forsaken her, now conjured them to be merciful—"Here is my purse," said she—"I beseech you, release me, and let me go."

"No, no, Lady, we know better than that," said one of them: "however, as you offer us your purse so kindly, we will take it; and this pretty bauble," observing the diamond cross in her bosom, "we will make free with it too: and now, fair Lady, as we have no time to parley, you will please to accompany us." As he spoke, he took her into his arms, and assisted by his comrade, in spite of her screams and struggles, conveyed her up the mountain.

When they had arrived at a turn in the path, still pursuing their way along the side of the wood, one of them tied a handkerchief over her mouth, while the other placed her upon a mule, which was fastened to one of the trees. Having bound her feet, to prevent her attempting an escape, the ruffian who first seized her took his place before her: the other proceeded on foot; and his frequent hallooings seemed to intimate they were at no great distance from some fellow-travellers.

Resistance was now found to be in vain; and Adelaide, after a few ineffectual attempts to interest the compassion of her guides, resigned herself to her fate. They travelled with as much speed as the ruggedness of the road and the encreasing darkness of the hour would permit, sometimes through deep glens overshadowed with lofty trees, sometimes along the sides of precipices, and generally along tracks so rugged, that, as it seemed almost impossible for the animal to keep his feet, she expected every moment to be thrown, and dashed against the rocky heights, or precipitated and drowned in one of those lakes or *tarns*, lodged in the hollows of the mountains, and which the torrents, heard, on all sides, brawling down the neighbouring cliffs, seemed abundantly to supply.

They had travelled near a league through some of the wildest scenes of the Pyrenees, without meeting a human being, or distinguishing any sound than those of the mountain-stream, and occasionally the howling of the wolf, when the moon arose, whose confusing light contributed greatly to augment all the terrors which her busy imagination had hitherto formed, and she found them horribly confirmed by the prospect she was now enabled to discover. She perceived they were beginning to descend into a steep woody valley, extending as far as eye could trace, and which seemed to offer a horrible kind of security to the business of the ruffian and the murderer. Remote from the abode of man (for no trace of any human habitation was to be seen), the victim might there in vain call for help, or implore for mercy; the miseries of woe could not be seen through its dreary masses of shade, the shriek of death would not reach the ear of man across the heights. As they advanced deeper into the lonely valley, she seemed to be familiarized with the thoughts of death; her apprehensions became more and more terrifying—"It is here then," said she to herself, with a sigh of agony, "it is here I am to die." She shuddered, and daring to speak, besought her silent, stern conductor, to tell why she was thus taken, and whither she was to be carried. His answer was—"You shall see—Be silent, and be wise."

Another league brought them to the opposite borders of the forest, and Adelaide seemed to experience a reprieve from the horrors of a bloody death, when she found they were ascending from the valley; and the moon being now no longer hid by the high tops of the pine woods, she perceived they were approaching one of the wildest passes of the Pyrenees.

After winding for some time among the frowning cliffs, they began to descend; and she beheld, at some distance in the valley beneath, the towers and walls of one of those fortresses built to guard the communication of France and Spain. On approaching the edifice, she observed it stood on a rocky eminence in the valley; and the approach was through a narrow defile, cut in the stone. Its structure was massively solid, with only a few loop-holes; but yet so ruinous, as scarcely to allow of the possibility of its being inhabited.

They entered, over a tottering bridge, through a wicket in the gate, into a court overgrown with weeds and elder-bushes, when the ruffian dismounted, and sounding a whistle, which was instantly returned by another from some part of the building, two or three men came forth, and Adelaide was assisted to alight from behind her conductor. She trembled, again conjured him to be merciful;

but her entreaties were no further noticed by any of them, than by a single assurance that she had now but little further to go.

They led her onwards; and Adelaide, utterly hopeless of being able to move their compassion, or divert them from their purpose, whatever it might be, silently addressed herself to that Being from whom alone she could hope to obtain protection or support. The ruffian that led her, as he approached the entrance into the building, chancing to stumble, cursed the moon for withdrawing its beam; for a clouds was passing over it.

They entered a large hall, when one of them struck a light, and Adelaide now, for the first time, perceived that her companions were both masked. The villain who had first seized her, grasping her arm rudely, as if to prevent her attempting an escape, though no means of escape seemed possible, led her into a passage, at the end of which was a door, massive, and strengthened with iron. One who had gone before was busied in the removal of some stones, and other loose rubbish, lying on a few steps which descended to it; and when these were away, by the means of a lever moving in the wall, the gate or portcullis, as it might be called, was drawn up with a grating sound, which echoed back from what seemed a vast cavern below.

The silence of night, the gleam of the taper borne by the stern conductor, lost in the lofty space, the mysterious reserve of the ruffians, and the horrid dimensions of the prison she was about to enter, which might perhaps be her grave, produced impressions too powerful for female nature to endure, she faintly streaked, and fainted; nor did she awake to the consciousness of her situation, till she found herself in a large dismal-looking room, hung with tattered arras, and which contained only an old bedstead, with a mattrass, upon which she was laid, a table, and a few broken chairs: all these objects she dimly discovered by the light of a lamp, which had been left burning by the side of the bed; and by going to a little grated opening, which served as a window, she discovered that her apartment was not, as she expected, a dungeon, but a chamber of one of the turrets of the Castle; but by what passages she had arrived at her present abode, was a mystery which the present harassed state of her mind and feelings did not enable her to solve or conjecture.

In a few minutes, however, when somewhat more composed, she recollected the iron gate or portcullis, which she now, with every appearance of probability, supposed to be the entrance into some subterranean passage communicating with the vaults of the Castle, through which she had been led to her present place of confinement. These conjectures seemed to say, escape was impossible; yet so naturally, so irresistibly does hope cling to the heart, even under circumstances the most adverse and discouraging, so eagerly do we cherish even its faintest gleam, that she arose with a determination to attempt an escape, and to meet even death in the effort, rather than idly await the destiny intended for her by her ruffian conductors, in her present dreary solitude.

CHAP. XV.

She was engaged in this research, when she was startled by the sound of an approaching footstep. Instantly the door opened, and a man, whom she recognised to be one of the ruffians, entered the room. As her eye glanced over his figure, the blood chilled in her veins, and she uttered a faint scream; but in a moment her fears began to subside, and surprise, not unmingled with hope, succeeded to the terror his first appearance had excited. Instead of the weapon of death, which her imagination led her to suppose he carried, he had brought her some cakes and a little wine, which he set down in silence, and was departing, when Adelaide, in a soft and agitated tone of voice, entreated he would inform her where she was, and why she had been brought thither.

The man, a tall spare figure, clad in a cap and jacket of deer-skin, stopped, and gazed stedfastly in her face, apparently deliberating whether or not to answer her inquiries.

"I conjure you," resumed the trembling prisoner, "to tell me where I am, and what is this place."

The man still paused; at length he said—"This is the Castle of Ponteville."

"Ponteville!" repeated Adelaide, with astonishment.

"Yes—do you think I lie?—it is called the Castle of Ponteville."

"And for what dreadful purpose, oh tell me!" cried Adelaide, with trembling tongue, "have I been conveyed hither?"

"I am not to answer inquiries," rejoined he—"you will know more anon. In bringing you, I have only obeyed my orders." He then set down the wine and cakes, adding, "you have had a long journey, and must, to be sure, be in want of refreshment; so eat, and be content." He then quitted the room.

The door of the apartment, which, to the utter distress of Adelaide, was found to have no inside fastening, was then secured by a bolt, which, from long disuse, seemed to be drawn with difficulty; the retiring steps of the stern attendant sounded as though descending down steep and narrow steps, and presently all was silent.

"I am then indeed a prisoner!" exclaimed Adelaide, bursting into a flood of tears, "and in the Castle of Ponteville!—Gracious and merciful Heaven! for what am I reserved?—If to murder me be their object, why did they delay the execution of their horrid purpose? why bring me here, to make me die with terrors?—Would not that forest, those dreary wilds, the mountain-dells, and gloomy caverns of the rocky valleys we have passed, have afforded scenes as secure for their purpose, nay better, than even the solitude of this Castle? Perhaps then," said she, a gleam of hope beaming upon her mind, "my death is not intended. But why, then, am I brought to this dreadful place?—Oh!" cried she, with a shriek of horror, "surely it cannot be intended that I am to be kept for those brutal purposes for which lawless men sometimes, as I have heard, destine our unprotected sex!—Oh that I had but, even in this place, the reassuring presence of the Countess! or that the arm of the Count could but be raised for my defence!—But you, my beloved friends, know not of my anguish, or of my fate: alas! while I most need your aid, your affectionate hearts are racked by anxiety on my account. Too well I know the distress you feel for my extraordinary, my unaccountable disappearance: surely you will not think I have fled from you; no, you will not—you are too good to deem me base, your hearts will vibrate with tender sorrow; you are now, I am sure, anxious to render me that assistance I so much want." A flood of tears burst from her eyes, and somewhat relieved her aching heart.

After some pause, her feelings softening into the most tender sensations of regret—"Here," she cried, sighing, "perhaps I must remain, wretched, disconsolate, and a captive; nor can you, my friends, reach to comfort, to protect me—within these walls you cannot enter; nay, there is no clue to lead you to the gates."

From the recollection of the Count and Countess, her thoughts wandered to St. Angouléme—"Oh, could he know—could he know," said she, "the fate of his unhappy child! his beloved, his once-darling Adelaide! But perhaps, a benignant spirit, he now hovers over me unseen; perhaps gently reproving my want of reliance on the great Ruler of human actions, the Director of all mortal events."

This thought was peace; for, soothed and comforted by the reflection, it seemed that, in the excess of her terror, she had yielded to a greater degree of despair than her situation, melancholy as it was, could fully justify. She was indeed a prisoner, but it was by no means certain that her captivity would be of long duration. The circumstances of her conveyance to her present abode were so mysterious, that it was scarcely possible to form any reasonable conjecture concerning the purpose of her silent conductors; so little connected did they appear with her life and fortune, that she even began to imagine she had been mistaken for some other. Should this really be the case, a speedy deliverance from her present melancholy abode might perhaps quickly happen.

The person who had last quitted her had said—"Soon you will know more—I have only obeyed orders." Why then, her conductors belonged not to any of those numerous bands of robbers that infested the mountain-regions of the Pyrenees, but were men employed upon some other purpose. To muse upon the extraordinary events of the night, was but to add to a perplexity it was in vain to attempt to unravel: wearied with the endless, useless task, she, with much submission, again recommended herself to the merciful protection of Heaven, and then sunk, overcome with fatigue, upon the mattrass, and fell into a quiet slumber.

CHAP. XVI.

SHE was awakened by a noise near her bed; she started, and looked wildly around the room, but could discern nothing—"Good Heavens!" exclaimed she, in terror, as if the reflection had but that instant occurred to her, "this then is the Castle of Ponteville!" when, recollecting the Countess's words—*"A mystery hangs over that Castle, which never has, and probably never will be unravelled,"* she shuddered, a superstitious dread crept through her frame, and she lay for some minutes, overcome with horror and perplexity.

The moon shone full upon the high-grated casement of her window: she raised herself half way from the bed, and looked calmly, but not fearlessly, around the chamber—all was still. It was then nothing but the wind, thought Adelaide, and she again endeavoured to compose herself; but an apprehension of she scarcely knew what prevented the return of sleep, and she arose.

The moon still shone bright into her chamber; she advanced towards the window, and glanced her eye over the western wing of the building, of which that window commanded a full view. In several of the apartments of that wing, she observed lights flitting from window to window, with meteor-like rapidity: it was strange—she trembled, and immediately bethought herself of the relation given by the Countess of this Castle—the moving lights, the supernatural figure: a sudden faintness came over her, her limbs tottered, and she leaned against the stone-work of the window-frame for support.

While she stood thus terrified and aghast, the great clock of the Castle struck the hour of twelve. Its melancholy and deep-toned sound increased the awe of the present circumstances, and harrowed her feelings: she remained motionless and appalled—"At this hour," exclaimed she tremulously, "at this hour——" As she spoke, she stole another fearful glance toward the window; but in an instant retreated, overcome with terror and amazement. Either her imagination had deceived her, or she had seen the very apparition the Countess had described. A figure resembling the human form, pale, ghastly, and smeared with blood, covered with a sheet, and bearing in its hand a lighted taper, moved, or, to the awe-struck terrified imagination of Adelaide, seemed to move, in one of the apartments in the same side of the edifice where the lights were seen. With a desperate sort of courage, she again turned her eyes toward the window where the apparition had appeared: it was not illusion. She screamed—it beckoned her; she darted, almost flew from her window, and with a loud shriek fell senseless on the ground.

When recovered to a sense of her situation, and the alarming circumstances attending it, she accused herself of presumption, in having formerly dared to doubt the reality of the appearance of this spectre; and though it was possible that the Castle might contain some inhabitants beside herself and the men who had conveyed her thither, the tenor of her feelings did not immediately allow her to deliberate upon the probability of the figure she had seen being human rather than supernatural—"If human," said she at length, "it is some unfortunate being like myself, who has been brought, and left to perish in this gloomy solitude."

Apprehensive of encountering further trials of her fortitude, she flung herself upon the mattrass, and with trembling fear endeavoured to hide herself from alarm, by wrapping herself close in her dress. She lay and listened, yet dreaded to hear, for every sound seemed supernatural: she feared to look around, and almost to breathe.

Long laid she thus—sleep fled her pillow; and though weariness brought her to a kind of stupor of repose, yet terror failed not to keep her waking, by picturing to her fancy new apprehension, as torturing, and scarcely less dreadful, than those she had already suffered. The wind blew high; and as it whistled through the desolate apartment, and shook the loosened hinges of the door, she often started, and sometimes thought she heard shrieking voices in the pauses of the gust.

While racked by these alarms, a noise seemed to proceed from that part of the chamber in which she lay; it was like the undrawing of a bolt. The lamp was now extinguished, and the beams of the moon afforded only a dim uncertain light, when, raising her eyes towards the place from whence the sound seemed to issue, she perceived something move in the shadowy space, and advance slowly towards the bed. Terror again overcame her, and uttering a loud scream, she sunk back upon the mattrass, from which she had partly arisen, and covered her face with her hands, lest her eyes should encounter some other horrible apparition.

She lay, and all was silence, except the storm without. After some interval, she assumed courage to uncover her eyes: she gazed around, but could perceive nothing—dreadful was the stillness of the hour, but it did not intimate danger. Again a sudden gust shook the door, and agitated the arras, the figures upon which (for it represented a number of men at arms of gigantic stature) were strangely exhibited by the beams of the moon, which shone full upon them. The apparition, if apparition she had really seen, was gone; but the sound, and the object she had observed, reminded her that the room might be entered from without; and under her present circumstances, the idea of a spectre could not be more dreadful than that of being intruded upon, thus unprotected and alone, and in the darkness of night, by ruffians, such as those who had hurried her from her home, to whom deeds of horror were familiar, whose designs were yet unknown to her, and who, for aught she knew, might purpose mischiefs more dreadful than death itself.

These reflections, and the apprehensions that had given rise to them, operated so strongly upon her mind, that she did not venture to close her eyes till the light of morning began to disperse the glooms and dismal visions of the night; when, exhausted by the agitations she had undergone, she fell into a deep sleep.

CHAP. XVII.

She was awakened by the entrance of the ruffian who brought her daily supply of food: Adelaide viewed him attentively, almost expecting harm; but finding he was about quietly to retire, she resumed inquiries of the preceding night. At first he seemed resolved not to speak; and was moving toward the door, without making any reply, when Adelaide, impelled by despair, besought him, with clasped hands and streaming eyes, to pity and to save her.

Touched, as it seemed, by such energetic distress, he turned, and looking steadily at her, as before, said, in rather a feigned voice, "What is it you fear?"

"Alas! I have every thing to dread," rejoined Adelaide, "and, I fear, nothing to hope. Oh release me from the horrors of this place; and believe me, when I solemnly declare, I will divulge nothing that it may be your interest to conceal. Oh stop, and hear me, while I swear by the holy Mother, and by every saint, I *never will;* let me but without the gates of this Castle, and no ear shall ever learn that I have ever been within its walls."

The man paused; at length he said—"Fear not—be not perverse, but wise; to-morrow mayhap your fate may be known—all may yet be well." Saying this, he hastened from the room, bolting the door without, a caution hardly necessary to prevent her escape, for it was scarcely possible that she should find her way alone, through the subterranean labyrinths by which she had been carried, in a state of insensibility, to the turret.

"To-morrow then," said Adelaide, as soon as he had withdrawn, "to-morrow my doom may be fixed. He says *to-morrow*—What can this mean? Merciful Powers! in what a cloud of mystery am I now involved!—*Be not perverse, but wise*—What can he intend by this?—*All may be well*—Why then, according to this declaration, my fate is, in some way or other, dependent upon my own decision. But how can this possibly be? Shall I, a wretched, helpless prisoner, become to-morrow the arbitress of my own destiny?—How shall this be?—It baffles comprehension. Is then another night to be passed in the gloom and solitude of this apartment?" cried Adelaide, recoiling at the thought; "am I again to be exposed to other hours of agony? am I again to witness scenes of horror, dreadful enough to appal the stoutest mind, and subdue even the most fearless?"

She regretted she had not questioned the man, whom she now considered as keeper, respecting the lights in the western building. That these lights were supernatural, she scarcely ventured to doubt; that she had seen a spectre, the same the Countess had once described to her, seemed equally certain: she trembled at the recollection of her last night's watch, and feared that a repetition of such terrors might overturn her reason, and bring on madness.

Amid these fears and conjectures, the day passed heavily to its close: her masked keeper did not appear—she was not interrupted by any one—"To-morrow, to-morrow," she again repeated, "I am to know my fate; and oh what may that be, which is so near, and so important?" She paced repeatedly her prison, or seated herself in the window-seat, large, from the thickness of the walls.

Wearied with conjecture, she strove to amuse herself, by gazing upon the dark precipices, the wooded knolls, and rocky peaks of the mountains, till the splendour of the day began to yield to the sober tints of evening, and the veil of twilight to clothe, in misty garb, the rich and varied objects of the landscape.

Though deprived of liberty, a blessing which, like many others, we rarely know how to appreciate duly till it is lost, but which Adelaide had now learned to value, it was sweet to look, even from her prison-window, upon beautiful nature; to listen to the evening song of the feathered songster; to mark the dying breeze, as it idly rustled over the tops of the woods, or now varied the thunder of the distant cataract, which was heard tumbling from rock to rock in the higher vale, as it hastened to half encircle with its rapid stream the eminence on which the Castle stood.

Scenes like these are calculated to impress, upon the feelings of taste and sensibility, all the affections of the sublime; but the sublime is seldom pleasing, except to minds exempt from danger, and at ease: yet their effect was not lost upon Adelaide—she had been taught not to reject the good, because it came accompanied with evil: hence, though a captive within those walls, those horrid walls, yet still health and a pure conscience enabled her to look out from her window upon those scenes with pleasure, to fill her mind with admiration of the Author of nature, and to feel the liveliest gratitude for his many mercies.

She saw the mountain-cliff had been bared of all verdure by the beating of the storm; yet now all was tranquil; and an eagle soaring around it, in safety and delight, had fixed there its eyrie, and its home. Lower down, the woods had been stunted in their growth, or bared at top by the winds, which often took their tearing course along the vallies; yet their depredations were now forgotten, and the oak and chesnut, firmly rooting in the rock, exhibited vigorous life in their happy verdure. The river, even now, rolled swiftly along its stony channel; and in the grey gravelly bank shewed that oftentimes its current was ruinously irresistible. But now the grayling and the trout, leaving their haunts, where, during times of flood, they skulked in precarious safety, gambolled lively in the stream, regardless of dangers past or future, intent wholly on such joys as the present hour afforded.

"Let these objects," said Adelaide, as she contemplated them, "teach me to be patient, and wise. I am, at this moment, unassailed by any positive sufferings; I will not then trouble myself with the dread of harms, which may or may not come. Let me take consolation from the good even now allowed me, and be thankful I am not bereft of more. I am a prisoner, it is true, but not in a dungeon, and in fetters; I have not companions, but I am allowed food; I may perhaps expect personal injuries, but I may say, I have not, I think, deserved them. These reflections tell me I am happy, compared to many who might suffer here, nay, compared with many whom the world calls prosperous. I am afflicted, but yet I see I ought to hope; and I will try, in despite of terrors and dangers, to await, with cheerful patience, my hour of deliverance."

Musings such as these afforded a pleasing relief to her harassed mind; they even gave delight, for they excited something resembling the fervour of devotion; of course, she willingly indulged them: and remained thus occupied, till her apartment was almost hid in gloom; when she heard a noise on the other side of the wall, the same as had alarmed her on the preceding night, like the undrawing of a rusty bolt; she had scarcely time even for apprehension, for the arras near the bed was immediately moved aside, and a man entered from behind, and advanced quietly along the chamber.

Adelaide instantly perceiving it was not the person who used to bring her food, felt a degree of consternation, which almost deprived her of the power of utterance.

"Do not be alarmed," said he, respectfully approaching her; "the only motive of this my visit is to serve you. Do you wish to be released from your captivity in this Castle?"

"Do I wish it!" reiterated Adelaide—"Need the question be asked?"

"Will you accept of my protection?"

"Are you in earnest?—Do you indeed offer it me?"

"I have no hope or desire equal to my wish of serving you."

"What is it I hear!" exclaimed Adelaide—"Have I then a friend where I least expected to find one—in a place surrounded, as I believed, with enemies?"

"Soon, very soon," said the stranger, "though, as yet, I know not the time, I will convey you beyond the reach of your persecutors, whose power you too justly dread. Will you confide in me? Will you commit yourself to my protection?"

Adelaide, to whom these words, if sincere, would indeed be words of comfort, listened, half doubting; then, in a voice rendered tremulous by emotions of hope and fear, she begged he would inform her who he was, and how an escape might be accomplished?

"By my means, and mine only," resumed the stranger, "you may avoid the dangers that await you in this Castle. Place yourself under my directions, rely upon me, and fear nothing."

Adelaide gazed upon the figure of the person who spoke to her, whose countenance was obscured by the darkness of the evening hour, with a look of mingled astonishment and joy—"Is it possible!" she exclaimed, in an ecstasy of delight—"But inform me," added she, "I conjure you, stranger, to whom I owe this offer of deliverance?"

"The offer," he replied, "is wholly mine. I am one who, like yourself, have been basely seized, and detained a prisoner in this place; where, had I not been able to interest the compassion, or rather the avarice, of my keeper, who has consented, on a promise of an ample recompence, to afford me an opportunity of effecting my enlargement, I might have worn out, in a wretched captivity, a wearisome life. To dwell upon particulars, might be to endanger our mutual safety: the villains who conveyed you hither believe I am yet ignorant of your arrival, and consequently are entirely without suspicion of my attempts to liberate you; we must not therefore be seen together, nay, I must hasten away, lest my keeper should visit my prison, and finding it unoccupied, search for me in this turret. With the secret of your arrival, and the motive of these men, or rather that of their employer, in bringing you hither, I was last night informed, by a conversation I overheard between my keeper and his companion; for I had made a discovery of a trap-door opening upon a flight of steps, by which I could descend this tower, and visit various parts of the Castle."

Adelaide, sensible that any such conversation must be highly important under her present circumstances, entreated to be made acquainted with its import.

"I will inform you, Lady," said the stranger; "but I dare not stay here long—it would endanger the success of my design."

"But first," said Adelaide, "let me ask who is the owner of this Castle?"

"The present possessor of the estate in which this Castle is situated," rejoined the stranger, "is the Marquis de Ponteville. It was by this nobleman's orders you were seized, and brought hither; and if you do not shortly leave the Castle, you will have no chance of escape from his villainy, or what he may term his love."

"The Marquis de Ponteville!" exclaimed Adelaide, in amazement—"I know him not—never, to my knowledge, have I even seen him. My captivity must have been intended for another—it is impossible I can be known to him."

"You mistake, Lady; he has seen you. A deep and deliberate scheme of wickedness has been for some time forming against you. Count St. Angouléme——"

"Ah! what of him?" interrupted Adelaide.

"He has betrayed you into the hands of a villain."

"Impossible!" exclaimed Adelaide—"he could not be so base!"

"He has; nor need you other assurances than I can give."

"Oh be quick then," cried Adelaide, "lest we be interrupted, and discovered."

"It is now near the hour," continued the stranger, "when my keeper usually visits my prison; I must therefore hasten back. As soon as he has seen me, and all is safe, I will return to this turret, and afford you the information you so anxiously desire. Trust to my honour and exertion, and you will have no cause for fear or apprehension."

Adelaide waved her hand, she dared not speak, for a light now gleamed through the chasms of her door; and in a moment after the bolt was undrawn, and the keeper entered with her supper. The mysterious reserve of this ruffian attendant did not affect the imprisoned Adelaide as before; and she was now only anxious for his departure, lest she should not be able to disguise the emotions of joy and anxiety which the hopes of escape had excited, and which her countenance might but too readily betray.

The man acted exactly as she could wish; for, having left her a lamp ready trimmed upon the table, with a dish of some kind of meat stewed with vegetables, he withdrew in silence, of which Adelaide did not now complain, and was by no means disposed interrupt.

That Count St. Angouléme could be the abettor of such a scheme of villainy so atrocious as the stranger had described, seemed almost too monstrous to be believed; but every conjecture she could form was perplexed by the busy joy she felt at the prospect of deliverance, and the distressing reflection that, if the declaration of the stranger was really true, she could not return to her former residence in the Castle of St. Angouléme; and consequently that, after her escape, she would be without a place of refuge—a wanderer, and an outcast in the world.

CHAP. XVIII.

SHE was labouring under the alternate influence of hope, fear, joy, and regret, when an hour having nearly elapsed, she heard the bolt of the concealed door slowly undrawn, and again the stranger appeared—"We are safe," said he—"all is favourable to our purpose."

Adelaide trembled, and betrayed symptoms of confusion, as the stranger again entered, and thus spoke; she was fully sensible of the perplexing and awkward situation into which she was thrown.

He observed her alarm and uneasiness, and earnestly entreated her to place in him that confidence which his conduct would be found to merit—"Let me," added he, "assure you, that I am incapable of being actuated by any motives inconsistent with your honour and happiness."

"It would be painful to me in the extreme," said Adelaide, whom these words had greatly reassured, "were I to doubt the honour of a man who so generously offers assistance to one so unfortunate and unprotected as myself. For this kind, this noble effort, accept my most grateful thanks, which no term I can select will sufficiently express: I will rather say, may that self-approbation, which naturally results from the performance of actions truly virtuous and meritorious, be yours!"

The stranger was about to reply, but Adelaide proceeded—"May I be informed," said she, "of the name of the person to whom I am about to be so signally obliged?"

"My name," rejoined the stranger, "is Perouse. My father was a native of Paris, where I also was born. My story, till the incident which preceded the event of my being captured, and brought a prisoner to this Castle, contains nothing remarkable; I shall therefore hasten to those particulars which are more immediately interesting, as connected with our present meeting.

"With the Marquis de Ponteville I have only a mere personal acquaintance. My endeavours to save from dishonour a young female, a distant relation of mine, whom the Marquis had accidentally seen in Paris, and with whom he became suddenly enamoured, drew upon me the resentment of this nobleman, who, in order to prevent any future interference on my part, in the cause of distressed beauty, contrived that I should be waylaid on my journey through a part of this forest, and confined within these walls. The whole was managed with so much secresy, that it was some time before I knew even the name of my persecutor; and longer still, ere I could obtain any certain information of his intentions concerning me. At first, I had reason to imagine his design was to murder me, or leave me to perish by hunger; afterwards, I had sufficient grounds to apprehend that it was intended I should remain a prisoner here for life. My condition seemed now altogether hopeless, for I had been robbed of the little property I had about me by the banditti who had seized me, and had nothing to offer to bribe my keeper and attendant.

"Several weeks passed away in various ineffectual contrivances to escape from the gloomy horrors of the room in the great tower where I was confined, when one night, as I was walking in my chamber, I thought I perceived a board of it shake beneath my steps; and on examination found it, as well as two more, were loose and removable, and under them a trap door. Curiosity and the hope of escape determined me to open it, which with some difficulty I effected; beneath was a small dark passage of steps. I closed the door, and replaced the boards, resolving to explore the place that very evening, when my keeper had left me my night's repast. I did so, and taking my lamp, descended a considerable way down steps, often much broken, which convinced me my track was not in common use. At the bottom, I found myself in a narrow passage, along which I proceeded with caution, fearing not only lest my light might be seen through some of the loop-holes, but lest the dank vapours which curled around should extinguish my light.

"The passage was of a considerable length, and led to a door, which was fastened. I placed my lamp at some distance, to avoid the current of air, for I dreaded being left alone in darkness, and tried to open the door: it was bolted on the other side, but it was loose; and after some cautious efforts, I was enabled to push back the rusty bolt with my hand, and open it.

"I then found myself in a large, square, stone room, with two doors on opposite sides. I was deliberating which of them to open, when I distinguished the sound of voices in the next apartment; and in a few minutes, plainly heard that of my keeper, in conversation with some other person, whom at first I imagined to be the Marquis. Fearing they might enter the room and discover me, I was about to retreat; but a few words convinced me I was mistaken in supposing either to be the Marquis, and their import rivetted me to the spot.

"The substance of what I heard, though it occupied a conversation of some length, may be briefly stated. I found that a lady, whom I discovered, by their description, to be both young and beautiful, and consequently yourself, had been betrayed by Count St. Angouléme, one of our Gascon nobles, into the power of the Marquis de Ponteville, who, it seems, had not some accident intervened to prevent the accomplishment of his project, intended, by a pretended rescue of her from the hands of the ruffians by whom, on his orders, she had been seized, to convey her, in the character of a deliverer, over the mountains, to a splendid villa he possesses on the banks of the Ebro. The Marquis, I heard, was now daily expected; and immediately on his arrival, was to conduct his lovely prisoner from the Castle to the elegant habitation prepared for her, where she was to be compelled to accept of such proposals as he might choose to offer.

"Of the Marquis I know enough to be convinced he is capable of any species of villainy, when the gratification of his own passions is the object. The only part of the discourse which seemed to me at all extraordinary, was, that Count St. Angouléme should consent to sacrifice, to the intriguing purposes of the Marquis, a young creature, whom, according to their account, he once supposed to be his niece, and the heiress of a very considerable property, but who had been since discovered to be a changeling, and the offspring of some peasant near Avignon, of the name of De Launé.

"This, I afterwards gathered from the conversation of these men, he was induced to agree to, in consequence of the Marquis having lost a large sum of money at cards to a set of sharpers, with whom the Count was connected.

"On the discovery of this act of perfidy of the Count and his associates, the Marquis, in the violence of his rage, threatened them with an exposure; and, though the sum he had lost was thrice offered him, would listen to no terms of accommodation but such as he afterwards proposed, and which were at length acceded to: these were, that the Count should, by some contrivance, assist in throwing the young lady into his power, whom, though he had seen her only for a moment, and had not even spoken to her, he professed to love with the most violent passion.

"I was now in possession of a secret which filled me with the most tender concern: all I had further to learn was the place in which the fair prisoner was confined; this most valuable information was conveyed to me by the conversation which followed, and of this I resolved to make instant use. I returned therefore to my chamber, and waiting till past the hour when I knew my keeper and his comrade would have retired to rest, again descended the trap, determined, if possible, to enter the place of your confinement.

"I need not detain you with an account of the many difficulties I encountered; I will only say, that, after various exertions and much hazard, having entered this tower, I arrived at a small door, which led to the prison-room of my fair unfortunate fellow-captive: for I heard a deep sigh within, which convinced me my search had been crowned with success.

"I waited till the stillness that reigned around convinced me you slept, when I undrew the bolts, and presumed to enter your apartment. As I approached the side of the bed on which you lay, you screamed, and seemed, for the moment, bereft of sense and motion. I dreaded lest your cry should have reached the ear of my keeper, whose apartment might too probably be in the same part of the edifice, and therefore I precipitately retreated, satisfied with having discovered your confinement, and pleasing myself with the hope of being able to deliver a sufferer, so fair and so injured, from the mischiefs intended her."

The stranger having proceeded this far, discontinued his narration. Adelaide, for some time after he had ceased to speak, could not otherwise express her feelings for this promised deliverance, than by a copious shower of tears, which now streamed down her cheeks. Her heart beat quick with the emotions of her gratitude: how kind, how generous, seemed his purposed exertion in behalf of an unfortunate unknown, to whom accident had so strangely, yet so providentially, introduced him! hardly could she find terms expressive of her sensations—they were too refined for language; yet she strove to render him sensible of the high sense she entertained of his generosity and benevolence, to which she felt no acknowledgments could be in any degree adequate.

"Load me not thus," cried the stranger, "with the effusions of your gratitude: in delivering you from the injuries and persecutions preparing for you, I am but barely performing my duty, both as a man and a Christian." As he spoke, he pressed devoutly to his lips a small ivory crucifix, which hung suspended on his breast; and seemed, by the movement of his lips, to be engaged in mental prayer to the Virgin, or some saint. After a pause—"Let us not," said he, "waste our time in mutual compliments—these moments are precious: let us think only of the future." He then hastened to inform Adelaide of the scheme he had suggested for her enlargement; and gave such directions for her conduct to her keeper, as he conceived necessary to the occasion.

While they were engaged in discoursing upon their plans, and revolving in their minds the most probable means of escape, as also those by which they might elude the Argus-eyed vigilance of their ruffian attendant, a subject which now wholly occupied the thoughts of the prisoners, they were startled by a deep groan, which seemed to issue from an adjacent part of the building: it was repeated—they gazed upon each other, in terrified astonishment.

To Adelaide the idea almost instantly occurred, that there was near them, in that turret, some other unfortunate fellow-captive, whose condition was perhaps far more hopeless than their own. Ere she had time to express the nature of her surmises, the arras on one side of the chamber was gently agitated, and a thin spectre-like figure emerged from behind the walls, and gliding along the darkening space, vanished suddenly from view.

Adelaide shrieked—"Great Heaven!" exclaimed she, in agony, "it is here—the figure, the same figure I once saw!—Oh save me! save me!" She could add no more, but sunk fainting into the arms of Perouse, which were extended to receive her sinking, and now lifeless form.

On recovering, she found herself upon the bed: she started, and looked fearfully around the chamber. A man was standing by the side of the bed—but it was not Perouse. Scarcely had she awakened from this trance of terror, when a hoarse hollow voice sounded in her ears, and demanded the cause of this disturbance.

"Did you not see it?" said Adelaide, forgetting, in the agitation of her feelings, that the person whom she now discovered to be her keeper, was not present at the moment when the apparition had appeared.

"See it! See what?" reiterated the man angrily.

"The ghost!" rejoined the still-terrified Adelaide, "the ghost!"

"Oh, we have many of 'em in this place," quoth the man calmly, and without the least appearance of surprise; "we make no count of 'em here."

"How!" exclaimed Adelaide—"Can you behold unappalled the spirits of the dead?"

"Aye, marry, can we," rejoined the ruffian—"Why not, have we not less to fear from the dead than the living?"

"Yes; but surely," cried Adelaide, shrinking with affright, "these visitations are very horrible."

"Mayhap so, till people be used to 'em."

"Used to them! Can use reconcile you to such appearances as these?—Oh Heaven, protect me from them!"

"You had better be quiet," returned the ruffian, "and not squall so, or, by our Lady, you'll have all the ghosts in the Castle about your ears, and that'll be a fine posse, I can tell you."

Saying this, he went out, leaving Adelaide in astonishment at his extreme insensibility and audacious stupidity, and more than ever averse from the solitude of her prison, subjected, as she now was, to the most awful alarms and interruptions; so dreadful seemed the idea being left alone, that even the presence of her stern keeper would, under the present gloomy circumstance of her fate, have afforded comfort and consolation; it would have even been deemed a valuable acquisition. He was gone, however; and she waited with impatience, hoping for the return of Perouse; but, to her extreme disappointment, he came not. She feared he had been discovered in her chamber, when, it was but too probable, his design of releasing her would be suspected; and she would have every thing to apprehend from the watchfulness of her guard, who would doubtless exert every effort of his vigilance to prevent her effecting an escape.

The night was now far advanced, and as Perouse did not return, she imagined he had retired to his bed, and meant to see her in the morning. Hopeless of his appearance, she took possession of her mattrass; and after some time spent in the most agonizing conjectures, wearied by her late alarms and the emotions she had suffered, she fell into a fast sleep. She awakened not till her keeper entered with her breakfast, when having taken a small portion of the food he brought, she waited, with renewed anxiety, the arrival of Perouse.

Hour after hour rolled on, and still he came not: her heart now beat with expectation, now throbbed with agony. He had been detected then in his attempt to rescue her, and was now probably removed to some dreary dungeon in the vaults beneath, when, of course, every chance of escape would be lost; and she must have to lament, not only her own misfortunes, but those of that noble and disinterested friend, whose absence she now thus feelingly lamented, and whose sufferings she had perhaps encreased and prolonged.

CHAP. XIX.

The day was passed by Adelaide in the most terrifying apprehension for her own fate, and that of her intended deliverer—"Never, alas! I fear," said she, "but on conditions that I tremble even to think of, must I hope to be emancipated from my confinement within these dreary, these detested walls!"

Evening again advanced. What she had before imagined to be probable, now appeared certain; hope no longer enlivened the now-cheerless prospect, and seating herself in the recess of her window, she sat immersed in the most melancholy contemplations, till all nature seemed sinking gradually into a state of repose, which the tumultuous emotions of her heart allowed her not to partake. She remained at her window till the dusk of twilight thickened, and the last crimson glow of light receded from the horizon: she shuddered, as the deepening gloom of the night stole through her chamber; and recollecting the late awful visitation, the most horrible apprehensions took possession of her mind.—Hardly durst she venture to snatch a gaze toward that part of her dreary chamber, along which the spectre had seemed to glide; she trembled, as the wind shook the arras—every sound encreased her fears; now, in the pauses of the shrill blast, she thought she distinguished voices, sometimes deep groans, and at others the most dismal shrieks.

Involved in uneasy fears and apprehensions, lest their purpose should be prevented till after the arrival of the Marquis, when escape would be impracticable, she sat terrified, almost distracted with her surmises, when she heard the bolt of the concealed door hastily withdrawn, and Perouse entered the room.

The darkness that had gathered around prevented her from observing the expression of joy that beamed from his countenance as he approached; but who may describe her rapture, when informed that the plan for her deliverance was accomplished, that the keys of the outlets of the Castle were now in the hands of her fellow-captive, and that he was come, even then, to convey her thence!—"Our keeper," said he, "is safe in my power; and, once beyond the boundaries of this Castle, we shall, I trust, have nothing to apprehend. The moon will soon afford us some light; but I fear we shall have to encounter a storm." Saying this, he took her hand, and conveying her through the door behind the arras, they descended from the turret, and pursuing their way through a number of galleries and deserted apartments, proceeded down several flights of stone steps, to the vaults of the Castle. Having traversed the subterranean passage, they arrived at an iron gate; and Adelaide and her guide emerged at length from the gloom, and entered upon the forest.

When they had ascended the eminence, Adelaide conversed with Perouse concerning the lights in the western wing of the building, the figure she had seen at the window, and also of the apparition which had glided through her prison on the preceding night.

Perouse did not even affect to deny that the Castle was subjected to these horrible visitations, and began to relate an account of so many dreadful murders, said formerly to have been committed in it, that Adelaide shuttered, and entreated he would drop the subject.

The wind blew high; it was yet dark; and after travelling through a part of the forest, Perouse, having conducted Adelaide to a little retired spot among the trees, proposed they should remain there till the rising of the moon. Adelaide, already wearied with the haste she had used in descending the mountain, assented to the plan of her conductor, who, taking his seat beside her, on the trunk of the large tree which had been torn up and thrown aslant by the fury of the winds, being now, as he conceived, in a place of temporary security, in answer to Adelaide's inquiries how he had obtained the means of escape, he gave the following relation.

CHAP. XX.

"After the conversation I had overheard between my keeper and his companion, whom I afterwards learnt was one of the Marquis's servants, I returned to my prison-room, and waited in anxious expectation till I thought my attendant was in bed, when, solicitous to make further discoveries relative to the place I was in, I again ventured from my turret. Having reached the main building, I traversed, as before, several passages and stone chambers; finding, however, no door or outlet by which I could effect an escape, should my keeper, as I sometimes feared, fail in the performance of the promise he had once made, of restoring me to my liberty on the conditions I had offered.

"Disappointed in my attempt, I was returning pensively to my chamber, when, having crossed a large square room leading into the passage which terminated the flight of steps I had descended, my foot struck something lying on the floor, and lowering my lamp, I found a dagger: it was rusty, and of little worth; but it was a weapon which might be useful, and I placed it in my girdle. I returned to my chamber, and closing the trap-door, sat revolving schemes for your deliverance, which I was determined to effect at any risque, even of that of life itself.

"Last night, when my keeper appeared as usual, I made many inquiries about the apartments and offices belonging to the Castle; to which, though he returned very imperfect and cautious answers, they enabled me to understand as much as was necessary for effecting our escape. Among other inquiries, I asked who they were whom I had heard in conversation in a room below?—He was surprised that I should have heard them, but replied that some of the Marquis's pages had been there the night before, but that they were now departed, with others who usually resided in the Castle.—'Then you are the only one remaining here tonight?' said I. He answered in the affirmative, but pronounced the word *yes* with surprise and hesitation.—'Now then,' said I, 'you may, if you are willing, give me my liberty on the terms I once proposed—Will you do it?'—He said he had no objection, except from his fears of the Marquis, whose anger he was afraid to incur. I observed, the Marquis had probably now ceased to interest himself about me, 'and you may comply with my request' said I, 'without any danger.' I then, the more effectually to overcome his reluctance, promised a handsome premium, which I assured him he should receive as soon as I had obtained my enlargement, and was in a place of safety.

"He paused, and seemed to deliberate upon my offer, when, rushing upon him unawares, and casting him down, I exclaimed—'I will not continue one more night within these accursed walls: either resign to me the keys of the doors of the vaulted passages through which I entered,' drawing, as I spoke, my instrument of death, 'or I will plunge this dagger into thy heart.'

'At the sight of it (for he was unarmed), he submitted; and lying quietly at my feet, begged loudly for mercy; promising to do whatever I might require.—'Lead the way then,' said I, 'to the place where the keys are deposited; and, unworthy as you are of the reward I offered you, it shall still be yours.'

"He thanked me, and promised to do whatever I desired. I bade him give me the keys of the Castle: this he promised. I ordered him to rise, and holding the dagger ready to strike if necessary, followed him through a considerable part of the Castle, to a small room contiguous to the gateway of the inner court. There he reached from the wall a bunch of keys, which he delivered to me, with the assurance that they would enable me to open all the gates I should have occasion to pass, even that of the barbican, beyond the ditch next the forest.

"I told him he must now be my prisoner, to which he did not object; and desired to be locked up in the room we were then in, for that his bed was in a recess in one side of it; 'and there,' said he, 'I can rest till my companions return.' I had mentioned the trap-door: he requested that it might be left open, as it would favour his declaration that I had come through it upon him by surprise, when left alone in the Castle; and thus he should be able to escape not only punishment, but censure.

"With the rest of the particulars," continued Perouse, who had now concluded his narration, "you are already acquainted; and now, Lady, I am ready to convey you wherever you shall please to direct. It must be unnecessary to observe," added he, "that the Castle of St. Angouléme can no longer afford you a secure and honorable asylum; were you now to return thither, the Count, to escape public obloquy, must immediately resign you to the Marquis. But you have perhaps some other friend or relative, within a convenient distance from this place, with whom you may find a secure asylum, and, what is more necessary, a powerful protection?"

To this Adelaide replied only with a deep sigh. Her forlorn and friendless condition never struck her so forcibly as at this moment: Perouse's account, gathered from the conversation of the two men at the Castle, relative to herself, was too circumstantial to permit her to entertain a single doubt of their veracity; they seemed acquainted not only with her real name, but all the particulars of her situation. She knew the Count was fond of play, and that he indulged in it to a very culpable excess; she remembered also the alteration she had remarked in his manners for some weeks past, his melancholy, his abstraction, and the emotions he seemed to undergo from some unknown cause; nor did the till then seemingly unimportant circumstance of his pressing her to walk abroad the evening she was seized and brought to the Castle in the forest of Ponteville, escape her now busy recollection—all appeared thoroughly consistent.

The Countess could not receive her, without betraying her to the Count—whither then was she to go?—Perouse had twice repeated the question, before Adelaide could reply to it. Where indeed was she to go?—At length she answered, she had no friend near with whom to seek asylum; nor a single relative on earth, except her father, whom she had only once seen, and who resided, she believed, in some part of Provence.

"If you have no friends," said Perouse, "to whom you can instantly apply for protection, suffer me to convey you to the house of a female relation of mine, an aunt, who resides in a small village not many miles from hence. I have only to tell her your story, as far as you may allow me to reveal it, to interest her in your favour; and in the retirement in which she lives, you will have nothing I hope to apprehend from the future schemes of your persecutors."

Adelaide, to whom this offer appeared highly eligible, and, in her situation, truly generous, listened to the proposal with trembling delight; tears of thankfulness and joy again rushed to her eyes; nor did she fail to express, in the most lively and energetic terms, her high sense of the obligation he was about to confer upon her, in the promised asylum and offered protection of the lady to whom she was to be introduced.

It was now quickly resolved, that as soon as the moon should arise, they would commence their journey over the mountains, to the little village Perouse had mentioned as the residence of Madame St. Clair, his aunt. Their arrangements thus made, Perouse arose, and retired from the little embowered spot where he had been sitting, leaving Adelaide, with fresh assurances of protection and watchful care, to repose on a bed of leaves and grass he had collected for her.

She attempted to take that repose for which he had prepared; but she scarcely slept on her rustic couch, for her mind was occupied with impatient expectation for the rising of the moon. It arose at length, but it rose in a lowering and portentous sky; and her listening ear seemed to distinguish a low muttering sound, like the noise of distant thunder. A storm seemed to be gathering around; but, to Adelaide, the fury of contending elements offered nothing to her imagination which could bear even the most distant comparison with the horrors that had awaited her in the Castle of de Ponteville.

It was now light, though the moon was often hid by passing clouds rolling over it. She waited in eager expectation the return of Perouse, whom she supposed not far off, whose active benevolence in the cause of an unhappy stranger, and seemingly correct, if not polished manners, had rendered him an object not only of esteem but interest, notwithstanding the qualities she admired were combined with an ungraceful figure and countenance which, if not absolutely disagreeable, yet, seen at any other time, and under any other circumstances, might have excited aversion rather than admiration—"Surely," said she, shuddering, as the thought occurred, "nothing cannot have happened to obstruct our departure; surely no wild beast—no ruffian——"

While she spoke, Perouse entered with a sort of horseman's coat, which he said he had found, and which he desired Adelaide would put on, as it would not only afford her a complete disguise, and thus prevent their being traced, but serve as a defence against the weather, which seemed to threaten a storm.

Adelaide, delighted at his return, and sensible that the covering might be useful, took it without hesitation; and Perouse, slouching a large hat over her head, so completely concealed her figure, that, under this disguise, it became impossible to recognize the beautiful Adelaide de Launé. Thus clad, she hastened to accompany her conductor over the remaining part of the forest.

END OF VOL. I.

PYRENEAN BANDITTI.

A ROMANCE

IN THREE VOLUMES.

BY

ELEANOR SLEATH,

AUTHOR OF

THE NOCTURNAL MINSTREL, BRISTOL HEIRESS, WHO'S THE MURDERER, &c., &c.

Know'st thou not,
That when the searching eye of Heav'n is hid
Behind the globe, and lights the lower world,
Then thieves and robbers range abroad unseen,
In murders and in outrage bloody here?
But when from under this terrestrial ball
He fires the proud tops of the eastern pines,
And darts his light through ev'ry guilty hole;
Then murders, treasons, and detested sins,
The cloak of night being pluck'd from off their backs,
Stand bare and naked, trembling at themselves!

SHAKESPEARE.

VOL. II.

LONDON:

PRINTED AT THE

Minerva-Press,

FOR A. K. NEWMAN AND CO.

(Successors to Lane, Newman, and Co.)

LEADENHALL-STREET.

1811.

CHAP. I.

The travellers had not proceeded far on their journey, when the storm, which had been long threatening, burst over them. The tones of the thunder became deeper: and the moon, shrouded in clouds, emitted but a faint uncertain gleam. Adelaide gazed at the portentous aspect of the heavens, and often started, and shrunk with an emotion of unmixed awe, as while winding round the base of one of the mountains, she saw the lightning flash around her, and heard the hoarse voice of the thunder reverberating amongst the rocks.

"We are safer here," said Perouse, "than in the woods:" but as he gazed at the opening sky, and viewed the sheets of sulphureous flame darting from among the vapourous clouds till the horizon seemed all one constant glow of vivid flame, Adelaide thought she perceived an expression of alarm on his countenance, and she eagerly inquired if there was no place that could afford them shelter?

"I believe none," said Perouse: "there is no house or cabin within about two miles of this mountain, where there is a village, and where we may procure horses, and perhaps a carriage to convey us to Auboigne, the place of our destination. We had therefore better make the best of our way; for by stopping we do no good, and only augment our danger."

The storm, however, encreased: the rain began to pour in torrents, and they were obliged to take shelter in the cavern of a rock.

This sky was now completely overcast; the lightning flashed more faintly; the thunder rolled off into distance; and no light, except at intervals, appeared to disperse the gloom of the night, which to Adelaide appeared more terrifying, as she distinctly heard the howling of wolves, the sound of which seemed to approach the rock in the cavern of which they had found shelter.

The dread of being exposed to the fury of these animals made her eager to quit the place, though it was far from certain that safety could be found in flight. Perouse's apprehensions were scarcely less sanguine; he resolved, therefore, as soon as the storm should have subdued, to set forward with renewed speed, and reach, as soon as possible, the town, from whence they were to procure horses to convey them to Auboigne.

The rain at length abated; the clouds dispersed; and the travellers, eager to resume their route, pursued their way along the mountains.

Having reached the place where they were to stop, Perouse, after roaring himself almost hoarse with his holloings to the landlord of the inn, who had just fallen into comfortable sleep, procured a carriage with two mules, and a guide to direct them to Auboigne.

As Adelaide entered the carriage, she observed that the landlord eyed her attire, a circumstance which she readily attributed to the singularity of her appearance; for she had no fears of being discovered or traced; and felt that emotion of delight which liberty imparts to those who, like her, have been deprived of its enjoyment, though without a home to receive or friends to cherish her. Yet by Perouse she had been promised both, at the abode and under the protection of his aunt, of whom he now continued to speak in the highest strain of eulogium, and for whom he professed the most dutiful esteem and affection.

About the dawning of the day, they arrived at Auboigne, a village so surrounded by rocks and mountains, that the inhabitants might be considered as secluded by these barriers from the rest of the civilized world.

Perouse, observing that his aunt and her family would not be risen in some hours, proposed that they should remain at the inn, and that at a proper hour in the morning he should call on Madame St. Clair and prepare her for the reception of her new guest. Adelaide, who much needed repose, assented readily to this plan; beds were therefore ordered for the travellers, and Adelaide, recommended by her escort to the care of the hostess, was again condemned to witness the scrutinizing glances of the people by whom she was surrounded, but she had now thrown off her disguise, a circumstance which however rendered her not less than before an object for the prying eye of curiosity.

CHAP. II.

At a late hour in the morning, the hostess appeared to inform Adelaide that the gentleman with whom she came had, after an absence of about an hour, returned to the inn, and was waiting her rising below. Adelaide, who had just awakened from a sound refreshing sleep, instantly arose; and having dressed herself in haste, repaired to the room where Perouse was waiting with a message of welcome from Madame St. Clair, who requested to see her immediately.

They accordingly left the inn: and Adelaide proceeded with gleeful steps to the residence of Madame St. Clair, which was about a quarter of a mile distant from the village.

Adelaide, who had now leisure to contemplate the surrounding scenery, was struck with admiration at the sublime and beautiful objects of mountains, woods, and lakes, which alternately solicited her regard, and which viewed under a now cloudless sky, and brilliant sun, appeared charming.

The decorations of the chateau of Madame St. Clair were rather those of nature than of art. It was small, and had the appearance only of a beautiful cottage, retired amid scenes of romantic elegance. The pathway, leading up the ascent to a wicket gate, which opened to a rustic lawn, was bordered with groves of almond and citron trees, intermingled with a glowing profusion of flowering shrubs, forming altogether a "wilderness of sweets."*

At a little distance, almost concealed from the eye by the pinewoods, which here began to extend themselves, a cascade threw aloft its bright spray, glittering in the sunbeam: while from a lower part of the rock, a brawling torrent was heard coursing its way from cliff to cliff, as it hastened to swell the waters of a lake below, whose mirror-like surface and delicious banks, composed a foreground to a picture to which, with the mountain-wild above, hardly any pencil could do justice.

Immediately behind the chateau arose a lofty amphitheatre of hills, green with new verdure, and covered with flocks: and beyond these, the immense outline of that chain of mountains which divides the provinces of France and Spain.

Madame St. Clair was sitting in the recess of an opened window, embowered with clematis, when Adelaide and Perouse entered the lawn. On seeing them she arose, and came forward to receive Adelaide, whom she accosted with the freedom of an old acquaintance, and such expressions of welcome, and even marks of joy on seeing her, as made her almost from the instant forget they were strangers.

Adelaide's replies were fraught with the genuine sensations of a heart that knew no disguise; and she endeavoured to make Madame St. Clair sensible of the feelings which her friendly reception of her hed inspired in her warm and grateful bosom.

"Oh talk not of obligations," cried Madame St. Clair; "it is I only who am obliged; you know not how much happiness I promise myself in your society: nor could you, Pierre (addressing herself to Perouse, whom she embraced with all the ardour of affection), have conferred upon me a greater favour, then introducing me to so charming an acquaintance; for to speak the truth, I am heartily weary of the loneliness of this retirement: and had not something occurred to change the monotonous course of my life, and produce that variety, without which life is scarcely worth having, to escape the vexatious feelings of ennui, I should have taken my flight to Paris."

Adelaide, who perceived by this speech, as well as from her appearance, for she was highly rouged and dressed, although only in a morning dishabille, in the extreme of fashion, that Madame St. Claire was completely a French woman: yet all things conspired to persuade her, that though possessing all the levity of her country, it would yet be united with animated feeling and a susceptible heart: and combined with such an inexhaustible fund of vivacity and good humour, as would ensure her love and admiration on more intimate acquaintance.

The lady, whom Adelaide already loved by anticipation, appeared to be between forty and fifty. Her face bore traces of her former beauty; but there was a fierceness in her eyes, to which she was perhaps indebted, in great measure, to the embellishment of her cheek, which imparted to her countenance an expression rather striking than agreeable.

Her complexion was that of a sallow brunette, her hair of the darkest brown. She was rather above the middle size, and something inclined to what the French call *en bon point*,* though not sufficiently so as to appear clumsy. Her address was easy, yet totally void of elegance. In her conversation she was fluent, and extremely lively, but not always grammatically correct: nor had her manners any of that polish French women usually possess, but which is perhaps not always to be acquired, except by those who are accustomed to move in the public circles of the higher spheres of life.

During the morning's repast, which was spread on the arrival of the guests, Madame St. Clair discoursed with her nephew on the subject of his capture and imprisonment at the Castle de Ponteville. In the course of her conversation, it appeared she was not only acquainted with all the principal incidents concerning him, but even with many parts of Adelaide's history, particularly what related to the Count St. Angouléme and the Marquis. The latter she execrated as a monster disgraceful to human nature, and described as profligate, unprincipled, and vindictive.

Epithets not less expressive of abhorrence were applied by both to the Count, whom, like the Marquis, they affirmed had been instigated by the worst of passions to the commission of the most barbarous and disgraceful actions.

Madame congratulated Adelaide on her escape from so infamous a combination, renewed the promises of protection Perouse had before given her, and declared she would never part with her, while her place of residence should be agreeable to her, or till she could be more eligibly settled.

"You will guess," said she, "from the smallness of my establishment, that I am not rich; but I have enough for all the conveniences and comforts of life: and while I have the means of possessing these, you, my love, shall never want them." Adelaide made a suitable reply, while Perouse pressed his aunt's hand, in token of the most friendly affection.

After breakfast, Adelaide accompanied Madame St. Clair in a little stroll about the grounds. Madame then shewed her the apartment she designed for her, and conducting her to her wardrobe, presented her with several changes of dress, which she desired she would accept of her, as a token of her friendship, and also that she would apply to her for any thing further she might want.

Adelaide, though highly grateful for Madame's favours, would have declined the acceptance of these presents; but she would not be refused; and Adelaide perceived that by declining them, she would not only hurt, but offend her seemingly highly generous benefactress.

CHAP. III.

After dinner, Perouse, on the plea of some urgent business, which he had to transact at a village some few miles from thence, set off from the chateau, with the promise of returning to it at an early hour in the morning. As he was departing, Adelaide inquired if he was not afraid of meeting with the Marquis, or some of his people?

"Not at all," said Perouse; "I have no fears except for you. I shall not travel in the night unarmed or unattended: besides, as in all probability the object of my former quixotism is become indifferent to him, and he believes me too insignificant to cope with a man of his rank and fortune, I have, I think, nothing further to apprehend from him."

When Perouse had departed, Madame burst out into praises of her nephew, which, notwithstanding the signal services he had rendered her, and the esteem she felt in consequence, seemed to Adelaide almost extravagant. She described him as possessing every possible virtue and accomplishment; and concluded with observing, that on the death of an uncle, who was old and sickly, he would be heir to a considerable estate, which, in addition to what he now possessed, and what she would herself bequeath, for she had made her will in his favour, would enable him to maintain an appearance equal, and indeed superior, to many of the nobles of the country.

From Perouse, the conversation turned upon the subject of the situation of Adelaide, in respect of the family of St. Angouléme. The Countess was to Adelaide an object of the most tender interest; at her name her eyes swam in tears, and her bosom heaved with sighs, especially as she reflected on the sufferings she would experience on account of her sudden and extraordinary disappearance.

These reflections were so poignant, that she consulted Madame St. Clair on the propriety of sending a message to inform the Countess of her present situation and safety—a scheme which Madame declared to be highly imprudent, and extremely dangerous; and she spared no efforts to dissuade her from any such purpose. The arguments used by Madame, if not quite decisive, were sufficient to deter Adelaide from pressing the subject any further; and when added to this was the consideration that she could not make any communication to the Countess without criminating the Count, she determined to abandon it entirely.

"It is better," said she, "that the Countess should think I have fallen into the hands of banditti, and am murdered, than know her lord has been guilty of this act of treachery."

Perouse did not return according to his engagement, and Adelaide began to apprehend that he had been pursued and seized by some of the Marquis's people, and that they were probably even then in the neighbourhood. She communicated these apprehensions to Madame, who acknowledged them to be too just;

and they both now awaited his arrival with many expressions of solicitude.

Their fears and conjectures were at length dissipated by his return, though it was not till a day later than he had appointed. This he ascribed to a trifling yet vexatious occurrence, which he said would require his frequent attendance at a neighbouring town. What might be the nature of the circumstance to which he alluded, he did not declare; nor did anything transpire which could afford an explanation, or even the remotest hint upon the subject.

He came home, as he had went, unattended. He rode a mule which he had purchased, as he afterwards declared, on his way, for the convenience of passing and repassing the mountains; and he brought with him a kind of sack, which he himself took from the back of the mule, and carried into his own chamber.

As he entered the room where Madame St. Clair and Adelaide were sitting, they were both full of expressions of satisfaction at his safe return; and the latter, after the usual civilities were ended, began to speak of her father, who as being her nearest, and indeed only relative, ought, she thought, to be made acquainted with her situation; and she begged to be informed how this might be most conveniently done.

"Your father, Madam," said Perouse, "is probably not now in a situation to receive you. I think, however, with you, that he should be informed you are in safety; and yet, till we may have sounded his inclinations respecting you, it may perhaps be imprudent to acquaint him with where you are. Do not think, however, I even suspect that your father can be at all concerned in the schemes of the Count; I do not—I will not think so vilely of human nature; but it is necessary that we should first know on what terms he is with Count St. Angouléme, and whether he has sufficient power or discretion to defend you from any farther persecutions. This is certainly a matter which must be ordered with much delicacy; but leave the management of it to me. I will see your father: the journey is a long one; nevertheless I will undertake it—I will myself discover whether he regards you as he ought, and is inclined to afford you that protection which you, as his daughter, have an undoubted right to claim."

Adelaide said a few words expressive of her persuasion both of the inclination and ability of her father to protect her; and delighted with his proposal of visiting him, warmly expressed her thanks to Perouse for his friendly exertions in her cause, and received from him a promise that he would commence his journey to Avignon at an early day on the following week.

The better to secure Adelaide from the designs of the Marquis during his absence, and till she might be under the protection of her father, he proposed that she should take another name, since she was known by those of St. Angouléme and De Launé, and either might lead to a discovery of the place of her retreat. Adelaide instantly assented to this proposal; and it was resolved that she should pass for a relation of Madame's, and be called Adelaide St. Clair.

CHAP. IV.

THE next day, Perouse rode from the chateau, as before, on the plea of further business at the neighbouring town; and Adelaide and Madame St. Clair being again alone, the latter resuming her favourite theme, spoke of her nephew in her former strain of eulogium, describing him as the best and most honourable of men.

"Excuse my partiality," she said, "for it is impossible not to speak of him as he deserves. You are silent, my love," added she; "perhaps you think I say too much."

"If I am silent," cried Adelaide, "it is because I cannot say enough. Monsieur Perouse has done me services I can never repay."

"There are ways of returning obligations," observed Madame significantly, and with an archness in her smile, expressive of some latent meaning, "which are always in the power of youth and beauty."

"I do not understand you, Madame," said Adelaide.

"Oh no, I dare say not," said Madame. "Well then, to be plain with you, my dear, though your own penetration must ere now have discovered it, unless you have much less than I can imagine, or those charming eyes of yours indicate, Monsieur Perouse—may I go on, my love?"

"Certainly, Madame, said Adelaide, "if you please."

"Monsieur Perouse then loves you—loves you most passionately," pursued she; "and he has asked and obtained my consent to offer you his hand."

Adelaide started; a crimson blush suffused her cheek. "You are mistaken, Madame. I think—I hope," cried she, scarcely knowing what she said.

"Mistaken, you *think*, and you *hope*," said Madame, who by the emphasis she used, seemed not highly pleased with the concluding words of Adelaide's speech. "My dear young friend, my sweet Adelaide, can you deliberate even for a moment upon such an offer as this?"

"Pardon me, Madame," said Adelaide, "when I assure you that nothing could give me more serious concern, then that Monsieur Perouse should honour me with a proposal of this nature, and at present under circumstances which forbid me to entertain even a thought of marriage."

"The very circumstances to which you allude," said Madame, "suggest the propriety of securing a legal protector, and recommend an immediate marriage with my nephew. Beside, what objection can you possibly have to him?"

"As a friend, Madame," said Adelaide, "I shall always value him; as my protector, revere him; but as a lover——"

"Well, well," said Madame, "I will leave you to talk the matter over by yourselves; perhaps I was to blame to mention it; but many are the fair ones who would be transported at such an offer, from the amiable, the brave, the accomplished Perouse."

Adelaide, who was seriously concerned, and even hurt, at the idea of having inspired a passion which she felt it impossible to return, entreated that Madame would interfere to prevent Monsieur Perouse for making his intended declaration; adding, it was quite impossible that she could accept his proposals, and she therefore wished to be spared the pain of hearing them. Madame seemed disconcerted and chagrined, but she made no answer; and Adelaide, fearing she had offended her, hastened to change the subject of their conversation. It was not resumed.

When Perouse again arrived at the chateau, Adelaide, who went out with Madame to meet him, was uneasy and dispirited, and her distress was increased, when Madame having designedly left the room, Perouse declared his passion for her, and even urged an immediate marriage. Adelaide received his overtures with politeness, but at the same time firmly declined accepting them.

Perouse seemed surprised, and even agitated; but though he pursued his suit with passion and vehemence, Adelaide would not even promise to refer it to a future consideration. He left the room in much apparent emotion, and did not return to it for several hours.

When they next met, his behaviour was composed; but the traces of disappointment, and even anger, were yet visible in his countenance. These, however, were quite removed by the following morning, when he talked to her as before of her father; and fixed an early day for the commencement of his intended journey into Provence. But in this interval he repaired as usual to the town he spoke of: and did not return till after an absence of some days.

In the meantime, Madame St. Clair, who had seen much of the world, and was an easy and cheerful companion, endeavoured to amuse Adelaide with the most lively anecdotes; and to engage her in conversations of which Perouse was usually the subject. Of his family, except the uncle to whose estate he was to succeed, she never spoke: nor did she ever mention a single relative of her own. From these conversations Adelaide could only learn, concerning Madame, that she was a widow of genteel connexions, related on the maternal side to the family of Perouse; and that after passing several years in the gayest circles of Paris, she had repaired, with a handsome competence, to enjoy the pleasures of retirement in the chateau she now occupied. But though such was her purpose, it was evident to Adelaide that she had no particular *penchant* for the sublime and beautiful objects which surrounded her abode; and it was equally certain that she had none of those mental resources which are requisite for the enjoyment of the retirement she had chosen.

To one so oppressed with ennui, and so little able to contend with such a dreadful tormentor, a companion like Adelaide, gentle, amiable and obliging, was indeed a valuable acquisition; and either from the wish of retaining her, or for some other motive, she pressed the suit of her nephew with such warmth and earnestness as sometimes to surprise Adelaide, who wondered that on so short an acquaintance she should thus anxiously desire an alliance, which, birth and fortune considered, was certainly much inferior to what Perouse had a right to expect.

But whenever Adelaide hinted at this inferiority, Madame, who affected to disregard or scorn every mercenary consideration, would exclaim, "My dearest Adelaide, you know not your own worth, or half the power of your charms. If I cannot behold the beauty of your person, and the accomplishments of your mind, without wonder and admiration, is it possible that Perouse should be insensible to them, or refuse them that homage which is so indisputably their due?"

Observing Adelaide had a fine voice, and finding she had been well instructed in music, Madame St. Clair presented her with a lute; she also procured for her several volumes of books: and Adelaide, who now often employed herself in reading and music, felt her hours pass agreeably, and even profitably, for the books being such as she had herself desired, she was enabled to make an encreasing progress in the study of the belles lettres.

Sometimes, accompanied by Madame, she would stroll amongst the mountains, or along the margin of the lake, whose crystal surface reflected the bold outline of the rocks, and the green recesses that bordered its waves: and refreshed by the beautiful breeze, and enchanted by the rich scenery through which she passed, she would return with new zest and fresh pleasure to her literary pursuits.

One evening, when they had extended their walk for a considerable way from the chateau, Adelaide persuaded Madame to accompany her to the top of a rocky promontory on the lake, for the purpose of enjoying a more extensive view of the rich tints which at that season adorned the surrounding objects. Madame, less zealous and less active than her young companion, bade her proceed, and occupy the favourite station, and she would follow at more leisure. As the station was very near, though the approach was steep, Adelaide, after a few friendly expressions, hastened onward, and soon gained the point of the rock, when having feasted her eyes for a moment, she turned them toward her friend, when she saw her foot slip, and Madame instantaneously precipitated down the steep side of the rock, where it was several feet perpendicular. She was completely stunned by the fall, and lay apparently lifeless.

Adelaide, terrified beyond conception, uttered a loud scream. Her cry reached the ear of a young chevalier in a shooting dress, who, with dogs and a gun, was returning homewards from the pursuit of game, and was descending unobserved by Adelaide and Madame from the upper heights.

He saw the situation of Madame St. Clair, and the distress of her companion; and he reached her just as Adelaide had raised Madame St. Clair's head. She opened her eyes; but it was long before she was able to answer the affectionate inquiries of Adelaide, and to say she was not much hurt. She looked with earnestness on the stranger, who helped to raise her up; and finding herself utterly unable to walk without support, was obliged to accept the offer of his arm, which he tendered with looks expressive of the most delicate interest and compassion; and politely insisted that he should be permitted to support her to her home.

When the alarm at Madame St. Clair's accident, which at first had entirely engaged his attention, had subsided, and she had repeatedly assured him that she had not suffered materially from the fall, he turned his observation upon Adelaide; and while he expressed his satisfaction at being fortunately near to afford some little assistance, under an accident so alarming, he fixed his eyes upon her with a look of such earnest admiration, that her cheeks were suffused with blushes. This rendered him sensible of the impropriety of which he was guilty; and he afforded sensible relief to the embarrassed Adelaide, by his renewed attentions to Madame.

The good lady, although she seemed to walk with difficulty, and even pain, persisted she was not hurt, and would have declined his further attendance; but he insisted on escorting her to her residence, where they now arrived.

At the wicket gate opening upon the lawn, Madame St. Clair politely thanked the Chevalier for his assistance, but in a manner which forbade his entrance. This behaviour appeared very extraordinary to Adelaide, and occasioned no little vexation to the polite stranger, who did not attempt to proceed farther. But as they separated, he again rivetted his eyes upon Adelaide, with the same expression of tender admiration with which he had at first regarded her. He paused, as if unwilling to depart; and leaning over the gate, followed them with his eyes, till they had crossed the lawn; when Madame turning as she opened the door, as if suddenly awakened from a reverie, he bowed and departed.*

CHAP. V.

Madame St. Clair in her fall had sprained her ancle, and the next day was unable to leave or even walk across her chamber. Adelaide had just made her morning inquiries of Madame, and was descending the stairs toward the breakfast-parlour, when some one rapped at the door, and a servant attending, she heard the voice of the young stranger they had met with in their walk of the preceeding evening. He politely inquired after the health of Madame St. Clair, and entering the hall, was ushered into the room were Adelaide was now sitting.

"Excuse me if I have intruded, Madame," he said, observing Adelaide looked surprised. "I have called," with hesitation, and colouring highly as he spoke, "from an anxiety to be assured that the lady whom I had the happiness of seeing with you yesterday has not sustained any injury from her accident."

Adelaide replied that Madame was then confined to her room, her ancle having been sprained by the fall; but she had suffered no other inconvenience, and she hoped she would soon be well. "I am glad, Madame," said he, "very glad to hear this—very happy—(still much embarrassed)—I could not leave the neighbourhood without first informing myself of her situation, and this I hope will excuse my intrusion."

Adelaide thanked him for his politeness, and the chevalier, after a few minutes conversation, arose and took his leave.

Adelaide hastened to inform Madame that the stranger had been, and to deliver his message. "He has given himself more trouble than I think he need to have done," said Madame coldly; "it certainly could not be necessary for him to call here. I hope, however, my dear Adelaide, you said enough to satisfy him on all points, and have afforded him no plea for resuming his visits."

Adelaide related what had passed.

"Well, my dear friend," said Madame, "I do not doubt your prudence; I only fear your attractions: we do not know who this young man may be."

"Nor is it of much consequence, I believe, Madame," said Adelaide blushing, "as I find he is about to leave the neighbourhood, and there is, therefore, but little probability of our seeing him again."

At night, when Adelaide had retired to her chamber, Helene, Madame St. Clair's maid, inquired of her if she knew who the chevalier was that had that day called at the chateau? Adelaide replied that she did not, as by a seemingly strange neglect, he had never once mentioned his name. "But why," said she, "Helene, do you ask the question?"

"It is no business of mine to be sure," said Helene, "only I thought it a little odd, and so I said I would tell you."

"What is it you mean, Helene?" said Adelaide, "and what have you got to tell me?"

"Not much, Ma'moiselle; only the chevalier, if he is a chevalier, for nobody it seems knows who he is, has been making a great many inquiries about you in the village, and of Jacques."

"About me! inquiries about me!" said Adelaide; "what can he want to know about me?"

"Why, as who you was, and what was your name, and where you came from, and such like."

"And what did Jacques say to him?" asked Adelaide, tremulously.

"He did not tell me, Ma'moiselle, what he said," resumed Helene, "but he told me he had asked a great number of questions about you, and some about my mistress; and Jacques says he is sure the chevalier is in love with you, Ma'moiselle, for he saw him watching about the chateau this morning a good while, and leaning over the gate; and at last he plucked up a spirit, and came in, and, all by way of excuse, asked about my lady; for he is sure, he says, it was only to see you, Ma'moiselle."

"Jacques is under a strange mistake, I think," said Adelaide smiling, but with some confusion.

Helene was about to reply, but hearing Madame St. Clair's bell, she hastened to attend her mistress; and being tolerably communicative, repeated what she had said to Adelaide relative to the stranger.

In the morning when Adelaide, as usual, visited Madame St. Clair in her chamber, she evinced much uneasiness and dissatisfaction. "I hope," said she, "this young man will not think of calling upon us again, and if he does, that you will refuse to see him; for you must know, my dear, that I am not without my apprehensions that he may be connected with the Marquis; and that through him, you may, in some way or other, be made miserable by his artifices. Let me caution you not to go abroad till you are sure he has left the neighbourhood. There is something in his countenance that I do not like. He looked at you, I thought, very particularly. I would not for the world anything should happen to you here. I wish my nephew was at home, for I really feel very uneasy."

"My dear Madame," said Adelaide, "I think you disturb yourself without reason. The chevalier's call here this morning, after the accident at which he was present, had certainly nothing particular in it; it was an act of mere common politeness. Indeed, I think he could hardly have done otherwise—a person of your appearance."

"Yes, but why should he make inquiries about you?"

"This I conceive," said Adelaide, rather hesitatingly, "to have been quite accidental."

"It may seem so," rejoined Madame, "and so did the circumstance of your being seized and carried off from the neighbourhood of your former home, by persons whom you then suspected to be no other than common banditti. What appears to us to have been merely accidental is often the effect of design and sometimes of the deepest treachery. We cannot be too cautious; for should the Marquis once discover you in this place, we, your protectors, as well as yourself, have every thing to dread."

"Heavens!" exclaimed Adelaide, "is there no security from the power of that wicked nobleman?"

"None, I believe none," said Madame, "unless in the concealment which this retirement seems to promise. However, above all things, let me advise you to shun every future opportunity of seeing this stranger. I do not, as I told you before—I do not like his looks. His manners, his inquiries, his lurking about the chateau, are all circumstances too suspicious to escape the eye of friendship, and certainly forebode some evil intentions."

"I will promise to do anything, Madame," said Adelaide, "to avoid the danger you apprehend; but in this instance, I think your fears, and the generous solicitude you feel for my welfare, may have misled your judgment. The stranger who so politely offered assistance—"

"Well, well," interrupted Madame, somewhat pettishly, "I wish

I may be mistaken. I wish I may prove myself the foolish woman I suppose I am; but lest I should not, and the danger I apprehend be not merely imaginary, I shall desire Jacques to make inquiries about him in the neighbourhood, and to watch and inform me if he is again seen loitering about my grounds."

Thus ended the discourse upon this subject; and such orders were accordingly given to Jacques; but either they were entirely neglected, or but irregularly attended to; for he brought no further account respecting the stranger; and as he was not seen about the chateau for several days, the fears of Madame seemed to have subsided; and she agreed with Adelaide, that he had now in all probability left the country.

CHAP. VI.

Adelaide, wearied of confinement, at length resumed her walks about the chateau; and although she had imbibed none of Madame's suspicions in respect to the stranger, she adopted some of her cautious directions, and did not venture far, and avoided the more public ways, lest she should accidentally meet some of the adherents of the Marquis, who, it was but too probable, would endeavour to discover, and might easily, by the help of this pretended chevalier, (should he prove to be, as Madame suspected, one of his people), trace her to her present place of concealment.

Lost in uneasy conjectures respecting her future destiny, beset with evils, and threatened with persecutions, from which she seemed to be only partially, and indeed scarcely at all defended, dependant too upon the friendship of strangers for her comforts, and upon their bounty for the very means of existence, she sighed with deep regret for the society of the Countess, and bewailed the cruel treachery which separated her from the friend and mother of her early youth.

Occupied by the remembrances of the past, and the pains of the present time, she wandered on in mournful rumination, till she had arrived near the borders of the lake, when she seated herself in a little shady recess, formed by high trees, embowering a crystal stream, which poured its tributary waters down a small cascade, whose steady dripping sounds were well attuned to the melancholy reflections that now pressed upon her mind.

She had not sat many minutes, when she was startled by the sound of an approaching step. She turned her head, and perceiving the chevalier, with a heart palpitating with the emotions of surprise and fear, arose to depart. But as she was obliged, by the nature of the place, to pass by him, he had full opportunity to address her with his wonted grace, and renew his inquiries concerning Madame, who he hoped, he said, was now nearly recovered from the effects of her late accident, if not yet able to go abroad.

Adelaide curtsied, and returning a general short answer, was proceeding on her way toward the chateau. The chevalier, surprised at her needless reserve, followed and overtook her. "Pardon my presumption, Madame," said he, "if I again venture to intrude upon you, and as I once had the honour of attending you home, allow me again to be your escort; at least let me conduct you to within view of your residence."

Adelaide, whom this request had greatly embarrassed, knew not what to reply; for she was well aware that Madame would be seriously alarmed, and even highly displeased, should she learn she had been walking with the chevalier.

But before the confusion she felt would allow her to frame an excuse, to prevent his offered attendance, he had accompanied her part of the way along the path; and ere she could resolve in what manner to dismiss him, his amiable deportment, his open intelligent countenance, in which were expressed a happy mixture of dignity and sweetness, the gracefulness of his figure, the peculiar elegance of his manners, and the fascination of his discourse, had so entirely engaged her mind, that she ceased to remember it was her object to desire him to retire.

After a few just and tasteful remarks upon the beauty of the surrounding scenes, he observed, it was his intention to have left the neighbourhood some days since—"But there is a charm," added he, "or a fatality, I know not which, that detains me here, and chains me, as it were, to the place."

"Here are indeed objects," said Adelaide, "which might engage and delight the eye of taste for many months."

"Nature here seems resolved to shew the perfection of beauty in every thing," cried the chevalier. "You, I suppose, Madame, are a native of this soil?"

"France is the country of my birth," said Adelaide. As she spoke, he sighed; and gazing upon her for a moment or two with a look of peculiar earnestness, said—"Deem me not too bold, or rude, if I presume to ask whether you have long been an inhabitant of this province?"

Adelaide hesitated, and at length answered she had not.

"This place then," resumed he, "is probably only a temporary residence: do you propose to continue here long?"

"I do not know, Sir," said Adelaide, more and more confused; for she felt the impropriety of answering these interrogatories from a stranger, particularly under her present circumstances.

"Your home is probably at some distance?" observed the chevalier, with a look that seemed to express more than curiosity.

"Yes, Sir, I believe at a great distance."

"Your family, may I know the name?"

"Good Heavens!" thought Adelaide, "to what can all this tend?" An uneasy suspicion began to mingle with her surmises. "The name of my family, Sir," added she, blushing from the consciousness that she was now uttering an untruth, "is St. Clair."

"St. Clair! Is it possible that you can indeed be a relation of Madame St. Clair's!" He paused. "I fear," added he, "I must have seemed strangely impertinent; but your appearance—your manners—"

"You, Sir, I suppose," said Adelaide, anxious to change the conversation, "are not a native of these mountains?"

"No; but they are so congenial to my state of mind, so dear

to me, from the recollection of objects from whom I am now separated, so interesting, as having been the scenes—but why do I talk thus? Excuse me, Madame, excuse me, Ma'moiselle St. Clair. To-morrow I must bid adieu to them, and go hence, in order to accept an invitation from my commander, the Marquis de Ponteville, to attend him in an excursion through a part of this country."

"The Marquis de Ponteville!" faintly reiterated Adelaide. Had the dagger of an assassin at that instant been pointed at the bosom of Adelaide, hardly could it have produced an emotion of terror more exquisite than that she now felt at the name of the Marquis de Ponteville; notwithstanding his amiable appearance, and the partiality she already felt for the young and interesting stranger, the most terrible apprehensions of Madame seemed now fully confirmed. Fear so entirely overcame her, as to deprive her of all self-command, and even of the power of reflection. Her limbs seemed palsied; the blood forsook her cheek; she leaned against the trunk of a tree, and overwhelmed with her emotions, burst into a flood of tears.

The chevalier stood petrified and aghast. "You are ill, Madam," said he, "I fear very ill. Heaven!" exclaimed he, "what can be the matter?"

"Leave me, Sir," said Adelaide, "I conjure you, leave me, I am not ill—I am only—" she stopped.

"Not ill! why then so pale," said he, in a tone of the tenderest commiseration, "and wherefore all this seeming agitation? Not ill, and not alarmed, and yet—"

He looked earnestly and tenderly in her face; the paleness that had overspread it had disappeared, and it was now flushed with vermilion.

At that instant, the figure of a man was seen slowly moving amongst the trees. It was Jacques, the servant of Madame St. Clair, who, having been told that Adelaide was from home, had sent him in quest of her. On seeing him, she waved her hand in a signal for the chevalier to depart. He obeyed, though with reluctance; and, as she turned to observe if he was gone, she saw him leaning pensively against a tree at some distance.

She walked, with hurried pace, across the lawn, to the door of the chateau, and then flew to her chamber, where, throwing herself into a chair, she exclaimed, "It is true then; it is but too true! what else could mean all these inquiries, my name, my family, the place of my former abode, the probable time of my continuing in this place? Oh mischief! mischief! And yet it may not follow, that because he is acquainted with the Marquis, he must necessarily be implicated in the schemes designed by villains against me! If he is, if he should indeed prove so, let no one ever again depend upon externals, grace and elegance, all that is amiable and charming shall appear deformed; for never before did I behold a confidence so prepossessing, so noble, and full of sweetness; a form so interesting, or manners so engaging! Can vice, can falsehood," resumed she, "wear the semblance of truth and honour so successfully, so effectually to deceive the eye, and baffle the judgment? Yet why, if he had reasons for making inquiries so unexpected, so surprising, and to *me* so embarrassing, did he not assign them? But perhaps he was restrained by considerations not less powerful than those by which I was actuated, in withholding from him that confidence he so anxiously seemed to desire."

Such were the reflections which the partiality of her admiration urged in favour of the chevalier. Yet reason and recollection soon suggested the fallacy of these sentiments, and assured her of the justness of Madame St. Clair's suspicions; for he was, it appeared from his own confession, a dependant upon the Marquis.

The part she ought to act was now evident. It was necessary for her own safety, it was a duty she owed her friend and benefactress, to acquaint her with the unexpected intrusion of the chevalier, and the discovery she had made from his conversation.

To Madame St. Clair, whom she found alone in her chamber, she accordingly gave an undisguised relation of what had passed; concluding with a resolution of never more venturing abroad, till she was sure the chevalier had departed, or till the Marquis, who was now more than ever the object of her terror, should have left the neighbourhood.

The alarm which Madame exhibited, when informed of these circumstances, made Adelaide almost repent the communication. She screamed, sobbed, and wept, and wrung her hands in all the agony of distress; and with all the frenzy of despair; insisted that they were betrayed to the Marquis; and should Perouse delay to return, and the house not be properly secured and guarded, the doors might be forced open by a band of miscreants, and her Adelaide, her hope and only joy, would be torn from her, and hurried she knew not whither, to the castle—to a dungeon—to death—or to sufferings worse than death!

In vain Adelaide assured her, that as she had cautiously concealed her name, and since the person who called himself chevalier had before no personal knowledge of her, it was impossible for him to identify her as the object of the Marquis's pursuit, even if he were base enough, a supposition which, she must add, his appearance seemed to contradict, to assist in betraying an innocent girl into the hands of a merciless and abandoned libertine.

"Alas, my child," said Madame, "you yet know but little of the world, and of the artifices and contrivances of wicked men. I am glad, however, you have had the precaution not to declare your name; but I fear all we can do will be ineffectual."

"And do you indeed think there is so much danger, Madame?" said Adelaide.

"Danger!" repeated Madame St. Clair, "yes, certainly danger! and danger which I see but one way for you to avoid, and that is by an immediate marriage with my nephew. Perouse, my sweet Adelaide, loves you—he is worthy of your affections. The services he has rendered you demand some return. Think, my dear, of what he has done for you, and what, but for his generous interposition in your behalf, would have been your sufferings and situation in respect to the Marquis. The feelings of your pure unsullied heart must, I know, impel you to esteem the good and, in your cause, the brave Perouse; and would you but consent to receive his addresses, esteem would soon, in such a mind as yours, become affection. Why then continue to hesitate upon proposals so disinterested, and I may add too, so generous, as those of the man who loves you, and whose behaviour and exertions have been those of a brother, towards a suffering and beloved sister? Give him but the legal power of protecting you, and he will convey you beyond the power of the Marquis, and beyond the reach of his persecutions."

Adelaide, however desperate her situation, was never less inclined than at this moment to listen to the renewal of the overtures of Perouse. She coldly replied, that she could not doubt but that Monsieur Perouse's proposals were entirely disinterested; and if he had really the regard of her he professed, she had only to lament, that notwithstanding the esteem and respect she felt for his character, she could never return his kindness as she ought. She must therefore decline an offer, which, after such a declaration, it would be ungenerous for noble mind to press; nay, even highly dishonorable for a person of nice and proper feelings to accept.

Perceiving Madame was somewhat irritated by this candid and ingenuous declaration, and observing a fierceness in her eyes, and an air of haughtiness in her demeanor, very different from what she usually assumed, she took her hand, and assured her, in an affectionate tone, that notwithstanding what she been obliged to declare, as she was accustomed to be ingenuous, and feeling herself above the meanness of disguise or artifice, she had the highest sense of the obligation she owed to Monsieur Perouse; and that she should always think of him with sensations of gratitude, as lively and as sincere as those of his generous delivery of her from a dreadful captivity had at first excited.

Saying this, she withdrew, and repairing to her own apartment, placed herself upon the side of the bed, where alone and uninterrupted, she ruminated upon the subtleties and dangers of her situation—dangers to which the representations of Madame, influenced, as it appeared, by the most alarming forebodings for the fate of her charge, had given a colossal form, and difficulties, which seemed every instant augmenting, and swelling to a magnitude most dreadfully tremendous.

To remain long in the same house with Monsieur Perouse, should he, as she much feared, persevere in his addresses, would, she felt, be distressing to her delicacy, and even contrary to her own ideas of female decorum; and she had but too much reason to apprehend, from the altered countenance of Madame, when she persisted in the rejection of his offers, that the continuance of her protection was to be afforded only on the condition that she consented to accept them.

These reflections and considerations led her anxiously to desire the arrival of her father, an event which she thought would certainly take place as soon as Perouse should apply to ask her hand; though whether he could or would offer her an asylum from the dangers that now threatened her, and deliver her from the difficulties with which she was surrounded, appeared to her at present very uncertain. "Yet surely," said she mournfully, "he cannot be wholly insensible to the dictates of parental affection; he must know—and knowing, feel that I am his daughter."

CHAP. VII.

The next day passed without any new occurrence. Madame's alarms seemed, however, by no means to have subsided. She often spoke to Adelaide of the stranger, and betrayed various symptoms of distress and apprehension. In the evening, Perouse did not return as was expected, and his protracted stay increased the fears both of Madame St. Clair and Adelaide; the latter of whom, though she could not endure to think of him as a lover, yet reverenced him as a friend, and esteemed as the only person, except her father, capable of offering her the protection her situation required.

Ten and eleven o'clock struck, and still he came not. The conjectures of Madame and Adelaide became now more various and more painful; for they began to apprehend he had fallen a sacrifice to the arts and schemes of the Marquis.

Adelaide had retired to her bed, and, exhausted by the emotions of fear and anxiety, had fallen into a fast sleep, when she was awakened at an early hour by a loud knocking at the door of the chateau. Surprised by a circumstance so unusual, she arose in haste; and throwing on her night gown, flew to the window, when she perceived, by the light of the moon, which now rose high in the horizon, the figures of two men on horseback. Her terrors immediately suggested that they were some of the Marquis's people; and finding they were stationed immediately under her window, she drew back: while she stood in terrified expectation, the knocking repeated. Madame St. Clair's bell rang violently; and soon after she distinguished, with delight, the voice of Perouse, calling loudly for Jacques to take the horses.

The horsemen alighted, and Adelaide, satisfied that they were not, as she had apprehended, the Marquis's people, returned to her bed.

They remained for some time under her window, unloading, as she conceived, some kind of packages from one of the horses. After a while, they came in, and went into the room below the chamber where Adelaide slept. They continued there in conversation the greater part of the night. At some times Adelaide could distinguish only a low, murmuring, indistinct sound; at others they seemed to be talking loud, as if disputing, or, at least, in very earnest discourse.

At length she heard them ascend the stairs, and enter into their chambers. Jacques soon followed, and all was still.

In the morning, Adelaide was awakened by the entrance of Madame St. Clair into her chamber, who came to inform her of the arrival of her father, who, it appeared, was one of the two horsemen Adelaide had seen from her window. In answer to her inquiries, Adelaide was informed by Madame, that Perouse, as he was returning homeward, had stopped at an inn for refreshment, when accidentally hearing the name of De Launé pronounced by a traveller, who was talking with him in the stable, he had questioned the hostler, and learnt from him such particulars as served to convince him that the person of whom he spoke was the object of his intended search, the De Launé of Avignon, and the father of Adelaide.

"And how," said Adelaide, "did he introduce himself?"

"Why as the friend and deliverer of his daughter, to be sure," rejoined Madame, "though at first he was resolved not to be too explicit, but merely mentioned that he had had the happiness, or the honour, I don't know which, to extricate a lovely young woman, of the same name with himself, and probably a relation of his, from the snares of a libertine and a villain; and that she was then in a place of safety, but he did not say where; for, till he should know how he was disposed towards you, he thought it prudent to conceal the place of your retreat."

"Well, and how did he receive the declaration?" said Adelaide.

"Just, my love, as we could wish," said Madame; "so then our dear Perouse told him the whole story."

"And was he much affected with it?" asked Adelaide, looking earnestly in Madame's face.

"Oh, very much, indeed," said Madame.

"Was he—was he indeed affected?" reiterated Adelaide: "oh let me go to him!" hastily throwing on her clothes, "let me go to my father! But does Monsieur Perouse indeed think he feels for me; and oh, still more, does he love me? alas, except himself, I have no natural claims upon any one for tenderness and affection; and once, once I thought he did not love and regard me as a daughter."

"Depend upon it, my dear," said Madame, "if we may judge from appearances, he has the greatest possible regard for you. Indeed, I think his affection is wonderful, considering you were not brought up in his house, and are yet, in a manner, an utter stranger to him; for he wept, my nephew says, first for grief, and afterwards for joy; and embraced him over and over again, for his kindness, and the noble interest he had displayed for his poor unfortunate girl. He asked a thousand questions about you in a breath; and said he could not be happy till he had seen you; that you was to him the most dear of all human beings; and that nothing but your advantage, and the prospect of seeing you a rich heiress, could have induced him to impose you upon another family as their child. As things had fallen out, he could never, he said, love you too much. The sincerity of this declaration was confirmed by a tear trickling down his manly cheek. He then pressed my nephew's hand, and said he could never do enough for him, and that he was the best friend he had ever had, because he had been a friend to his dear persecuted little girl. But la! my love, we are wasting time, while we are only talking of him, and you are all over in such a tremble, I see, that you cannot put on your clothes; ah! well, I don't wonder at it, and the poor man is as bad; and so impatient to see you, that if it had not been for me, they would have had you called last night; but, poor thing, said I, she has had a sad fright, and so have I, about this young fellow; and then I told them the story, and what a fidget I was in about it, and how I had had him watched, and yet, how, after all, he had contrived to see you, and walk with you; and how impertinent he was in asking you questions, trying to get every thing out of you; and to know who you were, and where you came from, and how long you were to stay, and where you were going, and when, and how, and why——

"And then I told them what I thought of him; and they both agree with me that his coming hither, and following you, has a very ugly look; and that there is some mischief on foot; and they fear the Marquis——"

"Heaven forbid!" exclaimed Adelaide, "but they have neither of them seen the chevalier."

"No, but I have seen him," rejoined Madame, "and it was his appearance that first gave me the suspicion. I told you, as you must remember, that I did not like his looks; no, and I did not like them. I thought there was something very forward, and bold, and assuming about him. Compare him but with my nephew, and observe the difference."

"The difference is certainly very great," said Adelaide, whose gratitude toward the person to whom she owed her deliverance from the most formidable of all dangers, did not so entirely overrule her judgment, as not to suffer her to perceive that Perouse, both in face and figure, was completely disagreeable; that his manners were rude and unpolished, and even vulgar; and that his looks sometimes expressed an almost savage ferocity, calculated to excite fear rather than affection; and her sentiments were but too feelingly expressed by the soft sigh that gently and involuntarily heaved her bosom, as images of Perouse and the young chevalier presented themselves, in affecting contrast, to her mind.

"I am glad you think there is so much difference," said Madame, who either did not, or affected not to understand her meaning. "I am sure your taste is too nice, and your judgment too good, to suffer you to mistake in bestowing the preference."

By the time Madame had finished her speech, and made this last remark which she accomplished with a look of scrutinizing observation, Adelaide was completely dressed; and impatient to behold her father, and receive from him those testimonies of affection which his behaviour, as described by Madame, seemed to promise, she went down, with trembling steps, leaning on Madame St. Clair's arm, to the room where he was waiting to receive her.

CHAP. VIII.

De Launé and Perouse were sitting together at a small table, near the window, in the breakfast-parlour, apparently engaged in anxious conversation, which on the entrance of Madame with Adelaide they broke off suddenly. De Launé, on seeing his daughter, arose and came forward to meet her. He spoke, and she thought kindly. He rushed towards him, and, falling on her knees, faintly exclaimed, "Oh my father!" she could add no more.

"Bless thee, my girl, said De Launé, gazing upon her with a look expressive rather of curiosity than tenderness, yet of as much kindness as the harsh lines of his countenance were perhaps capable of expressing.

"Well, my child," added he at length, after a pause, during

which Adelaide arose, and Madame placed her on a seat between herself and De Launé, "so you have had some strange ups and downs, I find, since I saw you last. Things have not gone on straight with you, notwithstanding the fine promises of that smooth-faced rogue, the Count, who between ourselves, is as neat a villain as ever bilked the gallies. Come, don't hold your head down, my little girl, but cheer up, and look about you; we shall get a husband for you after all. By the mass, you were in high luck to find your way out of your cage, or out of the fire, as one may say, without singeing your pretty wings, or without being a feather the worse for it; and after all, having got your liberty, to light on so good a common as this. A pretty place—a very pretty place! I could not have provided for you so well myself; so be a good girl, and mind what you are about, and never think you can do enough for Monsieur Perouse, who, though he hears me say it, and I have not known him long, is the worthiest fellow in the world."

"Monsieur Perouse will never, I hope, find me deficient in gratitude for the great benefits I have received," rejoined Adelaide, who, observing a significant glance exchanged between Perouse and De Launé, pronounced the last words falteringly, and with an evident embarrassment, for she thought she discovered that her father was not unacquainted with Perouse's sentiments in respect to herself, nor yet of the proposals he had made. She imagined also, that she perceived an expression of exultation in the countenance of Madame, and in that of Perouse a degree of confident assurance, which made her shrink from observation, while at the same time it excited apprehensions the most painful; for she had but too much reason to fear that her father would approve his suit, and that he would spare neither argument nor entreaty, nor, perhaps, even force, to drive her to a marriage, which, on an examination of her own heart, she was afraid would entail upon her certain and lasting misery; for however highly she might respect Perouse, on account of the service he had rendered her, it was impossible she could ever love him; and, if pressed to an alliance so repugnant to her inclinations, even the sensations of gratitude she now felt toward him, might, too probably, be superseded by the coldest indifference, and finally be transformed into an unconquerable disgust and aversion.

Adelaide had not without reason received apprehension which now disturbed and agitated her mind. What she had feared was soon fully confirmed. De Launé, it seemed, had not only heard, but highly approved, of the proposed alliance, and he sought the earliest opportunity of speaking to Adelaide alone, when, after highly congratulating her on the prospect of wealth and affluence, which a marriage with Perouse would offer, he desired she would not hesitate about accepting it, lest, as he said, the young fellow, made mad by her refusal of him, should fly off from the bargain, when, as she could not possibly stay at Madame St. Clair's, she would be reduced at once from a comfortable living to a state of downright poverty and nakedness.

Adelaide, to whom no condition could appear half so wretched, as that of being the wife of a man for whom she felt it was impossible to entertain the least spark of affection, for his headlong application to her father, at a time when her rejection of his proposals had been so positive, had given her no very high opinion of his delicacy, entreated he would not press her farther on a subject, which had already given her much pain and anxiety, but consent to take her home with him, where she would do her utmost, not only to earn a subsistence for herself, but to assist and support him, should his situation in life be such as to require her labours.

"Urge me not," said she, "to a marriage of which the very thought has become hateful to me, and let not my father think me disobedient and ungrateful, when I only ask to be allowed the favour of returning to my home, a home I have never yet known, humble, perhaps, but not more so than are my wishes, and how humble I care not. Let me, my honoured Sir, strive to earn, by my own industry, my own support, and in some degree also ease your labours, and contribute, as much as my unwearied attentions may, to those comforts which age and increasing infirmities may ere long render acceptable to you, and even necessary."

"Poh, poh, nonsense, my girl," interrupted De Launé, pettishly. "Do you think I am one of those fathers who will sit quietly down to be fed by his children, preferring his own ease to their welfare and advancement? No such thing, my pretty one, no such thing; I know better; and I think you have too much prudence and good sense, or you are none of mine, to refuse a fine young fellow with a good fortune, a rich aunt, with a will already made in his favour, and a large estate in reversion, for the petty employment of waiting upon a crazy-boned old father, as you seem to think I shall soon be; though, by St. Jago, I have as tight a set of joints as any man in Christendom; and feel none of those increasing infirmities of age you speak of."

"Whatever may be my fate," said Adelaide, "I beseech you, I intreat you, if you are indeed my father, to permit me to go with you. Deny me not this one request, and assure yourself that there is no future act of duty which I will not cheerfully perform with gratitude and even joy!"

"Your duties just now, my pretty one," replied De Launé, sarcastically, but with an air of affected pleasantry, "lie in a very small compass. You have nothing to do but take to yourself a good husband and, with him, as much wealth as you can in reason desire. Those little hands were never made for hard labour; this pretty ornament (putting a ring upon her finger) will become them better than work. Come, come, take it as a gift from your father; and consent to have another from Perouse, who, having attained my consent and approbation, has no right to wait long before the ceremony be performed."

"Never," exclaimed Adelaide, frowningly, "will I ever be the wife of Perouse!"

She cast her eyes upon the ring; contained a device woven in hair, set round with brilliants, and seemed to be a valuable one. Suspecting it to have been sent to her by Perouse, she would have returned it, but De Launé assured her it was a present from himself, and desired she would put it on again.

Adelaide, astonished to find a man in the situation of De Launé should be possessed of a ring set with large diamonds, and which must originally have been purchased at a considerable price, inquired how he obtained it? He said he had been persuaded to take it in payment of a bad debt; "and so," says he, "wear it, and think I wish you well, and don't plague me with questions."

"What this ring may sell for, may some time be of use to us," thought Adelaide, who, having examined, and replaced it upon her finger, renewed her former entreaties that her father would take her with him to Avignon, and remove her from the vexation of Perouse's addresses, which, as she had resolved to decline, she was very sensible it was utterly improper that she could continue longer an inhabitant of Madame St. Clair's house.

De Launé affected to believe that she was not really in earnest, in her unwillingness to receive Perouse as a husband, which, he said, was nothing more than girlish tricks; while, at the same time, he convinced her by his manner, that no excuse would be accepted, and no entreaties avail, to alter the resolution he had taken of marrying her to Perouse. After listening to her pleading for some time, with a kind of stockish difference, he left the room, without betraying any symptom of anger, but certainly without being at all moved by her eloquence, or softened by her entreaties.

CHAP. IX.

From this behaviour of her father, Adelaide drew some very unfavourable omens, and particularly from his insensibility and indifference to her present distress, on being obliged to continue some time longer under Madame St. Clair's roof, where she would be constantly subjected to the intrusions and solicitations of her lover, who probably, having obtained the sanction of her father's approbation, would become more and more troublesome and importunate. She was seriously alarmed, and knew not where to apply for relief. In Madame, Perouse had a strenuous advocate; for she was evermore representing him as a model of all that was great and excellent in human nature. Of course she would be inclined, as she had always been, to condemn her rejection of him as ridiculously absurd, and as a denial of his merits; consequently as an affronting contradiction of those encomiums she never ceased to heap upon him.

Any application to her seemed very unlikely to be successful, yet was there no other person to whom she could unbosom herself; and hopeless as was the attempt, she resolved to make one effort to engage her in her cause.

With this view, she sought an interview with Madame in private, which, however, she, as if aware of her intention, seemed designedly to shun. It was some days before she could catch the opportunity she so anxiously sought; and when thus far fortunate, the conversation of Madame afforded her neither satisfaction nor comfort.

"I am concerned," said she, "Ma'moiselle," in a half angry tone, "that you should remain insensible of the happiness that must await you in a marriage with my nephew."

"Can that be happiness," said Adelaide, "which we do not know or feel to be such?"

"That hereafter may prove to be happiness, which you now, by a strange perverseness of understanding, choose to conceive to be misery," observed Madame.

"It is impossible, as the wife of Monsieur Perouse, that I ever can be happy," resumed Adelaide, "though as a friend I should always have esteemed him, and had it been in my power to return the obligation he has conferred upon me in any other way, I would never have been his debtor. Oh why will he persevere in addressing me? why continue to ask what I never will—never can grant him?"

"Hush," cried Madame; for at that instant the door slowly opened, and Perouse appeared. Seeing Adelaide, he entered; and Madame St. Clair, disregarding a signal from Adelaide, requesting her stay, hastily departed; and she was left alone with Perouse.

Adelaide regarded him as he approached with a look of severe displeasure, which Perouse too readily understood.

"Heavens!" exclaimed he with passion, "what is it I have done? Cruel, ungrateful girl! is it thus you treat the man who rescued you from the most horrible captivity, and would have sacrificed in your defence even life itself? is this the return I am to expect? are those scornful glances to repay my faithful affection, which, not satisfied with merely placing you in a situation where you have enjoyed every comfort which friendship could administer, seeks to render you mistress of a splendid fortune, and to shower upon you all the blessings which wealth can procure, or beauty like yours desire?"

As he spoke he seized her hand, and would have pressed it to his lips, but with an effort of offended pride, she loosened it from his grasp, adding, "If you indeed, Sir, wish me to be as sensible as I ought of the benefits you have conferred upon me, and desire that I should retain that warm sensation of gratitude which your former conduct seemed to merit, you must instantly withdraw your suit; and by reconciling my father to the relinquishment of your proposals, restore me to the enjoyment of the little comfort and happiness which my lot affords."

"Never, by Heaven!" exclaimed Perouse with energy. "No; even though you detest—though you will abhor me, you shall be mine. Your hatred may change the tone of my passion, but cannot check or destroy it. Your father has a right to dispose of you; he has promised; and he cannot—will not—dare not deny me."

"How?" interrupted Adelaide, "*dare not!*"

"He *will* not!"

"And would you, taking advantage of my unfortunate situation, meanly *force me* to a compliance with your wishes, when I solemnly assure you my affections are not, nor ever can be yours?" cried Adelaide, regarding him with a look of abhorrence. "Is this the treatment to be expected from the man who once nobly stept forward to rescue an injured unprotected female, and by a seemingly strict attention to the nicest dictates of honour, and the purest principles of benevolence, won from me my entire esteem, and caused my bosom to overflow with feelings of gratitude beyond what I had ever before experienced—sensations to me most delightful, for I then believed they were merited, and thought they might be safely offered?"

"Behold—survey yourself, too beautiful Adelaide," cried Perouse, pointing to a mirror opposite, "and then ask if it is possible to see you, and to love moderately; and loving, not wish to possess. Oh, be not thus cruel! Drive me not to extremities; but let me owe to your generosity, or even your pity, a return to that affection I have so long and tenderly indulged.

"Seek to deserve the continuance of my esteem," said Adelaide, "by an immediate compliance with my request; and let me again think of you as my friend—as my deliverer, more I cannot."

As she spoke she moved towards the door, which Perouse attempted to fasten; but awed to forbearance by the dignity of her deportment, and the emphatic tone in which she spoke, as she commanded him to desist and allow her to retire, he opened it, and she withdrew.

She repaired to her chamber, and for a while yielded to the sorrow that oppressed her heart. But recollecting that lamentations and grief would neither stay the persecutions of her lover, or the tyrannical disposition of her father, she determined again to have recourse to Madame St. Clair, and with more deliberation than before, to express her resolve never to receive Perouse as a husband. This determination, though it by no means abated that delicacy of manner for which the fair Adelaide was ever distinguished, yet it dried up her tears, and diffused a dignified firmness over her features, which, as she entered her room, Madame beheld with a degree of awe. Nor was this a little increased by the union of courage and good sense displayed as she expressed her resolution, at all hazards, to reject the offers of Perouse.

Madame was agitated with alarm, but she answered, in a soothing tone, "If such, my dear Adelaide, is your determination, I will try to persuade your father, and pacify my nephew; and yet I fear greatly, lest on receiving your positive refusal, he should commit some act of desperate violence, perhaps upon his own person; or probably, in revenge, he may betray you to the Marquis, who is certainly in this country; and every day, while you continue here, we are in danger of having our house beset by his people, coming to take you from us by force. You are determined; yet surely a marriage with Perouse, even if he is not the man whom perhaps your heart would choose, is preferable to a life of infamy, or one exposed to continual alarms and dangers from that Marquis. I cannot indeed bear the thought of compelling you to accept this alliance; yet think, my dear Adelaide, of the dangers you have lately escaped from—dangers to which you are still liable, and let your own prudence be your guide: you can only hope for security from the power of the Marquis, by removing to a distance."

"True, Madam," interrupted Adelaide, "and cannot I go to Avignon?"

"Why that, my dear, depends upon your father; will he take you? I am of opinion he will not; nor indeed would the house of your father offer you any absolute security from the wickedness of your persecutor. The Marquis, on the discovery of your escape from the Castle, would, I think, most certainly apply to the Count Saint Angouléme, his partner in intrigue, and not finding you there, both would conclude you had fled to your father's house. They would of course seek you; and a man in the situation of Monsieur De Launé could, you must be sensible, make but a very feeble resistance against the power or artifices of one of the greatest nobles in the country. He must therefore either instantly resign you to the wishes of your wicked lover, or probably be carried off, together with you, to an imprisonment in the very Castle from which you have escaped.

"In fact, my dear, neither your father, nor any reasonable man living, would dare to draw upon himself the resentment of a noble of the realm; or one whose court interest is so considerable as that of the Marquis De Ponteville."

"But might not my father," rejoined Adelaide, "convey me hence, and place me, if not in Avignon, in some distant province, or even in another country?"

"Why in this, my dear," said Madame, "you speak rather more reasonably; but I fear your father has neither money nor time to spend in remote expeditions of that kind. I will hear, however, what he says, and believe me, in every instance in my power, I will prove myself your friend."

Adelaide, comforted by these expressions of kindness, tenderly embraced Madame, who imprinting a kiss upon her cheek, said, "Do not flatter yourself too much; but I am willing to undertake anything, rather than see you thus distressed and unhappy."

Adelaide returned the friendly salute; and Madame, having obtained her promise to appear at supper, engaged, although Perouse and her father were to leave the chateau on the morrow at an early hour, and to be absent some days, to signify her determination to both; and to endeavour to persuade Perouse to be patient, and to prevent the enforcement of any arbitrary measures which a resolute father might design.

"Remember, however," said Madame, as she withdrew, "that my own opinion is unchanged; I think, nay, am certain, that you cannot take a more effectual method to secure your own happiness than that I have before recommended, and shall still continue to advise; though my wish is that nothing may be done without your consent and concurrence."

CHAP. X.

ADELAIDE appeared at supper with as much composure as she could assume; and taking her seat next De Launé, who spoke to her frequently, and with much kindness, she watched with an eager eye the countenance of Madame, who she knew must have had an interview with her father; but could discover nothing calculated to inspire either hope or apprehension. As to Perouse, he was more than usually attentive; and nothing unpleasant occurred.

Madame retired early; and Adelaide having taken leave of De Launé, and bowed politely to Perouse, though without speaking, or seeming otherwise to notice him, followed her directly to her chamber, where she anxiously inquired what had passed between herself and her father.

"Why he thinks," said Madame, "you are very wrong, and very obstinate; and at first was inclined to be extremely angry with you. He says, and for the reasons I mentioned to you, that he cannot take you with him to Avignon; and that if you do not marry my nephew, you will be a great trouble to him."

"Oh, then," said Adelaide, whom a gleam of hope had now somewhat revived, "he does not say I *shall* marry him."

"Why he did not positively declare this, though what he said amounted nearly to the same. You ought, he said, to marry him, and there was no other way by which you could ensure your own safety, and prevent the trouble and danger which he must incur on your account. But he would think, he added, about what was to be done when he came back, when something must be settled."

"Well," cried Adelaide, eagerly, "and have you seen Monsieur Perouse?"

"Yes, I have seen Perouse also," said Madame, sighing heavily. "Alas! my poor nephew, the disappointment, if he is disappointed, will be the death of him, and of me too. Oh!—oh that he had never known you!"

"Believe me, Madame," said Adelaide, "Monsieur Perouse's passion is not so violent, or rather so deeply rooted, as he and perhaps you may imagine. Let him be taught to believe that the marriage cannot take place, and he will soon cease to desire or even to think about it."

"Well I wish it may be so—I wish it may," said Madame; "but alas! I know him too well! he will become distracted; he will never survive your cruel unreasonable refusal."

"Do not give way to these afflicting fancies, my dear friend," said Adelaide (for Madame had sunk back in her chair, and covered her face with her handkerchief, and was sobbing and weeping bitterly); "the heart, or rather the inclination, which so soon became mine, may as soon become another's; and another object may approve and gladly reward that affection, which to me is unfortunately a source of severe distress."

"Your cruelty, unkind, ungrateful girl," cried Madame, still sobbing violently, "will certainly break his heart; and then, and when you are in the power of the Marquis, and it is too late to prevent the consequences of your own folly and rashness, you will repent the part you have acted, and wish you had accepted the offer of an honourable and true affection, and saved the life of one who deserved better at your hands."

"Trust me, Madame," said Adelaide, "the effects of my cruelty, as you term it, will not be what you imagine. With some minds, no property is more easily transferable than what is commonly called love; and if I mistake not, that of Monsieur Perouse is of the class I mention."

Madame shook her head and sighed, but made no answer; and Adelaide, pleased that her father had referred her fate to a future consideration, after some further attempts to sooth her, wished her good night and retired.

CHAP. XI.

The kindness expressed in the behaviour of her father, after he had been informed by Madame St. Clair of her fixed resolution in respect to Perouse, which she had feared would have greatly irritated him, was a balm to the wounded feelings of the unhappy Adelaide; yet the consolation she derived from this source was nevertheless embittered by the reflection that she was not only hourly exposed to the most dreadful evils herself, but while she continued, as at present, the object of illicit pursuit, must necessarily expose to difficulties, and even dangers, all those with whom she was in any way connected.

The apprehensions of what she might have to encounter from the persecutions of the Marquis, should they be continued against her, and there seemed no reason to hope they would not, together with conjectures about the many evils and distresses which seemed likely to attend her in her passage through life, engaged her mind in sorrowful rumination, and kept her waking many hours. Weariness at length overcame her, and she was sinking gradually into a state of repose, or rather insensibility, when she heard, or thought she heard, the door of Madame St. Clair's room, which was nearly opposite her own, cautiously opened. She perceived also a light gleaming through the crevices of the door; and soon afterwards distinguished the sound of footsteps, pacing slowly and carefully down the stairs.

This circumstance surprised her; for Madame, as on the preceding night, had retired early to her apartment, and was partly undressed, when Adelaide, after the conversation we have before related, withdrew from her chamber, Madame having more than once observed that she was extremely wearied, and could sit up no longer.

A considerable time had elapsed since she seemed to have retired for the night: how strange then, thought Adelaide, that she should leave her bed at this hour! Something extraordinary must have happened.

She listened: all was still. At length, she thought she distinguished a distant murmuring, as of the voices of people talking in one of the lower rooms of the chateau. But the sound was too indistinct to allow her to determine from which of the apartments it issued. She became anxious to ascertain whether Perouse and her father were in their beds; and having listened some time, and not hearing Madame return to her chamber, curiosity almost tempted her to rise, and endeavor to investigate what to her appeared now strangely mysterious.

But the caution with which the steps seemed to descend, which she could not doubt were those of Madame St. Clair, convinced her that whatever might be Madame's motive for leaving her chamber at that hour, it was a secret one; and an attempt to discover it might subject her to her displeasure, and appear, on her part, as the error of a prying curiosity.

The surprise of this incident prevented the approach of sleep; till her wearied attention could be kept no longer awake, when she sunk into a gentle slumber.

CHAP. XII.

When Adelaide arose in the morning, she found Perouse and her father had departed, and learnt that they had set off as early as daybreak. She inquired of Madame if she had been unwell in the night, and whether any thing had happened to disturb her? but upon observing a confusion in her air and look, as of that of a person suddenly embarrassed by some perplexing interrogatory, added, "I thought I heard somebody descend the stairs; but I was probably mistaken."

"Oh, very likely you did, my love," said Madame, as if suddenly recollecting herself; "I never told you before, and it was perhaps very foolish of me that I did not, as such a circumstance might have alarmed you; but you must know, my dear, I have an unfortunate habit of walking in my sleep, particularly when any thing has happened in the day to agitate me; and no wonder I did last night, after I had suffered so much, in consequence of the conversation I held yesterday with my poor Perouse, about yourself. Oh, pray did I come into your room? I am very apt to make these nightly expeditions; and might have been the cause of much terror to you, who knew not of this infirmity."

"And do you always take a candle in your hand, Madame," said Adelaide, "for I saw a light, I think, through the door?"

"Oh, very likely—yes, I dare say I do."

"Surely this must be very dangerous," cried Adelaide.

"Why so it seems," rejoined Madame; "but I believe some guardian spirit is appointed by a particuliar providence to watch over people who are addicted to this habit; for we seldom, I think, or never, hear of any accident. La, I could tell you a thousand laughable stories of which I am the heroine. You cannot conceive into what a number of almost unaccountable situations I have been brought by this unfortunate propensity."

"I was once ingenious enough, while dreaming of a voyage of wealth and glory to the Indies, to find my way into a bag which hung in my closet, and while I imagined I was rising myself up the sides of a splendid galley, in which I was to embark, was near suffering the effects of suffocation, from the tightness of the string by which I drew it round my neck. Nay, I should have been completely strangled, had not my groans awakened a part of the family, who came and liberated me from a condition the most wretched that can be endured, or even imagined. Never was so absurd an exhibition; nor one of which I was more heartily ashamed. My head alone was out of the bag. I appeared as though I had been in a pillory.

"Another time I was found sitting like the sign of the Jolly Bacchus, upon a wine cask in the cellar. I have prowled like the nightly thief, through every part of my own premises; and was once detected in the act of attempting to enter a henroost, dreaming that I was a fox. Oh, it would fill pages, nay, even volumes, to record half my adventures!"

She concluded this somewhat curious account of her nocturnal perambulations with a hearty burst of laughter, in which Adelaide also joined. She, however, requested of Madame that she would be more careful for the future, and not suffer a light to be burnt in her chamber; or that she would place it in some safe situation; lest dreaming that she was Eratostratus,* about to eternize her name by firing the temple of the Ephesian Diana, she should chance to burn herself in her own dwelling.

As the young chevalier, whose appearance and somewhat extraordinary inquiries had excited a strong interest in the mind of Adelaide, had not been seen or heard of some days, it was generally concluded that he had at last really quitted the neighbourhood—an opinion from which Madame seemed to derive much pleasure; nor was Adelaide without her share of satisfaction, since she seemed to be more secure from the designs of the Marquis. At the recollection of the personal charms and graces of this seemingly amiable and highly-accomplished youth, a sigh would sometimes steal involuntarily from her bosom, and a tear spring into her eye. "I shall see him no more!" she would exclaim mentally; then blushing, hastily turn her thoughts from the object, and wonder why he should have so much engaged them.

She now again resumed her walks, generally attended by Madame, and chiefly amongst the acclivities that rose high at the back of the chateau, where travellers did not, and indeed scarcely could come. When at home, she amused herself with her lute, or in reading and conversing with Madame St. Clair, who endeavoured, with all the arts of ingenuity, to reconcile her to the idea of a marriage with her nephew, which she presented not only as prudent, but wholly unavoidable.

CHAP. XIII.

THUS passed the time for some days,' and Adelaide experienced a suspension of her former stress and anxiety; for Perouse did not return. This calm, however, was soon disturbed, and Adelaide was again thrown into a state of tumult and apprehension, by the intelligence communicated by Madame, with all the symptoms of alarm, that a party of horsemen, supposed to belong to the Marquis, had appeared in the village, and also at the gate of the chateau opening to the lawn; that they had been making a number of inquiries at the inn, of which Adelaide was supposed to be the object, and had certainly gained all the intelligence which the host could give.

"Oh Heavens! I am betrayed then!" exclaimed Adelaide, "and who will protect me? you, Madame, you, alas, cannot!"

"I am as much alarmed as you can be, my dear," said Madame; "but I have taken such precautions as may serve at present to render their pursuit ineffectual. I have deceived the people at the inn, whose curiosity must naturally have been much excited by your arrival there at night in the disguise in which you came, with fictitious account of you, and which I think will satisfy them, and prevent them from directing these men to our habitation. But lest this should be insufficient, they are taught to believe you are departed in company with two travellers, by whom you are to understand I mean your father and Perouse."

"And are you sure they are satisfied?" demanded Adelaide. "Have they left the village?"

"No; they have been seen within this half hour."

"And how do the people at the inn know that they are the servants of the Marquis?" asked Adelaide.

"They do not know, they only suspect they are."

"Perhaps then they may be mistaken."

"I fear they are not," said Madame, "I fear they are not. So pray my dear, don't venture out at present, not even into the lawn; oh, oh, I am all over of a tremor! This young man—this young fellow has betrayed us; and we are ruined and undone for ever!"

"Where are these people?" asked Adelaide; "can I get a sight of them?"

"A sight of them!" interrupted Madame; "a sight of them! oh, no, no, no! not for the world! for Heaven's sake, child, keep away from the window; who knows but they may be at the gate? and if they should see you—oh that such a charge should have been left to me! upon me, a poor, weak, defenceless woman! If I could but have foreseen—if I could but have known—if I could have dived into futurity, never would I have been left to suffer these agonies of terror, unprotected as we are."

"But why not call the people in the village to our defence, Madame?" said Adelaide; "surely in a cause of humanity such as this, some benevolent being would step forward to give us that protection we require?"

"Not a soul—not a soul," cried Madame; "they are bribed—all bribed to assist in your destruction; nor dare they, if they would, protect you."

"Then we must place our dependence upon Heaven only,"

said Adelaide, "and that innocence which is sure to secure to us its promised mercies."

"Innocence!" repeated Madame, with a shudder, which seemed to shake her frame, and with her eyes cast down and fixed; "who is innocent?"

The remark drew the attention of Adelaide to the countenance of the person who uttered it; it seemed momentarily convulsed. She raised her eyes, and perceiving Adelaide was observing her, roused herself from the temporary reverie into which she had fallen.

"Can nothing then be done?" said Adelaide.

"I believe it has all been done very well," rejoined Madame, with an absent air.

"How, my dear Madame?" asked Adelaide.

"The report of the host at the inn may mislead, if it does not effectually deceive," said Madame, "and serve to direct their pursuit to some other quarter."

"You think then they are probably already gone?" said Adelaide, now somewhat re-assured.

"I fear not at present. But instead of troubling ourselves with vain alarms, let us consider how we may contrive to avoid these dangers; or what we ought to do, should that which we apprehend really approach. For this, it is necessary that you should keep concealed; for should you be seen, or if it be known by any one that you are still here, you will be discovered, and the consequences must be fatal."

"I will certainly not venture from the chateau, Madame, or even look out from the windows," said Adelaide, "if you think my appearance there subjects me to any hazard."

"You cannot, my love, as I have told you before, be too cautious," pursued Madame; "be careful only not to be seen; and I will go and give some further orders to Jacques, whom I have employed to watch the motions of these people, if they are still, as I fear they may be, loitering about the village."

With this she withdrew, leaving Adelaide, although seriously alarmed, more composed than when first informed of their arrival; for she hoped if she was indeed the object of their search, they had been told she was departed, and had taken another route.

CHAP. XIV.

The night passed on without any alarming incident. In the morning, intelligence was brought that the men had left the village, though probably with the design of returning, and Adelaide was in consequence still confined to the house, for she had received the most earnest request, nay, the strictest orders, from Madame, not to stir abroad, till it might be certain the horsemen had left the country.

After breakfast, as Adelaide and Madame St. Clair were sitting together in the parlour, discoursing on the subject of the alarm of yesterday, the conversation was interrupted by the entrance of Jacques, on some trifling occasion, who as he left the room looked significantly at Adelaide, and almost beckoned her to follow him.

Curiosity, which several late incidents had contributed to excite, rendered her anxious to know what he could mean; and she soon after went into the hall, where she found him loitering. The instant he saw her, he made a sign for silence; and beckoned her into a recess at the farther end of the hall.

"Well, Jacques, what is it you would say?" said Adelaide; "have the men been seen again in the village?"

"Hush, Ma'amoiselle, for Heaven's sake, speak lower; for if Madame should hear us, and come out, we shall both be as good as murdered!"

Adelaide now thought it was of the chevalier he was about to speak, and not of the Marquis's servants; for she recollected Helené having told her he had inquired and talked about her to Jacques. Hope palpitated at her heart, and she begged him to explain what he meant.

"Why, that is what I have been wanting all morning," said Jacques; "I have watched, and watched, for an opportunity of seeing you without Madame; and when I could not, came with excuses into the parlour, or loitered under the window where you sat, tying up the shrubs and flowers, and trying to catch your eye, till I was afraid Madame herself would see me; and all would not do."

"If you have any thing to say to me," cried Adelaide, "pray be quick."

"Yes, Ma'amoiselle; for if we should be seen talking together, and only a word or two be caught, we shall be all blown up. But I would do any thing to serve you, Ma'moiselle; and I could not bear to see so much villany on foot, and not tell you of it."

"For the love of Heaven!" exclaimed Adelaide, "if you know of any danger that threatens me, speak instantly, and to the purpose, or we shall be discovered."

"Well, but will you promise, Ma'moiselle, never to say it was I that told you?"

"Yes, yes, I will promise any thing and every thing, only be quick, or we may be interrupted. Have the Marquis's servants, or the Marquis——"

"Poh, poh, Ma'amoiselle, the Marquis! that's all a flam. The Marquis, I dare say, knows no more about you than the man in the moon, and not so much. I know a great deal; but I can't tell you now, Ma'amoiselle, for if Madame was to find us here—I would not for the world we should be seen together. Cannot you come out after dinner, when she is taking her afternoon's nap, and walk in the little shrubbery behind the chateau, and I'll slip out the back way and meet you?"

Adelaide promised she would walk there; and begged if Jacques had anything important to tell her, he would not fail in the appointment.

What she had already heard was sufficient to employ her surmises, and excite an eager curiosity to be acquainted with the sequel. She waited, therefore, with impatience till the dinner was over, and the cloth removed, when, as usual, Madame having taken three or four glasses of wine, and one or two of some famous liqueur, of which she was extremely fond, withdrew to take her *siesta*, or afternoon's nap, in her own apartment.

CHAP. XV.

ADELAIDE repaired anxiously to the shrubbery, where Jacques was already waiting, employed, as he pretended, in his garden-work.

"I thought you long, Ma'amoiselle," said he, "but perhaps, thinks I, Madame has not finished her drams. And now you are come, I'm almost afraid to tell you what I know. But as to staying here longer, I won't, and that's flat."

"Well, Jacques," said Adelaide, "and what is it you would tell me?"

"Hush," cried Jacques, "let us first see whether any body is about. I declare if I an't in such a fright, even the fluskering of a bird throws me all over in a sweat. But I could not bear to see such fine good young lady—hark! did not I hear a step?"

"No, no," said Adelaide, "pray proceed."

"I could not bear, as I was saying, to see such a sweet young lady—surely Ma'amoiselle, I saw something moving behind yon tree."

"Oh, do not trifle thus," said Adelaide, "if you have any thing to say, tell it me, or we may be observed."

"True, Ma'amoiselle; but where was I? I could not bear to see such a sweet good young lady—I was there I think."

"Pray go on," said Adelaide, with impatience, "you have told me this three times already."

"Don't interrupt me so, Ma'amoiselle," said Jacques, "or I shall never be able to get on at all. It grieves me to the heart to see you in so much danger," added he, "and so I determined to tell you. But you must be as mum as a maggot, Ma'amoiselle, will you? or I durstn't."

"I fear you have determined *not* to tell me," said Adelaide, whose patience was now nearly exhausted: "what danger is it of which you speak? and if not from the Marquis, from what quarter am I to expect it?"

"Why from that quarter, I dare say, Ma'amoiselle, between ourselves," said Jacques, "you least thought of expecting it; for if a child cannot depend upon its own father, I don't know who it can ever think to trust unto."

"My father!" cried Adelaide; "what of my father?"

"Why you must know, Ma'amoiselle, I've had my thoughts some time; but that's neither here nor there; a man may have his own private thoughts, without being obliged to speak 'em. But I'd a huge fancy that all things were not as they should be, ever since Madame's nephew, my master, as I call him, brought you, Ma'amoiselle, to the chateau. For what *argufies*, says I, all this hiding, and these nightly confabs, and such winkings, and whisperings, and closetings, and getting together in corners? If things are going on honestly, why may not they go on openly and above aboard? says I. Now you knew nothing of all this, Ma'amoiselle, but I had my eyes and ears about me; and I saw and heard a great deal more than they thought such a ninny as they took me for could. But what of that? well then, your father came, and then there was more of it; though I thought he looked more cunning than the others, and seemed more upon the sly; but I smoked him, for all that. Well, I found they made a pretence to go to bed, and then came down again in the night, when they thought all the rest of us were asleep, and that they sat up drinking and talking many hours. I should not have taken so much notice of this, if the men had been by themselves, and Madame had not been amongst 'em. But this, says I to myself, has an oddish look: so the last night, making a sham of going to bed with the other servants, knowing your father and my master were to be off in the morning, I came down again too; for I was strangely mistaken if some mischief was not a brewing. If, says I, it's all for merriment, why is not Ma'amoiselle there too amongst 'em? for I'm sure, though she has such sweet looks, and is so good tempered, and speaks so free to us all, like a true lady, she want something to make her merry as well as the rest of 'em; for I saw clear enough you wasn't so easy in your heart as you should be, Ma'amoiselle, or as I thought you deserved. So what does I do, for I came down a little before the others, but pop myself into a closet, where there was a little cranny into the room, where they had been colloguing the night before. Well, I had not been there long, when down they came pod, pod, pod, like so many spirits, one after the other, with candles in their hands, and in their night-gowns. Now, says I, I have you; so clapping my ear right to the chink, I got into all their secrets."

"And what did you hear?" said Adelaide, who had listened to this account with a trembling solicitude, which was every instant increasing; "if the matter concerns me, I pray you be brief, and let me know it."

"Concerns you, Ma'amoiselle! yes, it concerns you sure enough, and badly enough too, I may say, for they are nothing but thieves and murderers after all; and they want to get you into their gang."

"Merciful and gracious powers!" exclaimed Adelaide, clasping her hands and raising her eyes to Heaven, with a look of terrified astonishment, while the agony of her feelings almost suppressed her utterance, "is it, can it be possible! my father too—my father!"

"Well, and so when they were all at their talking, and their revels," pursued Jacques, "they began to say how well they had contrived it, and laughed, and chuckled, and seemed as merry as grigs;* and said the little fool, meaning you, Ma'amoiselle, was caught in the snare; and that they had you now as safe as a fox in a bag; and you might cry and toss a little, if you would, but could not get away. And then they laughed again, and said the story of the Marquis was a capital hit; and one said it was their contrivance, and another theirs; and all seemed so eager to be thought the first inventor of the scheme, that I thought they would have gone to loggerheads about it. 'Are you sure,' said the old one, 'she does not suspect the trick? does she believe the Marquis is in pursuit of her at this moment? for, by jingo, if we don't frighten her, she'll smoke us before we nail her; and may fly off like an arrow from a bow, and then catch her who can.' 'Never fear,' said Madame, 'she believes every thing; but you would have spoilt all, if you had not gone on as I bid you; for she is as shy as little chamois;* and would have bolted, had you offered what she would call a liberty, or spoke a word out of place. Poor thing, she will know better after a while, or won't fail of it for want of teaching.'—'Well but,' said Perouse, 'what must we do, if, after all, she should refuse to marry me?'—'Why force her, to be sure,' cried De Launé; 'am I not her father?' 'But what if she won't repeat her part in the ceremony?' cried Perouse.—'Poh, poh, she dare not hold out,' said the other, 'if she does, we'll bring some of our comrades to act the part of the Marquis and his servants, and pretend to force her from the chateau. Ods wounds, d'you think we have so little brave blood, my lad? we who have shed so much in the way of trade, and can't out-bravo a little simpleton of a wench of eighteen, who knows no more of the world than a child just born, and is as easily bamboozled?'—'I am afraid of nothing but that chevalier,' cried Madame; 'I wonder who he is.'—'No matter,' said De Launé, 'we can soon do for him; egad, I don't know whether we have not paid him already, if what she said about him was true; but I did not know who the party were till we had done with 'em. They stood to it bravely, that's certain, but we were too many for 'em. It was a devilish lucky accident, our gang just coming up at that instant, or they'd have given us no quarter. By the living jingo, I was afraid they had not been near enough to have heard the whistle.' And so then, Ma'amoiselle, they began to talk of their booty, and the number of travellers they had left dead, and laughed, and seemed so merry, while I stood trembling, Ma'amoiselle, from head to foot; for what, thinks I, if they should come round, and find me here? why they would cut me up into mince-meat. Lord a mercy, thought I, what will become of me! Verily, I think my hair stood on end with fright, as well it might; for I found they made no more of killing a man than they did of eating their suppers. My knees knocked together, till I almost thought they would have heard 'em. And there I stood, Ma'amoiselle, more dead than alive, for I knew how it would be with me if I was catched, till they had finished their palaver, when they got up, and went away, one after another, pod, pod, just as they came down. Well now, says I, I'm safe, and main glad I was to hear 'em go out. I waited till they had got up stairs; and then came out from my hiding-place, like a fox from his hole; and when I thought they were all asleep, pod, pod, I went too, up the stairs. Holy Saint Dominic! never was I so glad as when I got safe to bed, thinking of the 'scape I had had. And now, says I, if Ma'amoiselle does not know what sort of gentry she is with, she'll be nabbed; and so, come what will, I'll tell her; for it will be a sin and a shame to let so good a young lady be in such danger, and not give her the chance of getting away from 'em, all for want of a little warning."

Adelaide, whose feelings during this relation of Jacques's may be more readily conceived than described, now saw herself in a situation beset with dangers, from which it was utterly impossible to extricate herself but by instant flight. "And did my father," said she, "join in this iniquitous scheme against me? my father! then from henceforth I renounce the tie; no longer am I his daughter. Oh wretch!—wretch! forgive me, Heaven! a robber and a murderer! dy'd deep in blood. Horror on horrors! my pretended generous benefactress too, and him to whom I owed my seeming deliverance, both—both perfidious and deceitful! bent on my destruction, even while with smiles they seemed to court my affections, and flattered to betray me to my ruin!"

"Well, Ma'amoiselle!" cried Jacques, "but what do you think must be done to cheat 'em, as one may say, out of their contrivances? as to me, I'm bent upon going, if I don't get a single farthing of my wages."

"What if I should attempt an escape?" said Adelaide: "would you assist me, Jacques? You are an honest fellow; and if it should ever be in my power to recompense you——"

"Why as to that, Ma'amoiselle," cried Jacques, scratching his head; "but where are we to go? I'm stout enough, and don't fear but I could shift for myself; but you, lady——"

"Assist me but till I can get beyond the reach of my enemies," said Adelaide, "and I shall then comparatively have nothing to fear."

"Well I've been thinking a little bit of a scheme myself," said Jacques, "for says I to myself, Ma'amoiselle will be for getting off when she hears how she's like to be served, and what company she's got into; for I warrant she thought they were all as good as herself, or she wouldn't have been so contended among 'em, and have spoke so pretty to 'em all."

"And what was you thinking of, Jacques?" cried Adelaide; "be quick, pray, and tell me; for if Madame should awake, and come down, and find us here—"

"Aye, by our Lady, and that would be a bad find for us, I can tell you, Ma'amoiselle; for she's as cunning as a pickpocket, and not a whit the honester, or she would not have said what she did."

"But your scheme, Jacques—you said you had a scheme?"

"Aye, the scheme, lady."

"May I depend upon you, Jacques? will you assist me to escape the destruction that awaits me here? Alas! I have not a friend in the world, if I do not find one in you!"

"The more the pity—the more the pity, Ma'amoiselle; for I'm sure you deserve one."

"What plan have you?" said she, perceiving Jacques was deliberating.

"Why you must know, Ma'amoiselle," rejoined Jacques, "they have left a horse behind 'em in the stable: a bay jennet black mare, and tail and legs black, all but the near foot behind; fourteen hands and a half high; and as nigh as I can guess, Ma'amoiselle, for I looked in its mouth yesterday, not much above four years old."

"Never mind the marks, or the age," interrupted Adelaide; "can we have the horse?"

"Aye, marry can we; and for the matter of right, I dare be sworn we have as good a right to it as they have; and that's as good as no right at all."

"Well, and where shall we go?" said Adelaide; "have you thought of that?"

"Why, yes; I have been thinking a little about that, too, Ma'amoiselle, if so be we have the luck to get clear off without meeting any of the troop. I have a good old grandmother in Rousillon, please God she be yet alive, for I have not seen her for some years, who, when I shall tell her the story, will be kind to you, and make much of you for my sake; for she was always main fond of me; and when I left her to come on my travels—"

"Well then, to-night," interrupted Adelaide.

"To-night, Ma'amoiselle, or never; for as to shilly-shallying, it's of no use; and beside, who knows what may turn up to-morrow? But how are you to manage with Madame?"

"She is so sure, as she imagines, of the success of her own measures," replied Adelaide, "that she will have no suspicion of my intention. I will pretend, like her, to go to bed, and then come down again; take you care only to seem to be up the last, that the doors may be left unfastened."

"Right, Ma'amoiselle, and I will oil the locks and hinges well too, that we may go out without noise; and that will be only doing the Madame bid me. 'Jacques,' says she, 'the doors creak sadly; do get a little oil, for they make me quite nar—narvus,' I think that was the word; but I didn't do 'em for all that. Well, so about an hour after bed-time, Ma'amoiselle, do you be ready to steal out from your chamber, and meet me at the bridge on the other side of the lawn; where I will wait for you with the nag. The moon will be up; and if we meet with nothing to interrupt us, before Madame awakes in the morning, we shall be got a good way on our journey; and with the blessing of the Holy Mother (crossing himself) shall be out of their reach before my master and your father return; for Madame can't follow us herself, and she has nobody to send after us. Lord-a-mercy, how she'll stare when she finds us gone! I wouldn't be in her shoes when they come home, and hear we are missing, for all the money she's to have for tricking you, Ma'amoiselle, though I warrant it's a fine round sum; for by our Lady, I believe she'll be half murdered for't."

"Remember your promise, Jacques," said Adelaide, "and let us now part; you know it may be dangerous to our plans if we are seen together."

Jacques assured her he would not fail in the performance of his promise at the appointed hour at night, and Adelaide returned to the chateau.

On entering one of the rooms, she was soon afterwards joined by Madame, who had but just awakened from her afternoon's repose.

Aware that the means of her escape might be in an instant prevented by the slightest degree of alarm on the part of Madame, Adelaide carefully avoided every thing that could excite any suspicion; and she endeavoured to appear composed, and even cheerful. In this she was so successful that Madame did not perceive the emotions she thus concealed under the appearance of a fictitious and painful tranquillity.

CHAP. XVI.

Evening, at length, approached. Adelaide watched the dusk of the twilight as it stole over the features of the landscape, gradually deepening into the shades of night. To-morrow night at this hour, thought she, I shall, I trust, be far away.

As she gazed upon the outlines of the mountains, which now alone were to be discerned, she thought of the evening when she had walked with Madame and the chevalier. A horrible apprehension arose with the recollection; for she remembered De Launé and Perouse's words, as repeated by Jacques, which seemed to threaten his safety; or even to imply that they had probably already severely wounded, perhaps killed him in some late recontre.

The perturbation of her mind during her conversation with Jacques, had prevented her from dwelling upon this circumstance;

indeed she then scarcely remarked it. But now it occurred to her with increased force; and the certainty that he was not what her own fears, and the cunning artifices of Madame, had once taught her to suspect, rendered him now more than ever an object of the most tender interest and lively admiration. That this interest was of the most tender kind was incontestibly evident. The horrible idea that he might be murdered—murdered in consequence of his attempts to serve her, by delivering her from her present situation, occurred to her imagination. The sensations thus occasioned were most painful; a death-like sickness seized her, and obliged her to retire to her own chamber, to indulge in sorrow she could no longer suppress.

"In him," said she, weeping, "I might have found a friend and deliverer, had I but dared to confide in his zeal and affection; and he is now lost to me for ever." She remained agitated by these emotions, and racked by such reflections, till a message came from Madame requiring her presence at supper. "Is it the supper hour?" said she with surprise; for the time occupied in these tender sorrows had fled quickly; and assuming as well as she could that appearance of composure which was so necessary to prevent suspicion in Madame, and the interruption of the escape she was about to attempt, she went down stairs.

Madame seemed in high spirits; and Adelaide affected a cheerfulness very foreign to her heart, and which an attentive observer might have discovered to be fictitious. She waited with anxiety the hour when Madame would retire for the night; and the restlessness of her feelings led her to imagine it was protracted beyond the usual time; and various trifling incidents which retarded what she wished, became the cause of the most teazing vexations.

She withdrew, at length, and followed by Adelaide with quick and agitated steps, repaired to her room. Adelaide, after waiting a few minutes, as usual, in Madame's chamber, took her leave for the night, as she said, but inwardly hoped it might be for ever; and then retired to her own apartment.

The hour that was to intervene, ere the time appointed for

her departure would arrive, was passed in anxious alternations of hope and fear. The enterprise of that night—that important night, seemed the crisis of her fate. That it might be fortunate was the subject of a prayer not less devout than might be uttered by "the rapt seraph that adores and burns."*

She implored the Father of Mercies, he who pities the fatherless and the widow, to look down on her forlorn and destitute condition, and guide her on in safety through that course which could alone deliver her from the worst and most dreaded of all evils.

Those who know what it is to address their Father and their God in the hour of trial and of danger, will not hear with surprise that she arose from her posture of supplication with a composure of mind fitting her for the most effectual execution of her design, and with a secret assurance that if she could not ensure, she might at least hope for success.

CHAP. XVII.

THE hour now arrived when Jacques was to meet her at the little bridge beyond the lawn. She cautiously left her room, taking nothing with her except the clothes she had worn on her arrival. Those since received as presents from Madame were left behind; Adelaide conceiving it would be dishonourable to make use of them, after a step which the donor would most undoubtedly have opposed.

As she opened her door, she listened for a minute or two, to discover whether all was quiet throughout the house; not a sound was to be heard; she descended the stairs, and crossing the hall with quick, but trembling steps, reached the outer door of the chateau. It was unlocked, and stood ajar. She opened it without noise, and went out. A sensation of fear for a moment took possession of her mind, on finding herself alone in the silence of the night; but it was only for a moment. Hope fluttered at her heart; she tripped lightly over the moonlight lawn, to the wicket-gate at the further end. She went on, and turned down towards the bridge. The figure of a man seen below and advancing towards her, caused her to start and tremble; but all was well—it was the punctual Jacques.

"You are come just in right time, Ma'amoiselle," said he, "for it is a fine night, and the moon will be up for some hours. I hope you won't be tired, Ma'amoiselle," added he, as he lifted her upon the horse, "for we have a main long journey to go; and what's worse, we must stop nowhere within twenty miles of this town."

Adelaide assured him she was not afraid of fatigue, and then inquired if he was well acquainted with their route; and whether he thought there was a probability of their being able to prosecute their journey in safety, till they should have reached their destination?

"Why as to the road, Ma'amoiselle," answered Jacques, "I believe I know every step of it; but as to our going safe, it must depend upon meeting any of the troop who are generally abroad at night among the mountains. All we have to do is make the best of our way while the moon's up; and if we hear 'em coming, to skulk behind the trees, or under the rock, taking care to be neither seen nor heard, till they shall have passed us. Hold you fast by me, Ma'amoiselle, and don't be daunted, for the horse is able enough, and seems to know the road; so I shall put him on, come what will: only take care, Ma'amoiselle, you don't slip off behind; for the pillion* is but a middling one, though it was the best I could get."

They travelled with good speed over the rugged and generally steep road, so that Adelaide had some difficulty in obeying that part of her companion's directions, not to slip off behind. But his lively and good-humoured sayings were a great comfort to her; and the prospect of effecting an escape gave strength to her exertions, and courage to her heart.

Before the moon had set, they had proceeded several leagues, without any alarm or adventure; when as they were descending by a path down the side of one of the highest eminences, into a deep valley which fell at its foot, they were alarmed by the approach of horsemen; and Adelaide, whose fears instantly suggested they were banditti, trembled so excessively, that it was with difficulty she could keep her seat.

"They are here, Ma'amoiselle, for certain," cried Jacques; "but we must hold to the right, and get within that thicket; and then, with the blessing of Saint Dominic, I hope we shall be safe enough. Don't be frightened, Ma'amoiselle," though while he spoke, Jacques himself trembled like an aspen, "for if you squall out, or make any noise, they'll find us, and we shall have the balls of a brace of blunderbusses whizzing about our ears."

Adelaide gave proof of her attention to the advice of her conductor, by forbearing to make any reply; and Jacques turned into the thicket, and waited till the troop should have passed by. As they approached near, the pacing of the horses seemed to strike upon the heart-strings of poor Adelaide, and those of Jacques also; and they both almost feared to breathe, lest they should be discovered. However, the party passed right onward, and crossing the mountain by the track down which our travellers had come, were soon out of hearing and sight.

"I am glad we have met with 'em," said Jacques, whose courage had returned with his security, "now they have gone away so quietly, as we shall now have nothing to fear from 'em; for it will soon be day-break; and before to-morrow night we shall be in Rousillon."

At the thoughts of being so soon in a place of safety, and, as she hoped, beyond the reach of these outlaws, Adelaide's spirits also revived; and she amused the tedious journey by inquiring of Jacques concerning Madame St. Clair, of whom, however, Jacques could give only a very imperfect account.

According to his report, she had resided only a few months at Auboigne, and had taken the chateau ready furnished, as it was only a little time before Adelaide came there with Perouse; and the term for which she had hired it was almost expired. Who she was, and where she came from, was a subject which had supplied materials for the curiosity and inquiry of all the people in the village, ever since she had arrived. But as she made no acquaintance in the place, and seemed scrupulously to avoid all opportunities of intimacy, and even intercourse, with the inhabitants, they had no means of satisfying themselves on these points.

Various rumors had, however, of late arisen from some intimations made by two travellers, who had stopped at the village inn, from which it was believed that she had led not long ago a disreputable life. But it not being quite certain that Madame St. Clair was the person whom the travellers said they knew, their declarations were not much regarded, and served only to keep alive suspicion.

On the arrival of Perouse, who was considered as a person of very suspicious character, the story of these travellers, which had before begun to die away, was revived. It was not generally believed that he was her nephew, though it was impossible to prove that he was not. As Adelaide had accompanied him to the inn, and afterwards to Madame St. Clair's house, it was universally believed that she was of the same description of females to which Madame herself was supposed to belong. "Though when they talked to me about you," said Jacques, "as they often did, and said as how you were no better than you should be, meaning Ma'amoiselle, I suppose, not so good, I always told 'em what a sweet kind creature you was, and how modest and pretty you behaved; and bid 'em look to themselves, and mind their own business, and not sit in judgment upon others, but try to look and behave as you did; 'for,' says I, 'she's a gentlewoman, I know she is, let her be who she will, for she always speaks like one, and knows how to conduct herself like one too, and that's more than every body can say,' meaning them I spoke to. And then they laughed, and jeered; but what of that, since it *argufied* nothing but to prove my own words. When Madame first came," pursued Jacques, "she had no man-servant; but I having lost my master, who died in the neighbouring village, and thinking she must want one, went and offered myself, and was immediately hired, which might be about a week before you came."

"Then," said Adelaide, "you had seen Monsieur Perouse before his coming with me."

"Oh la, yes, Ma'amoiselle, several times, and Monsieur De Launé too; and they had many a confab together, I assure you; and when you came, I thought they must all have been about you; but that, you know, Mamoiselle, was no business of mine. But when I saw my master come home at night, sometimes by himself, and sometimes with one or two, I did not know who, and carry packages into his chamber, and hide 'em, or lock 'em up, I do not know which, thinks I to myself, it's time to look about me; for I thought those things could only come from travellers, and muleteers, which I heard were often robbed by a desperate gang of thieves, as they were conveying their commodities over the mountains which separate the two kingdoms."

While they were thus engaged in discourse concerning Madame St. Clair and Perouse, Adelaide, whose fears had almost wholly subsided, perceived, with delight, the dawn of day streaking the eastern clouds; and soon afterwards beheld the sun, rising in all its splendour. She hailed with welcome the glorious orb, and felt the cheerfulness its beams diffuses. "A few hours," said she, "and I shall be safe from the dreaded power of my enemies."

The idea inspired gratitude and hope, but succeeding reflections sunk her into thoughtfulness, and spread their saddening influences upon her mind. She was again, she recollected, about to be dependant upon the protection and bounty of strangers, destitute not only of a home, but even of the means of subsistence. She was without a friend, or any regular connexion. She was doomed also to feel all the miseries of suspense, and all the tortures of surmise; for she imagined she had been the occasion of exposing to the fury of her persecutors, the chevalier who had so benevolently interested himself in her welfare; though her fears had prevented her from allowing him to render himself actively serviceable in her cause. These her apprehensions were indeed but too well-founded; for it was evident, from the declaration of the cabal at the chateau, that they designed his death, and that they even thought it likely that he had fallen in the rencontre they had described.

CHAP. XVIII.

It was not till some hours after noon, that our travellers, who had stopped only once for refreshment, passed the borders of Gascony, and entered upon the wild and romantic province of Rousillon. Pursuing their way through a country rich with olive-groves, and abounding with the sublime features of mountain scenery, they arrived at an obscure village, deeply embosomed in a valley, formed by two ridgy hills, covered in part with wood, and partly rugged with the most grotesque rocks, and watered by a mountain-stream, which darted clear and rapid down its stony course.

The scene as they advanced became so beautiful, that Adelaide could not restrain the expression of her admiration. Of these kind of remarks Jacques took little notice; his attention was indeed otherwise engaged. At length he exclaimed—"There it is, Ma'amoiselle, there it is! And see how merry they are yonder," pointing to a group of peasants dancing on a green between the rivulet and a vineyard. "It is the vintage, Ma'amoiselle, and, now they have done their work for the day, they are footing it away to the sound of the tabor and flageolet. Ah! it reminds me of the time when I was a lad, Ma'amoiselle. And look there, against that grove, Ma'amoiselle, with the olive-ground below," directing the attention of Adelaide to a fine old gothic chateau, a little without the village, "there lives my old grandmother, God bless her, if she be yet alive."

"Your grandmother!" exclaimed Adelaide; "does your grandmother reside at that chateau?"

"Yes, Ma'amoiselle," returned Jacques, "and has done for many years. She lived servant there in her youth, and afterwards, on the death of my grandfather, who died before I can remember, was hired again as housekeeper; and a fine place she had of it, till the family went abroad, when the rest of the servants were discharged, and she was left in the chateau to take care of it, in order that the windows might be opened, and the rooms kept in airing, that the furniture might not be spoiled by the damps."

"And does she continue there alone?" asked Adelaide.

"Yes, Ma'amoiselle, except at night, when a neighbour comes from the village to sleep there, my grandmother thinking it somewhat lonely to lodge in such a great old rambling place by herself."

"And have you any other relations in the village, Jacques?" said Adelaide.

"Yes, Ma'amoiselle, I've a sister that's married, and lives a little lower down in the valley, in that cottage there, with the smoke curling from the top," pointing to a little rustic habitation, whose simple dome-like roof was seen just peeping from a luxuriant grove of chesnuts: "but she has a large family," resumed Jacques, "and lives hardy enough, I warrant; though I'm not sure, Ma'amoiselle, when she knows how you have been used, she will be main kind to you, though it's I that says it."

Adelaide, aware that if Jacques was allowed to disclose all the particulars of her story with which he was acquainted, he might involve her in some distressing embarrassments, and this not so much from a fondness for the marvellous, as from ignorance of the real circumstances of her situation, requested he would say nothing amongst his friends about the conversation he had overheard at Madame St. Clair's, and that he would leave her to disclose what she should think proper; to answer no inquiries concerning her; and above all things, not to mention that De Launé was her father, or that he was one of the troop of banditti that infested the mountains, and had been long the scourge and terror of all Gascony.

"However cruel may have been his conduct, however unjustifiable, and even wicked, Jacques," pursued she, "he is still my father; and I must not implicate him in the villainy of which he now stands charged."

Jacques promised carefully to follow these injunctions, though evidently not without some reluctance at being denied the pleasure of telling a story which he conceived to be both interesting and extraordinary.

They had by this time arrived at the village, which was extremely neat, but simple, and promised but indifferent accommodation. Scarcely had they reached the first cottage, when Jacques was accosted by one or two of his old acquaintance, who shook him by the hand with such earnestness of regard, that it seemed as though they were unwilling any other of their neighbours should shew him like tokens of friendship and affection. He inquired of his grandmother and sister, and was told they were both alive. Having passed the village, they ascended a gentle acclivity to the chateau, where the old woman whom Jacques had described resided.

CHAP. XIX.

THEY passed through two or three courts, the gates of which were unfastened, to the entrance, when Jacques, after first peeping through two or three of the lower windows, rang the bell at the door. It was opened in a few minutes by an old neat-looking woman. She uttered a loud exclamation of joy on seeing Jacques, who leaped from the horse, and ran and embraced her with great affection. On seeing Adelaide, she seemed surprised, but assisted her to alight, and conducting her through a spacious hall to a parlour at the farther end, received her with a ready warmth of benevolence, which would have done honour to a person in a much higher station.

Adelaide, who felt the necessity of accounting for her appearance, acquainted her with such particulars of her history as might answer that purpose, and then inquired if she could be accommodated with lodgings in the chateau?

"Aye, that you may, Ma'amoiselle and welcome, replied the good old Genifrede, for that was the name of Jacques's grandmother; "there is a deal of room in the chateau which is of no use now but to make it look more lonesome and desolate; I will air a bed for you directly, Ma'amoiselle, and to-morrow you shall see the rooms. But you must want your supper, and we will look first to that;" and immediately she went out with as much expedition as she was capable of, and in a few minutes returned with the materials for an omelet, of which Adelaide, who was almost fainting for want of food, thankfully partook.

"I wish I had something better to offer you, Ma'amoiselle," said Genifrede; "but alack, living here, by myself—there was a time indeed, but that is all over," added she with a sigh, "and now I am old, and must not expect better days. But my poor dear," said she, "thou lookest tired—thou shalt have another faggot to warm and comfort thee, and by the time that is out, thou shalt go to rest in a good bed. I have kept all things tight and wholesome, but it is many a day, aye and many a night too, since this house had a guest."

Jacques, who had been absent in order to procure some provender for the horse, and serve him properly in the stable, now entered the room, and attacked the portion of the omelet reserved for him with an appetite pretty keen; nor did he hesitate at emptying the stoup of the *vin de pais*, which his careful grandmother had prepared for him.

Genifrede returned; and Adelaide, who felt the fatigue of so long a journey, performed with such haste, and with little or no intermission, requested to be shewn to her apartment.

She was conducted by Genifrede, who talked all the while about the rooms and the curiosities she would shew her the next day, to a large old chamber, furnished in the ancient style, and hung with tapestry. A fire had been previously lighted, and every thing prepared with so much attention to her comfort and convenience, that Adelaide felt as though she were already under the protection of friends highly interested in her welfare and happiness, and her heart seemed disburthened of half its load of wretchedness.

She took possession of her bed, which was adorned with drapery once extremely magnificent; but now in many places tattered, and much faded. The furniture consisted of several old-fashioned, high-backed, stuffed chairs, and low settees, covered, like the bed, with crimson damask, and decorated with fringe of gold, now tarnished by time, but which seemed once to have been extremely rich and splendid.

The chamber was lofty and spacious, and had the appearance of having been formerly one of the principal rooms of the chateau. It opened into a corridore, which extended through the whole wing of the building, and formed the entrance into a long suite of apartments, with folding doors, opening one into the other.

The fire diffused cheerfulness and warmth; but the size and dreariness of her apartment, the mournful sighings of the wind, and occasionally the shrill shrieking of the blast, as it howled through the gallery in which her chamber was situated, and sometimes shook a jarring door, excited sensations of melancholy, and even those of superstitious dread; for she thought of the castle of Ponteville; and while she shuddered at the recollection of the horrible apparition, which had more than once glanced before her eyes, she felt a dreadful persuasion that she had been conveyed there, as a punishment for her presumption, for having formerly dared to treat with irreligious levity what she then conceived to be nothing more than a mere idle superstition, but which she now no longer ventured to doubt, the doctrine of the appearance of spirits after death.

"Dreadful murders," said she, "have been committed probably in that castle, and the ghosts of the dead, for reasons we are not allowed to comprehend, are permitted to wander at night amid its awful solitudes. But here, surely here I have nothing to fear; this, too, cannot have been the scene of midnight assassinations, and crimes humanity shudders but to think of; within these walls, I may be safe from the horrible intrusions of the nightly phantom!"

The subject of her reflections was a dreadful one, and she strove to turn the current of her thoughts, by endeavoring to suggest to herself some plan of humble independence, to be pursued by her own industry and exertion. But before she could propose to herself anything likely to be productive of the intended purpose, it was necessary she should consult with Genifrede, by whose advice and assistance she would probably be enabled to put some such plan into execution.

These thoughts, for some time, fully engaged her mind, but fatigue soon overcame them; sleep was not long a stranger to her eyes; nor did she awake in the morning, till her good old hostess had entered with her breakfast: "which," says she, "my dear Ma'amoiselle, you shall take in bed; for I'm sure you have not had rest enough yet from the fatigues of yesterday's journey. And, when you have had another nap, you shall get up, Ma'amoiselle, and I will shew you the chateau."

Adelaide took a hasty repast, and soon afterwards arose, for the sun shone bright in her window; and after a little conversation with Genifrede, the good old creature set about the task of which she had scarcely ceased to talk since their arrival, of shewing the mansion committed to her care.

It consisted of two wings, approached by long corridores, communicating with a large hall in the centre, and leading to numerous suites of rooms, lofty and spacious, but antique. Those on the right were all furnished, though the furniture was faded and old. The rooms of the left wing were scanty of furniture, and mostly locked up, being entered only occasionally for the purpose of admitting the air and sun, to prevent the damp from injuring the floors and decaying the timbers. The whole exhibited proofs of ancient grandeur, and though impaired by time, and discoloured with the dews, bespoke the wealth and consequence of its former possessors.

Of these, the family of the Montrois, Adelaide obtained some account of Genifrede, who had spent the greater part of her life in their service.

"Aye, aye," said she, "it was a noble place once, Ma'amoiselle, but for want of being inhabited, is going fast to rack and ruin, and if something be not done to it soon, it will all be in a manner bare walls."

"It is a pity," said Adelaide; "but how happened it that the family left it?"

"Ah, well-a-day," answered Genifrede, "because they are all dead and gone! who would have thought I should have outlived 'em all? The young heir, too, that I used to dandle on my knee! It was a great grief, Ma'amoiselle, (weeping,) a great grief; but my years are many, and I cannot expect to live long, to see what more will happen."

She then proceeded to inform Adelaide of further particulars relative to the family of the Montrois, whose extinction she thus feelingly lamented. The late heir, it seemed, a young man not then of age, had died of a consumption, during a residence at Nice, whither he had been ordered for the recovery of his health. On his death, the chateau, with the estate adjoining, and some others in another province, had devolved to a collateral branch of the same family. The present heir, who had taken with the estates of that house the name of Montrois, although now in France, had not yet visited the place, but had sent some orders by his agent, who had been to inspect the premises, from which it appeared that he had some intention of repairing it.

Whoever he might be, he had excited in Genifrede a high opinion of his liberality; for he had desired that her stipend should be increased, and that she might have sufficient to provide her, not only with a bare subsistence, but to supply her with such comforts as her age and circumstances might require. "And God bless him for it!" said old Genifrede; "he is, I am sure, a sprig of the old stock; for they were all kind and charitable, and though I have never seen him, he deserves, I will say it, all he has got; and may he live long and enjoy it!"

"I hope he will," said Adelaide, "both for your sake and his own."

In the same suite with the chamber in which Adelaide slept, was a room with an oriel window, which commanded a beautiful view of the mountains, and of the distant waters of the Mediterranean. It contained furniture sufficient to render it completely comfortable, and this Genifrede proposed should be Adelaide's apartment. "It was my dear lady's morning sitting-room," said she, "and shall, if you please, be yours. I will see first, however, that it be well aired, and the dust rubbed off the furniture; and there you may sit, Ma'amoiselle, when you wish to be by yourself, though I fear you will find it very lonesome and solitary."

Adelaide admired this apartment, and Genifrede, eager to accommodate her with whatever the chateau afforded, opened a pair of folding doors, leading to a little library, which Adelaide perceived, with pleasure, contained several volumes of books, some of which were by the best French and Italian authors. These were indeed a treasure; and Adelaide gladly accepted Genifrede's offer of appropriating this apartment, which, for comfort and convenience, seemed superior to any she had yet seen.

CHAP. XX.

In the course of a few hours, Jannette, Jacques's sister, who had heard of his arrival, came to welcome him, and brought a present of fruit to Adelaide, who, receiving every instant fresh testimonies of the kindness and disinterested benevolence of her new friends, felt a degree of tranquillity she had been long unused to. With her story they were only partially acquainted. All they seemed to have understood was, that she had been unfortunate, and had fled from persecution, but of what kind they were left to imagine. During her continuance at Madame St. Clair's, Adelaide, as it will be remembered, had changed her name, and taken that of St. Clair. It is now necessary that she should assume another, as by that of St. Clair she might be known and traced to her present place of concealment, should De Launé, as was but too probable, attempt to pursue her. She therefore resolved to take that of D'Ainville, the name of the family of Madame St. Angouléme, her supposed mother. She imparted this resolution to Jacques, who had orders to introduce and speak of her as Mademoiselle D'Ainville, and preserve the strict silence he had hitherto maintained, relative to her real circumstances and connexions.

Every possible attention was paid to Adelaide by the faithful Genifrede; and nothing was omitted which could contribute, however slightly, to her comfort and satisfaction. Her repasts were simple, but they were wholesome and neatly prepared, and presented with a welcome so hearty and sincere, as would have rendered even the coarsest meal delightful.

The apartments allotted her were made clean and comfortable, and the furniture so arranged as to be conducive to every purpose of convenience. "In that set of drawers, Ma'amoiselle," said Genifrede, pointing to a large old cabinet with an escrutoire, in the corner of her chamber, "you may lay your clothes. But where are they, Ma'amoiselle? for now I think of it, I saw no bundle. But here are some of my poor lady's things, which she left behind her, dear soul, when she went abroad, little thinking she should come back no more, and they will fit you, Ma'amoiselle, to a tittle, for she was tall, like you, and had just such a sweet shape. 'What,' says I to the steward, 'must be done with my lady's clothes?' 'I don't know, Genifrede,' answered he; 'you may keep 'em, or sell 'em, for my master won't inquire about 'em.' 'I'll never sell 'em,' says I, 'for that won't be shewing respect to my lady; and as to wearing 'em, how I should look in those rich suits of silk and velvet, and those fine gold and silver trimmings, that my lady used to wear at court!' So you see, Ma'amoiselle, you may use 'em while you are here."

With this she opened the drawers of the cabinet, and drew from thence two full-dress suits, one of rich brocade, the other of dark green velvet, ornamented in the manner she had described, with three or four undress suits of plain silk, several changes of linen, and some other articles of dress, which, she said, had laid there ever since her lady had left the chateau, which was now more than ten years ago.

"Take what you please, Ma'amoiselle," said she, "and wear 'em, for they belong to nobody, now my poor dear lady's dead and gone, and I am sure you are hardly welcome: and so she would say herself, God bless her, if she was here and saw you wanted 'em."

There was a degree of generosity in this offer from the humble

Genifrede, and in her refusal to dispose of the clothes, because they had been the property of her beloved mistress, a refinement of attachment, if we may be allowed the expression, seldom to be met with even among persons of the most elevated stations, which particularly endeared her to Adelaide; and though at first, from motives of delicacy, she objected to accept or wear any part of the clothes, yet the urgent pressure of the occasion, and the repeated earnest solicitations of the good old motherly Genifrede, overcame her reluctance; and she consented to select such articles as might be useful and necessary to her present convenience.

Amongst other things, was a box of crayons and a *port feuille* containing several sketches of landscapes, and some highly-finished drawings, which were executed, she was told, by Madame Montroi, and proved that she possessed a correct judgment, and a highly-cultivated taste.

CHAP. XXI.

Employed in necessary arrangements, supported by hope, and soothed by the kindness of those around her, Adelaide almost ceased to recollect, that, notwithstanding every precaution used by Jacques, it was yet possible they might be pursued, and their asylum discovered, by her father and Perouse, who would, doubtless, employ every means they could devise to acquaint themselves with the place of her retreat. The next day, however, and the next elapsed, and nothing transpired to authorize the apprehension that the pursuit, if they had pursued them, was successful.

When Jannette again appeared, which she did on the evening of the second day after their arrival, Adelaide was struck with the resemblance she bore to someone whom she had seen, though she could not instantly recall the person to her recollection. "Have you any more grand-daughters?" said she to Genifrede, who was present when she had made the remark. "Yes; I have one more, Ma'amoiselle," rejoined Genifrede, "but she has got a service in

Gascony, in the Conserance; and we have not seen her of a long time. She has a rare place on't, I warrant, and fine wages; for her lady, the Countess St. Angouléme, is a noble lady, and——"

"The Countess St. Angouléme!" interrupted Adelaide; "is Bertha, the Countess's chief woman, your grand-daughter, and the sister of Jacques?"

"Aye, marry, that is she," resumed Genifrede; "do you know her, Ma'amoiselle?"

"Yes; and do you ever hear from her?" eagerly asked Adelaide; "for she hoped to learn something relative to her beloved friend."

"Seldom, Ma'amoiselle," cried Genifrede, "very seldom; and now, not for a long time; for it is a great way, and cross roads, and very mountainous. Though I says to Jacques, says I, yesterday, 'Jacques, what if, now you have taken to travelling, you would to make another tour to see poor Bertha? I warrant the steed you have got would carry you as far. For,' says I, 'while you're here, though you may pick up a little matter of work in the vineyards, yet as you're out of place now, and when you get into service again, mayn't be at liberty in a hurry—"

"And oh! will he go?—will he go?" interrupted Adelaide.

"He said, Ma'amoiselle, he'd been thinking a little about it himself; and if so be that you had no objection, and would agree that he might have the horse."

"The horse! oh yes, let him go! let him take the horse. Where is he? cannot I speak to Jacques?"

"He is somewhere about, Ma'amoiselle," said Genifrede; and she went in search of him.

As soon as she was gone, Adelaide, to whom the idea of Jacques's visiting the Castle of St. Angouléme opened an unexpected source of joy and comfort, since, as the brother of Bertha, he might easily gain admission to her lady, resolved to send the Countess a little narrative of her misfortunes, taking care, however, in her recital, not to criminate the Count, though she resolved, at the same time, to enjoin secresy as to the particulars she meant to unfold, since, should the Count be informed, or even suspect, that she had written to his lady, and her present place of asylum be known, the most unhappy consequences might ensue; for with all the native candour of her disposition, it was impossible for Adelaide not to believe, that the Count was an auxiliary in the horrid scheme which had been devised for her ruin, though yet there were times when she was almost inclined to doubt it.

Her next resolve was to dispose of the ring given her by her father, as it would afford a sufficient supply for her present necessities, and serve to defray the expences of Jacques's journey into Gascony. As it was necessary, before he could set out, that the ring should be sold, she consulted with Jacques (who readily undertook to go on the intended mission to the Castle of St. Angouléme), about the manner of disposing of it; and it was agreed that Jacques should, on the following day, visit Arles, and gain directions to some jeweller who might be likely to purchase it.

Jacques set off on his errand with glee, at the thoughts of the expences of his journey being thus borne; and he used such speed, that he returned in the evening, much sooner than was expected.

"Well, Jacques," said Adelaide, who went out into the court to meet him, "what have you done? have you succeeded? have you sold the ring?"

"Why no, Ma'amoiselle, not sold it," said Jacques, "not to say sold it."

"Not sold it!" interrupted Adelaide; "what then, my good fellow, have you done with it?"

Jacques gave a long and circumstantial account of his journey; the substance of which was, that on arriving at Arles, he had inquired, and been recommended to a jeweller of the greatest respectability; but the master of the shop, for whom he asked, was unluckily from home; and the person he saw, after examining it for some time, said he could not buy it till he had shewn it to M. Barreux, who would not be at home for several days. On Jacques's refusing to leave the ring, he offered to lend him a little money upon it; and after asking a number of questions, which Jacques at first refused to answer, laid down five marks, with a promise that the ring should be valued, and the estimate paid on the return of M. Barreux, who he dared say, he said, would be glad to purchase it.

"But I could not even get him to give me the five marks," resumed Jacques, "though he said it was not a quarter of the value, till I told him your name, and where you lived. When I said you were at the chateau de Montroi, he said, if you could wait about a month, or so, they should have some goods to send that road, and that you should hear from them; and then he gave me a card with an account of things sold in his shop, which he desired me to deliver with Monsieur Barreux's dutiful respects to Ma'amoiselle D'Ainville, who he supposed, by her living at the chateau, was a relation of the family of the Montrois, and might want something. I wondered, if he believed this, that he should think you would sell the ring; but I thought it was as well he should suppose so, and I did not undeceive him."

"You have done your business as well as you could, Jacques," said Adelaide, "and I am much obliged to you. The money you have brought will be sufficient for our present use; and when you return, and we have expended what the ring may produce, we will sell the horse, for which we shall then have no further occasion."

"True, Ma'amoiselle, and so we may, and I shall easily enough get a chap for that. It would have done your heart good, could you have seen how he was admired yesterday at Arles. Where did you get that horse? says one; a fine horse that is of yours, says another, if it is yours; and then they looked at me and my nag, wondering, I reckon, how I came by it, as well they might; and then they *axed* me questions about it, but I nodded, and said nothing. A nod, they say, is as good as a wink to a blind horse."

The next day was appointed for Jacques to set out on his journey into Gascony. Adelaide having written to the Countess, gave the letter to his hands, with orders that he should deliver it to his sister as soon as he arrived, and that he should give it to her with the utmost secresy, so that nobody but Bertha might know of it. He was cautioned against mentioning her name before any part of the family, except Bertha; and she desired him not to travel after twilight in the evening, lest he should meet with some of the gang of the banditti.

Jacques promised a punctual observance of these directions; and Adelaide having given him money to defray the expence of his journey, bearing with him many presents and good wishes to his sister Bertha, from Genifrede and Jannette, he departed for Gascony.

CHAP. XXII.

Adelaide, who was now assured that if her father had attempted a pursuit, he had certainly mistaken their route, ventured to ramble from the chateau. She had visited the cottage of Jannette, which exhibited a blooming family of boys and girls, healthy indeed, but not very well clad, who crowded about her, and being told she was the lady at the chateau, with an emulation natural to their age, seemed to contend for her notice; and the ready smile, and glowing kiss, repaid their little efforts to please.

But her chief amusement was to indulge her usual propensity of rambling, to view the fine scenery of the adjacent country, seldom with any other companion than a book; and indeed the good-humoured civility of the peasantry, to many of whom she was known, seemed to render no other companion necessary. She was soon acquainted with all the wild walks of the neighbouring mountains; and sometimes indulged herself with traversing alone their unfrequented paths, meeting only, now and then, a peasant from the village, or a shepherd with his dog, driving the sheep from the valleys, to graze on the fine herbage of the upper downs.

Sometimes, in these quiet excursions, she would seat herself upon a cliff, and meditate on such fancies as past occurrences, or present objects, might suggest; and often would the image of the stranger she had seen at Auboigne arise in her mind, when tears would start to her eyes, and she would exclaim, "Oh, could I know that he yet lives!"

At the chateau, she usually employed herself in reading and drawing, or in assisting Genifrede in airing and putting in order the apartments. This was an employment of which Adelaide was very fond. She loved to converse with this good-hearted creature, to listen to narrative old age, and learn the histories of times and persons now no more.

Often would she accompany her through the gallery where hung the portraits of the family; and visit the chapel, where their remains were deposited. In one place, she beheld the blooming knight, and beauteous damsel, as represented by the pencil, in the glow of youth and health; and in the other the same features, delineated by the statuary, wrought on the monumental marble, fixed and stiffened in death. There, too, the sculptured saints and crucifixes, at which the knee of devotion had so often bowed; the banner above, in memory of former victories and former valour; the rich escutcheon, the last appendage of expiring pomp; the painted arch, or crowned with ivy, obtruding through the shattered window into the holy edifice, where the bat, forsaking the glare of day, flitted briskly up and down, what time the evening cast its sombrous shade, with sublime solemnity over the lonely mansions of the dead.

Indulging the pensive enthusiasm of her character, she would muse on the melancholy scene, and experience a mournful kind of pleasure in reflecting upon the instability of every human state. "A few years," said she, "a very few years, and I shall be like one of these, over whose unconscious remains I am now treading. But what may be, ere then, alas! I know not! May I in every state adhere to my duty, and submit patiently to the decrees of him who judges rightly, and being infinite in wisdom as in power, cannot err! may his law be my guide, and then may I trust, and not trust in vain, that his mercy shall be my protection, even through the most mazy and difficult course of life!"

The same contemplative turn of mind, and that high sense of religion, which a variety of circumstances had excited in her heart, rendered her peculiarly susceptible of whatever was sublime or beautiful in nature, and led her to admire and love the author of nature. Seated in the oriel window of her apartment, she would mark with earnest observation the almost boundless diversity of objects and the prospects before her. Often did she arise to behold the sun emerging from the bosom of the ocean, dispersing the wreathing mists that hung upon the mountain tops, and as often, in rapturous enthusiasm, saw it sink beneath the blue and distant waves, to rise and enlighten another hemisphere. How beautiful, to behold the rocks tinted with its parting beams, assuming every variety of hue, then fading and softly blending into the uniform gloom of night! Often did she attempt to sketch the scene, and combined tints to express their wonderful and sweet varieties; and as often resigned her pencil in despair: "for who can paint like nature?"

CHAP. XXIII.

One day, while Adelaide was engaged in endeavouring to sketch the contour of a mountain group, whose sublime and shapeless heights were just emerging from the cloud of mysterious vapour that hung over them, her attention was recalled from the sublimity of the object of her regard, by the sudden entrance of Genifrede, whose looks announced hasty intelligence. Adelaide trembled as she approached, and seated herself, for she thought of her father; the pencil fell from her hand, and she falteringly demanded whether any one had been at the chateau, or if she had heard anything in the village?

"Oh, Ma'amoiselle, the strangest thing—the strangest thing has happened! and yet not very strange neither; but I am old, and a little thing puts me into a flusker. Been! yes, somebody has been, sure enough. Alack, alack, who would have thought of his coming here!"

"Has any person been inquiring for me?" resumed Adelaide; "if so, oh, let me hide myself," grasping Genifrede's arm. "Do not, do not say I am here."

"Inquiring for you, Ma'amoiselle! la, bless you, not a soul! who should know anything about you? and as to your hiding yourself, I'm sure there can be no occasion for that, for he's one of the kindest souls alive! and speaks so prettily about you, Ma'amoiselle, for I told him you was here."

"About me!" echoed Adelaide, in amazement, "about me! for Heaven's sake, tell me who you are talking about. If it is known I am here, I am undone for ever!"

"La, Ma'amoiselle, why do you put yourself into such a pucker?" cried Genifrede. "Undone! I'm sure he wouldn't hurt a hair of your head!"

"I beseech you," said Adelaide, "be explicit. Torture me not with this suspense! who is it you have seen?"

"I will tell you, Ma'amoiselle, if you will but give me time," said Genifrede; "but la, how pale you look! shall I fetch you a little water?"

"Oh no, no, only tell me."

"I wish Monsieur Montroi was here," said Genifrede, "for I'm sure the very sight of him would do you good. Oh, such a shape, and such a leg! I am old; but for my own part, never did I see a *properer* man! as much like my young master too as he can stare!"

"Monsieur Montroi!" repeated Adelaide, who now comprehended the purport of Genifrede's information; "has Monsieur Montroi been at the chateau?"

"La! have I not told you this yet? *Been!* aye; and he's a gentleman every inch of him, and speaks as free and as pretty to me, as though I were my lady, forsooth!"

"But did you tell him I was here?" asked Adelaide; "and will he not think it strangely impertinent in me, who am entirely unknown to him, thus intruding myself beneath his roof? did you expect him, Genifrede? for such intelligence would have greatly perplexed me."

"Expect him!" continued Genifrede, "no, no more than I expected the man would come out of the moon! But come he is, that's sure, and what's more, means to stay here some days. And it was upon the upshot of this that I told him you, Ma'amoiselle, was here; and how it happened that you came, as far as I knew, and such like; for says I, if he goes prowling about the chateau, and pops upon Ma'amoiselle, not knowing she's here, it will throw 'em both into a *quandary*, as she's not a common body; so after I'd talked to him awhile, I out with it; and so prettily he spoke, hoping you would make what use you pleased of the rooms, and said he was very glad to have it in his power to accommodate you; and desired you would count the chateau as your home, as long as you wished to stay in it. 'Why as to that,' says I, 'Ma'amoiselle won't be at all in your honour's way, for she's for the most part in a room by herself, reading or drawing pictures, or else goes wandering amongst the mountains, and is no trouble at all to anybody. When I told him who you was, he said he thought he had heard that name; and then he asked me where you came from. But this I could not tell him; upon which he looked, I thought, a little surprised, but said no more."

"And he is coming to stay at the chateau?" said Adelaide.

"Yes: and is to have a bed made up in the suite next yours; and the steward another. Guillaume (Jannette's husband) is gone to the market-town for provisions; and Jannette will be here to light the fires, and do a few little matters for me in the evening. Alack-a-day, that he should come in this manner, and throw us all into heaps!"

"And he is to be here to-night?" said Adelaide.

"Yes, to-night. 'I am come very unexpectedly,' said he; these were his words, 'but I want nothing that may not easily be procured.' La bless him! Said he then, 'I am a soldier, Genifrede, and have been used to hard fare, and do not, therefore, need delicacies;' and so then he went out, saying he should be back in the evening, when his servant would be with him, who would help him to get ready his rooms."

Adelaide desired Genifrede would convey a message from herself to Monsieur Montroi, to thank him for his polite offers of accommodation, which gave her the highest opinion of his benevolence; but desired that Genifrede would not, except on this occasion, even mention her name; and should he propose to visit the suite of rooms of which hers were part, she would take an opportunity to inform her, that she might avoid seeing him.

Genifrede, who saw not the propriety of this request, would have persuaded her to alter the resolution she had made of remaining secluded in her own apartments till Monsieur Montroi should have left the chateau, but she continued steady in her determination; and Genifrede promised to give her early intelligence, should he intend to visit the rooms.

The arrival of Montroi, who returned according to his engagement in the evening, deprived Adelaide of the liberty she had hitherto enjoyed. During this her confinement, she received frequent visits from Genifrede, who, delighted with her new master, was always eloquent in his praise. His generosity—his manly beauty—and the amiableness of his behaviour, had won her warmest affections; and she seemed never so happy as when speaking of him.

The next day Adelaide was informed that Monsieur Montroi and his steward meant to survey the apartments of the chateau, for the purpose of ascertaining what repairs might be wanting. "I promised to tell you, Ma'amoiselle," said Genifrede; "but la, if you were once to see him!"

"That is what I, of all things, wish to avoid," said Adelaide, pensively; "for how could I see him without accounting for my situation? and to account for it, under my present unhappy circumstances, is impossible."

"Well, Ma'amoiselle, if you will have it so, I will tell you when they are coming; but they are to see the other parts of the building first, and I'm to go with them to carry the keys; and this, with riding about the grounds to look over the estate, will take them the best part of the morning."

"You think, then, they will not be here at present?" resumed Adelaide.

"No, not of several hours; so walk about, Ma'amoiselle, or amuse yourself as you can; they won't see you, and I'll pop up, and tell you when I know they are coming."

It was not till the evening that Genifrede appeared. "They will be here directly, Ma'amoiselle," said she, "and if you would not be seen, you must go round by the library through the gallery, and down the back stairs, leading to the servants' hall; I will meet you there, and let you out a little door at the end of the passage."

Adelaide hastened to obey these directions, and Genifrede retired.

END OF VOL. II.

PYRENEAN BANDITTI.

A ROMANCE

IN THREE VOLUMES.

BY

ELEANOR SLEATH,

AUTHOR OF

THE NOCTURNAL MINSTREL, BRISTOL HEIRESS, WHO'S THE MURDERER, &c., &c.

Know'st thou not,
That when the searching eye of Heav'n is hid
Behind the globe, and lights the lower world,
Then thieves and robbers range abroad unseen,
In murders and in outrage bloody here?
But when from under this terrestrial ball
He fires the proud tops of the eastern pines,
And darts his light through ev'ry guilty hole;
Then murders, treasons, and detested sins,
The cloak of night being pluck'd from off their backs,
Stand bare and naked, trembling at themselves!

SHAKESPEARE.

VOL. III.

LONDON:
PRINTED AT THE
Minerva-Press,
FOR A. K. NEWMAN AND CO.
(Successors to Lane, Newman, and Co.)
LEADENHALL-STREET.
1811.

CHAP. I.

Adelaide proceeded, as directed, to the servants' hall, where she was met by Genifrede, who conducting her through a narrow stone passage, opened a little door at the farther end, which admitted her, through an avenue of lofty trees, to a lonely little shrubbery she had before visited; for it led to her favourite walk along the mountains. Here she sauntered safe from interruption, hearing only now and then the notes of a distant flute, which the breeze wafted sweetly to her ear, or the low tinkling of the sheep bell, till the sun had left the scene, when she hastened back toward the chateau.

Ere she had arrived at the avenue, she came to a shady path she had never before observed: and curious to know whither it led, she advanced hastily beneath the branches of overhanging trees, till she arrived at a gloomy little glade in front of the door of the chapel, which stood nearly open. The deep solitude of the place, encreased by the twilight of the evening hour, was in unison with her feelings, and she entered it.

Wrapt in mournful contemplation, she gazed with awe on the shrines and images that adorned its altar, now forsaken and despoiled; the cross, the stones, "which holy knees had worn,"* the monuments, the tombs, with figures piously recumbent, now mouldering into ruins, and discoloured with the damps. While she gazed, she reflected on her own melancholy condition, remote, unfriended, solitary, at an age too when she needed the advice and protection of kind relations; the impression was deeply affecting, and tears streamed fast from her eyes—"To you, whose remains are here deposited," said she with a sigh, "the call of death was perhaps an unwelcome summons; for you had friends to love and to protect you. The crimes of a father never tinged your cheek with the blush of shame; you were not compelled, like me, to seek an asylum amongst strangers, and depend upon them for that support and succour which those bound by the ties of blood ought to have afforded."

Thus, at the shrine of devotion at which she bowed, did Adelaide, yielding unrestrainedly to the effusions of a too poignant sensibility, breathe the language of discontent, a language which subsequent reflection, and her own native good sense, soon severely reproved; for, in thus repining, she felt she had been guilty of an act of ingratitude toward that Being who had so providentially preserved her from the worst of all evils: and when she compared her present lot with her past danger, what she was with what she might have been, the misfortunes of which she complained appeared to sink nothing in the scale of comparison; despair, or even discontent, seemed to be injustice; and she regretted that she had ever once harboured a thought of their suggestion. The idea of Jacques's return, and the hope of soon hearing from her beloved friend the Countess, was a balm to her heart—"I will still," said she, "trust in him to whom I owe my preservation; I will think I may not always be unhappy." She stopped; for she thought she distinguished the sound of a step of some person near, advancing up the chapel; and turning her head, she could with difficulty suppress the scream about to issue involuntarily from her lips, when she beheld, or thought she beheld, for the lateness of the hour, and encreasing gloom of the place, did not allow her to be certain, the young chevalier she had met at Auboigne. His voice, as he pronounced the name of St. Clair, which was that by which she had formerly been known to him, that voice, the accents of which were indelibly impressed upon her memory, convinced her she was not mistaken. The blood faded from her cheek, as he addressed her by a name she had now relinquished: and she stood trembling and abashed.

Montroi, for it was Montroi that stood before her, viewed her with looks of mingled joy and astonishment; for he knew not that, in Mademoiselle D'Ainville (the young lady of whom Genifrede had spoken), he should behold the object of his former curiosity, of his admiration, of his enthusiasm, of his love; if he could have allowed himself to have indulged a sentiment so tender and impassioned for one situated like Adelaide, surrounded, as she was, with mystery, and in whose story, as far as he could inform himself of it, there were circumstances so suspicious as to justify almost any unfavourable opinion he might form. The admiration he felt for Adelaide had induced him to make the inquiries which had so much alarmed her; and the result of these inquiries had determined him to overcome those feelings by which they had been prompted, and forget, if possible, a beautiful young creature, who, from her connexions, and probably her habits, must be unworthy of his regard.

From his conversations with Jacques, he had gathered nothing satisfactory: but, on the night previous to his quitting Auboigne, was informed by his servant, who had obtained intelligence of the hostess of the auberge, that Adelaide had arrived at the inn, seemingly after a long journey, in the middle of the night, wrapped up in a horseman's coat, and with a hat flapped over her face, evidently for the purpose of concealment, in company with a man of a very suspicious appearance, and believed to belong to the banditti of the mountains; that both Adelaide and her companion lived with a person of the name of St. Clair, a woman who had just come from Paris, and was known to have led an irregular and even vicious course of life; and this left no reason to doubt that the young lady had eloped with the fellow, to whom, however, though she had surrendered herself, she certainly was not married.

Thus did the hostess, without knowing scarcely any thing of our heroine, patch up a complete history of her, and sullied her with the darkest shades of obloquy; and thus Adelaide, though beautiful as the Grecian Hebe, graceful as the airy sylph, correct in principle, refined in sentiment, and in mind so pure as to shrink with delicate apprehension from even the shadow of wrong, was transformed by the venomed breath of slander, from the most innocent and lovely, to one of the most depraved and worthless of human beings.

The surprise and agitation experienced by Montroi, at a *rencontre* so unexpected and extraordinary, produced in him an embarrassment not less apparent than was that of Adelaide: he addressed her, and it was with more warmth and tenderness in his look and manner than he had ventured to express at any former interview—"To what happy accident," said he, "am I indebted for the pleasure of a renewal of so interesting an acquaintance? for, when my good old Genifrede informed me that she had afforded an asylum to a lady of the name of D'Ainville, she did not in any way hint, that the fair Adelaide St. Clair had become one of her inmates also."

"Circumstances of a very extraordinary nature, Sir," said Adelaide, with a look indicating a sensation of distress, "have obliged me to assume a name to which I have no legal claim; and Genifrede knows me only by that of D'Ainville."

"Your name then, Madam," resumed Montroi, "is, I presume, St. Clair?"

Adelaide hesitated, and at length answered in the negative.

"Neither D'Ainville nor St. Clair!" exclaimed Montroi, much astonished. He paused, still looking at her, in the expectation that she would mention her real name; but she was silent, and confused.

By this time they had reached the door of the chapel, toward which Adelaide had been moving during this conversation. They passed out in silence, occasioned by a mutual perplexity, and an almost equal embarrassment: and Adelaide was preparing to take her leave, when the chevalier proceeded—"It is late for you to ramble abroad, thus unattended; permit me to conduct you to the chateau." As he spoke, he took her hand, which he pressed tenderly; and drawing it within his arm, while she gently strove to disengage it, said—"Nay, you must, you shall allow me to attend you home;" and then, scarcely knowing what he uttered, he began to expatiate on the honour, the joy, the happiness he felt on seeing her again—"Little did I expect," said he, "when I came hither, to find, in my chateau, so lovely an inhabitant as Mademoiselle——" He stopped, not knowing what name to annex.

"And in the stranger I had the honour of meeting at Auboigne," said Adelaide, "I as little expected to find the owner of this mansion, and the person to whom I am thus signally obliged."

"Is it then to accident, to chance only, that I owe my present happiness?" continued Montroi significantly.

"Yes, Sir; a combination of strange unhappy events," cried Adelaide, endeavouring to recollect her scattered thoughts, "has rendered me unexpectedly and unavoidably dependent upon the protection of strangers, of whose benevolence, I thank Heaven, I have already had repeated proofs, and in whose honour I may, I trust, fearlessly confide." She pronounced these last words with more energy than she had before expressed; but, ere she had finished, her voice faltered; and as Montroi gazed earnestly in her face, he saw her eyes were filled with tears.

"I will not allow you to call them unfortunate," said he, "since they have been the cause of such exquisite, such unlooked-for felicity."

"To me, Sir," cried Adelaide, interrupting him, "they have been most unfortunate; and but for the protection your house affords me——"

"Ill should I deserve the noble confidence you repose in me," exclaimed Montroi, with warmth and earnestness, "nay, I should be unfit to live, were I to refuse you that protection you, Madam, have a right to claim; think, nay, believe me to be your friend."

Again he pressed her hand, again fixed his eyes upon her now pale but lovely face, with a look so expressive and full of generous feeling, as awakened all the tenderness of her soul, all the gratitude of her overflowing heart: she wept, but could not speak. In an instant all he had heard to her prejudice was forgotten, or, if remembered, remembered only with the contempt it really merited; and Adelaide, as she seemed the most beautiful, so also did she appear, to the eye of the delighted, the almost adoring Montroi, the most interesting and amiable of human beings.

She was come, how and why he knew not, but she *was* come, to claim his protection as a man, his compassion as a suffering, if not an injured fellow-creature. She was deprived, it appeared, of friends, or why else had she flown to ask protection of strangers? of a home, or wherefore sought she an asylum?—To a heart like that of Montroi, the single circumstance of having been unfortunate was a sufficient recommendation to its favour; and when, added to this, he beheld so much beauty, such sweetness and apparent refinement, the claim became altogether irresistible; and he resolved, by a behaviour the most respectful, to encourage her to repose in him sufficient confidence to communicate to him all her griefs, and explain her story, which had so much surprised, and still greatly perplexed him. Every word, every look, encreased his persuasion of her innocence and integrity.

On their arrival at the chateau, he respectfully took his leave of her for the night; for whatever pleasure he might experience from her presence and conversation, and however desirous he was of learning her history, he feared to offend her delicacy by the least semblance of boldness; and he knew it would be unworthy of a man of honour, to avail himself of any advantage which the circumstances of her situation might seem to offer.

CHAP. II.

Adelaide, upon parting with Montroi, repaired to her apartment, where, when alone, she reflected with astonishment upon the singular adventure of her having met, in the person of Montroi, the chevalier she had seen at Auboigne. The first emotion his appearance had inspired, was that of joy for his safety; the succeeding one, an undeserved, yet keen sense of shame at being obliged to become known to him by two names, neither of which was her true one. She derived, however, some degree of satisfaction from the confession, that she had no legal claim to either: but still this had only changed the nature of her own embarrassment; for, while the declaration naturally led him to expect to hear her real name, necessity still compelled her to conceal not only that by which she had formerly been known, but that to which, as the daughter of

De Launé, she was now entitled. The distress she felt from this occasion, was encreased by the recollection that, as she was now circumstanced, it would be improper, because highly dangerous to her father, to make any disclosure to Monsieur Montroi of the real incidents of her story; and this determined her to remain very close in her apartments, and to avoid, as much as possible, all conversation with him.

Such was her resolve; but Montroi, to whom every hour seemed an age, till he could again behold and converse with his lovely and interesting visitor, and who had waited with extreme impatience, watching every avenue from the chateau, in the hopes of seeing her, sent a message at length by Genifrede, soliciting permission to pay her his respects. Adelaide felt uneasy at the request, yet she knew not how to refuse it; and she sent an answer, that she should be happy to see him; but desired that Genifrede would continue with her, in whose presence she hoped Montroi would make no particular inquiries, and that their conversation would necessarily be general.

Genifrede almost instantly returned; and Montroi soon afterwards entered the room. Reassured by the continuance of Genifrede, Adelaide received him with less embarrassment than she had ever before felt in his presence: his manners were even more engaging and fascinating than at any former interview; and every sentiment he expressed was so entirely her own, every remark he made so exactly what she would herself have uttered, that she was astonished at the congeniality of their tastes and feelings.

In the course of their conversation, he spoke of the evening when he had last seen her at Auboigne: he informed her that, in pursuance of his engagement, he had, the next day, set off to accompany his Colonel, the Marquis de Ponteville, in his route through Gascony; and that, in the evening, on the borders of a wood, the party had been attacked by a troop of banditti, who overpowering them with their numbers, had left two of the Marquis's servants dead upon the spot; the Marquis himself having narrowly escaped with life, being dangerously, but not mortally wounded.

It was with the utmost difficulty that Adelaide could command her feelings during this recital: she feared to look up, or speak, lest her countenance, or the tremulous tone of her voice, might betray the painful interest she took in it; for that her father and Perouse were among the banditti he had described, the intelligence she had obtained from Jacques did not suffer her to doubt.

"It is unnecessary," resumed Montroi, "to add, I escaped unhurt. Would to God the rest of them had been as fortunate!"

"It would have been a most happy circumstance," said Adelaide falteringly, and with an abstracted air, while her eyes were bent downward, and fixed, with a seeming earnestness, upon some object she was unconscious of regarding.

"The Marquis is however determined to pursue the most active measures for the detection of the leaders of this ferocious and lawless gang," resumed Montroi; "detached parties are already employed to explore thoroughly that part of the country; and, should their place of rendezvous be discovered, I am persuaded they cannot escape the arm of justice.

At these words, Adelaide became more and more agitated; for she thought of her father; and her terrified imagination already suggested him in the hands of the *marechaussée*, and about to atone for his offences, by a painful and ignominious death.

Montroi observed her agitation, with surprise and wonder; but unwilling to distress her, by seeming to perceive it, or by continuing the subject, immediately turned the conversation. His visit lasted about an hour, during which Genifrede remained in the room; and he therefore forbore to make any reference to what had passed on the preceding night, a subject which Adelaide dreaded of course, and anxiously wished by all means to avoid.

CHAP. III.

Could any thing have afforded consolation to the unhappy Adelaide, whilst under the influence of these apprehensions for the fate of the wretched De Launé, it would have been the society of Montroi, could she have enjoyed it without the restraints which delicacy imposed, and by a candid of her reasons for adopting such a mysterious line of conduct, gain his friendship and esteem—"Oh could I tell him," exclaimed she, "could I tell him my sad eventful history! how would his generous breast have glowed with tender commiseration for the sufferings which have driven me to seek a refuge beneath his roof! Yes, he would pity, he would not condemn. But amongst the gentlest feelings of compassion, would he not reject with disdain the daughter of——Oh, let me not speak of him, let me not name him, whom I must ever blush to call my father—a companion of banditti, a robber, and a murderer! No, buried for ever in my heart, shall remain the sad secret of my disgraceful birth. Fear not, unworthy parent, if I must call you so, your Adelaide will not betray you; she will mourn and weep for the crimes you hourly commit, and of which your hardened unrelenting nature yet suffers you not to think with remorse; she will pray that, ere punishment overtake you, repentance may have worked its way to your heart, and so have changed your nature; that, ere the mandate of death arrives, your pardon may be sealed in Heaven, that Heaven whom you daringly thus offend, while you violate the order of society, and the peace and welfare of mankind."

While her heart was thus torn by the most painful sensations and apprehensions on account of her father, it had others not less distressing, arising from the reflection of the agitation she had shewn while Montroi was speaking of the banditti of the mountains. She could not doubt but he had observed the emotions she had endeavoured to conceal; and how, should he desire another interview, or should accident again throw him in her way, was she to evade an explicit account of the circumstances under which she had entered her present abode? Would he not think that fear alone prevented her from entering upon the explanation necessary to convince him he was not harbouring a person undeserving of his protection? and what but guilt (for such must be his conclusion) could hinder the communication he sought?

Montroi, as we have before observed, had certainly imbibed some suspicions respecting his guest, from the intelligence of the hostess of the *auberge* at Auboigne, who, like most other women of her description and rank in life, had a particular *penchant* for the marvellous; and was not less disposed than others of her profession, to cast an eye of scrutinizing inquiry upon the travellers who occasionally stopped at her house: the incident of Adelaide's arrival with Perouse was remarkable, and she failed not to make upon it such comments as the singularity of it would admit of. But whatever attention might have been paid by Montroi to the representations made in consequence of it, he was soon charmed into a state of disbelief, or rather of forgetfulness, by the impressions produced during his conversation with Adelaide in the chapel of the chateau: at this meeting, as it may be remembered, his manners were more tender and impassioned than at his former interview with her at Auboigne. Joy, on thus beholding one whom he hardly dared to think he ought ever to hope to see again, but whose beautiful image still haunted and troubled his repose, was perhaps the predominating emotion of his heart, as his eyes again met those of Adelaide de Launé; joy, accompanied by an admiration not less ardent than when he had before viewed her, but unmingled with that chaste esteem which he was nevertheless desirous to indulge for her, gave a sort of wild hilarity to his air and manners, very different from their usual character. He had taken her hand, that hand, than which no alabaster could be whiter: it trembled as he held it; yet he grasped it still. The tremor encreased. As he felt it tremble, his heart smote him: he had caused alarm, he had addressed, with the warmth of a lover, instead of the respectful freedom of a friend, a fair young creature, whom, he felt, at that moment he could have defended from any similar rudeness, at the risk even of life.

As they quitted the deep covert of the trees around the chapel, he had been enabled to observe the expression of a countenance, at all times too full of meaning to be misunderstood: he gazed, and saw "a thousand blushing apparitions,"* which seemed to refute accusations, and confirm her innocence and truth—"She may be mysterious," said he, as he mused on these particulars, but she is not guilty even of unintentional error. She has been slandered, cruelly slandered; but her heart, if the countenance is a true index, is as pure as heaven itself. She is—she must be innocent!"

The unaffected delicacy of her manners, the justness of her sentiments, and the graces of her conversation, when the embarrassment produced by his first entrance, on his next interview with her, had subsided, were considered by him as further testimonies of her worth and goodness, as also of the respectability of her birth and connexions: he perceived she was not only easy and elegant in her general deportment, but that her mind was highly cultivated and accomplished; her birth, therefore, could not, he thought, be mean. How strange then, that she should be left thus destitute and unprotected!

The curiosity he had before felt was now encreased to a degree almost painful, and he resolved to spare no efforts of the most obliging respect and attention, to induce her to repose in him the confidence so necessary to his happiness; for, with Montroi, the idea of happiness and Adelaide were already so united, as to have become inseparable in his imagination. To him, the accidental advantages of rank and fortune appeared as considerations wholly unworthy of his regard; and so tender and warm was the admiration he now felt for her, that he waited only till he should have obtained a satisfactory explanation of that part of her story which appeared at present so extraordinary and unaccountable, to disclose the real state of his heart; and, should his love meet a return of the same ardent affection which glowed in his breast, to attach her to himself, by the most holy and indissoluble of all ties.

CHAP. IV.

The next day, Montroi sent a message by Genifrede, to inquire after Adelaide's health, and solicit the favour of her company at dinner. Delicacy, and a high sense of female decorum, prevented Adelaide from accepting the invitation; and Montroi, though disappointed by her refusal, forbore repeating the invitation. But what pained him with disappointment, encreased his esteem and admiration, and caused him to reject, with fresh indignation, what he considered as a wicked slander of the object he adored. He grieved to be denied her company, but he reproached himself for having either forgotten or overlooked the impropriety that would have attended the acceptance of his request, and of which, he feared, and the thought filled his eyes with tears, Adelaide might be painfully sensible—"Sure," said he, "the lovely angel cannot think I mean to take advantage of her defenceless situation, to treat her with unbecoming boldness and familiarity? she will not, I hope, think me so devoid of principle, so regardless of the dictates of honour, as to be capable of such a conduct?—But she does not yet know me; and, if she did, she has perhaps only acted agreeably to the rules of female delicacy and prudence. Yet," added he, "I am to blame—I ought not to have made the request; not, however, till our friendship had been cemented by a longer intimacy."

The apprehension that he might have wounded her feelings, by seeming to presume upon her situation, was the occasion of another message, in which Montroi apologized for the liberty he had taken, and solicited the favour of being sometimes allowed to see her in her apartment.

Adelaide's reply, which was couched in terms of the most delicate politeness, released Montroi from the tyranny of uneasy fears; and he gave orders that she should be treated with the respect due to a female visitant of the highest rank, that her table should be furnished with every delicacy that could be procured, and that the daughter of one of the villagers should be immediately engaged as her *femme de chambre.*

Adelaide, although highly gratified and flattered by these acts of kindness and liberality, would have declined them, as inconsistent with her birth and condition, which, she observed, was too humble to allow her to take place, even of those to whose services she was obliged.

Genifrede, who, from the first moment she had seen Adelaide, had declared that she was a gentlewoman bred and born, was astonished at this declaration; and Montroi, when informed by her of what Adelaide had said, heard it with surprise, and could not credit the assertion.

In the evening, as soon as Adelaide had dined, Genifrede entered, and informed her that one of Jannette's youngest boys, a child of about eighteen months old, was taken suddenly ill, and thought to be in great danger. Adelaide, who sometimes visited Jannette, and had often nursed little Claude, which was the name of the infant, no sooner heard of his illness, than she set off for the cottage, where she found Jannette weeping immoderately, with the child in her arms: it seemed to be convulsed, and to respire with difficulty. Adelaide seated herself beside the distressed mother, upon a low bench by the fire; and was making some attempts to console her, when the village doctor, a respectable looking middle-aged man, entered with Guillaume, who had been dispatched to procure assistance.

The doctor having examined his little patient, pronounced his complaint to be spasms, arising from indigestion; but said there was little cause for apprehension: and having given him a cordial, which seemed to revive him, and a few directions to Jannette, respecting her treatment of him, said he had little doubt but he would soon be well, and departed.

Adelaide, who was a general favourite at the cottage, continued there till little Claude was nearly well, and then returned to the chateau. She had scarce entered the grounds, when she was met by

Montroi, whose eyes sparkled with the transport he felt on seeing her—"I will not say this meeting is accidental," said he, colouring highly—"I learnt you were absent, and knowing the occasion of your walk, expected, or rather hoped to meet you. How is the poor infant? is its situation as dangerous as has been described?"

"I believe not, Sir," said Adelaide, over whose cheek a blush had mantled, on being thus surprised by Montroi—"I am happy in saying the child is already very much better; I should grieve indeed were he to die, for he is a sweet infant, and the darling of his mother."

"It is then a favourite of yours, I presume," said Montroi, gazing tenderly in her face—"Fortunate little fellow! Who, were he sensible of it, would not envy him the happiness of engaging the favour of Mademoiselle D'Ainville?"

These words, and the ardent look of admiration that had accompanied them, were ill calculated to relieve Adelaide from her embarrassment; a deeper glow now took possession of her cheeks, she cast her eyes to the ground, and was silent.

"Have I your pardon," at length resumed Montroi, "for the liberty I took this morning? Your answer convinced me I had been guilty of an act of presumption, of which I was not, till then, aware."

Adelaide, scarcely knowing what she said, replied, she was highly obliged by his request; but that she had reasons for remaining as much retired as possible, while she continued at the chateau, or till she had heard, as she hoped she soon should, from a dear friend, to whom she had applied for advice and assistance.

"Oh why," said Montroi, "can it be necessary that you should, even for the shortest interval, live thus secluded and unknown, and hid under a borrowed name?" He paused—"Am I too bold," said he at length, "when I say I would claim the privilege of a friend, and be informed of the reasons which induce you to adopt a line of conduct seemingly so extraordinary? Speak, Mademoiselle D'Ainville, speak," with faltering voice, "dearest Adelaide; to this feeling, this sympathizing heart, unbosom all your cares, all your sorrows; if any communication made to your Montroi should enable him to contribute, in any degree, to the peace of one so lovely and excellent as yourself, how highly would he value, how would he delight in such communications, even though it subjected him to the most painful difficulties, the most dreadful dangers! These, any, or every thing, he would gladly encounter, for the sake of the pleasure such sweet confidence would afford."

"Had I the power, Sir," said Adelaide, with almost breathless confusion, "to make the communication you thus honour me by soliciting, I should not withhold it a moment from one so deserving of my confidence, and to whom I am so highly obliged. But know, sir, there are objections which are indeed insurmountable; be assured also, that it is not in the power of any one, not even yourself, warmed, as I perceive you are, by the most honourable and generous friendship, to afford me any other assistancc than a continuation of the benevolent protection you now afford me in your house, till I have received advice and instruction how I ought to act, from the lady to whom I have applied."

"And will you then cruelly refuse to afford me any share of that confidence you so readily give another?" said Montroi, with a reproachful glance—"Oh, why, why all the secrecy, this unkind, I would almost add, this ungenerous reserve?"

"Oh, do not say ungenerous," said Adelaide, bursting into tears; "rather candidly conclude, that there are circumstances which, if known, would reflect dishonour upon——" She paused.

"Dishonour!" faintly reiterated Montroi.

"That, in short, there are certain incidents of my life that I cannot unfold without injury to others, or without involving myself in some disgrace by the communication."

"Heavens!" exclaimed he mentally, "what can this mean?"

"Yet think me not ungrateful," resumed Adelaide, "or that I am insensible of the honour your friendship, Sir, would confer upon me, by desiring to become the sharer of my heart's sorrows: strange as the assertion may appear, especially when made by one who has known the sweets of confidential intercourse, yet I must add, that any endeavour to lighten them by participation, would only add to their weight. Seek not then, with kind concern, to know the cause of my concealments and my griefs; the one is necessary to my situation, the other is the consequence of events unforeseen, and not to be prevented. To a mind unaccustomed, till of late, even to the shadow of disguise, this single circumstance of being compelled to assume the mantle of a mysterious secrecy, must be attended with a sensation painfully acute. Believe me, Sir, that I lament the silence I must preserve, even towards you; but, could you know my reasons, I am certain you would agree that I am impelled by a necessity which is indeed insuperable."

"After such a declaration," said Montroi, "I am content to cease from all inquiries. But is it necessary that this silence should be *for ever* maintained? Can I never be able to tender with effect my most zealous services? and may not time allow you to unfold these mysteries?—But to this question I do not ask an answer. In the meantime, however," added he, tenderly taking her hand, "permit me to assure you, that there is a heart in this breast," laying his hand upon his own, "which sympathizes with your cares or misfortunes, whatever they may be, with the sincerest, purest affection; and this hand, and all the means which it can use, will be ever ready to be exerted in the cause of beauty, merit, virtue, such as yours."

The honest earnestness with which these words were uttered, produced the deepest impression on the heart of Adelaide; but they rendered her fully alive to all the misfortunes of her situation. She looked the look of gratitude on Montroi, which she could not utter—she was for a moment unable to speak; at length, perplexed, distressed, bewildered by confusion, and forgetting, in the agitation of her feelings, that he had resolved to desist from further inquiry, she exclaimed, with tears—"Urge me, Sir, no further, I conjure you—I am wretched, very wretched; and, most of all, unfortunate, in having excited a curiosity I am utterly unable to gratify."

"Curiosity! call it not curiosity," exclaimed Montroi, pressing her hand to his lips—"it is friendship, it is affection; it is an eager wish, arising from the hope of being able to extricate you from all your difficulties and distresses, and to make you happy. Oh, that it were indeed in my power to bestow felicity on one so loved, so honoured!—But I have been too busy with inquiries—I ought not to have been thus importunate; I have distressed, I have afflicted you—those tears reproach me. Oh that I should have been the cause of them, I that would give worlds——Forgive me, charming Adelaide, forgive the rash, the inconsiderate Montroi: he will not again offend, he will not wound your feelings by a repetition of his former fault. Yet, as the dearest treasure he could retain, he will not relinquish the hope, that you may one day relax from your reserve; and as a proof that he is not hateful to you, honour him with, at least, some share of your confidence; and impose upon him some task, some arduous task, in which he may promote your interest, your welfare, your happiness."

Adelaide, sensibly affected by Montroi's manner, which shewed how greatly he was disappointed and perplexed by her refusal to impart what he was thus anxious to learn, returned an answer, which did not absolutely forbid him to hope that an alteration of circumstances might enable her to act as he now wished.

By this time they had reached the great steps of the principal entrance into the chateau; and, from the hall, each took the different corridors leading to their respective apartments.

CHAP. V.

Montroi loved too tenderly not to avail himself of every possible opportunity of meeting and conversing with Adelaide. She felt uneasy and disturbed by his constant attentions; for her heart told her his society might be dangerous to her future peace, and even sometimes suggested, that she ought not long to remain an inmate in his house. It was impossible for Adelaide not to perceive that, to Montroi, she was already an object of the most tender love, as well as the most anxious curiosity: the soft melancholy that sometimes overspread his countenance, convinced her that, though blessed with affluence, and in the possession of every thing which might seem to constitute felicity, he was yet far from happy. But it was when discoursing upon the delight resulting from the intercourses of a refined friendship, or upon the painful sensations occasioned by the sufferings of amiable and respected relatives, that this expression was most observable; and often then, his eyes filled with tears, he would hastily draw from his bosom a miniature, which he constantly wore, and gaze upon it, or press it to his lips; then heaving a deep sigh, remain for a while immersed in thoughtfulness and abstraction. Sometimes, after these fits of melancholy musings and saddening recollection, he would take his oboe, and strive to dissipate his sorrows with the charms of music; and would often attempt a transition from moody care to blithsome gaiety, by varying from notes of tender woe, to those of some light and popular air of his native province.

When, as was now usually the case, though she had sometimes strove to prevent it, he accompanied Adelaide in her walks, he would take with him his instrument, and at the foot of an overhanging cliff, or on the margin of some lake, perform with an exquisite taste and pathos, one of his most favourite compositions. At other times, he would amuse himself in sketching the features of the landscape; one of these, in particular, he finished; it was a view of the chateau, with the shady mount on which Adelaide loved to sit. This he presented to her, and she reserved it as a treasure, which she might preserve as a memento of him from whom she was soon to be separated, and, in all probability, for ever; yes, for ever; for how was it possible to imagine that Montroi, notwithstanding the diligence with which he sought her society, and the thousand little elegant gallantries he daily practised towards her, would ever think of her as one whom he could make his wife? This was impossible. Propriety, therefore, strongly urged the necessity of that separation, which she at once dreaded and desired, and which must seemingly be the act of herself, since Montroi appeared not to have any intention of leaving the chateau, or of discontinuing, or abating his attentions to her. But although steady in her opinion on this point, she was yet unable to take any step, till the return of Jacques from his journey into Gascony, of which, however, she was now in daily expectation, for Jacques had set off before Montroi's arrival at the chateau.

Montroi had now been many times in the company of Adelaide; not a day indeed passed, in which he did not visit her, or overtake her in her rambles about the grounds, or attend her to the cottage of Jannette, whither she frequently took a stroll, or along the side of the woods and thick plantations of olive groves, which almost surrounded the village, and nearly hid it from view. But, in all his walks, in all his conversations, no word, or even the most distant hint, was dropped by Adelaide on the subject of his former curiosity: he had already urged that subject as far as politeness would allow; indeed he even promised not to touch upon it again.—Though she was sensible that she must appear reserved and disingenuous, and the idea of this was most painful, yet Adelaide continued firm in her purpose of concealing her name and birth, and especially the late events of her life. Thus her resolution was chiefly, as she supposed, owing to a sense of duty towards her father, since a disclosure of these particulars might expose him to the greatest dangers; and partly, and indeed in a greater degree than she was perhaps fully aware of, to a lively sensation of shame, at being born of parents who were dishonest, and consequently far more disreputable than poverty alone could possibly have rendered them.

These reasons operating powerfully on the mind of Adelaide, and confirming her purpose, grievously disappointed the expectations of Montroi; for he had hoped that time, and a nearer intimacy, would have induced her to lay aside that impenetrable veil of mystery in which she had hitherto been involved: but finding that it still continued, torturing as was the idea, he began to suspect there must be something in her story highly dishonourable, which could induce one so young to wear so deep a disguise. Again he thought of the tale told his servant by the woman at the *auberge*. But could Adelaide, the correct, the lovely, the attractive, the delicate, the bewitching Adelaide, be the character the hostess had described? Impossible!—Yet, who was she?—Twice already had she changed her name; and according to her own declaration, on the night he had met with her at the chapel, neither of the names she had assumed was that of her family.

The uneasiness experienced by Montroi, while ruminating upon these circumstances, was excessive; it preyed upon his health, and became too evident to pass unobserved by Genifrede, with whom Montroi sometimes conversed concerning Adelaide; and Genifrede had soon penetration enough to discover that nothing but this unfortunate, and, to her, seemingly unnecessary concealment, prevented him from declaring his passion for her, and making her, as she conceived, the happiest and most envied among women—"You know not what you are about, my dear Ma'moiselle," said she one day to Adelaide—"Monsieur Montroi loves you; he has as good as told me so himself, though I should have found it out, if he had not; or why did he look at you so, and talk of you thus continually; and go sighing about the chateau, as he did this morning, as if his poor heart was breaking? and all for nothing, but because you won't out with it, and tell him who you are. What need of all this secrecy, and these mysteries, as he calls 'em? Why cannot you make a friend of him at once, and be the happy lady of this chateau?—'Genifrede,' says he, 'I have no one to controul me in my inclinations; my fortune is large, it is even larger than my wishes; and with such a woman as Mademoiselle D'Ainville, I could be the happiest of men. But how can I offer her my hand, when I know not even her name?'—Dear Ma'moiselle, do but consider what you are doing; and don't stand in your own light, and distress him so any longer. I'm sure, so good as you seem, you can have done nothing amiss; but who can tell what he may think of you?"

"Genifrede," cried Adelaide, "I am the most wretched, the most unfortunate of human beings."

"God forbid, Ma'moiselle! God forbid!" exclaimed Genifrede.

"And whatever may be the nature of the regard with which Monsieur Montroi condescends to honour me," resumed she, "it is impossible I can ever be——" A stream of tears suppressed her utterance.

"Mercy on us!" exclaimed Genifrede; "so fine a chance, and all to be lost, for want of a little courage to speak out, and tell the truth!"

"Was Monsieur Montroi to be made acquainted with the events I am determined to conceal," continued Adelaide, "he would never see me more; he would abhor, he would detest me: and oh! never, never will I deceive him!"

Genifrede shook her head, and looked earnestly at Adelaide—"I fear I understand you but too well," cried the good old creature feelingly, and with a deep sigh—"But don't cry so, Ma'moiselle; it'll make your head ache; and all, you know, can do no good now.—Oh, who ever could have believed it, so good, so innocent as she looks?" thought Genifrede, rising to depart—"Alack, alack! poor Monsieur Montroi! what news will this be for him!—It is all over then, and she can never be my Lady."

"What is the matter, Genifrede?" said Montroi, who met her as she was passing through the last room in the suite, on her way from Adelaide's apartment.

"Nothing much, your Honour," replied Genifrede; "only—only——"

"Only what, my good woman?" said Montroi eagerly—"How is your charge? how is Mademoiselle D'Ainville?"

"Well, very well, your Honour," answered Genifrede; and was passing on, when Montroi, looking steadily in her face, said—"Are you sure, Genifrede, that nothing is the matter?"

"Nothing," replied she; "only I have just been having a little talk with Ma'moiselle, and she has confessed——"

"What, what, my good Genifrede?" interrupted Montroi.

"Oh, I can't tell your Honour what she says; it grieves me to the very heart but to think of it."

"Speak, Genifrede," said Montroi; "I am all anxiety, all impatience. Has the dear lovely creature made you the confidant of her misfortunes? has she—"

"Yes, she has had a misfortune, a chance, I warrant; for what else could she mean? Alack, alack, poor soul! and so young too! and now to be left all forlorn, with not a soul to care for her—Ah, well-a-day! it's a hard case."

"Has she told you," resumed Montroi, to whom the terms, a *misfortune* and a *chance*, thus used, were wholly unintelligible, "of those sorrows which unhappily prey upon her spirits, and, I fear, injure her health?—Oh tell me! let me fly to her, and pour into her gentle bosom all the consolation my tenderness can afford! Be quick, Genifrede, and inform me—What is it that she has confessed?"

"She says, your Honour, that she is the most unhappy woman in the world; and so, in truth, I think she is. But she can never tell your Honour her story, or any part of it, nor even her name; and she says besides, if your Honour was to know how she came to be so unfortunate, and all about it, you would never see her again, and that you would hate her; but, for all that, she scorned to deceive you: and then she cried sadly, and sobbed, till I thought her poor heart would have broke. Alack! it is a pity so sweet a young lady—But men are very wicked; and when people have no friends to look after 'em—I had a sister once, God bless her! for never was a sincerer penitent; but she died, as one may say, by inches, of a broken heart; all for grief at having been led astray, and brought to shame, by a cruel false-hearted man. Oh it was a grievous sight to see her in their last days, wasted to skin and bone, and——"

"Eternal and merciful Powers!" exclaimed Montroi, striking his forehead with vehemence; "all then is true, too, too true!"

"I doubt it is," resumed Genifrede, though without knowing to what he alluded; "I doubt it is all very true."

Montroi made no reply, but hastening down stairs, entered one of the apartments; and throwing himself on a settee, remained for several hours alone, a prey to sorrow and despair. In the evening, being somewhat more composed, he informed Genifrede that it was his intention to leave the chateau, at an early hour on the following day; and that it was probable he should not return for several days: That, during his absence, it was his desire that Adelaide should continue to receive every possible attention, and all the accommodation his house could afford; and that it was also his wish, that she (Genifrede) would use all her efforts to persuade her to disclose the most material events of her life, as, without such a disclosure, it was impossible for him to render her any actual service: above all things, he observed, it was necessary he should know the name of her friends, and learn the reason why they had thus abandoned her.

"And does your Honour mean to depart without seeing Ma'moiselle again?" eagerly asked Genifrede.

"Were I to follow the impulse of my feelings, Genifrede," said Montroi, sighing heavily as he spoke, "I should see her again; but propriety tells me I ought not, at least for the present. I do not say I will see her no more; she may want my services, and they are hers whatever she may require them. Oh that she had deserved—But, no more; I must not, dare not think," said he, softening, as he spoke, into tears of the tenderest regret—"she is lost to me, for ever lost; and I must not give way to these unmanly expressions of distress. Oh, Adelaide, were you but as you seemed!"

"Ah, well-a-day!" cried Genifrede piteously—"But what excuse," added she, "must I make for your Honour's going away, and not seeing her?"

"Tell her I am gone unexpectedly, and in haste," said Montroi; "and that, after an absence of about a week, I mean to be here again."

Genifrede promised to execute these orders faithfully; and the next day, at the appointed hour, Montroi, who had passed a night of extreme anguish, and the most painful irresolution respecting his purpose of departing without again seeing Adelaide, a resolution which he was more than once on the eve of violating, attended by the steward and his own valet, set off from the chateau.

CHAP. VI.

Adelaide was surprised, and cut almost to the heart, when she found that Montroi had departed, even though in great haste, without bidding her adieu: a conduct so extraordinary could not fail to occupy her thoughts, and awaken all her solicitudes. Did this agree with what Genifrede had so lately told her, and with what she had herself observed? Was this his friendship, his tenderness, his love?—"If he had regarded me with those feelings of affection which I, alas! indulge for him," said she, "never, never could he have left me thus unkindly, without once bidding me farewell."

She questioned Genifrede, but of Genifrede she could learn only what she had been desired to say, which was, that he was gone unexpectedly from the chateau on business, which would detain him about a week, when he should return, and would then see her again. The coldness of this message struck like ice upon the heart of Adelaide; she turned away, to hide the emotions of mortified tenderness that pained and agitated her bosom, and to wipe away, unobserved, the tear that trembled in her eye.

Scarcely had Montroi departed, when a messenger arrived at the chateau and desired to speak with Mademoiselle D'Ainville. The person who appeared, and was shewn into the apartment of Adelaide, was the junior partner of Monsieur Barreux, the jeweller, at Arles, at whose house Jacques had left the ring given to Adelaide by De Launé. He introduced himself as the person in whose hands it had been deposited, and had brought a letter for Adelaide from Monsieur Barreux, requesting information as to the manner in which she had become possessed of it, and demanding an immediate and unequivocal answer.

There was something in the style of the letter, and in the request it contained, calculated to excite apprehension and uneasy suspicion in the mind of Adelaide. The circumstance of her having received it from her father, was of itself sufficient to authorise the suggestion, that the ring might have been unfairly obtained: but that Monsieur Barreux should be informed of this, supposing it to be really the case, seemed extraordinary; and she demanded if any person had seen the ring, or if he knew Monsieur Barreux's reasons for a requisition she considered as inconsistent with the laws of politeness, and which she was, therefore, not bound to answer?

The young man, who either was, or affected to be wholly ignorant of Monsieur Barreux's reasons for making the above application to Adelaide, said he was not to depart without an answer; and Adelaide was therefore obliged to return one, which she did in writing. In this she briefly informed him, that she had received the ring from a friend, whose name she was not at liberty to mention. She desired, in case Monsieur Barreux meant to buy the ring, he would let her hear from him as soon as possible; but, should he determine to decline the purchase, that he would return it immediately on the receipt of her letter.

This somewhat singular event employed her surmises, though without exciting any extraordinary degree of fear respecting its consequences, till she was awakened to other apprehensions, and fears not less distressing than any her imagination had yet suggested. The time appointed by Jacques for his return from Gascony had transpired some days since, and the punctuality with which he usually performed whatever he undertook, rendered it but too probable that he had fallen into some unexpected difficulty or danger; for that he should have staid at the Castle longer than he had first proposed, seemed unlikely; though it was possible, at such a distance, he might have met with some unexpected delays.

The length of his absence appeared, to Adelaide, to be prolonged, by the eagerness with which his return had been anticipated; for nothing could have afforded her more joy and satisfaction than to hear from the Countess, between whom and herself she had no doubt, on Jacques's introduction by means of Bertha, who was always about her Lady, a regular correspondence might be established, unknown to the Count. To the affectionate and sympathizing bosom of her more than mother, Adelaide could have confided every sorrow; and her heart, by such friendly communication, would have been eased of the heavy burthen that oppressed it.

Another, and another day passed, and still he did not return; and Adelaide had now not only to sustain her own surmises and uneasiness, which became every hour more painful, but those also of Genifrede and Jannette, each of whom betrayed the utmost anxiety, and indulged various distressing apprehensions for his safety.

CHAP. VII.

Jacques had not yet arrived, nor had any thing been heard of him, when one day, as Adelaide and Genifrede were sitting pensively at a window in one of the lower rooms in the chateau, talking of him, and hoping for his return, they were surprised by the appearance of a cabriolet drawn by a single mule, driving through the inner court, followed by two horsemen, all armed in the manner of the *marechaussée*. Before they had time to conjecture who they could be, or what could be their business, a middle-aged man, genteelly dressed, alighted from the carriage, and came up to the window, and addressing Adelaide, said—"I presume, Madam, you are Mademoiselle D'Ainville?"

She was surprised, but immediately answered—"Yes, Sir, my name is D'Ainville."

In the meantime the two horsemen, who had dismounted and entered the house, burst into the room, and seizing her by each arm with the most violent roughness, cried out together—"You are our prisoner, Madam, and must go with us."

Their words and manner convinced the unfortunate Adelaide that they were the officers of justice: she shrieked, and fainted; but this did not for a moment delay their purpose; and utterly regardless of her condition, and of the entreaties, the tears and remonstrances of the astonished and terrified Genifrede, they forced her into the carriage. The person who had alighted from it, placed himself by her side; and either touched by her distress, or moved to admiration by the youth and beauty of his prisoner, insisted that means should be used for her recovery before they proceeded. The attendants reluctantly consented; for they were preparing to set off, without attending to the state in which they had carried her to the carriage.

When she recovered, he said something which he seemed to intend as a kind of apology for the force employed against her: pleading, however, the necessity of doing their duty. He then informed her that his name was Barreux, and that she was arrested on the information of the Marquis de Ponteville, for having in her possession a ring, which, together with a diamond star and some other valuables, was taken from his Lordship by a set of banditti infesting the Pyrenees, who had attacked his party as they were crossing the pass of Mount St. Andero, and killed two of his servants, the Marquis himself being dangerously wounded.

Adelaide listened to this account with a look of terror; and when she heard of the murder of the attendants, burst into tears.

Monsieur Barreux observed her narrowly, and proceeded— "The ring I well know; it contains a device with hair, and is set round with diamonds of the finest water. It was committed to my hands not many weeks before the robbery, to be altered in the setting; and, of course, it was impossible for me not to know it immediately to be the property of the Marquis. I accordingly sent it to his Lordship, with an account of the manner in which I had become possessed of it; and the Marquis, on receiving it, said he was sure the person having it must be connected with the robbers, and ordered that proper measures should be immediately taken to apprehend you, Madam; and now you will be considered as an accomplice, and exposed to the utmost rigours of the law, unless by a clear confession of the manner in which you got the ring, and all particulars, you will direct the *marechaussée* to discover the offenders, and bring them to justice."

"And whither am I to be conveyed?" said Adelaide.

"To prison, Lady," returned Monsieur Barreux.

Adelaide shuddered, but made no reply.

"In a few days," pursued Monsieur Barreux, "your examination will be taken; and if you will confess the truth, you will obtain your enlargement without much trouble, and probably with little or no expence. And should it appear, on inquiry, that you had no commerce or connexion of any kind with the persons concerned in the robbery and murders, you will be discharged without punishment."

"What if I refuse to give any evidence whatever?" said Adelaide.

"You will be put to torture, Lady," returned Monsieur Barreux—"The safest way will be, to give a plain and honest account of the manner in which you became possessed of the ring: if you prevaricate, you are undone: you will be considered as an accomplice, and your punishment will be proportioned to the degree of guilt of which you are suspected. Do you intend to adopt the plan I prescribe?"

"No, I will not confess from whom I had the ring."

"You will not? Astonishing!—This is a desperate resolution, young lady," at length he added—"How then do you mean to act?"

"There are but two ways in which I can act," said Adelaide—"I have already said I will not declare from whom I had the ring. The consequences may be dreadful, but I am determined to abide them."

"Good God, you cannot be in earnest!—Are you aware of the penalty which the law exacts in such cases?" at length he added.

"I will prepare myself to endure its utmost severities," said Adelaide, "rather than make the confession required."

"You amaze me," said Monsieur Barreux—"is it possible that you, Madam, can have been concerned in this daring and horrible transaction?"

"It is impossible that I should," said Adelaide—"I have not; but it is possible, at the same time, that I may have my reasons for withholding the information you, Sir, seem to consider, and which is perhaps necessary to my own safety: such I have; and while these reasons exist, whatever may be my fate, I shall persist in withholding it."

"Will you not take advice how to proceed?"

"Yes; but I will take it of my own heart, which, while it acquits me of intentional wrong, exhorts me how I ought to act in this arduous and trying case."

"Do you intend to employ an advocate?"

"It is proper I should have some one to plead my cause."

"Allow me then to recommend a friend of mine, a man of profound judgment and proved integrity, now resident at Arles, and within a street or two of the place where I live. Shall I call upon him? Will you permit me to engage his interest in your defence?—Depend upon it, he will do you justice."

Adelaide received Monsieur Barreux's proposal with thankfulness; adding, she was a stranger, and without friends, and knew not herself where to apply for counsel.

Extraordinary as it may appear, Monsieur Barreux, notwithstanding Adelaide's words contained as full an evidence as could be required, that she was engaged in some connexion with the persons by whom the robbery had been committed, felt the deepest interest in the welfare of his fair unfortunate prisoner. Her beauty, her youth, the sweet, yet energetic tones of her voice, the tender melancholy that overspread her charming features, conspired, with a high degree of pity for her situation, to awaken in his breast feelings of which he was perhaps hardly ever before conscious; and the sentiment of compassion, mingled thus with admiration, he now indulged for her, led him to state, with renewed urgency, the necessity of her giving up the name and the residence of the person from whom she had received the ring, and thus to escape the dangers which she must otherwise incur.

Perceiving all he could urge was of no avail, he threw himself back in the cabriolet, which, on the arrival of the orders for Adelaide's arrest, he had hired at his own expence, and fell into a profound rumination, which Adelaide, occupied by her own melancholy reflections, was not disposed to interrupt, till, after some hours' travelling, they reached the town of Arles; and driving through two or three of the principal streets, stopped at the gate of a high building, whose massive architecture and grated windows marked the entrance of the prison.

As soon as they arrived, the officers, one of whom had preceded the carriage, the other followed it, dismounted from their horses: the door of the cabriolet was opened, and Adelaide assisted to alight. She uttered a deep sigh, as she surveyed the gloomy structure of the place, its high and ponderous walls, and heard the large key turned in the sounding bolt of the door; and started, with a look of horror, as the rattling of chains in the prison-yard below caught her ear, and told her she was entering the abode of vice and misery.

When they had entered the outer gate, Monsieur Barreux conversed a few minutes apart with the warder, who looked at Adelaide with surprise, and then turning to the right, led them through a grated door, across a yard, into a more private area; and afterwards up a stone staircase, in the tower belonging to the keep, or central building of the prison, and looking into the courts or wards below. The room, though small and with bare walls, was yet clean, and decently, indeed almost comfortably furnished, having a bed, a table, and a few chairs, with some other articles of convenience. But the massive thickness of the door, and the extreme height of the windows, with the heavy stanchions of iron fixed across, gave it, with the security, all the dreariness of a prison. This room, which was superior, in point of comfort, to most in the building, had been procured for her, she was told, by the interest of Monsieur Barreux, who had desired she might not be put with the rest of the criminals, and that her situation should be rendered as easy as circumstances would allow.

Adelaide was highly sensible of this indulgence; and she pressed the hand of Monsieur Barreux presented on parting, in token of the gratitude she felt for this kindness—"I am not," said she mentally, "to accuse him as the cause of my misfortunes; he is performing only what his duty requires from him, both as a citizen and a man. The guilty ought to undergo the punishment due their crimes: but it is not for a daughter to arraign a father at the tribunal of justice; there is a moral obligation, even though there shall be no filial respect to strengthen the bonds of union, which cannot, without sin, be violated. I may suffer, but I will suffer unworthily, and endeavour to endure with patience a destiny I cannot alter."

CHAP. VIII.

When Monsieur Barreux had departed, and Adelaide was left alone in her prison, her feelings, notwithstanding all the efforts of her resolution, partook of the melancholy of her situation; but, after some further trials of exertion, a philosophic calm took possession of her spirits, and she became thoughtful, but composed.

It is the property of some minds, and perhaps, in some measure, natural to all, to yield to trifling evils, and rise superior to great calamities. Adelaide's was perhaps of this cast, or probably a long course of sufferings had rendered her less susceptible of their influence. By a habit of enduring misfortunes, she had learned to endure them patiently: she had been taught, however, to bear them without that impatience of distress in which some are too apt to indulge, and which serves only to render them more sensible of the miseries under which they labour.

There is something flattering to our feelings as human beings, in the idea of being engaged in the performance of some difficult duty, something, if we may be allowed the expression, that aggrandizes the mind, calls forth its latent energies, and makes us feel that we have powers of which we were not perhaps before fully sensible. It was her duty, she was persuaded, not to assist in criminating her father, even though her own life should fall a sacrifice to her perseverance in this opinion: it might be said to be a duty difficult to perform, because she had no motive of affection and reverence to induce her to skreen him from punishment, at the expence of her own character and life; but yet this difficulty was overcome, by the operation of a principle, with her very powerful—a high sense of moral rectitude and filial obligation, which, she felt, she ought not to violate: from this principle, and this only, she now resolved to act. It was impossible that for De Launé she could entertain any feelings of respect or tenderness; for his conduct towards her had been marked with deeds of cruelty, even at the moment when he had affected to be most kind, and to receive and think of her as a daughter; throughout the whole, it had been unnatural, unfeeling, or at least highly culpable. As a member of society, he was a being to be feared, abhorred, and avoided—dangerous in his habits, and hateful in his character—"Who is there," said she, "that can, or ought to love De Launé?—But he is my father;" and she was firm.

The advocate recommended by Monsieur Barreux had sent word that he would call upon her on the following morning. Adelaide passed an easy, though, for the most part, a sleepless night: she prayed often, and fervently, that her father might repent of his lawless and guilty course of life; "and then," said she, "I shall never think I can have suffered too much for him."

Tears would sometimes flow from her eyes, but it was when the image of Montroi was presented to her fancy, who had left her so hastily, so unexpectedly, and so abruptly, that she knew not whether she might hope he would ever think of her again—"Oh, would he grieve," said she, "was he to see me here? Will he pity me, when he shall know I am a prisoner?"—To be pitied, to be loved, by one so highly revered, so tenderly beloved, seemed, at this instant, a more than sufficient recompence for any sufferings she could undergo; for, to Adelaide, Montroi seemed the best, the most perfect of human beings: and when she thought how she must have suffered in his opinion, from the mysterious secresy she had been obliged to observe relative to her family and name, and it occurred to her that this might probably be the reason of his sudden and abrupt departure, it was then that Adelaide was most wretched. To have lost the affections of the most esteemed and beloved of men, seemed the very acmé of misery: compared to this, the rack, the wheel, pain, agony, even the pangs of death, were but inferior calamities, unworthy of a sigh, a tear.

Yet Montroi did believe her guilty; and this suspicion would be corroborated and confirmed by the circumstance of her arrest, and detention in the public prison: her former reserve would now be rendered intelligible. He would condemn her, for he must think her an accomplice with those desperate criminals, of whose outrages he had himself been an eye-witness, and by which he had indeed nearly fallen.

Against such strong presumptions of guilt, her own innocence could avail nothing; and even should she be acquitted of the crime of which she stood charged, could he think of regarding with feelings of affection, or any feelings but those of a contemptuous pity, one who had been rendered, not indeed by her faults, but her misfortunes, an object of distressing and disgraceful publicity? or, could he know every incident in her unhappy story, would he ally himself with the daughter of a robber and a murderer?

It was fortunate perhaps for Adelaide, if any thing in her situation could be deemed deserving of the epithet, that she had never been deluded by her hopes into that fairy field of love and joy, to which the declared admiration of Montroi might have led her: she saw at once the utter impossibility of his marrying a woman so situated, and with a virtuous energy of which few minds are perhaps capable, resolved to combat those feelings of refined affection, which agonized, but could not sooth. She therefore shunned rather than sought his acquainted; though his society, had it been less dangerous, would have been the sweetest solace she could have known.

It was not till he had left her, that she knew how dear Montroi was to her heart; and in proportion as he was beloved, the idea of his being lost to her for ever became more and more intolerable, and her feelings were more acute and agonizing. Could she have preserved his esteem, she believed, even now, she could be happy; at least this dear, this exhilarating hope, would have added a portion of sweet to have assuaged the bitterness of her present cup of affliction: but this, even this was denied; and her condition became altogether wretched.

CHAP. IX.

In the course of the morning, at the hour appointed by Monsieur Barreux, Monsieur Monét, the advocate, arrived at the prison, and was shewn into the apartment of Adelaide. She was sitting attentively by the side of the bed, her hair dishevelled, and her cheek leaning upon her hand, in an attitude of deep reflection, when the door of the prison was unlocked, and starting from her posture, she beheld the man of law, who having announced himself as the person sent thither by Monsieur Barreux, bowed profoundly, and seemed to await her orders.

Adelaide inquired if he had been informed of the reason of her arrest? and being answered that he had, Monsieur Monét, as if desirous to give Adelaide a specimen of his professional abilities, entered into a tedious harangue, interspersed with so many law terms and phrases, that it was with difficulty she could understand a single sentence he said. Adelaide, more wearied than instructed, and certainly not comforted with this technical jargon, interrupted it, by simply stating the case, as to the manner of her having received the ring, now known to be the property of the Marquis de Ponteville; persisted, however, in her refusal not to mention the name and abode of the person by whom it had been given her.

The advocate assured her, that unless such particulars were declared, she would be subjected to an indictment, as an accomplice of the persons who had committed the robbery; and if she refused to confess all she knew, she must at least offer some reason, which might have weight and influence with the court; otherwise her allegation relative to the means by which she had obtained it, would be considered as an idle defence, and she would be judged and treated accordingly—"You, I presume," said he, "Madam, mean solemnly to declare, that you were not engaged, either directly or indirectly, in the robbery?"

Adelaide answered she did.

"You have some strong reasons, I understand, Madam," resumed he, "for concealing the name and residence of the person from whom you received the ring, and who, you do not deny, is one of the perpetrators?"

Adelaide replied, that the person who gave it her said he had taken it in payment of a debt: it did not therefore, she observed, necessarily follow that this person was one of the robbers.

"Not absolutely, Madam," said Monsieur Monét, "not absolutely; yet, consistent with your resolution of not giving up his name, a strong presumption—An extraordinary affair, a very extraordinary affair indeed; I never, I think, met with one so peculiar in all my practice: a lady, too, of your appearance—The person, Madam, I presume then, is—has the happiness—in short, Madam, I suppose there is some acquaintance, some attachment—very extraordinary else, very unaccountable indeed; and unless you make the confession the court requires, it will be very difficult—I will try what I can do, certainly try; but it is a very great undertaking, Ma'am, a very great one. You mean to stick to this declaration about the debt and the ring indeed; but this, I fear, will do little, very little, unless you can get somebody to speak for your character. Have you no friend, Ma'am, no evidence of any kind, to appear, and speak in your behalf?"

"None that I know of, none, however, that can be of any use to me in this business," said Adelaide; "none indeed that——"

"Wonderful!—Good God, Madam, there must be something surely very extraordinary in your history!—*No friends!* I am sorry to say it, but, upon my word, Madam, your situation seems very hopeless. I'll try what I can do, as I said before but really——"

"Heaven is my witness," interrupted Adelaide, "I have done nothing which ought to have placed me in the predicament in which I now stand, a predicament which you, Sir, think, and I myself conceive, to be very awful. You know my resolution, it is unnecessary therefore that I should repeat it: the law must have its course. I am well aware of the consequences which may ensue on my refusal to answer all the questions concerning the ring which will be put to me; I am therefore prepared to meet them. The world, Sir, of late, has offered to me little else than adverse circumstances, and scenes of sorrow and persecution; and there are times when I think I could leave it, even without a sigh. My destiny is not, however, in my own hands; I await the decree of Him on whom I rely, the decree of a wise unerring Providence; I trust in him in life, I will confide in him in death. It is in his power, and perhaps in his only, though he may choose to accomplish his purposes by means seemingly accidental, to release me from my present most calamitous condition; he may please, on the contrary, to take me hence, and make me everlastingly happy, in a state of eternal blessedness."

"You astonish me, Lady—such sentiments; and yet——"

"The forlorn, despised inmate of a prison," said Adelaide.

"You deserve, or I greatly mistake, a better fate.—She is, she must be innocent," thought he; "yet how very wonderful!"

"I have now, Sir, I believe," said Adelaide, mentioned all that can be necessary to my case: it is perhaps, as you say, most hopeless; I fear—I think it is."

"Could I be acquainted with your reasons, Madam; or would you but afford me some hint or clue, by which I might understand, and which might serve——"

"Simply then, Sir, they are these," said Adelaide: "I must not even run the risk of criminating the person by whom that ring was given me—it would be a sin, a sort of parricide, an act by which I could incur more positive guilt, than, where I utterly unconnected, in concealing the perpetrators of this daring outrage."

"Ah, that alters the case a little. A relation," said Monsieur Monét, "or some near friend—*a sort of parricide*; not, I presume, exactly a father, but——"

"What I have said, Sir," said Adelaide, "must suffice. You will plead what you can in my defence."

"Certainly, certainly."

She then inquired of Monsieur Monét whether he knew when the trial was to come on?—He answered, that the advocate for the prosecution was already engaged, and he believed it would be brought forward early in the following week, but that her examination would be taken in a few days, when he would not fail to attend.

Adelaide again observing to the advocate that she had nothing further to add, desired she might no longer detain him; and Monsieur Monét, with a promise that he would exert all his power in her cause, arose, and bowing most profoundly, withdrew.

Leaving Adelaide to prepare for her public examination, and the trial that was soon afterwards to ensue, we return to Montroi, whose object in thus hastily quitting the chateau, was to solicit the advice and assistance of Father Athanasa, a monk of exemplary character, and of a most amiable disposition (who had acted as chaplain to the regiment to which Montroi belonged, and was then in a monastery at Aix, in Provence), to whom he resolved to mention every circumstance concerning Adelaide, and to bring him back with him to the chateau; for such an entire confidence and affection subsisted between Montroi and Father Athanasa, though the latter was more than twenty years older than himself, that Montroi consulted him on all occasions; and from the friendly sympathy of the benevolent monk, he hoped to find a soothing consolation for the painful perplexities under which he now laboured.

Adelaide, since the day he had first seen her, had been making a constant progress in his affections: nor could the very suspicious circumstances under which he had met with her, or the reserve she maintained at his chateau, respecting her real name and connexions, however perplexing, and calculated to fill the mind with uneasy doubts and surmises, check the progress of his love, or lessen the persuasion he entertained of her innocence and virtue. The declarations of Genifrede were, however, too forcible not to open the eyes, and produce conviction even in a lover; and he owned with sorrow, that they annihilated his hopes, and overshadowed his future views with clouds of wretchedness and despair.

To Father Athanasa he gave an undisguised relation of all that had occurred since his acquaintance with Adelaide; and the good monk easily perceived that Montroi, even while he confessed she was unworthy of his love, felt the fondest affection for this unfortunate and mysterious girl, an affection which, as it had no longer esteem for its basis, he at once pitied and reproved. That universal benevolence for which he was distinguished, rendered him nevertheless ready to engage in any plan which might possibly be serviceable to an erring fellow creature, perhaps, as he imagined, less guilty than unfortunate; and he willingly agreed to accompany Montroi into Roussillon, to see and consult with him concerning the object of his seemingly ill-placed affection, in hopes, if not already penitent, he might reclaim her from the path of vice; and if sensible of her follies, confirm and strengthen her in her purposes and habits of virtue. But the principal motive which determined him to accept the chevalier's urgent invitation to accompany him to the Chateau de Montroi, had its origin in the purest friendship: he dreaded the effects of this unhappy attachment upon the mind of his young friend, for whom he felt the affection of a father, and all those anxieties which belong to the paternal character; he knew the purity of his heart, but he knew also the power of temptation and the force of passion upon the conduct of youth and inexperience. From the portrait Montroi had given of Adelaide, she seemed to be possessed of every thing but that which is most estimable in her female character; her beauty, her accomplishments, the apparent sweetness of her disposition, even her modesty, if but assumed, seemed as so many lures held out for his destruction: he feared not only for the happiness, but the honour of his friend; and resolved, by endeavouring to render him sensible of the dangers to which so unfortunate an attachment might expose him, to convince him of its impropriety, and persuade him to use his utmost efforts to surmount it.

Montroi had hoped that, before they should have reached

the chateau, Genifrede would have obtained some insight into Adelaide's history; and the eagerness with which he entered upon his inquiries, on his return with Father Athanasa, shewed how much he hoped for the intelligence he thus anxiously solicited. But who may express his astonishment, his grief, and his despair, when told that Adelaide had been been taken from the chateau under an arrest, and that she was now in the prison at Arles!

To his eagerly-vociferous interrogatories, Genifrede could afford no answers at all satisfactory: she had sent Guillaume, her grandson, she said, to Arles, to inquire after Ma'moiselle; and but that she was old and hobbling, she would have gone thither herself—"Alack, alack!" said Genifrede, weeping, "I have had nothing but troubles and misfortunes ever since your Honour left the chateau. There is my other grandson, poor Jacques, the Lord knows what has become of him: he went to see his sister in Gascony, and was to have been back a week ago, and he is not come yet: and so, what with one thing and what with another, I have well nigh gone beside myself."

"But what said Guillaume about Ma'moiselle D'Ainville?" hastily interrupted Montroi.

"Why he said, your Honour, when he got to the prison, he asked to speak with the warder, who looked very surly at him, and would hardly give him an answer; but on his saying he must not go home till he knew what Ma'moiselle had done to be put into prison, he said she had committed a robbery, or was colleagued with those that had, which was the same thing; upon which Guillaume said he stared with all his eyes, and said he would never believe it. 'Won't you?' said the warder—'But I reckon you'll be made to believe it, or she will, which is as good; for the trial is to come on to-morrow, and they say there's not a chance but she'll suffer."

Montroi waited not to hear more—"Let us go," said he to Father Athanasa, "let us fly. It is false—I'll gage my life upon it. A robbery!—Fools!—villains!—Can they look at her, and believe——"

"Be calm, my son," said Father Athanasa, "nor suffer your rage to transport you thus beyond the bounds of reason and discretion. Whither would you go?"

"To Arles—to the prison! Oh do not stay me!—This instant, yes, this instant, I will see her, I will know all, I will force her into explanations!" Saying this, he ran out, and mounting his horse, never thinking or asking whether Father Athanasa would follow him, galloped off for Arles.

CHAP. X.

Adelaide had undergone her first examination, and the next day was fixed for the trial. Having been told she had but little to hope, she had desired to be attended by a confessor: her request was readily granted. The holy priest had been with her at her devotions for near an hour, and was departing, when Montroi arrived at the prison: she was kneeling at the side of the bed, with her hands clapsed, and her eyes raised toward Heaven, with a look of earnest supplication and saint-like devotion, when he rushed into the room. She screamed—he caught her in his arms—she looked at him, almost doubting—Could it be Montroi, Montroi who, with all the fondness of affection, clasped her to his throbbing, bursting heart, who wept over her, like a father over a fondly-beloved child, calling wildly upon her name, and entreating her to confide in him all her sorrows, all her misfortunes, and above all, the cause of her present calamity?

From the warder he learnt the reason of her arrest; and he hoped, by his interest with the Marquis de Ponteville, who was then at Arles, to stop the prosecution. With this view, as there was no time to be lost, he flew from her chamber as precipitately as he had entered it, leaving Father Athanasa, who had just arrived, to console and question Adelaide in his absence, and went in quest of the Marquis. He found him at an hotel in the next street, and immediately informed him of the reason of his haste and intrusion. From the Marquis he learnt further particulars of the case; and he heard with agony the declaration of the Marquis, that he was determined to proceed with the prosecution; nor would he assent to a proposal made by Montroi, that he would visit Adelaide in her prison; fearing, perhaps, lest the sight of so much beauty in distress, should shake the resolution he had made of bringing the offenders, whoever they might be, to justice. The trial, however, the Marquis observed, must necessarily be postponed a day later, a man, supposed to be one of the gang of banditti by whom they had been attacked and robbed, having been seized and taken into custody, for having in his possession a horse belonging to the Marquis, which had been taken from his party by the banditti, at the time of the robbery, and had been claimed by one of his attendants, who had accidentally met him on his way to a part of Gascony. The man, he said, who had been in confinement about a week, was to have been at Arles that evening; but, owing to an unexpected delay, he could not be conveyed thither till a late hour on the following day. It was therefore judged proper, that the trial should be postponed till his arrival, when the prisoners would be confronted together—a measure which, he observed, was the more necessary, as the woman had refused to impeach, or give any evidence about the matter, even though she had been told that her silence would be interpreted into the strongest proofs of her guilt, and that she would be judged and condemned as an accomplice in the robbery.

This extraordinary firmness on the part of Adelaide, Montroi pleaded as an evidence of her innocence; which indeed the utter impossibility of her taking a part in an outrage such as this, rendered sufficiently clear. These, and other like arguments of Montroi, though followed by entreaties the most urgent, were not able to make any impression upon the Marquis, in the business upon which he had entered, and he determined that the prisoners should be tried; when, if innocent, he said, she would be acquitted; if guilty, she ought to suffer the penalty of the law.

The Marquis being thus inexorable, Montroi, almost distracted at the utter failure of his hopes, retraced, with melancholy pace, his way back to the prison, where he found Adelaide attentively listening to the discourse of Father Athanasa, whose eyes beamed pity upon the hapless sufferer, while he inculcated the duties of her present situation, formed upon the principles of his holy religion; and endeavoured so to fortify her mind, that she might be enabled to bear with becoming firmness, the trial she was shortly to undergo.

The presence of Montroi, of Montroi whom she so dearly loved, and whose attentions to her in her present fallen state made him appear more amiable in her eyes than ever, imparted a gleam of joy almost amounting to rapture, to the sorrow-softened heart of Adelaide; nor were the emotions of Montroi, occasioned by the present circumstances, less agitating and affecting, when, gazing on her lovely form, he perceived the havoc which grief, and the exhausting efforts of resolution, had already made on it; when he saw her pallid cheek, her sunken eye, so very, very different from what she was when rosy health, associating with innocence, or what then appeared such, and supposed serenity, gave more than human splendour to her beauty, and exhibited her to his enraptured fancy as something truly angelic; when he beheld her in her present languid state, although it rendered her a thousand times more interesting than before, his heart was unable to bear the pang that tortured it; the big tear glistened in his eye, yet even this gave no relief, but left him in silent misery, to feel all the anguish of despair.

Thus afflicted, he continued rivetted by his attention to the conversation of Father Athanasa, and the beautiful, yet patient prisoner; nor did he or the father think of their departure, till the warder entered to inform them, that the doors of the prison were about to be shut for the night. They then, with many mournful adieus, took their leave, and retired to an hotel, where they passed the night, and where they resolved to continue till after the trial, and till Adelaide's fate should be determined.

The distressing state of Montroi's mind during this momentous period, can only be imagined by those who have experienced similar distresses. Not satisfied with the advocate recommended by Monsieur Barreux, he engaged an eminent pleader to take the lead in the defence; but this advocate did not afford him much food for hope, while Adelaide continued steady in her resolve by withholding the necessary information; and he passed the night in the most gloomy apprehension, and in the morning arose from his bed, without having once closed his eyes in sleep.

CHAP. XI.

The day appointed for the trial at length arrived; and Adelaide, attended by the warder of the prison and a few officers with staves, was conducted from the prison through the streets, to the hall of justice. The feeble frame of Adelaide, so long harassed by grief and anxiety, almost sunk under the agitation of her feelings, when, placed at the bar, she saw herself standing, a conspicuous object, in front of the grave and venerable judges of the parliament of the district, and surrounded by a large concourse of spectators assembled to witness the trial, and who seemed to regard her with looks of particular interest.

The trial now commenced, after the usual formalities, and the Marquis came forward to afford his evidence on the case. He deposed that, in crossing the pass of St. Andero, in the mountains, accompanied by a party of about fifteen friends and attendants, he was attacked by a gang of banditti, whose number he could not ascertain; that two persons, his servants, were slain in the conflict, and several, together with himself, wounded; that, unable longer to withstand the attack, they had fled, leaving their baggage to be plundered; that many articles of value were taken from him, and amongst others, a diamond ring, which had long been the property of his family; that this ring had been traced to the prisoner; but farther he could not speak.

Monsieur Barreux deposed, that the ring was offered to him for sale, by a person who affirmed that it was the property of a lady, calling herself Mademoiselle D'Ainville; that he knew it to have been the property of the Marquis de Ponteville, for that it had been entrusted to his care for the purpose of some alteration, and that he suspected it was the one which had been taken from the Marquis by the banditti of the mountains; he therefore detained it under a pretence: and his opinion respecting the ring being abundantly confirmed by the Marquis, he proceeded to the place of the abode of Mademoiselle D'Ainville, and assisted in apprehending her person.

This part of the evidence being closed, the advocate for the prosecution arose to observe, that the prisoner must necessarily be guilty; for unless she could prove that she had obtained honestly what had been dishonestly taken from the noble Marquis, she must be presumed to have obtained the articles dishonestly; in which case it was evident she stood in the situation of an accomplice, and was guilty of the crime by implication: and though it might not be just to condemn her, upon such implication, to the heaviest punishment, as though she were a principal, yet the prisoner ought not to be discharged as innocent, when it was evident she was guilty to a certain extent, by withholding such communication: that the perverse silence of the prisoner in this respect, was an offence of the highest degree, not only as it obstructed the proper course of justice, but as it could not be owing to any worthy motive; since no private obligation, attachment, or tie of blood, could justify the aiding, abetting, or concealing a crime like the outrage committed upon the person and followers of the honourable Marquis, which being perpetrated by a body of men in arms, was of a deeper dye than robberies committed by one or two persons only, and amounted, in effect, to the crime of *léze majesté*. On these grounds it was to be maintained, that the offence of the prisoner was such as justly subjected her to the *question*; and that the force of torture ought to be applied, to draw from her such a confession or declaration as might promote the peace and security of the subject, by enabling justice to discover, overtake, and punish offenders, so atrocious as to dare to associate in bands against the public peace, and to raise the weapons of death against the life and honour of a person who occupied a rank and station but little inferior to that of the monarch himself. That these observations were strictly agreeable to the established law of the land, he knew the august court would not gainsay; he therefore left the cause for which he pleaded to the judgment of the court, humbly praying that justice might be done, as he had said, upon the person of the prisoner.

During the delivery of this speech by the advocate for the prosecution, the attention of a very crowded court was alternately directed to the animated speaker and the beautiful prisoner, against whom these observations were directed; some of them had indeed excited considerable emotion in her feeling mind. The arguments respecting the principle of duty by which she was actuated, in her refusal to make any confession respecting the person from whom she had obtained the ring, were heard with astonishment, since she had never doubted the solidity and the truth of the principle upon which she acted; and her habit of considering it a duty on the part of a child to support the interests of the parent, in all circumstances and on all occasions, led her to consider the whole of this speech as an artful piece of chicanery, intended to shut her from the mercy of the court, or to draw from her those declarations she had resolved not to make: her looks of surprise, therefore, soon subsided into a steady indifference to these arguments, which the mention of the torture scarcely altered; for she expected, and was prepared to endure that punishment. Yet when, in energetic language, the advocate prayed, at the conclusion of his speech, for punishment to be inflicted upon her as a culprit, she considered herself as already under sentence of condemnation, though innocent of the intention of any crime: she was affected, but not moved; and only cast her eyes for a moment up to Heaven, as if in resignation to her fate, and looking there for that comfort and support, which, guileless as she was, she no longer expected from her fellow man, whom now she considered as deluded into hostility against her, and as regarding her, without exception, as infamous, and a felon.

The speech of the advocate had produced a very considerable effect upon the minds of all present; and it was followed by a pause of some moments, during which the eyes of all were fixed intently upon the person of our heroine. They had been taught to consider her as guilty, though they yet knew not to what extent; but the thoughts of censure were, in an instant, changed to pity and to tears, when they beheld her beauty, clothed in a dignified simplicity and elegance.

At length the clerk of the court, on an intimation from the president, proceeding to the discharge of his office, loudly cried—"You, Adelaide D'Ainville, have heard the charges alledged against you, and also the evidence by which they are supported; what have you to plead why sentence should not be pronounced upon you?"

These words seemed to sound like thunder in the ear of the unfortunate arraigned: she heard them with an inward shudder, but was firm; and bowing with modest timidity, replied, that she begged the favour of the court, and left her defence to her advocate.

The clerk then cried—"Let the defence of the prisoner proceed; and first let the evidence in her favour be heard."

At these words the Chevalier de Montroi came forward, and having been sworn on the holy evangelists, proceeded to declare, that, on his unexpected arrival, a few weeks since, at the Chateau de Montroi, he found Mademoiselle D'Ainville an inmate with the aged housekeeper left there by his predecessors to take care of the mansion: that he learned from that faithful domestic, that Mademoiselle D'Ainville had been brought thither only a few days before, by the grandson of his old servant, who had acted toward the lady, the prisoner, as *valet:* that he himself had held but little conversation with her, she always acting towards him with greatest reserve, but conducting herself with the utmost delicacy and propriety, which produced in his mind the highest opinion of her virtue, and rendered it impossible for him to doubt her honour and integrity.

The chevalier having concluded his evidence, the advocate for the prisoner arose, and looking first at Adelaide, and then bowing to the president and seated judges, thus began:—"Most honourable Seigneur the President, and you right honourable Seigneurs the Fellow Judges, in this ancient and high court, I rise to plead the cause of one who stands here charged with the crime of *léze majesté*, and upon whom my brother advocate has now just prayed that judgment may be done; yes, judgment *may be done.* But, with submission to this high and venerable court, I ask, judgment for what? and on whom?—It appears clearly from the undisputed evidence of the noble Marquis, that a certain ring, I will allow of value, had been taken from his person by a party of outlaws, who infest the passes of the mountains, and had attacked the Marquis and his followers in the vicinity of their wonted haunts: it appears also, from the testimony of Monsieur Barreux, a jeweller of known and acknowledged respectability, that this ring was offered to him for sale, by a person confessedly sent by this lady, the prisoner; for it was sent without any attempt at secresy, and the lady herself does not even wish to deny it—all is open, fair, and candid, and bears the stamp of honesty and integrity. Had the case been otherwise, the ring would have been sent under some colour of secresy, some pretence would have been made when it was offered for sale, some evasion to the inquiries likely to be made by the merchant, would have been planned, and the name of the seller and the place of her abode, and that a near place, would never have been given: indeed, had the ring been dishonestly obtained, it would not have been offered for sale in a provincial town, as Arles is, and to an honest trader, but would have been sent to some of those marts of villany with which Paris abounds; or might have been hurried beyond the limits of the kingdom to some foreign city, where detection would be impossible, and our laws do not reach. Or again, had circumstances rendered this impossible, or inconvenient to the lady who sent the ring to Monsieur Barreux, yet, had she felt any, even the slightest guilt, attaching itself to the possession of the ring, neither herself, or the person (her *valet*) who offered it for purchase, would have left it in the hands of a man of Monsieur Barreux's extensive acquaintance with articles of such value, subjecting themselves to an almost certain discovery; assuredly not: they would either have parted with it at any price, to be paid in ready money, or they would have sold it to some petty dealer, some itinerate chapman, who could neither trace them, or be traced, perhaps, himself. And what conclusion are we to make from these obvious undeniable circumstances? Why certainly, that the lady for whom I plead is innocent, and ought to be acquitted; yes, with all due deference to the honourable judges here assembled, I say she ought to be discharged, without pain or penalty. Observe her, and consider whom it is you would condemn as a robber and an assassin; behold her, mark her well, and see if there be any trait of villany or depravity in that fair and graceful form; observe her intelligent, her sweet and animated face—She holds down her head; her modesty will not suffer her beauty to plead for her deliverance. Is this the part of one corrupted with vice, a profligate, a robber? She seems willing to die, rather than do any thing inconsistent with the modesty of her sex, or else she would display, to obtain the compassion of the court, eyes beaming with all the lustre of life, joy, and benevolence; lips fair, and softly fitted to speak words of kindness and love; features from which an Apelles might gladly study how to draw the lineaments of an Helen; a complexion which might make Hebe herself blush for envy, while she administers the cup of nectar to celestial Jove.

"But my respect for the court bids me restrain the zeal which, old as I am, and long unused, as I have been, to contemplate beauty with rapture, animates me on the present occasion; and while I crave indulgence, I am sure it will be granted me, for I am persuaded that there is not one in this crowded court, who does not sympathize in the sufferings of this interesting unknown: and yet this is her whom you say is an accomplice with the banditti who assaulted the Marquis and his train of followers at the pass of Mount St. Andero; and public safety requires that a lady (blush, ye men of gallantry, while I go on), a lady, young, beautiful, and virtuous, should be torn by the rack, buried in a dungeon, or broke upon the wheel; and for what?—She has had a ring, you say, in her possession, which once belonged to the Marquis, or rather, she does not choose to declare how she obtained it; although it is evident she never could suspect, for a moment, that it was wrongly procured. The great Judge above alone can see our hearts; and I am persuaded that some great judge sees now that she withholds the declaration, which, I am sure, might in an instant effect her discharge, from some honourable motive; yes, the venerable judges will see that her silence cannot proceed from personal guilt, but from personal virtue; and with this persuasion upon the public mind (for I cannot doubt but that it is impressed deeply and strongly upon all present), I conclude my pleadings in the cause of one whose innocence can scarce, I think, have needed it; and with full confidence in the integrity of the fair prisoner, leave her cause to the wisdom of the court, humbling moving that she be immediately ordered to be discharged."

As the advocate concluded his harangue, a buzz of approbation sounded from every part of the court, and all confidently expected the acquittal of the prisoner.

The pleadings ended, the judges consulted together respecting the sentence: to the surprise of all present, they continued long in deliberation, which augured no good to the unfortunate Adelaide. At length the president thus addressed her—"Prisoner, were the court to regard your appearance, or the general circumstances in which you stand, they would instantly give orders for your discharge; for they are inclined to believe that, however you may have obtained the ring, you could not have been actively instrumental in the robbery and the assaults of the Marquis de Ponteville, nor criminal in the means by which you obtained it. They therefore are persuaded that you can, and the laws of the country say you ought to explain how it came into your hands, so that the offenders may be traced, and brought to condign punishment. Are you willing to make the confession the court requires? This done, you have your discharge. An interval of three hours is graciously allowed you, to determine upon your reply; when, if your answer be not such as the law requires, the sentence of the judges will be passed upon you: this is, thrice to undergo the severities of the *question* within ten days; after which, should you persevere in your resolution of skreening the offenders from the just judgment of the law, you are to undergo a solitary imprisonment of seven years, in one of the castles on the shores of the Mediterranean Sea. Your answer is expected."

Monsieur Monet, now leaning towards the resigned, yet firm Adelaide, pressed her to the declaration; Monsieur Barreux also came, and with friendly solicitude urged her to compliance; a message from the Marquis was to the same effect; for all were persuaded of her innocence: but Adelaide, more than ever convinced that, if she confessed from whose hands she had obtained the ring, she should convict and condemn De Launé, did not falter in her purpose, resolving rather to sacrifice her own life than endanger that of her father. At the idea of the dreadful suffering that was preparing for her, she shuddered, but endeavoured to assume fortitude to meet her approaching fate with resolution and firmness. But when, casting her eyes to the opposite side of the court, she perceived Montroi leaning for support on the arm of Father Athanasa, pale and agitated, and saw him gazing upon her with looks of indescribable agony, the anguish occasioned by the view of his sufferings pierced her to the soul; and no longer able to struggle with the tumult of emotions that now rushed upon her heart, she heaved a deep sigh, and fainted.

When the confusion occasioned by this circumstance had subsided, the court next proceeded to the trial of another prisoner, who was put to the bar, and arraigned by the name of Jacques du Bois, who had been apprehended about a week before, on his return from Gascony, and had been brought, the preceding evening, to the prison at Arles, under a charge of having stolen the horse he rode on, which had belonged to one of the attendants of the Marquis, who was slain in the rencounter with the banditti.

In this person the reader will, of course, recognize the identical Jacques, to whom Adelaide owed her preservation and escape from the house of Madame St. Clair, and her reception in the Chateau de Montroi. A similar misfortune, arising from the same cause, had involved them both; but Jacques had the advantage of being known in the neighbourhood, and in the few hours he had been at Arles, he had gained several persons of respectability to appear and bear testimony to his former character and good behaviour. On seeing him, a flush of surprise passed over the cheek of Adelaide, as she was seated in the prisoners' box; but it instantly yielded to the paleness of fear, when, on entering upon his deposition, she found it would necessarily involve her father.

It is needless to recapitulate the forms of the trial, which were the same as those just described; suffice it to observe, that Jacques, who had felt no small degree of terror on being apprehended and brought before a court of justice, though to answer to a charge of which he was confessedly innocent, felt his courage revive on seeing Adelaide, whom he viewed with looks of joy and astonishment.

On being asked whether he had ever before seen the prisoner? he answered that he had, having known her several weeks. He then proceeded to give an account of the manner in which she had been brought to the house of his late mistress, Madame St. Clair, by a person of the name of Perouse; of the arrival of De Launé, Adelaide's father; he related the substance of the conversation he had overheard between him, Perouse, and Madame St. Clair; by which it appeared they were connected with a party of banditti; and that Madame St. Clair was an auxiliary in a scheme, which was to force Adelaide, contrary to her inclinations, to marry the man called Perouse; to escape which marriage, she, on the discovery of their measures, and the characters of the persons in whose power she was placed, determined to quit Madame St. Clair's house; and had persuaded him (Jacques) to accompany her. In pursuance of this plan, as their object was to escape secretly and without delay, they had been obliged to take a horse out of Madame St. Clair's stable, brought thither either by Perouse or De Launé, which, except a ring given by De Launé to his daughter, the same which he had lately offered to sale at the shop of Monsieur Barreux, was all the property they had between them. Of Perouse and De Launé he could give no account, except that they were occasionally at Madame St. Clair's house, which was at the village of Auboigne, in Gascony.

The junior partner of Monsieur Barreux, the person to whom Jacques had offered the ring, was then called to give evidence, and he deposed that Jacques was the person from whom he had received it.

The punishment of Adelaide, who was now publicly acquitted, if the testimony of Jacques should prove true, was immediately suspended; and though she was discovered to be the daughter of one of the gang, yet she was only remanded to prison as before; and, together with Jacques, was to remain in custody till Madame St. Clair should be apprehended, and other measures taken to ascertain the truth of his testimony, of which there was little doubt, for the Chevalier Montroi had confirmed it in many particulars. Adelaide was to remain in the town of Arles, but with liberty to go abroad, under certain restrictions, attended by a guard; and was to be considered as a prisoner at large.

CHAP. XII.

Montroi, who had awaited, in terrified expectation, the event of the trial, was overwhelmed with joy, when he found Adelaide was acquitted of the charge which had been brought against her. Of her innocence he had ever been persuaded; nor could the circumstance of her being proved to be the daughter of a robber, alienate her from his affections; for it convinced him she possessed a sense of filial obligation, which, though exercised, in the late instance, on an erroneous principle, was yet utterly inconsistent with any moral depravity; and when he found she would have sacrificed her own innocent life rather than endanger that of her father, even though she had been obliged to fly from him, to escape the prosecution of the treacherous and hateful scheme which had been devised for her destruction, she seemed to him more than woman. All that had appeared mysterious in her conduct, was now fully explained; though, that she could really be the daughter of such a father, and yet have imbibed principles so noble and truly honourable, seemed so extraordinary as to mock all belief; and he would often exclaim—"It is impossible she can be the daughter of that De Launé!"

On the day after the trial, Adelaide was removed from the prison to an hotel in the suburbs, where neat and handsome apartments were provided for her. Genifrede, by Montroi's orders, was sent for to attend upon her.

In the meantime, Adelaide was impatient for intelligence from Jacques; and she resolved, as soon as Genifrede should arrive, to send her to make inquiries concerning the success of his late journey, in hopes of hearing something of the Countess, who, she thought, if yet living, would certainly write to her.

Montroi, who was now almost continually in the society of his Adelaide, appeared more tender and affectionate than ever. But, though a faint ray of hope seemed now to beam upon her prospects, yet the situation of her father filled her with the most anxious fears for his safety; and she reflected with tears upon her hard condition in being thus unhappily allied, and the sorrow to which this alliance might one day expose her.

One evening, while she was sitting in conversation with Montroi and Father Athanasa, a carriage stopped at the hotel: as she looked from the window, she saw a lady in deep mourning, and covered with a black veil, which entirely concealed her features, enter the court. In a few moments, the door of her apartment was thrown open, and a female, the same which had just alighted from the carriage, rushed into the room, and in an instant was in her arms.

The tide of joy which rushed irresistibly through the heart of Adelaide, almost deprived her of sense, when she heard the well-known voice of the Countess St. Angouléme, and, her veil thrown back, beheld that countenance, lovely, though pale with suffering, which she had so often contemplated with delight and affection truly filial. But the feelings of transport which burst forth at this unexpected and happy incident of her arrival, soon yielded to sensations of wonder-struck astonishment, when the Countess, turning from her embrace, uttered a loud shriek and fainted in the arms of Montroi, who caught her ere she fell, exclaiming—"Great Heaven! can it be possible? Do I indeed behold her whom I have so long mourned as lost to me for ever? My friend! my more than parent!"

"Theodore! Theodore!" repeated the Countess. She could add no more—the sudden emotion of joy that darted through her frame, was too exquisite for feeble nature to support. She reiterated his name, but it was faintly; snatched another hasty gaze, as if doubting the reality of what she saw; and then sinking again into his arms, rested her head upon his shoulder, and sobbed and wept in ecstasy.

The name of Theodore, thus uttered by the Countess, explained what would otherwise have appeared strangely mysterious both to Adelaide and Father Athanasa. The latter had been acquainted with Theodore St. Leon before he took the name of Montroi; but he had never seen the Countess St. Angouléme, though he had frequently heard Theodore speak of her; and having heard she was insane, and constantly confined to an apartment in the Castle, where she saw no one but her keeper, it had never till now occurred to him, that the stranger could be the amiable and long-lamented aunt of his beloved friend.

But Adelaide, who had believed that Theodore had died abroad (for so artfully and so successfully had the Count spread the report of his death, in order to obtain the residue of his wife's property, that no suspicion was entertained as to the truth of it), what she saw and heard appeared most wonderful. But every thought and every feeling was arrested and suspended in her care and anxiety for the Countess, whom this sudden emotion of joy had so completely overpowered, that, when she spoke, it was only in half-formed words, which seemed rather like the utterings of anguish, than the expressions of delight and rapture.

By degrees, however, the violence of these emotions subsided, and she enjoyed a cool, yet lively perception of her happiness. Theodore was alive, and all she had felt and suffered for his sake was effectually done away, by the discovery that he had survived the accidents to which, it had been reported, he had fallen a sacrifice. But she had still to learn that he was no longer the indigent youth, with no other dependance but his sword, as when he left her, but the possessor of a noble fortune; what she had once suggested as possible, had really happened; and if any thing could have increased the happiness she felt on seeing the adopted child of her affections restored to her, as from the grave, it would have been the intelligence obtained from Father Athanasa, of this unexpected change of fortune in his favour.

How the Countess came to be unacquainted with the death of the late heir, to whom she was herself distantly related, may seem somewhat extraordinary; this, however, will be accounted for, when we proceed to give a relation of such events as occurred at the Castle de St. Angouléme, after the departure of Adelaide.

When the necessary explanations were over, and the Countess's spirits somewhat tranquillized, she arose, and taking Adelaide's hand, said—"Let me not, in the joy I now feel, forget the important commission on which I came. You will guess, by my appearance, that I am now a widow: Count St. Angouléme, my unhappy Lord, expired about a week since. The circumstances of his death are extremely melancholy—I shall not describe them at present. Conscious, my dearest Adelaide, that he deeply injured you, he desired me to solicit your pardon, and also to request your prayers for the repose of his soul, that soul which, as it quitted its earthly habitation, sent you," delivering to her hands a writing, "this, his dying bequest."

Adelaide opened the writing, which was folded up, and sealed: she read, started, and turned pale—it was a formal renunciation of all right and claim to the estates and other property of his deceased brother, the late Julien St. Angouléme, in favour of Adelaide St. Angouléme, his daughter and only heir; and contained a document of her birth, sufficient to reinstate her in her possessions without the interference of the parliament.

The surprise and joy of this discovery deprived her, for some moments, of the power of utterance; at length she exclaimed— "I thank thee, Heaven, for having relieved me from so grievous a burden of obligation, by informing me (Oh most happy intelligence!) that I am not the daughter of a robber and a murderer: and thanks be to thee also, oh most gracious Power! for having given me him for a father, whom I always revered as a father. Oh this, this is indeed happiness! and, but for my unfortunate uncle, whose death presents a subject for melancholy regret, I should say I had not a wish ungratified."

"The remorse he expressed, and truly penitential tears he shed in the presence of his confessor, who administered to him the last holy offices," said the Countess, "will, I hope, with the prayers and masses which I have ordered to be performed weekly for the repose of his departed soul, be accepted as an atonement for his past faults."

"I hope—I trust they will," said Adelaide, and she gave a sigh to the memory of her unworthy relative.

Theodore, although previously prepossessed with the idea that Adelaide was not the daughter of De Launé, was nevertheless overcome with amazement, when informed she was the niece of Count St. Angouléme.

The Countess then related the most important events which had taken place at the castle since the departure and supposed death of Theodore. Pity, however, if not respect, for the memory of her late Lord, induced her to suppress some particulars which might have been introduced, and to touch upon others so lightly, that her narrative was, in many parts, imperfect. The real occurrences were more accurately as follow.

CHAP. XIII.

When Adelaide, by the will of her father, was committed to the joint guardianship of the Count and Countess, extravagance, and an indulgence of the pernicious passion of gaming, had rendered the Count's situation and his future prospects alarming, even to himself, thoughtless as he was of those expences into which his libertine inclinations constantly led him, and the consequences which must inevitably ensue. He had, by a daring act of falsehood, imposed upon the Countess, and gained from her that portion of her fortune which she had reserved for her nephew; but this acquisition, instead of satisfying the craving passion it was intended to gratify, served only to lead him into deeper schemes of desperate and wicked policy; and the success which attended his first enterprizes, lured him to attempt the commission of another, if possible more atrocious than that he had already practised. The guardianship of his niece, a minor, with which he was invested by the will of the chevalier, offered another immediate supply of wealth, of which he availed himself to the utmost of his power. But even this supply, though ample, was insufficient for the gratification of his increasing avarice, and passion for expence: it was not till he visited Avignon, in order to arrange the affairs of the Chevalier Julien St. Angouléme, that he formed the daring design of seizing for his own use the estates of his deceased brother; and perhaps he would not have had courage to have undertaken an act so replete with difficulty and danger, had not accident thrown in his way a person fated, as it should seem, by Nature, for deeds of villany and oppression: this person was De Launé: the Count had met him accidentally in the streets of Avignon. On looking at him somewhat particularly, he perceived his features were not unknown to him; and at length recognized him as a man who, some years before, had been a servant in his establishment at the

Castle; but had absconded from his service, and had carried off a considerable quantity of plate, and several jewels of considerable value, the property of the Count.

The fellow appeared confused at the sight of the Count, and endeavoured to retire from observation. The Count, perceiving his embarrassment, passed on, without seeming much to regard him: he, however, made inquiries concerning the man, and learnt that he had resided at Avignon for some years, and had married, for his second wife, a young woman, once a servant in the family of the Chevalier St. Angouléme, till Mademoiselle Adelaide had been sent to nurse, almost immediately after her birth. The woman had died but a short time before the Count met De Launé, without leaving him any children, she never having had more than one child, a daughter, born at the same time nearly as Adelaide, but which died soon after the Chevalier St. Angouléme had placed his infant under her care.

The Count ruminated upon this intelligence, and devised at length a scheme, from the very thought of which a mind endowed with the smallest sense of rectitude would have shrunk with abhorrence and self-reproach; he resolved to have it proved, that the daughter of the Chevalier, and not that of the nurse, had died; and that she had imposed upon the family of St. Angouléme her own daughter, as the real heiress of that house.—The assistance of De Launé was indispensable to this plan; but of this assistance he entertained no doubt, for the man was already in his power; and it was easy, by bribes and threats, to bend him to his purpose.

He succeeded but too well in the scheme he had formed, which was artfully carried into execution. At first it was thrown into circulation, that the present wife of De Launé (for he had been three times married) had, in a quarrel with her husband, charged him with such an imposition. This the Count pretended to notice with anger, and a determination to resent the falsehood, and vindicate the birth of his niece; but his noisy measures were stopped, by the discovery of what was merely a forged confession of his former wife, said to be her dying declaration, made in the presence of a neighbour, who was also since dead, and committed by herself to writing, in the last stage of a lingering illness.

De Launé affected a wish to conceal this instrument, which the Count compelled him to produce; and at last, with much difficulty, as was pretended, the man owned the circumstance, which, though uncommon, was not altogether unprecedented; and the tattling gossips of the city, more eager for the marvellous than the acquisition of truth, anxious to tell the story in the most wonderful way, represented the circumstance of Adelaide's been changed at nurse as a fact; and in a short time, nobody seemed to doubt but she was a changeling, and certainly the daughter of De Launé.—What perhaps promoted the almost general delusion was, that Adelaide had been educated in a convent at Marseilles, and, owing to the retirement in which the Chevalier had lived after the death of his lady, had been but little seen and known in the neighbourhood of her late residence. By these means, the villany of the Count and the roguery of De Launé succeeded with the public; and the Countess with sorrow, and poor Adelaide with resignation, submitted to the general opinion, neither of them having any suspicion of the fraud.

Adelaide, being thus lowered from the rank of nobility to the condition of a domestic, would have been allowed to remain with the Countess (for the Count had not the least fear or apprehension that the forgery would be detected, and brought to light), and, as such, she was detained, till the Count was informed by De Launé, that a woman, who had lived servant in the family of the Chevalier at the time of Adelaide's birth, had declared that she should know the real child of St. Angouléme, by a particular mark on her left arm. This assertion, the Count was told, had been made so publicly, as to endanger the success of his scheme, and threatened to involve him, in the issue, in disgrace, and even punishment.

The Count was alarmed at this intelligence, and much embarrassed, for he knew not how to avert the consequences: in his fright, he condescended to ask De Launé what could be done? for his situation seemed now highly perplexing, and full of danger.

De Launé, after much apparent deliberation, observed, that it was now too late to recede; and that there was but one way in which he could escape the consequences which, on the discovery of the cheat, would certainly ensue. The Count desired him to explain himself. De Launé hesitated, and was for sometime silent; but at length, on the repeated inquiries of the Count what he meant? and how the dreaded evil might be avoided? he said it would be better, as they had proceeded so far, to go through with the business; and as things had since fallen out, the safest way was to do something with the girl, to prevent her from being troublesome in future.

The Count looked earnestly in De Launé's face, as if doubtful whether he understood his meaning—"I see the necessity," he said, at length, "and would dispose of her, if I could; but I know not how."

"There are sure and easy ways," said De Launé.

"Ah! what are they?" cried the Count.

"She would die sometime," said De Launé.

The Count started—"To what," said he, "would you urge me?"

"You are alarmed at my measures, I see," cried De Launé—"they are desperate, but I see no other way by which you can escape the disgrace that will attach to you, when——"

"I see it all," said the Count, "I see it all very plainly—it was a rash, imprudent act: would to Heaven I had not entered upon it so hastily!—But is there no way to silence this woman?—A mark on the left arm, say you?"

"She is said to have declared so, my Lord," cried De Launé.

"Cannot we bribe her to our interests?"

"The attempt would be hazardous, my Lord: she is attached, they say, to the family, and eager to assist the claims of the young heiress. She says, too, she has other proofs."

"She must die some time, as you observe," said the Count.

"These mountains are the haunts of banditti," cried De Launé.

"I understand you," said the Count tremulously—"You are willing then—"

"Not I, my Lord; but——"

"I would not employ a third person in a business of this kind," said the Count.

"You may do it safely, my Lord."

"How safely?"

"Robberies and murders are not unfrequent among these mountains," said De Launé—"I know a man—When she is rambling abroad——"

"I will trust no one but yourself," cried the Count—"Will you undertake the business? If so, name your terms."

De Launé hesitated—"My Lord," said he, at length, "I am bound to serve you; but——"

"What farther have you to say?" cried the Count—"Robberies and murders, as you observe, are not unfrequent amongst these mountains; yet," said the Count, "I have traversed them often, and have never met with any accident; it will, of course, not easily be believed——"

"We must then employ some stratagem, that may serve to render the event which is to follow less extraordinary," cried De Launé.

"How? what stratagem?"

De Launé paused, and looked thoughtfully, as if meditating some plan; after a few minutes deliberation, he proposed that the Count should pretend to have been assaulted, as he was travelling along the mountains, by one of a gang of banditti, who, he must say, had attempted his life, and but for the interference of his servants, who were to be ordered to follow at some distance, would have effected his purpose: and as it was necessary that the farce of this assault should really be performed, De Launé was to act the part of the robber, and be bound, and brought by the Count's servants to the Castle. This, he said, would take from the improbability of Adelaide's being seized and carried away, as it would be supposed, by banditti; for as the pretended attack upon the Count would pass almost under the eye of his servants, who were to be near enough, on his calling out to them, to gallop to his assistants, no suspicion would be entertained as to the reality of the event;

and while in seeming custody at the Castle, he (De Launé) and the Count could meet, and consider what was farther to be done; after which, the latter was to contrive some way of dismissing his prisoner, before he was delivered up to justice.

The Count observed, that De Launé had been seen at the Castle; it was therefore necessary that he should assume some disguise, which would prevent his being known as the person who had lately appeared as Adelaide's father.

Although De Launé had persuaded the Count to consent to the death of his niece, who, according to their plan, was, in one of her rambles amongst the mountains, to be seized and murdered by De Launé, in a forest about two leagues distant from the Castle, nothing was farther from the intentions and wishes of this villain, than the actual accomplishment of the horrid deed he had recommended; he had a scheme, from which he promised himself a much higher advantage than he could possibly gain by her death: this was, to marry Adelaide to his son, young De Launé, who has been better known to our readers by the name of Perouse, the same who had pretended to rescue her from the power of the Marquis de Ponteville, and by whom she was afterwards conveyed to a house which had been hired for her reception by De Launé, who had previously taken all measures preparatory to his projected enterprize: he, too, had placed in that house the woman called Madame St. Clair, whom he had brought from the brothels of Paris—she was, of course, base and profligate; and being clever, was equally versed in all the arts of intrigue, or rather wickedness.

Perouse was one of the ruffians by whom Adelaide was seized and conveyed to the Castle of Ponteville; De Launé was the other: they were both of them masked; and as they seldom spoke, and then only in feigned voices, Adelaide, in the characters in which they afterwards appeared, did not recognize them as the banditti by whom she had been surprised and carried off to her horrid place of captivity in the Castle of Ponteville.

Perouse, or, as we shall now call him, young De Launé, had formerly served the office of *valet* to a young nobleman of loose principles and a debauched life, with whom he resided some years—a circumstance which may perhaps account for his manners being less disgustingly vulgar than those of the elder De Launé. He left his service to join a party of gamblers, and entered afterwards into some swindling transactions with a set of wretches, who rambled about the country acquiring money by various rogueries; and at last, gradually proceeding in his life of vice and guilt, had subjected himself to various criminal charges, and the officers of justice had long sought to apprehend him. To avoid these, he entered into a troop of banditti, infesting the Pyrenees—De Launé had not, for some years, seen his son, nor did he know where he was, till he accidentally met with him on his way through Gascony, when he learnt his profession, and the principal place of rendezvous of the gang. He described the life he led in such glowing colours, that he easily persuaded his father to join thc troop. It was after this step that he formed the golden scheme of uniting his son, now called Perouse, to the wealthy and beautiful heiress to the house of Angouléme—a scheme which, under the advantages which the designs of the Count and his connexion with the banditti afforded, he imagined would be accomplished almost without difficulty.

The place of rendezvous for the banditti, was a large, castellated, and now ruined mansion, belonging to the Marquisate of Ponteville: it had long been abandoned by the owners to neglect, and the artifices of the robbers effectually prevented the intrusion of all prying visitors, by the practice of tricks, which established the belief that it was haunted by horrible and dangerous spectres. To this place Adelaide was brought, as above described; not to be murdered, as the Count had agreed, but to be practised upon in a manner likely to persuade her to accept, with joy and gratitude, the protection of her pretended friend and deliverer; and finally, by the united influences of terror and apprehension from the feigned pursuit of the Marquis, to consent to a marriage with the young De Launé, the pretended nephew of Madame St. Clair, whom she had been taught to consider as a man of fortune and respectability, and her superior, both as to birth and connexions. Should artifice and persuasions fail in their effect upon Adelaide, actual force was to have been employed, to oblige her to become the wife of De Launé.

CHAP. XIV.

The Count, as it will be remembered, had for several days previous to the time in which Adelaide had been yielded into the power of these ruffians, betrayed various symptoms of an uneasy and distempered mind: bad as he was, he could not reflect upon the guilty part he had acted to one so innocent and lovely, one, too, so nearly connected with him by the ties of blood, and whose general behaviour had been so uniformly affectionate, and void even of just suspicion, without horror and self-reproach: thought was agony; and he sought to silence that busy monitor within, which was continually picturing his cruelty and wickedness in the most terrifying colours, by plunging anew into scenes of pleasure and debauchery: but, even in his wildest hours of riot and excess, the image of the unhappy victim of his ambition and avarice would start up before his maddening fancy, and involve him in all the horrors of guilt and shame.

His parties of friends, as he called the heterogeneous sets of visitors at the Castle, were more frequent and numerous than ever; but they were composed of the most licentious of both sexes, for persons of honour and respectability refused to mingle with the motley groups. Signora Violanta Sforzo, who was one of the most unprincipled and profligate of his female favourites, after repeated visits to the Count, became a constant inmate at the Castle: she presided in the place of the Countess, and was soon publicly recognized as his mistress.

This woman, by her wily arts and cunning fascinations, had so insinuated herself into the affections of the Count, that she was enabled to exercise over him an almost boundless dominion. She detested the Countess, because she easily perceived she was considered by her rather as an object of contempt than jealousy: this was agonizing to her pride, and she exerted all the blandishments of her beauty, all the witchery of her charms, to involve in deeper wretchedness an unhappy, persecuted woman, whose severest misfortunes has originated in one single fault, that of having suffered herself to be persuaded to an alliance with a man every way unworthy of her, and who had ever since treated her with almost every species of cruelty and unkindness.

In a mind like that of the Count, unprincipled, and destitute of every feeling of humanity, it was easy to convert indifference into absolute aversion; and he became in this, as in various other instances, a mere instrument in the hands of his insidious and haughty mistress.

Through the deadly hatred of the Signora, the Countess was confined to an apartment in the Castle: nor was this all; a report was spread in the neighbourhood, that she was insane. The story of her derangement was managed with sufficient art to gain universal credit, and she was considered and treated as a maniac.

Such was the situation of the unhappy Countess, when Theodore's regiment returned to France, an event which took place almost immediately after the death of the late heir of the house of Montroi, to whose estates he succeeded. His first inquiry, when he reached the borders of Gascony, was for his aunt, who, he was told, was in a state of mental derangement, and was to be seen by no one except her keeper.

Theodore, who had anticipated with delight the hour of his return, and who was already, in imagination, locked in the maternal embrace of his beloved and honoured relative, who, if not allowed to invite him to the Castle, would, he was persuaded, contrive some means of seeing him unknown to her Lord, was almost frantic at this intelligence. He wrote to the Count, who having pretended to believe that he had fallen in battle, affected great surprise on hearing he was yet living. He had requested an interview with his aunt, but all access to her was positively denied; and he was commanded not to attempt to see her, or even to visit the Castle.

The circumstance of Theodore's return was cautiously concealed from every member of the family at the Castle; the Count being apprehensive, if the secret was known, it would in some manner be conveyed to the Countess, who might avail herself of his assistance to escape from her confinement, and thus publish to the world the story of her wrongs and her husband's perfidy.

Theodore, wearied out and baffled in all his endeavours to obtain an interview with the Countess, and believing her to be, as she was represented, really insane, after loitering for some time about the Castle, he, with many tears, and much heartfelt regret for the fate of his revered friend, quitted the neighbourhood, and pursued his solitary ramblings among the Pyrenees. Chance, or rather perhaps the romantic style of the country, and the profound retirement of the reposing scenes, congenial to the present temper of his feelings, thus saddened by disappointment, directed him to the village of Auboigne, where, under the name of St. Clair, he first met with the interesting, the mysterious Adelaide.

The arrival of Theodore in France, and a knowledge of the consequence which he had acquired as heir of the house of Montroi, were circumstances little calculated to calm the perturbed mind of the Count; he dreaded him as an enemy, because he had never deserved that he should be his friend, and was in perpetual fear lest the artfully-fabricated tale of the Countess's derangement should be discovered to be false, when he well knew that the chevalier would interpose in her behalf. But, in the unsuspicious nature of Theodore, he had a security of which he was himself quite unconscious; for however circumstances might seem to favour such a surmise, the thought never once occurred to Theodore, that the Count, or any man, would be base enough to confine, under a false pretext, an amiable and still-lovely woman, whose unoffending manners, and almost unequalled sweetness of disposition, had rendered her an object of affection to all who knew her.

CHAP. XV.

While the Count was thus brooding over the numerous evils which might befal him in consequence of his own folly and wickedness, he was soon roused to thoughts of the most awful vengeance, by the perfidy of the woman at whose base suggestion he had ventured upon an act of cruelty almost unparalleled, an act for which conscience, when not deadened by the inebriating potion employed to lull it to repose, assailed him with its most poignant sting.

Amongst his most frequent visitors at the Castle, was Count Roviné, a young nobleman, who possessed, beside the usual qualifications of a man of gallantry, a person more than ordinarily elegant, a fine voice, with some skill in music, and a most insinuating address.

The Count's health had been for some weeks declining, though so gradually as not to create alarm; and he often rode abroad, usually accompanied by the Signora, but sometimes alone. He had set out one morning for Barrége, meaning to try the effect of the waters of that salubrious spring, which had been recommended to him by his physician: he had not proceeded far, when, finding himself suddenly indisposed, he resolved to return home. On arriving at the Castle, he inquired for the Signora, who, he was told, was in her chamber. Thither he was going, when he was stopped by Signora Violanta's woman, who informed him her lady could not then be seen, but that she would go and tell her of his Lordship's return.

Her agitation, and the embarrassed tone in which she spoke, led the Count to suspect some mystery in the business, and he rushed forward, in spite of her remonstrances. He entered an anti-room, and was proceeding to the Signora's chamber, when he stopped, on distinguishing the voice of a man; and he soon discovered it was that of CountRoviné, in conversation with the Signora Violanta. He listened, and caught the following words— "Is it possible you can conceive you have a rival in my affections? Do me not the injustice to believe it, even for a moment. You know my heart—its best feelings are yours: wait until I obtain possession of the Angouléme estates, when we will revel together in every luxury which art can furnish or wealth procure."

"You have never loved," said the other, who was Count Roviné, "if you know not the anguish of protracted hope, and the miseries of suspense. May he not, even now, live to prove that the sweetest hopes may prove fallacious, and to sadden the present with the dread of future disappointment?"

"It is impossible," rejoined the Signora, "that he can survive many weeks; and immediately on his death, a deed of gift puts me in undisputed possession of what I have long panted to enjoy."

"But what do you propose to do with the Countess?" inquired Roviné.

"Why need you ask?" said the Signora—"Are you not already acquainted with my plans?"

"How!" cried Roviné—"have you courage to do what I once suggested?"

"Courage! Am I not an Italian?" exclaimed the Signora; "and think you, after the professions of attachment I have already made, I have so little enterprize in my nature, so little of the Roman energy in my soul, that I would not, Cæsar-like, wade through seas of blood, rather than abandon any purpose of ambition I had once formed? Nay, start not; if I have meditated her death, it is to be accomplished by the same gradual means—You understand me?"

"Speak low," said Roviné.

"You are a fool, if it needs that I say more," cried the Signora— "Mark you how thin he looks, and what a jaundiced blackness steals round his sunken eye. How now? You are pale!—Think of what may follow, not of the present, my dear Roviné."

"Ah! think indeed *of what may follow!*" reiterated the Count, in a tone like thunder. He rushed forward—the Signora shrieked; her guilty paramour, urged by his terrors, leaped from the balcony, and escaped.

"Wretch," cried the Count, seizing the Signora's arm, "think not to escape my vengeance, and the punishment your crimes deserve! I convict you, on your own words, of an attempt upon my life, and that, too, of my innocent and much abused Countess." With these words, he rang a bell violently; and a servant appearing, he commanded the astonished attendants to convey the Signora thence, and confine her in the north tower, till they should have further orders. He then sent for his physician, and informed him he had reason to suspect that he had taken a slow poison, which might be the cause of his present illness, and desired that he would immediately supply him with something by way of antidote.

The physician felt his pulse; he looked earnestly at the Count—"Your disorder, my Lord," said he, "has for some time baffled all my skill." He then, with evident marks of apprehension for the fate of his patient, wrote a hasty prescription: the necessary drug was procured, but it was ineffectual for the purpose for which it was employed; he languished through two or three days, in the interval of which he desired that the Signora might be brought forth, and examined.

She refused to confess that she had administered poison to the Count, or that her words would bear that import: she was nevertheless committed to close custody, till the event of the Count's illness should be determined, when the affair was to undergo an examination in a court of justice.

The Count's disorder increased daily, death seemed to approach with rapid strides: the horror of his feelings while he contemplated this event, surpass all the powers of description. Dreadful to him was the retrospect of a life marked with such deeds of guilt, as seemed now on reflection, to harrow up his soul;* hardly dared he to hope for mercy, hardly did he venture to lift an imploring eye to the Author of his existence, or endeavour to deprecate his just vengeance; conscience-struck and appalled, it seemed as though the gates of mercy were now for ever closed against him: his looks, his words, every gesture bore testimony to the agony of his feelings. Let us draw a veil over the horrid scene; suffice it, that, all hopes of recovery at an end, he was solicitous, as far as was in his power, to make amends to those he had injured: with this view he sent to the Countess, requesting to see her ere he departed.

The summons of a dying, though unworthy husband, was not to be resisted by a being generous, noble, and forgiving, like the ill-treated Countess—a sense of his condition had obliterated from her heart all former resentments: she flew to his bedside, gazed with pity on a countenance now almost stiffened in death, pressed his hand to her lips, and uttered a blessing on the pale conscience-tortured wretch, who now solicited her pardon and compassion.

The name of Adelaide faltered on his quivering lip. "She lives!" exclaimed the Countess, who had that day, by a contrivance of Bertha's, received Adelaide's letter. A flush of joy passed over the pallid cheek of the sufferer, as he faintly caught the sound—*she lives!* He looked doubtingly and intreatingly at the Countess: she repeated her words with energy. As she spoke, he clasped his hands, and turning his eyes upward, seemed for some moments as though engaged in mental prayer. He then made a sign for ink and paper, and desiring the Countess to sit down, dictated the paper already mentioned; as also a short deed, by which he gave all the property he died possessed of to the Countess. By this act the deed of gift, then in the possession of the Signora Violanta, was rendered utterly useless, even should she escape the ignominious punishment due to her crimes.

This done, overcome with the fatigue of his exertion, he remained for several minutes in a state of stupor. The physician, who, during his interview with the Countess, had retired, now re-entered the chamber. The Countess was ordered to withdraw. A medicine was administered—it revived him. He inquired for his confessor, who was summoned to attend him, and he continued alone with him for some time.

In the course of a few hours, he betrayed symptoms of

approaching dissolution. A servant was dispatched in haste for the Countess, who, on entering the room, found him already dying. She pressed his hand—it was cold, and almost lifeless. He looked wistfully in her face, faintly articulated the name of Theodore, and seemed struggling to unburthen his mind of something which still obstructed its quiet: the effort to speak was ineffectual—he heaved a deep groan, and soon afterwards expired.

His remains were deposited in the chapel of the Castle: the Countess and her domestics attended them, in solemn procession, to the place of interment.

This duty performed, in compliance with the request of her dying Lord, the Countess set off for the Chateau de Montroi, to perform the act for restitution of the estates of the house of St. Angouléme to their rightful heir—an act of justice which, she felt, ought not longer to be delayed; nor was she less urged to hasten her journey thither, by an eager wish to behold, and clasp to her maternal bosom, the child of her adoption, her beloved and long-regretted Adelaide.

On her arrival at the Chateau de Montroi, she learnt from the weeping Genifrede of the extraordinary event of Adelaide's imprisonment, and the cause of her arrest; and the rest of the circumstances of her situation, as far as the old woman was herself acquainted with them. This intelligence seemed like a dreadful dream to the astonished Countess, who, hoping to prevent any future evil that might threaten the injured and lovely heiress of the house of Angouléme, by producing a document of her birth, and appearing as an evidence in her behalf, should circumstances require her presence, immediately set off for Arles.

On inquiring at the prison, she was informed of the event of the trial, and directed to the hotel at which Adelaide lodged. The joyful discovery that awaited her in that place, and the scene that followed it, has already been described.

CHAP. XVI.

Adelaide, on discovering that she was indeed the daughter of the Chevalier St. Angouléme, and consequently the niece of the late Count, put on mourning for her deceased uncle. Theodore paid the same respect to his memory; and, with Adelaide, often heaved a sigh of generous commiseration for the sake of his cruel but unfortunate relative.

Meanwhile the most active measures were employed by the court for the discovery of the two De Launés. Madame St. Clair's house was searched; and she was seized, and brought to Arles. Adelaide and Jacques du Bois were cited to appear, in order to certify the identity of her person. The circumstance of the horse having been taken from her stable, was sufficient to convict her of having been an accomplice in the robbery; and she was ordered either to confess, and yield the culprits into the hands of justice, or suffer the torture.

The wretched woman, finding she could not, in any other way, extricate herself from the horrors of her situation, than by giving up her accomplices, answered, without reserve, all the questions that were put to her; and the De Launés, with the rest of the gang, were accordingly seized at their place of rendezvous, and after a short trial, their guilt being fully evident, were condemned and executed.

The Castle de Ponteville, long distinguished by the appellation of the Haunted Castle, was, from thence, known to have been the resort of a banditti, who, by the trick of the spectres above mentioned, had ensured to themselves a retreat, where they had long lived undiscovered and unmolested. As they gained admission into the Castle by means of a subterranean passage, terminating in the valley below, and not easily discoverable, they were never seen to enter it: this favoured the success of the various artifices employed to establish the belief of its being subjected to supernatural visitations. Lights were placed at midnight in the western side of the building, which might be seen at a distance; and tapers carried by the banditti, were seen flitting, meteor-like, as has already been described, from window to window. Whenever any persons approached the place, to examine into the causes of these appearances, some of the gang acted the part of a spectre; and, wrapt in a bloody sheet, generally prevented any from entering, by the terror they seldom failed to excite. But if any more daring, or trusting to numbers, did enter, they were lured along, and bewildered among intricate passages; and were often struck and wounded by invisible hands; and if they did escape, which was not always the case, they never failed to relate with exaggerations, the terrors and dangers of the Haunted Castle. Such were the practices which had long alarmed, and were now made known to the surrounding neighbourhood.

Shortly after the trial and execution of the De Launés, Signora Violanta was led to the bar of justice, on a charge of having administered a poison to Count St. Angouléme, which, though given only in small potions, and at different periods, was supposed to be the cause of his death. She was acquitted, for want of sufficient evidence to prove the crime, of which she was nevertheless believed to be guilty: but she did not live long to enjoy her fortunate escape from public ignominy and a disgraceful death; for, riding out one day in a carriage with Count Roviné, her paramour, the horses suddenly took fright, and she was thrown out; and being dashed against a rock, received a contusion on the forehead, of which she almost instantly expired.

Count Roviné escaped with life, but his leg was fractured near the hip; and that beautiful person, of which he was so vain, became, from thenceforth, crippled and deformed.

In the lives and fortunes of the persons of this history, it is easy to discover how great are the miseries that attend those who venture into the paths of vice, and how certain is the punishment that never fails to overtake them. The Count, from the moment when he conceived the horrible design of sacrificing his niece to obtain her possessions, had never enjoyed the calm comforts of a peaceful hour; and he fell, like many others, a sacrifice to the unrestrained indulgence of an overruling passion. The De Launés present an awful example of the power of a depraved principle leading, by imperceptible degrees, to the commission of crimes of the blackest dye. In Madame St. Clair we have an example of the force of habit, and the tendency of corrupt communication to deaden all the gentler feelings of the heart, all that humanizes and ennobles the mind. Signora Violenta presents to our reflection a character nearly of the same stamp, but somewhat altered, from the different circumstances under which they acted.

Let us turn from these with the abhorrence they so justly incur, and shew that the good are ever the peculiar care of Providence, by describing the happiness of those who, having passed with integrity through scenes of unmerited persecution, and arriving at the goal of virtue, receive the rewards which virtue only can deserve, or enjoy; let us behold Montroi and Adelaide blessed with reciprocal affection, found on the purest esteem, ennobled by friendship, enjoying together all the felicity which an attachment so fervent and so elevated is calculated to afford.

The life of Adelaide, since the death of her father, presents little else than scenes of sorrow and persecution. How auspicious then appeared the present! how bright on the horizon of her prospect, arose the star of hope, which, till now, had seemed to set in thick clouds, portentous only of future evils! The storm which had been gathering over it was now disbursed—all is serene and cloudless. She had heaved a sigh of commiseration and tender regret for the death of her unnatural but repentant uncle; she had even dropped a tear of pity for the fate of the unfortunate De Launés, not that she deemed them worthy of such a tribute, but because she had known them, and it was by her means, although innocent of such intention, that they had been brought to the wheel, to answer, by the commission of a single crime, for a long list of enormous and atrocious offences. But the tear that gemmed her cheek was soon chased by the smile that glowed over it; for Montroi, the enraptured, adoring Montroi, was her companion; and could Adelaide, in the full possession of his love, be otherwise than happy?—The Countess, too, her beloved aunt, was now always her companion.

Accompanied by her delighted lover, the Countess, and Father Athanasa, she left the town of Arles, and repaired to the Chateau de Montroi. About a week after the arrival of the party at the chateau, they received a visit from the Marquis de Ponteville, whose admiration and esteem for Adelaide had been the cause of various uneasy sensations, and even those of self-reproach, in thus bringing her to a public trial; and he sought to lessen the remembrance of the prosecution he had instituted, and which was too recent to be as yet forgotten, partly by apologies, but chiefly by availing himself of every opportunity to testify the high respect he felt for her character, and his admiration of the filial piety shc had displayed in her conduct towards her supposed father, in risking her reputation, her liberty, and perhaps her life, for his preservation. He congratulated Theodore on having found a woman of such superlative excellence; and resolved to remain at the Castle, to witness the celebration of the marriage, an event he desired might not be unnecessarily delayed.

From Adelaide he heard of the extraordinary circumstance of his having been represented to her as her persecutor, whom she was instructed always carefully to avoid; and also of the astonishing appearances she had seen during her imprisonment in the turret at the Castle de Ponteville. With the stratagems that had been employed by the banditti to impose upon the fears and credulity of the public, the Marquis was already acquainted.

CHAP. XVII.

In the course of a few weeks after the death of Count St. Angouléme, Theodore received at the altar the hand of his beloved

Adelaide: Father Athanasa officiated at the ceremony, the Countess and the Marquis de Ponteville attending.

Immediately after the celebration of the nuptials, a liberal entertainment was given to the neighbouring poor, who were feasted at the chateau in the true baronial style. In the festivity of these scenes, none partook more largely than the kind-hearted Genifrede, who, old as she was, joined the dance in an avenue of chesnuts, with her children and grandchildren, among whom Jacques was most forward to express the exultation of his feelings on the happy occasion of Adelaide's marriage with his young master—"Who would have thought," said he, shrugging his shoulders, and dancing about for joy, "that, when Ma'moiselle and I left Madame's house with our stolen horse, I should ever live to see her the Lady of this chateau?—Oh la! oh la! what odd things come to pass! and after we had both been put in prison too!—Well, who knows but I may be a Lord myself some time? stranger things methinks have happened."

Adelaide, in her present good fortune, did not overlook the services she had received from Jacques and his family, all of whom, by her bounty, were placed in what, by them, was deemed affluence; but Genifrede and Jacques earnestly requested to continue at the chateau, and were retained in the service of their noble master

So many claims had been made by his creditors upon the property of Count St. Angouléme, that, when his affairs were arranged and settled, but little remained for the Countess. The deficiency was, however, amply supplied by a splendid present from Theodore, whose fortune, with the addition of the estates of the house of Angouléme, on his marriage with its heiress, might now be called immense.

The Countess, in the union of her adopted children, who seemed formed for each other's happiness, found every wish of her heart fulfilled; and so dear to her were both of them, that it was difficult to determine which were pre-eminent in her affections.

Father Athanasa, after a visit of several months, returned to his convent, having previously pronounced a blessing upon the happy pair, who placing their felicity upon the surest foundations, those of piety and virtue, felt that every revolving year brought a fresh accession of happiness; for, constantly engaged in acts of real benevolence, and considering such employment as their chief good, every year contributed something to their general stock of enjoyment. They disdained to pass their time in frivolous amusement, or in courting the pleasures, or rather the pains of idleness and folly: their affluence was not lavished in the purchase of luxuries, and the mean, unworthy gratifications of the table, or of unnecessary splendour and equipage; it was employed in the encouragement of industry, and the relief of helpless indigence: it was used, not to oppress, but to support; not to mortify, but to console. It comforted the afflicted, when languishing under the sufferings of poverty and sickness; it dried the tear of the orphan, and made *the widow's heart to sing for joy.** Such were their objects, such their occupations, such their pleasures. May all, who, like Theodore and Adelaide, possess the means of diffusing happiness in the possession of wealth, *go and do likewise!**

FINIS.

NOTES.

PAGE

3 French Protestants, who, for the most part, were Calvinists. In 1562 some twelve hundred Huguenots were killed in Vassey, starting a protracted religious conflict which lasted until 1598 with the Edict of Nantes, which gave the Huguenots some freedoms. Many Huguenots emigrated to avoid persecution.

22 Cornetcy: the commission of a cornet, the lowest rank of commissioned officer, a junior cavalry officer.

44 Courtesan.

55 A small wooded valley.

89 From John Milton's *Paradise Lost*, Book 5, line 295 describing Eden as seen by the angel Raphael for the first time.

91 *embonpoint*: meaning stout or plump.

100 It is interesting to note that Jane Austen's *Sense and Sensibility*, which also features a sprained ankle as a device to introduce a dashing, handsome, and mysterious stranger was published in 1811, the same year as *Pyrenean Banditti*.

129 Also called Herostratus: a Greek arsonist who burned down the temple to Artemis/Diana at Ephesus to earn eternal fame.

137 A merry child.

138 A small goat-like creature indigenous to Europe.

144 From Alexander Pope's *Essay on Man*.

145 Either a padded saddle for women or a cushion behind a regular saddle for a woman to sit on.

171 From *Eloisa to Abelard* (1717) by Alexander Pope: Relentless walls! Whose darksome round contains / Repentant sighs, and voluntary pains: / Ye rugged rocks! which holy knees have worn; / Ye grots and caverns shagg'd with horrid thorn! (16-20).

180 From Shakespeare's *Much Ado About Nothing* Act IV, Scene 1: I have marked / A thousand blushing apparitions / To start into her face, a thousand innocent shames / In angel whiteness beat away those blushes / And in her eyes there have appeared a fire / To burn the errors that these princes hold / Against her maiden truth.

239 From *Hamlet*, Act I, Scene 5. Hamlet's father's ghost is speaking to Hamlet of the conditions in Purgatory: "I could a tale unfold whose lightest word/ Would harrow up thy soul . . ."

247 Job 29:13 "The Blessings of one ready to perish came upon me. And I made the widow's heart sing for joy."

247 Luke 10:37, the parable of the Good Samaritan: "Then Jesus said unto Him, Go, and do thou likewise."

www.ingramcontent.com/pod-product-compliance
Lightning Source LLC
Chambersburg PA
CBHW030811310726
48980CB00006B/453/J
* 9 7 8 1 9 3 4 5 5 5 9 2 7 *